My fellow Royal,

Thankyou for purchasing MTTAK and supporting it through out our journey! We made it!

All of my love
&
until the next,

-J

Jennise

Typewriter Pub, an imprint of Blvnp Incorporated
A Nevada Corporation
1887 Whitney Mesa DR #2002
Henderson, NV 89014
www.typewriterpub.com/info@typewriterpub.com

ISBN: **978-1-68030-820-4**

DISCLAIMER

Royal's Tale

MATED TO THE ALPHA KING

JENNISE K

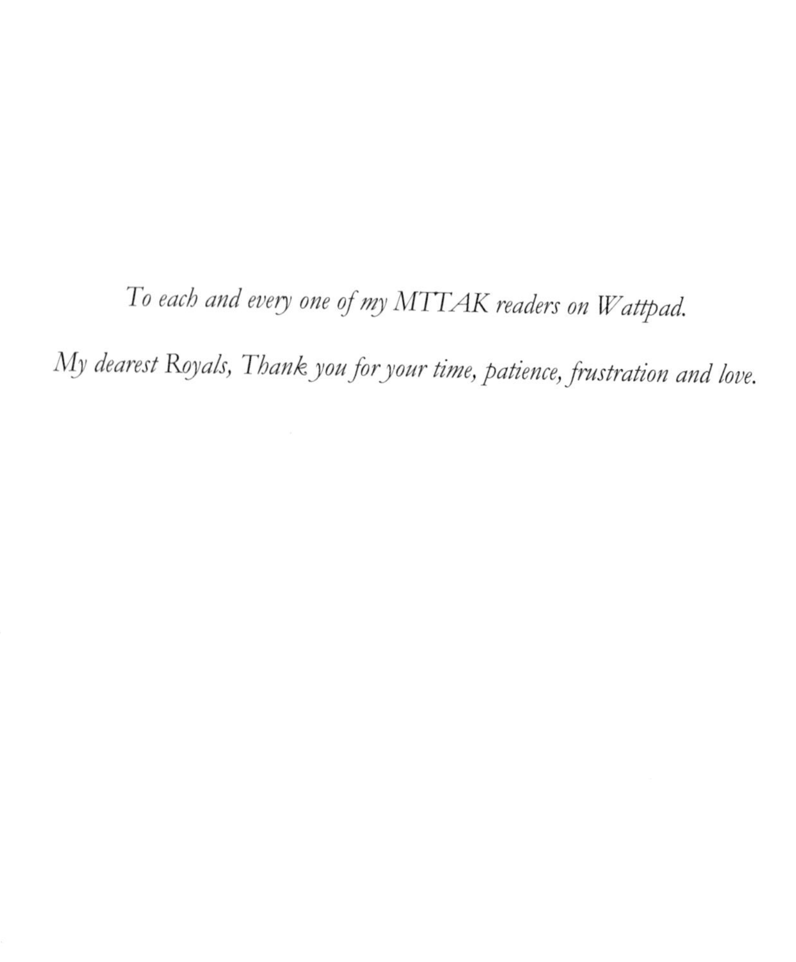

To each and every one of my MTTAK readers on Wattpad.

My dearest Royals, Thank you for your time, patience, frustration and love.

PROLOGUE

Dear Reader,

It is with great pleasure that I present to you a brief introduction to the new world you have decided to enter, a new life you have decided to live. Let it be that it will only last for some chapters, but I hope you enjoy it until it lasts.

Let me introduce myself first.

Hi, I am Theia Anderson. I am just like any one of you, human, alive, and breathing. (Unless you are a zombie, in which case I am not, and I especially do not have brains!)

Just putting it out there!

I am eighteen, and currently a senior in Rosenberg High. (I'm what they call a nerd. But let us face it. Nerds nowadays are hot!) I have also only recently moved from the sunny state of California to a city called Peidmond, just beside Seattle. Needless to say, it rains here a lot.

When I moved here, I imagined finally living in a cold state and thought that it would be an amazing experience. Although, the fact that it was in the middle of the year, and I would have to settle in as the "new girl" was very well placed in my mind.

New friends, new teachers, a new environment—everything was new. But that all was well-known and understood. I had expected those.

However, what I certainly didn't expect was to meet the man who owns the castle I gazed upon from my window every morning and night. Yes, a castle…A castle I am now living in.

This is my story. A story I am now willing to share but only if you can keep a secret.

Do you remember the stories your grandma used to tell you every night about cursed beasts, village beauties, girls in red capes, and wolves in disguises?

Well, maybe, just maybe…they actually do happen. Maybe beasts do exist.

They do. I would know. I am bound to one.

Whom, you may ask?

Well, I am mated to the Alpha King.

How?

You will see.

You will live through it with me.

I hope you enjoy the ride.

Best wishes,
Theia

CHAPTER ONE

Done finally!

Packing had never been my forte. In fact, I absolutely detested packing. Maybe it was because the amount of books and other things I possessed seemed impossible to place in tons of boxes.

Slapping duct tape across the box, I picked up a marker and marked it as Theia's Books #3.

When the box was pushed aside carefully, I finally let out a sigh of relief as I wiped away a layer of sweat that had accumulated on my forehead. I lived in the warm state of California. It was summer. So naturally, the heat was killing me.

A single thing one should always know about me—I was not much for heat.

When my dad came home one afternoon and declared that we were moving from California to a cold city just near the outskirts of Seattle called Peidmond, I was actually very excited.

Well, that was until I realized that I had to attend a new high school in the middle of the year and leave my best friend, Casey, behind. And since it was senior year, with prom and all, well, it sucked.

Had I been in my old school, Stinson High, I would have at least had my best friend to accompany me. The thought of being home, all alone on prom, only helped me sweat more.

We were a small family—my dad, Arthur Anderson, a professor of history and literature; my mom, Maia Anderson, a designer and entrepreneur; and me, Theia, currently a senior student in high school and hoping to become a criminologist or psychologist—whatever came first. I also had a very strange fascination with history.

I guess Dad's genes rubbed off on me that way.

Another soft huff of sigh left me as I lazily picked myself off the floor and dragged myself towards the bathroom. I only had two hours before we were to load everything and leave, and I knew, in this heat, I would need every minute of it.

Minutes later, as I stood under my cool shower and slowly observed my bathroom for the last time, I let a few stray tears flow with the water as I washed the tiny ache in my chest away.

It seemed like a day had passed when I found myself scrubbed and fresh, walking out into my bedroom in a towel.

A loud yelp left my lips when I suddenly found myself on the floor and a heavy weight on me.

"Don't go!" Casey cried hysterically against me. I would have cried too, but the fact that I was currently sprawled on the floor with a towel on and my hundred-something-pound best friend was on top of me was a little suffocating. Especially in my part, I was merely five feet after all.

"Need…to…breathe, Casey!" I managed to gasp as I writhed under her, trying to escape her deadly grip. Immediately, Casey stilled above me.

"Oh, I'm sorry!" She apologized hurriedly, blushing beet red as she got off me, and stood. She gave me her hand and helped me stand up.

On my feet, I sighed as I brought her in for a hug. "We will talk every night on Skype or FaceTime, and then there is Messenger! We will always talk. It'll be like I'm not even away, I promise." I assured her as I pulled away. Losing my towel, I pulled on my clothes.

Casey sighed a little heavy and a little scared. "What if we don't?"

I smiled a small, broken smile. My hand found Casey's again, and I gave it a comforting squeeze. "No matter what happens, whether we talk every day or not at all for months, when we do talk or meet, we will always be the same best friends."

A small tear dropped down Casey's cheeks, and she nodded, chuckling.

"You better tell me everything when you get there!" she blurted out, smiling a bit as she folded and placed my towel inside a plastic before packing it into my suitcase. My room was nearly empty. It was literally stripped bare except for the built-in bookshelves and a few boxes and suitcases that were still lying around waiting to be hurled into the moving truck.

Smiling, I nodded and pulled Casey in for a final hug. "We'll visit each other during breaks. I'll miss you, you know."

Casey nodded. "I'll miss you too, Thi."

The loud stomping noises alerted us both of someone coming up the stairs, and soon enough, there was a knock on the door. "Theia, are you done?"

"Yeah, Dad, come in!" I replied as I picked up my jacket—just in case it got cold—and slipped into my flip-flops, which seemed like an irrational choice considering the two contrasted each other, but I wouldn't need my shoes in the car, anyway. I'd probably just tuck them under me throughout the ride.

The door opened instantly and in walked my dad with two bulky men. Smiling at me softly, they strode towards the boxes and picked them up.

Again, Casey and I stood in my empty room—a room we had dozens of sleepovers in, a room we played doll in, a room we gossiped, planned, and plotted in, and a room we did our homework and fangirling in. I sighed.

"I think we should go now…"

"Uh-huh."

Casey and I walked downstairs hand in hand. I took a deep breath as I stood in the living room.

The place had a lot of my memories. I grew up in this area. Well, that was until I turned sixteen and got the television setup in my own room. My eyes were closed. I let out a deep breath and whispered, "I'll miss you, home. Goodbye."

"Theia, sweetie!"

My mom's voice rang out to me like a fire truck's siren. I instantly opened my eyes and walked out of the threshold, letting Dad lock the door and hand over the keys to our real estate agent, who had managed to sell our home for a very, very reasonable amount.

The day outside was bright and happy, vibrant and warm, yet the heat suddenly didn't bother me anymore. I looked around my neighborhood and smiled. I would be taking all the good memories as I went. But as much as I was sad, truth be told, I was also secretly excited.

I didn't know what it was, but I felt like something was waiting for me in Peidmond. An adventure was waiting to be lived—maybe a mystery waiting to be unraveled. The little knowledge about the new feeling in me was all the more alluring, and somehow, secretly, I couldn't wait to reach Peidmond.

"Bye, Cas. I'll call you when I reach there okay!" I muttered, suddenly holding back my tears as I was pulled into a hug.

"Uh-huh, we will always talk! And if we can't, we will at least message when we can." Casey assured me as she hugged me back.

Smiling slightly, I pulled out of the hug and with a final wave, climbed into our SUV, watching my best friend stand in my yard and my neighborhood for the last time as my dad drove off.

It felt like I was leaving a part of me here. But then again, I was going whole.

***

"Are you excited, darling?"

Mom suddenly asked me, cutting the silence that had been building up since we left seven hours ago. The ride from California to Peidmond was fifteen hours and thirteen minutes, and already in these seven hours, we had stopped twice to fuel up the SUV and buy some snacks for along the way.

"Yeah, Mom, are you?" I murmured back, knowing well that both my parents were extremely excited for this "new chapter" in their life. Dad would not stop talking about the amount of brilliant literature his new university had, not to mention the immense raise in wage and position. He was ecstatic. For Mom, her boutiques and salons around California were still running. And although she would have to fly back and forth occasionally, her excitement with opening a new boutique and salon in Peidmond was especially overwhelming.

"Oh, I am so excited!" She squealed, clapping her hands together before turning towards Dad and placing a loving kiss on his cheek.

It was normal for me to witness their weird romance, so I just rolled my eyes and looked at the passing views.

"The new house is bigger, Theia." Dad chuckled and looked at me from the review mirror.

I knew he was trying to make me feel better about moving, leaving my old friends and life behind, so I just grinned at Dad and spoke the first thing I thought would make him worry less. "I get the room with the best view!"

Dad chuckled and nodded, making my grin widen. It was not hard to notice that I was a papa's girl. And with me being the only child, he doted on me. I was his little Fuzzybottom—not that my bottom was fuzzy, but just because—well, he was my hero.

"One of the best things about the house is that it has great views all around the rooms. But you'll receive the one with the best view, we promise. We should be settled by tomorrow. Hopefully, the day after, you and I could go shopping!" Mom said as she turned to look at me. Not excited at all, I somehow managed to produce a fake smile and plaster it across my face.

Nobody messed with Mom when it came to shopping. Nobody!

Once her attention was elsewhere, I turned around to see how far off our moving truck was behind us. Before turning around, I brought out a book from my backpack and plugged my earbuds into my iPod before playing "Davy Jones Music Box and the Rainy Mood." Somehow, the rumbles of thunder together with the soft tunes created a more reading mood for me. Shoving the iPod inside my pants pocket, I flipped through the pages of my newest read, Indiscretions, slumped back into a more comfortable position and began journeying once again into a different time and a whole different world—this time, into the world of Lord Lockwood.

***

"Thi, we are here!"

I mumbled a few incoherent words before turning in my bed. Need sleep.

"Thi, wake up!" Dad's voice urged before I was shaken on the shoulder and lightly tapped on my face. What the heck?

"Alright, alright!" I grumbled as I sat up on my bed and peeped my eye open.

I gasped. My face becoming warmer by the second as I finally realized that I was in our SUV and a couple of people were staring at me, smiling like a bunch of weirdos. My folks included.

My cheeks burned as my eyes rested on a blond-haired guy smirking at me, an axe in his hand as he rested it on his shoulder.

What was he? A huntsman? I rolled my eyes in my mind as I pushed any budding crush away. I was more of a Beauty and the Beast girl, anyway.

Finally managing to look away, I smiled at the rest of the folks smiling at me, two slightly elder couples.

"Oh, she's so beautiful!" The red-headed one gushed as I shoved my iPod and book into my backpack and got out of the SUV.

"Thanks," I mumbled back, knowing full well that the blond was still staring and smirking at me.

"Hello, dear. Welcome to Peidmond! I'm Jane, and this here is my son, Alex, and my husband, Hugh. We live just there beside your house. That one there is Mary and her husband, Grant. They have a son too, Matthew. He is good friends with Alex here," Jane told me excitedly, and I smiled back, brightly mirroring her excitement.

"It's nice to meet you all. I am really excited to be here," I replied back happily as I extended my hand towards each one of them, shaking their hands softly but waving awkwardly at the smirking blond, Alex.

That boy seemed as beautiful as he seemed arrogant. But then, arrogance trumped beauty any day.

My new home stood tall and proud—red bricks and a posh-looking French door. It seemed to have at least three floors, including the small attic on the third floor. Even the front yard seemed beautifully cultivated. I waited for Jane and Mary to start talking to Mom and Hugh and Grant to start helping my dad and the movers place all our stuff into the house before picking up one of my smaller book boxes. I made a run for it.

Making a dash into the house as quickly as I could, I stopped only to grab Dad and drag him away, begging him to show me my room.

He grinned excitedly and exchanged a knowing look with both Hugh and Grant who led me upstairs until we came to a stop on the very end of the hallway. He unlocked the room and opened the doors, motioning me to walk in.

I walked in and froze.

There, in front of me was the most amazing view of a castle perched on a mountain, surrounded by pine trees and fog. Beyond it, I could see water, maybe a lake. Maybe a sea…It was actually hard to say through the fog.

I turned around, already readying myself to leap on Dad but frowned when I noticed that I was now alone in my room. The blond Alex was standing in the doorway with the usual smirk on his face and his axe missing.

I frowned. The urge of just smacking his smirk away seemed quite strong now, and it would be easy too.

"That is the Castle Dovelore, owned by His Grace, Alexander Whitlock. 'His Grace' because some say his grandfather was a duke, and that has now been passed over to him. He is also very rich if the castle isn't proof enough. But not by heritage, most of it is self-made and all. We are supposed to visit that castle this year, you know. Mr. Whitlock is providing one lucky student with a full-time scholarship to any university he or she wishes to attend and another lucky student a chance to stay in his castle for the breaks with the full usage of his library and a full tour around the castle if he or she wanted to, that is," Blond spoke, but his gaze did not once shift from the castle, which although looked quite brooding, looked equally inviting as if charming me into visiting. There definitely was something about that castle.

Suddenly very curious, I turned towards Blond and asked, "What would you like?"

He turned his attention towards me, and for the first time since the fifteen minutes that we had known each other, he smiled at me—a real smile.

"Although the most brilliant of literature are available in the castle library and I would love to roam the dungeons and secret pathways where the pirates were slain and beasts held hostage, I want the scholarship." I nodded and turned back to look at the castle.

What beasts was Blond talking about?

The feeling of my feet pushing itself forward registered slowly before I found myself staring at the castle and my hands, sliding the window open.

Is someone living there right now? How many rooms can there be?

I swept my gaze along the windows of the castle but stalled when I saw someone staring back at me. It seemed a he. His bulky built made sure of showing no confusion even if he was so, so far away. It was quite distinguishable that he was wearing a white shirt, but that was all that could be made sense of. The rest was a blur.

"Hey, Blond, come here!" I whispered, motioning Blond to move forward.

"Blond?" he asked quite confusedly and sounding outraged as he made his way to me.

The man was still staring. His stare seemed so intense it made hairs stand at the back of my neck. I turned towards Blond, wishing he could see the strange man just as I did. Castles were always haunted. But the one I would see day and night could not possibly be haunted, could it?

"Can you see the man?"

"What man? I see no man," he whispered back, scrunching his eyes as he looked in the direction of the castle.

I turned towards the castle, and the man was gone.

"He was just there! I promise!"

He looked at me frowning for a second before his smile came back.

"I can help you decorate your room." He offered, looking as if he really were interested in sorting out my mess.

I smiled as I brushed a stray of brown hair behind my ear, silently thanking God for his sudden offer to decorate my bedroom. It would have taken me all day and night, otherwise.

"Let's do this."

CHAPTER TWO

The sun had begun to sink, and darkness was making an entrance when Alex and I finally managed to complete setting up my bedroom.

I slumped on the comfortable alcove by the window as I heaved out a sigh of relief. I had a feeling this part of the room would be my favorite. Dad did give me the room with the best view. I could see the castle from most of the windows here. But the best view was provided by the window by the bench and the full glass walls where Blond and I had decided to place my two tiny sofas.

The brilliant thing about this was that there were bookshelves around the bench. It was the perfect spot for reading.

I smiled and turned towards Blond who was currently slumped on the sofa. "Well, I'm glad it's over. Thank you for helping me with the lights, moving stuff and everything."

"It's alright. Dad was an electrician before, so he taught me a few things. Besides, it was fun. Who knew you could rock to Mayday Parade like you did?"

Thinking of all the ridiculous dance moves I had bolted out while decorating my bedroom, I giggled. "Thanks. You're not so bad yourself. I'll buy you smoothies for this, you know?"

Letting out a chuckle, Blond casually got up and began walking towards me lazily, making me tense immediately.

With the same old smirk I had grown to so lovingly hate now plastered onto his face, Blond strode his way towards me, and I watched wide-eyed as he bent down to level himself with me.

"I ask not much for the help I provided, but a small token of gratefulness, a kiss, fair maiden, for the help I provided?" Alex murmured, still smirking slightly as he stared straight into my wide eyes. *Wait, what?*

"Or maybe a staring competition?" I croaked out, moving back slightly.

I felt like hitting myself. *Idiot!*

Alex confused me when he grinned. "I accept."

Chuckling nervously, I shook my head and nodded. "Let us commence the battle!"

Looking straight into each other's eyes, I popped out my tongue trying to distract him, but apparently, Blond seemed learned and didn't lose his concentration for a second.

"You wanna play dirty, aye?" He chuckled, still staring straight into my eyes.

A small giggle left my lips but stopped instantly when Blond started to come closer, all the while not breaking eye contact once.

I began to sweat. This was definitely getting heated. His beautiful face just inches before me. His smirk was slightly edgier, but I still managed to maintain eye contact. This was not something I had expected to be happening on my first day in Peidmond.

"You could look away, you know?" Alex whispered as he inched closer. Our nose slightly brushed together, making me gulp nervously.

This was definitely something I hadn't expected to happen on my first day here. Sure, I had hoped that there would at least be a cute guy living next door. But nearly kissing that cute boy next door, in my own room on my first day, was something I was not expecting. Looking at Blond's personality, I wasn't sure it was something I wanted. Heck, I had never been at nose distance from a guy before except my cousin Ronny, but that fella was three, and he had burped on my face just seconds later. Kids these days!

"Look away. You'll just lose, nothing more," Alex smirked as he continued to inch closer, and I narrowed my eyes at his egotistic self. Despite my reservations on kissing Blond, I continued to stare back. I never backed down from a challenge, and I was definitely not going to let the arrogant blond huntsman win.

Blond moved closer. Despite the nervous sweats beginning to trickle down my neck, despite the blush that must have practically made me look like a darned tomato, and despite the fact that what could be an Abercrombie model was barely brushing noses with me now, I stared back.

Alex suddenly grinned, and my eyes widened as a spark shot across his eyes, slightly glazing his beautiful blue orbs over. He inched close, only for a second, as if going in for a kiss, and I fisted my hands tightly on my sides before moving back to brushing noses again.

This was bad. I felt more nervous than when I had to sit for the surprise quiz for AP Calculus. I was sure I was going to die of intense heart palpitations. This was that bad.

Suddenly, Alex's expression turned more serious, and the smirk disappeared. It was then that I knew that this was never about the game. He had just wanted to kiss me. *Get ready to initiate a punch.*

He moved slightly closer, and I stilled, realizing that my back was now pressed against the bookshelves. Either I would lose this game or get kissed. *Lose, it is.*

Just as I was about to push Blond away, a very loud yet distant growl rung out from the direction of the castle. I shot my head towards the window to see a blur of white run past one of those windows. *Strange.*

Blond stilled instantly. I stilled, glued looking at the castle. *Ghosts*...The whole world came to a standstill.

Alex grimaced slightly and moved back until he sat on the other edge of the bench. His face shone true horror as if he had just encountered a ghost or realized the woman he wanted in his bed was, in fact, a man.

Oh, makeup! Shine thy light upon my beard for I want smooth cheeks too!

"You alright there, Blonds? I wonder what that was, though," I asked him, awkwardly placing my hand on his shoulder. I silently hoped he would tell me what he knew about the growl because it was clear he knew something.

Disappointment on my part, Alex nodded before looking at me and smiling slightly.

"You lost," he stated, got up, and moved towards the door. Opening the door, he turned back and smirked. *Damn that smirk!* "See you in school, Theia."

I slumped slightly onto the bench and sighed, my mind whirling with Alex's reaction after the growl. It was clear he knew something; his face had been too scared not to know. What was Alex hiding?

Turning to look at the castle once more, I opened the window wide open. Bright lights now illuminated half of the castle windows and grounds. The other half, however, still stood in darkness because of its little usage, perhaps. *It made sense.* That castle seemed big enough for a thousand people or more, actually. Still, though, to see the soft glows of the castle against the slightly bluish grey color of the skies made it look magical. Then again, how could it not? After all, who would have thought that there would be such a big splendid castle in a city like Peidmond, just in the outskirts of Seattle?

Thinking of city, maybe shopping wasn't such a bad idea. I straightened on the bench. My face suddenly brightened up again with excitement. Yes, maybe, shopping was not a bad idea, after all. I had school on Monday, and the weekend provided a great time to get up and prepare for that.

With my mind made up and a smile gracing my lips unconsciously, I closed the window shut. After opening the other window near the couch, I paced to the bathroom. I had checked the bathroom out earlier. It was more than enough compared to what I had in my previous home. Everything looked great and new.

Moving towards the shower, I realized I had left my essentials behind. Shaking my head as a chuckle passed my lips, I slowly walked out into my bedroom once again, but stopped when I noticed the curtains from the window flew in one direction very strangely.

I stopped in my steps. The image of the curtains flowing in one direction shot up in my mind again. They were flowing in one direction as if something had just rushed past it.

My eyes widened, and I looked around my empty room. Suddenly feeling stupid, I dismissed the idea in my head.

"Theia, you're an idiot," I muttered under my breath while I went over to my untouched suitcases. I hadn't let Blond touch any of the suitcases that contained my clothes and showering essentials. That boy was too naughty for his own good.

Grabbing onto the bag with my body washes: shampoos, conditioners, and scrubs; I walked into the bathroom and set everything up. I walked back out once done and grabbed onto the creams and body lotions I knew I would most probably use after showers, moved them into the bathroom, and placed them in front of the mirror. Finally done, I dumped my nightclothes onto the bed before shutting close the suitcase and placing it beside the ones packed with clothes.

Feeling my muscles ache with the day's work and travel, I groaned as I turned the main lights off and turned on the string lights around the room before grabbing the clothes and marching into the bathroom. A bubble bath was very much in order.

Food was the one and only thing I could think of as I made my way out of the bathroom, all scrubbed and brushed, clad in a tiny boxer shorts and tank top.

Unwrapping the towel from my wet hair, I gave my hair a final rub and hung the towel on the towel hanger before padding my way towards my backpack.

The sooner I plugged both my iPod and phone into the charging dock, the faster I could get to the food. The hunger hazed my senses so much that I didn't even notice the man standing by my window, wearing a black shirt and grey trousers, never moving his gaze from me.

And I surely didn't notice the faint whisper when he simply frowned and said, "Mine."

CHAPTER THREE

I groaned as the harsh morning sun danced over my face, toying with me and coaxing me to get out of bed, and I so desperately wanted to pull the drapes close. But my bed was inviting. The want to stay cuddled against my various amounts of comfy pillows outweighed the need to close the blinds. I decided to stay in bed and grumbled out a million very colorful profanities, hurling each one to this current morning. To be defined as a morning person was nothing I'd be accountable for.

"Honey, get up! You have to go to school, remember?" Mom yelled and knocked on the door twice before the sound of her footsteps faded. Suddenly, with all sleep forgotten, I shot up in bed and stared ahead wide-eyed.

It was Monday. I had school. It was the middle of the year, and I had a new school. *Kill…me…now.*

"I hate this," I grumbled out to the empty air as I moved into the bathroom, my morning voice sounding as gritty as an amateur trying their hands at a violin. *Horrendous.*

Picking up my toothbrush, I quickly brushed. After, my crying bladder decided to make its agony known. It seemed like minutes later when I found myself walking out of the bathroom freshly bathed and brushed, and I padded my way lazily into my bedroom.

A cold gust of wind hit my wet skin, and I shivered. *Strange. I don't remember opening the window since I closed it last night…*

Maybe Mom did, I assured myself as I ignored the open window and walked into the closet, picked out an outfit that would go well with my well worn-out white sneakers. Once all dressed up and ready, I made a check for my iPod, phone, and books before walking towards the window and glancing at the castle once again.

I just couldn't stop looking at it. The tales spun as I watched and analyzed each and every window. The tiny glimpses of halls and the grounds usually brought up images of beasts and pirates, of lords and ladies, of Belle in her yellow gown, gliding along the ballroom and her beast. Yes, the tales I spun while watching the castle were truly beyond what would even be considered possible. And with every tale I spun, I couldn't help but wonder how would it be like to live there.

With a final glance and a faint smile lurking on my lips, I walked downstairs and into the kitchen.

I had come to appreciate my new home the past weekend. The brick house was actually very homey once I managed to get used to it, such as making sure that the hallways turned right instead of left if I wanted to go downstairs, and there were now four bedrooms and not three. But despite all facts, I still liked this house mainly because of the views. In fact, I personally believed it was very cleverly designed to have all the views in every room possible since one side of the house actually sat on the edge of a cliff and faced the countryside and the castle while the other faced the distant city.

My gaze stopped on a small note. I quickly picked it up and began reading. It seemed that my mom and dad were already gone. I suppose I had stared at the castle a little too long.

Gone to work. Blueberry pancakes in the fridge. Eat before you leave. We are not kidding! Alex will give you a ride to school. (Thank the sweet boy after the ride, Thi.) See you by 7!

Love,
Mom and Dad

I glanced at my wristwatch quickly before picking up two granola bars and moving towards the front door. I was possibly late, not a good sign for the new girl. The pancakes would have to wait for later.

"About time she walked out!"

Looking up as I closed the front door and turned around, I saw Blond seated in a black Range Rover with a brown-haired boy with glasses in the passenger seat. I smiled at the two boys awkwardly. I hadn't seen much of him all weekend. My attention moved back to the nice-looking boy riding shotgun. *Hmm. Maybe that's Matthew.*

"I'm sorry for being late," I murmured apologetically as I opened the back door and got in. Even though I was not a morning person, I still managed to get to school an hour early and have myself a good library session. My attendance record was spotless so far.

"It's okay. We like to make banging late entries, anyway. I'm Matthew by the way. You're pretty! Alex here wasn't lying." The brown-haired boy looked back and smiled at me, extending his arm.

I took it and gave it a shy handshake. The heat on my cheeks made sure Matthew saw exactly how surprised I was by the compliment. Apparently, Blond thought I was pretty.

Blond suddenly coughed, violently shoved his arm into Matthew's side, and then glanced at me from the review mirror. His cheeks flushed slightly. *Oh, so he's shy.*

"Oh, so Blond thinks I'm pretty, aye? Well, good. I'm glad our thoughts are so similar. Thank you, Matthew. That's very sweet of you. How is Rosenberg High School, though?" I chirped brightly as I smirked at Blond before turning towards a smiling Matthew.

"The House of Wolves," Alex replied, still smirking and turning to look at me before turning his attention on the road. The fear of a car accident began flashing in my mind.

"You didn't exactly answer my question," I responded, cocking an eyebrow up at Alex, and turned towards Matthew. "But wolves are my favorite animals."

Matthew turned back and looked at me. A grin set on his face. "How so?"

I shrugged. "They are beautiful."

"We are here," Alex declared suddenly.

Turning into the parking lot, he found a parking space and drove in. After we parked the car into a good enough spot, I got out of the car first and turned to say my thanks when two arms linked themselves to mine. I yelped as the two boys began walking towards the school.

"What are you guys doing?" I whispered as a dozen stared us.

"Helping you around." Matthew chuckled and pulled me closer as he tightened his hold on my arm.

Blushing beet red, I shifted my gaze towards Blond, who was looking at me with a very amused smile.

"What?" I demanded, frowning slightly.

Was there something on my face?

"You look like a tomato." He chuckled, causing Matthew to let out a loud laugh.

I huffed as I felt my blush deepen. The nagging feeling of knowing that the attention of the whole student population, who were currently standing outside was on the three of us—myself, in particular—was extremely awkward.

The glares thrown my way were also something that didn't go unnoticed. I shuddered because I knew that if it could hit, the glares would definitely shrivel me up to a pulp.

However, the analyzing gazes from the guys were not exactly subtle either, as Matthew soon pointed out. "Awkward how the boys are looking at us. We've never experienced this sort of look before."

Blond growled. "They're looking at Theia, Matt. They really should look away. I hate being stared at…and my fists are itching for a brawl."

"Hey, Matt, who's the new girl? Cousin or something?" a buff, blond dude asked as we entered the hallways.

"Whose? Yours? Good to know at least one of the girls here at Rosenberg is your cousin, Jared." Matthew chuckled and pulled me away, leaving the guy gawking at us.

Turning towards Matthew, I giggled. "That was really good!"

"Hey, guys, er…I need to be somewhere. See you during lunch," Blond suddenly spoke up, unlinking his arm from mine, and walked away.

"Where's he going?" I questioned Matt, who continued to lead me towards the office. Come to think of it, he was actually very cute.

"Probably gone off to meet Diandra." Matthew shrugged.

"Who's Diandra?"

"Alex's girlfriend of two years, didn't you know?" Matthew asked, turning towards me incredulously.

I frowned. Blond tried to kiss me. Blond tried to kiss me but had a girlfriend. Blond tried to kiss me but had a girlfriend and never told me. *Well, shit.*

It hurt a bit that someone would do that, and suddenly, the fact that I had initially found him attractive made me cringe at myself. *What an idiot, Theia.*

"You okay?" Matthew nudged me as we turned towards the hall that led to the office.

I glanced at him and smiled slightly. "Dandy."

Rosenberg High was incredibly large, not as large as my previous school but large, nonetheless. Its facilities looked newer, and although I didn't appreciate the slight cream and blue combination, it seemed to fit perfectly well around the halls.

"Good morning. How may I help you, Matthew and the lovely lady you have clenched beside you?"

I smiled at the lady at the counter, ignoring her slight emphasis on the word *clenched.* She seemed nice enough with a navy blue suit on. Her gracefully greying hair was rolled up in a bun, and those twinkling eyes assured a good sense of humor. A tag was pinned by her breast; it read *Marilyn Jeffrey.*

"Good morning. I'm Theia. I'm new here," I mumbled sweetly, not at all trying to move out of Matthew's grip even though Marilyn kept on glancing at it and smiling to herself.

"Oh, yes, dear! Here are your schedule, your locker number, and pin. Also, we were informed by your previous principal that you were one of the top students and an avid reader. Hence, here is a library pass to make you feel more at home. It will enable you to use and issue out just about any of the library books available, even the reference if you need it, that is, and you will have your own little space."

Shocked for a minute, I quickly regained myself and beamed as I took the papers and card from her. "Thank you, ma'am. It means a lot! Have a nice day."

Still beaming that Mrs. Ambrosia had actually made a note of calling my current school and helping me get an all-access library pass, I had only just turned to leave when Marilyn said, "I'm glad you've finally found a girl, Matthew. She seems like a keeper! Just keep her glued to you like you are doing right now and everything will be fine."

Matthew stilled. I stilled. Marilyn let out a slow giggle.

I turned towards Matt, who now looked like he would rather have the floor open up and swallow him alive. It made me giggle.

"Thanks, Mrs. J," he murmured before pulling me behind him as he quickly fled the area.

I couldn't breathe.

"Let's find my locker." I let out in huffs, still trying to catch my breath as I was being rushed out of the reception area.

***

"We have Math now," Matthew declared as he scanned through my schedule while I, on the other hand, stood in front of my locker, placing all my books, pens, pencils, tapes, paint brushes, and paint into it.

Once done, I picked out the books and things I would need for math and closed the locker shut.

"Well, let's go then," I declared, hooking my arm with Matt.

The occasional jealous glares I had thought to be receiving only for Alex actually was equally being handed my way for Matthew too. Apparently, his cute-geek-slash-angry-young-man look appealed to the ladies at Rosenberg High. I could see why, though. He was actually very handsome.

As we walked into class, the loud and obnoxious whispers floating around the classroom instantly came to a halt. I made a quick scan through the crowd.

Smiling girls, *check*. Oblivious boys, *check*. Glaring girls, *check*. A slightly alarmed Blond sitting beside another blonde-haired girl, *check*.

Ignoring my urge to land a swift slap on Blond's face for even attempting to cheat on his girlfriend, I made my way to the only vacant desk in front of him and as gracefully as I could, placed my butt on the seat.

I knew it wasn't worth it. Good-looking guys were hardly ever faithful, and I was never one to end up in these type of dramas. As long as I didn't let myself get into such situation again, I would be fine by ignoring Blond.

Matthew, however, grinned a little at the counted amount of glaring boys and made his way over to the seat beside mine before plopping down on it.

"H-Hey, Matthew! Is she the new girl?" a new voice spoke up from behind me, and I turned around to glance at a timid girl sitting just behind Blonde's girlfriend, Diandra.

The girl smiled at me shyly, and her lips crinkled slightly as she did. She looked about my height, which wasn't much, only 5'3." Her soft red hair glowed slightly as she tilted her head nervously.

I smiled back and waved in greeting, not missing the eye roll Diandra sent my way as she pulled Blond's arm more. Blond, however, looked at me as if apologizing for his act, but I shrugged it off without handing him a reaction to work with.

Serves him good. That attempted cheat!

"I'm Theia Anderson. It's nice to meet you."

"H-hi. I'm Marley! Theia as in 'goddess of light,' right?"

I giggled and nodded. I had also wondered why my mother and father had decided to name me Theia since it was a Greek name, and we were anything but Greek. The curiosity led me to do a bit of research as any twelve-year-old might do once a sudden topic of interest sparked, and it was then that I found the meaning of my name. Later, I learned about Dad's fascination with Greek mythology during the days of Mom's pregnancy had gotten the best of him, and well, that was that. I was thus named Theia.

"Yeah, that." I giggled, still nodding to a now giggling Marley. I had a feeling we were going to be great friends!

"Good morning, class. How are you all this fine Monday morning?"

I turned towards the white board to see a quite handsome man wearing glasses, standing in front and smiling at us students with a strange sarcastic humor.

His eyes did a small sweep around the room until it landed on mine. I barely held off my head as a sign of approval flashed in his eyes and he smiled rather nicely at me.

"If my sources are correct, we have a new student here, Theia Anderson. I'm Mr. Phelps. Could you please stand up and tell us a little about yourself?"

My eyes widened, and I turned to look at Matthew frantically. The last thing I needed right now was to make a complete fool out of myself. It wasn't hard to see I had trouble speaking in front of large crowds without mucking up. When Matt refused to offer me anything except a sad smile that barely said, 'I'm sorry,' I slowly got up and instantly felt my feet give way. This was bad.

Breathe, Thi! Breathe! Imagine them wearing coconut shells and leaves and doing the hula!

"Hi, my name is Theia Anderson, and I have just recently moved here with my family from Los Angeles, California. And, er…that's all?" *Phew, that was good!*

Mr. Phelps nodded approvingly, and I gladly slumped back into my seat, Avoiding the glares from every girl, Marley excluded.

"Well, Ms. Anderson, I hope you enjoy studying here at Rosenberg High. Now, class, let's start with AP Calculus."

"Bring it on, baby! This is a piece of candy," Matthew whispered as he held his pen with much more vigor.

So I was right! He is a nerd! Thank you, God. I have found my people!

"Let's do this!" I whispered back and grinned towards Matt.

Maybe this new school wouldn't be as bad as I thought.

***

Dipping my toe into the miniature man-made stream, I sighed happily as I felt the water flow right past my toe.

So cool!

I had barely the time to check out my backyard the past weekend since I helped Mom and Dad decorate the house and all, and then, the shopping wasn't easy as well. So naturally, I thought to remedy that after school.

The day had gone through as smoothly as it could. I had gained myself two friends—Marley and Matthew—and although I wouldn't mind calling Blond a friend, even after his kissing stunt, Diandra seemed to think it fit to keep her boyfriend at least five feet away from me.

Not that I minded that or anything, the last thing I was looking for was drama. And Diandra spelt out drama with a capital D, although a capital B for *queen bee* would also fit perfectly.

After math class, Marley and I had discovered that we had the rest of the classes together and ended up being teamed as desk mates in art class. We had to paint each other as our project, which I found awesome.

From what I had seen, I personally think Marley seemed to have a crush on Matt. I mean, not that that's impossible; he was handsome and smart too. I definitely saw myself playing Cupid when it came to both of them, though.

Mathew, on the other hand, shared every class with Marley and I except Arts, and that was sad since I had a feeling he had amazing art skills.

The day had ended quickly, and before I knew it, classes were over, and I was boarding the bus. I made a note to myself: beg Mom and Dad to let me buy my Audi. I had been saving up for it for forever. I turned eighteen a few weeks ago. I deserved a car. Besides, after the kiss incident, I refused to travel in Alex's vehicle. That would be wrong.

Shrugging the thoughts away, I made a sweep across the backyard and noticed a swimming pool near the tiny patio, which led to a bench area that was surrounded by rose bushes and vines. I stared in wonder at its beauty. With the pink and white roses in full bloom, it looked like a scene just out of a romance novel. *Mental note: spend time reading here.*

After five minutes of staring at the beauty, I finally managed to tear my eyes off the gorgeous bench area and continued to look around the backyard. There were roses bushes planted firmly along the fence. But the fence ended, and it appeared as if our backyard led straight into the woods.

Strange. Why not fence the whole yard?

All of a sudden, my eyes landed on the large apple tree in the far corner of the yard. It was plain and barren, nary a fruit or flower in blossom. But what caught my attention was the swing that was attached to one of the thicker branches.

As a child, I loved swings and would make Dad take me to the park every afternoon just for that. Now, to have my very own swing seemed like the best thing that could happen, and although it was fairly plain, it would do perfectly.

Sighing contentedly as I ran my hand along the strong rope, I finally gave it a try and sat on it. I dragged the swing back a meter, and I let go and let it soar above the ground.

It was the best feeling I felt all day. I felt free as the birds, and it felt so elevating. I couldn't help but let out a low giggle.

***

"It's getting dark," a deep voice spoke up from behind me as I felt my swing come to a sudden stop. Clearly caught off guard, I gasped with a sudden stop. A stranger was in my yard. He was right; it was growing dark.

Damn it, Thi!

My mind was everywhere. The deep voice was very alluring. The person also had a very distinct British accent, so trying to imagine a dangerous face with the voice was nearly impossible.

Shut up, Theia! What if he's a killer? What if…Oh my god, I can feel him breathe behind me! Oh my god! Shit, Theia! Do something! Run! Okay! One…Two…Thr—

"Ah!" My sudden scream echoed around me as the stranger pulled me back into the swing, mid-way from my escape. His large hand clasped around mine while I still gripped tightly around the ropes.

I was stuck.

What does he want? Does he want to kill me? Why does he want to kill me! I am too young! Damn it, I haven't even finished the book I was reading! What about Mom and Dad? Oh, why is life so cruel?

"A-are you going to kill me?" I whispered, not wanting to let my voice waver. I was too proud to show my future killer how scared I actually was. If I were to die, I would die bravely.

The stranger let out a chuckle, and my eyes widened as I felt a warm feeling run through my belly. *I wonder how he looks like.*

"No, I am not going to kill you."

Despite the warm tingles bubbling inside my belly, I stiffened. Feeling calm enough, I let out a deep breath, a big one for good measure. *Turn around...slowly.* I mustered enough courage to do so. It's like I died and went straight to paradise and came back.

Standing behind me was a duplicate of the Greek god Adonis. Standing behind me was the sole epitome of perfection, the type of man who deserved to be in movies or on magazines. His deep baritone voice fit his face perfectly. Everything from his clear blue eyes to his beautiful cleft chin to his strong aristocratic jaw to his dark wavy hair spelt power and dominance.

When he realized I had been staring too long, his lips pulled up a ghost of a smile, and my wide eyes found another thing to marvel. This man's smile was officially to die for.

How could someone so beautiful be bad. What the hell are you doing, you stupid girl? He could kill you! He is trespassing on private property! He could be a looter!

Suddenly seeing sense, I shook my head and looked away.

He couldn't want anything good, could he?

I sighed. There was no escaping him. The man was built like Hulk.

"What do you want?"

"A name," the man responded, his voice a bit on the huskier side.

I frowned. "Whose?"

He smiled, his cleft chin becoming more prominent. "Yours."

"Why?"

"You ask too many questions, *amore mio.*"

"A name for a name?"

I really did want to put a name to his beautiful face. Okay, I had officially lost my mind.

The man smiled. "You may call me Bryce."

Bryce, huh? This will need some getting used to. Wait, you probably won't ever meet this man again.

"Now, your turn," he added, moving to stand in front of me while I still sat on the swing. He placed his palm on mine as he switched his position.

"T-Theia," I mumbled. Suddenly too shy to match eyes with him, I turned my gaze towards my lap.

"It's an honor to finally meet you, Theia. *Ti ho aspetatto per tanto tempo*," Bryce's deep voice spoke softly, making me glance at him in disbelief.

Finally met me?

Still holding onto my hand, he slipped my hand off the rope and slowly brought it to his lip. His soft, warm lips pressed gently against the back of my palm, a little while longer than normal as if holding a promise that this would not be the last time his lips would grace my skin. I shivered at the thought.

Stupid Thi, he is a Greek god and you, an English milkmaid. Chill out. You're weaving worthless romances.

"I have to leave now," he announced all of a sudden. Letting go of my hand, he stepped back, his stance stiff and his facial expression a little distant.

I nodded and instantly stood up, half-disappointed and partially overjoyed that he had to leave. Why couldn't I just feel one thing?

You're never going to see this beautiful face again, Thi. Of course, you would be sad. Hell, even Grandma Lidia would be disappointed at the thought of never seeing this beautiful face again.

"You're tiny." The stranger chuckled, pulling me a little closer. My head barely reached his shoulders, well, almost. Damn him for being so tall!

"Or maybe you are just too tall," I retorted lamely, folding my arms in front of me.

Bryce grinned. "Touché. Now, close your eyes."

My eyes did the contrary. They widened.

"Why?" I demanded, stepping back for a bit. Bryce's eyes narrowed at me, his anger apparent although he quickly shook it off and a smile appeared on his lips.

Damn that smile!

"Just close your eyes. I promise I won't bite…yet." He assured me. Finally sighing in defeat, I closed my eyes slowly.

The sound of shoes crunching onto leaves drifted to my ears, and before I knew it, a voice whispered in my ear. "Until we meet again, my love."

A sudden rush of wind hit my face as if slightly urging me to open my eyes, as if informing that he was gone.

So, I did. And he was. Bryce was gone.

His words seemed to echo around me even though it was only a soft whisper against my ear. And at that moment, I knew. This was not the last of Bryce. We would meet again.

CHAPTER FOUR

Finding out that we were moving a month ago never had me daydreaming about a lot of things. On most parts, I'd wanted to let the mystery continue because the less I daydreamed, the less disappointed I would be. I forgot that the less I daydreamed, the more shocked I'd be too.

What had occurred three days ago, though, seemed like a very good candidate for a perfect daydream. A historical lord-like being descended from the heavens above talked to me and held my hand.

I would have thought I was crazy, but the marks that remained from his grip on my arm was proof that I had in fact talked to the epitome of every girl's fantasy and imagination when they read a historical romance.

There was no way to deny it; Bryce had been a beautiful possible killer. But truth be told, that wasn't it. His beauty, his charm weren't exactly what had me so intrigued. There was just something about him. Something just pulled me in, something warm and comforting. I didn't know what it was, but I found myself back in the swing each day after the end of school, waiting. And he would come.

Sometimes he would sit in front of the swing. Sometimes he would stand at the back and pull. And every day in these past three days, all we ever talked about were those tiny things, the likes, dislikes, jobs, and dreams.

I noticed, though, Bryce had seemed to avoid some of the questions, and although normally that would alert me, I didn't know why, but I couldn't bring myself to suspect him. And then I'd spend my nights telling myself how much of an idiot I was.

The same sound of a bat's cry ran through the woods, reminding me of the setting sun every day, and I slumped in the swing a little.

Again, I sat on the swing again today, hoping he would come. He didn't. My nagging conscience that almost always turned out correct couldn't help to warn me that being this friendly with a stranger was incredibly stupid and all because he looked really, really, really handsome.

I sighed as I turned towards the darkening sky and finally got off the swing. Maybe he wouldn't come today. With each step towards the back door, I felt the lump of disappointment settling in my throat. I climbed on the first step, my hand reaching for the doorknob, and I stilled when a hand wrapped around mine.

"I'm sorry."

I stared down at my feet as I let him hold my hand. "What for?"

He took a step closer, his footstep thumping on the patio floor. "Being late."

"It's almost dark." I shrugged. Turning around, I looked up into the bright blue pools of ocean staring at me.

A small smile teased the edge of his mouth, and he leaned down lower. "I know," he mumbled, curling a strand of hair behind my ear.

"How was your day?"

"Profitable. How was school?"

I shrugged. "Educational."

Bryce smirked and began striding towards me. He dropped on the sofa beside me. It felt strangely good. This was the first time we'd actually sat somewhere together.

"You're angry."

I was a little. I shook my head. "No, I'm not."

Bryce's smirk widened. "Yes, you are."

Looking at him smirk, I slumped in my seat. "Okay, a little." I admitted in a small voice.

Bryce edged closer, and for the first, time moved his hands over my shoulder. I stilled. All the gnawing questions in my mind suddenly just slipped in one go.

"Are you engaged? Married? In a relationship? Do you have a kid? Or kids? Are you really even twenty-four?" I blurted out hurriedly as I asked him the questions I'd been wanting to ask him for days.

Bryce stilled beside me, and his grip on my shoulder tightened. I cringed a little at his strength.

"No. No. Maybe. No. No. Yes."

Maybe…

"So…It's complicated?" I mumbled out slowly, my mind on his relationship status. So there was another girl.

"Yes."

Yes…

It was already dark now. The moon was making itself known, another night, and another silky silver ball gown dazzling us with its rays.

"Oh…"

I inched out of Bryce's arms and smiled awkwardly when I stood up and turned towards him. "It's getting late. I have to make dinner."

Frowning slightly, Bryce got up, rubbing his hands on his pants. "Want some help?"

Hands on the patio door, I opened it up and looked back at a smiling Bryce. I shook my head. He was in a relationship, and I didn't want the other girl to feel cheated.

"I'm sorry, but Mom said no strangers allowed in the house."

I didn't wait to see Bryce's face or hear his response. Moving back quickly, I turned away and closed the door behind me, locking it.

Two hours later found me in my room, a cup of forgotten chilled coffee on my study table, and lying numb on my bed.

The sound of a car entering the garage settled through the air, and I let out a small sigh. Mom and Dad were home.

My thoughts waded back to the blue-eyed man I met for the last time just hours ago. A glance at my grandma's wedding ring had me falling deeper into melancholy because his eyes were so like their shade, Swiss blue topaz.

I closed my eyes shut and turned away. Maybe something in Peidmond's water had every taken guy flirting with other girls. This was the second time this happened to me: first, Alex and now, Bryce. It hasn't hurt so much with Alex, though, but Bryce…Despite my closed eyes, a tear slipped out to its doom. It hurt more for Bryce.

"Honey, we're home!" Mom yelled as I heard the front door shut.

Our home was fairly moderate in size, somewhat leaning towards the large side, but the neighborhood was quite quiet during the dying hours of the sun, so hearing the front door shut or open was easier during these periods.

Feeling lame for falling into the same trap again, I shook my head. Immediately pulling on the happy face, I decided I was going to smile until my face hurt.

"Hey, Mom! Hey, Dad! I'm just up in my room going to do some homework, alright?" I yelled as I stuck my head out of the doorway, waiting for a reply.

"Okay, sweetie! We will let you know when dinner is ready! I feel like grilling chicken tonight! What do you say?" Dad yelled back.

Despite my smile, another tear slipped out, and I shook it away with an image of Dad seated on a high chair. I could practically picture him sitting in the high chair, placing his glasses aside and watching Mom as she stretched out a bit before cooking. It had been twenty years since their marriage, but their love was still very apparent.

I wanted that. Whenever I saw them holding hands or sneaking kisses when they thought I wasn't watching or when Dad whispered into Mom's ear and she turned red before hitting his arm—yes, I wanted that.

I sighed and replied, "Sure, Dad! Chicken sounds great! Let me know if you guys need help!"

Maybe someday I will find my very own Mr. Soulmate.

A pair of blue pools flashed before my eyes, but I chased them away.

Not him…

Still mentally scolding myself for acting so stupidly, I walked into the bathroom. A shower was in order.

***

I smacked the laptop shut before picking up the papers that had just been printed. A 5,000-word essay done and compiled. Stapling the papers together, I placed them into the file and padded my way to bed. I sighed in content as I slumped down, and my sore, strained back eased up.

Damn, I need to take posture lessons or something. This back pain is horrible!

Beside me, my phone flashed up instantly catching my attention.

"Oh, lord," I muttered as I reached for the phone and unlocked it.

```
I know you're mad. I know you think that I'm a dick, but I swear it I don't love Diandra! It's just…please just give me a chance to explain myself properly. Tomorrow, after school. Let me drive you home please! - Alex
```

"What a dick," I muttered, moving back to my messages section. I kind of felt bad for Diandra. I mean, sure, her soul seemed to be made up of castor oil, squids, and everything nasty, but she did not deserve to have her boyfriend cheat on her. Alex was wrong.

Deciding to avoid Alex from now on, I tapped onto *Create Messages* and typed up a text to Casey. It had been days, and I missed her badly. I made a sure note to invite her over for holidays.

A beep sounded through the room, and I tapped on it eagerly thinking it to be Casey.

`Please, Theia. I apologize. I just want friendship, nothing more. Even Matthew kinda hates me now. Please just…Text me back? - Alex`

My eyes stopped at Matthew, and I sighed. I didn't exactly want friends fighting because of me. Just then I noticed a reply from Casey, and my face brightened.

`And you remember me now? I WANT TO SHOOT YOU! How dare you not text me all day! (Am I clingy enough? Are you pissed yet? ;]) Jesus, woman, you have to give me a detailed description of that Adonis guy! I am so jealous! By the way, Brian here was asking about you; said, he sent you a request on Facebook (ACCEPT IT I SAY! That boy is a hunk!). Text me back as soon as you can! - YourBabyMomma x`

I rolled my eyes, barely holding off a chuckle as I typed a reply before curling up in bed. This time, however, thoughts of Bryce didn't come crashing in, my mind too preoccupied with Alex and Matthew.

"Theia! Dinner is ready, sweetie!" Mom called out suddenly.

"Oh, thank God! I was dying," I murmured, picking up the plate and cup and then proceeding to make my way downstairs.

Time for some grilled chicken and cheese!

***

The first thing I noticed as I entered my bedroom was the open window. The night air filled the room as a breeze danced past the light curtain, moving it in a waltz. I didn't remember opening the window.

Had someone been in here?

I turned to make a sweep around the room when my gaze catches the unlocked phone resting on my bed. Its screen showed my wallpaper—the castle.

A shiver ran through my spine. Someone had been in my room a second ago and had been going through my phone. Gulping down bile, I feebly walked towards my bed and picked up my phone for any evidence of what the person would have wanted.

I quickly tapped onto the call log and froze. There were a missed call from Alex and a received one. The call had been received only five minutes ago and lasted for ninety seconds. *So does that mean Alex knows who was here?*

My hands shaking, I moved back and into the messages section. There were new messages from Casey and Alex—both I hadn't read yet but already marked as read.

That's it. Someone wants to kill you, Thi.

As if automatically, my feet pulled me towards the open window. I leaned against it cautiously, trying to make out any moving figure in the woods. But the night was stripped bare of the moonlight, and the woods looked nothing but a dark game of Snakes and Ladders, where there were more snakes than ladders.

A howl rang out through the air. Nobody had told me these woods had wolves. Oh God, wild wolves could be highly unpredictable!

As if the fear in me bubbled beyond the extreme, I quickly grasped onto the window to shut it down but stopped when my gaze fell on a looming figure on the balcony of the castle. His silhouette slightly illuminated by the castle lights, the man turned, leaned onto the balcony, and faced me and then as if without a second doubt, jumped right off the fourth floor!

A shrill scream ripped out of my lips as I stared at the same spot—now empty! My heart beat frantically. A man just jumped off the castle balcony! A man had just…What the hell had just happened?

Everything seemed silent. Even the crickets ceased to chirp, and I still stood there staring at the spot the man had jumped.

Why would someone do that?

A deadly howl rang through the night, and I almost peed my pants. It wasn't every night you could hear a wolf howling, and that too right after someone sneaked into your room!

Come to think of it…Maybe I should call Alex.

"Honey, honey, are you okay?"

Whirling around, I came face to face with my parents. Their panicked face settled into a curious look when their eyes landed on me.

I shook my head. "Everything is fine, guys. I just screamed because an owl just flew into the window."

"An owl?" Mom cocked an eyebrow up, looking suspicious.

"The window?" Dad followed.

"Honey, do we need to give you 'the talk?'" Mom cringed as she made quote marks with her fingers. Dad looked like he wanted to hide.

Despite my fear and rotten mood, I smiled and shook my head at them. "No, guys. It's alright…Honest."

Looking a little skeptical, Mom nodded. Dad, however, smiled at evading the talk.

"Alright, if you say so, fuzzy."

The sound of the door closing echoed around the room, and turning towards the window again, I roughly closed it before glancing at my iPhone. I pressed a call to Alex.

"Hello?" I mumbled.

"Theia, oh my God, it's you! I thought that guy was going to murder me!"

Guy? So there was a guy in my room! Should I tell Alex I didn't know who he was talking about? No…Play along, Thi.

"What happened?" I asked him, trying to sound as calm and concerned as I could.

The phone was silent for a bit, and I frowned as I pressed my ears against the cellphone trying to hear the background voices.

Why isn't he replying?

"I really wanted to talk to you, so I called you…The first time, no one accepted the call. So I tried again. A man picked up."

I heard as my voice hitched in my throat. My grip tightened on my cellphone.

It was official. I had a stalker.

"And?" I urged him to continue.

"And he told me to leave you alone, or he would kill me, and how you belonged to him. He sounded very deadly. You didn't tell me you had a boyfriend, Theia." Alex's voice sounded a little bitter by the end of his reply, but I ignored that. I didn't care whether he was bitter. However, the fact remained that someone had been in my room and had called me his.

"That's because I don't. Thanks, Alex. See you tomorrow," I mumbled back, distracted by what Alex had just told me.

Who could it be? I barely knew anyone. And who could climb the mountain to get to my room? No…It seemed impossible.

But then…who had picked up?

Suddenly, the ground began to move, and the walls spun around me. The lights kept on fluctuating from dim to bright and then…nothing.

The last thing I felt was the sharp pang as my head collided to the floor.

***

A groan left my slightly chapped lips, and I rubbed my eyes, trying to rid the last pieces of darkness. The softness under me seemed inviting as if coaxing me to stay. But I couldn't…I had school.

Getting up and moving against the headboard, I finally decided to open my—wait…headboard?

Where the hell am I?

Immediately, my eyes shot open, and the familiar soft cream walls welcomed my still jaded vision.

What was I doing in bed? The last thing I remembered was…oh my god. I fainted! How did I get in bed?

I clutched my hair.

Relax, Thi. It must have been Dad. He checks up on you occasionally. He must have put you to bed. Calm down.

A sigh of relief left my lips as I got out of bed and walked over to the bathroom.

Walking out of the bathroom, I marched my way to the closet while humming the tune to "Million Dollar Man" by Lana Del Rey.

"Keeping it simple today, Theia," I mumbled to myself as I quickly brushed down my hair before pulling it up into a messy bun. Smacking on some lip balm and putting on winged eyeliner, I grabbed onto my essentials and files before marching downstairs.

"Good morning, Thi!" Matthew beamed at me as I walked into the kitchen with a very confused look on.

Mom grinned at me, wiggling her eyebrows as she motioned to Matthew, who was busy happily munching on the French toast on his plate.

Mom loved cooking. Her love for food kept her trying out new things and creating her own versions whereas her passion for looking good usually kept her running for hours at a time after eating a hefty meal.

Often times, I found myself wishing I was like her, but apparently, walking around for five minutes cut it for me. I couldn't work out to save myself.

"Hi, Matthew." I smiled as I slipped onto a high chair beside him and Mom immediately passed me a plate full of French toast and coffee. I smiled in thanks to her before proceeding to munch on the delicious toast.

"Hey!" I yelled suddenly when a chuckling Matthew stole a large gulp of coffee from my cup.

"Sorry, I finished mine." He shrugged sheepishly, and my mother, who I had forgotten was observing our every move, giggled as if she were a lovestruck teenager.

God, that's it. I'm going to get the talk about the birds and bees again for the tenth time!

I rolled my eyes. "Clearly!"

"So Dad finally got me that Jeep Cherokee I wanted. I paid the down payment, though," Matthew mumbled as he managed to steal a piece of my French toast. *What's it with this boy and stealing my food?*

I narrowed my eyes and glared at him.

"Mine," I muttered stubbornly as I popped the last bit of toast into my mouth and gave him a very wide smile.

"You're weird, Anderson," Matthew muttered, looking at me with a weird look.

"Same to you, Jefferson." I grinned back, quickly gulped down the remaining coffee, and made my way to the sink.

"Can we go now?"

"Sure!" I chirped up. I waved a goodbye to Mom, and flinging my backpack over my shoulder, I quickly rushed behind him as he made his way to the black beauty standing outside.

Damn this vehicle looks amazing!

***

"So what's the equation between you and Alex?"

I shot my head towards Matthew as he continued to look onwards at the road, his face free of any emotions.

"We had a fallout."

"What? He tried to kiss you but didn't tell you about Diandra and is now begging for your forgiveness like a madman because he suddenly finds himself liking you?"

I stared at Matthew wide-eyed. How could he know these things? Was he—No, no.

Matthew turned towards me and smiled.

"He actually texted me instead of you last night."

Oh!

I shrugged. "I don't care. It doesn't matter, actually. But I don't appreciate him attempting to cheat on the girl. No matter how awful she is."

I smirked at Matthew as he chuckled at me and shook his head.

"You're unlike anyone I know, Theia Anderson,"

"Well, it's an honor, Matthew Issac Jefferson," I replied in my British woman impression. Matthew turned to give me a sour face when I mentioned Issac; that made me giggle.

I took a quick glimpse at my wristwatch and smiled. 7:45 AM. *Loads of time to have a library session.*

As Matthew turned the car around the corner, I sneaked a glance at him. His brown hair was styled to form a slight quiff today, and the low lights on the tips of some of his hair shone blonde as the light touched them. He had a stubborn jaw paired with that beauty spot I knew he possessed in the left of his cheek. It was adorable. His warm brown eyes glowed red under sunlight. Usually, glasses hid the beauty of the eyes, but the nerd glasses Matthew wore today actually made them look more cute and innocent.

Now, I knew why the female population of Rosenberg High fancied Matthew I. Jefferson so much. The guy was the perfect blend of adorable and badass.

"Are you done staring at me?" Matthew chuckled.

I quickly glanced away as I felt the heat on my cheeks rising. *Oh shit! Damn it! He had caught me staring at him!*

"Er…Shut up!" I retorted lamely.

"Alright, alright." Matthew chuckled again as he drove into the school parking lot and found an empty spot.

"And we are here!" he declared as he removed his keys from the ignition, turned towards me and smiled.

Maybe I should talk about Marley to him.

I knew it could ruin her image in front of him, but hey, it could also help her out! *Well, worth a try I suppose!*

"So…er…I had to talk to you about something!" I chirped up, doubtful still of whether I should tell him or not.

"Yeah?" Matthew drawled, still smiling at me.

"What do you think about Marley?" I asked him, trying to read any expressions I could get from him.

His smile faltered a bit. *Oh shit!*

But then gained its original position again. *Hope!*

"She is a great girl. She's pretty too," Matthew replied.

He thinks she is pretty…Progress!

"So…I totally think you should take her out sometime!"

Matthew stilled. *Crap! You ruined it, Thi!*

"I'm sorry, Thi…I…She isn't my type. And my friend Keith likes her," Matthew mumbled, looking down at his palms as if disappointed.

I frowned curiously. "Well, what is your type?"

Matthew looked up at me for a bit before returning his gaze back on his palm.

"Well, spit it out. Come on tell, Mama Thi," I said in my best Jamaican accent.

He sighed.

"The girl I would want will have brown hair and shiny hazel eyes. Her lips will be as pink as a baby's. And when she would blush, her nose would turn the color of a tomato. She'd be simple, sweet, and innocent. And when we hug, her head will tuck underneath my chin. She will be that tiny." He stopped and chuckled. "Her laugh will be the brightest thing in my world, and she'll love books just like me. Yep, that's my type of girl."

I stared at Matthew. "And here I thought I had high expectations!" I blurted out and instantly gasped, slamming a hand over my mouth.

God, Theia! Filter that mouth of yours! What if he takes offense?

Matthew passed me a light chuckle.

"I guess I do have high expectations," he replied and got out, closing the door shut behind him.

I followed his lead as I got out and closed the door shut, walking with Matthew and proceeded towards the school.

"I'm sorry!" I mumbled as my hand found the back of his shirt.

Looking back, he smiled and shook his head.

"It's fine. Don't worry about it." And he walked away, and I stood there rooted to my spot.

Oh well. I am coming, my beloved library! At least, you don't get mad at my bluntness.

***

"Can you quit ruining the quotes from Hamlet?" Marley demanded as she slammed a palm against her forehead.

I wiggled my eyebrows and popped my tongue out.

"To pee or not to pee, that is the question!" I mock cried out quite loudly, forgetting that the English class was in progress, and Mr. Harway was currently grading our homework. Yes, it had been an assignment. Too bad for kids who skipped, though.

Rounds of laughter and giggles surrounded me, and I gasped and looked around the room, even Mr. Harway seemed to have heard!

"You may go to the washroom if you need to Ms. Anderson," he spoke up, a mischievous smile still on his face.

I nodded and cussed myself for the embarrassment I caused myself, slumping back into my chair. There was no way I was going to the washroom in this class, no way!

"So, you came with Matthew today, didn't you? I heard he has a new Jeep. I was thinking of finally asking him, you know?" Marley whispered shyly.

Crap! Matthew...I turned around a bit and instantly locked eyes with him. *Shit! I hope he didn't hear Marley!*

Giving him a soft smile, I quickly turned to face Marley. "I asked him today about maybe asking you," I whispered back, slightly nervous on how she was going to receive the news.

"OMG, what did he say?" Marley whispered back, grabbing hold of my arm and pulling me closer.

Mr. Harway looked up at us but smiled when he saw me. *I frowned at the thirty-two-year-old man.*

"He said you're pretty, but he doesn't like you like that. He has a different type. Plus—uh—his friend likes you," I mumbled back after a slight pause.

Gosh, I hope she doesn't take it to heart or something!

"Oh…And then, what did you say? Which friend?" Marley whispered back, her voice sounding sad.

I glanced at her, but she looked expressionless, so I continued.

"Are you okay? Well…I asked him what his type was then. I can't tell you the guys' name. Wait till he approaches you."

"And?" Marley urged.

I sighed. "Honestly?"

"Go on!" Marley urged me, pulling me closer.

"Please, don't change yourself for him."

She sighed. "Okay…Now, tell me."

"Well, brown hair, hazel eyes. She should like food. She should love reading, and when she blushes, her nose should resemble a tomato. Oh, and she should be tiny…like, reach up to his chin or something."

I quickly glanced at her to find her staring at me with a weird face.

"Are you okay?" I asked Marley.

She smiled. "Yes…And hopefully, he asks that girl out soon."

She knows who he was talking about?

"You know who she is?"

She smiled and nodded.

"We—"

Just then, there was a knock on the door, and Mr. Bishop walked into the class. He and Mr. Harway whispered amongst themselves before they both faced us with an excited look on their faces; well, on Mr. Harway's face, anyway. Mr. Bishop wasn't much for smiling. In fact, he reminded me of Professor Snape.

"Well, as you all might know, we are to make a class trip to the Castle of Dovelore," Mr. Bishop spoke out, instantly silencing the whole class. I supposed everyone wanted to visit the castle.

I felt a glare on the side of my face and turned just in time to catch Diandra give me the evil eyes before pulling Blond closer, who was giving me apologetic looks of his own.

I narrowed my eyes at her before looking back at Mr. Bishop. They didn't deserve my time of the day, anyway.

"The visit has been rescheduled and will now be on the eighteenth of this month. As you all know, one lucky student will get a full-time scholarship to any college he or she may obtain an admission. And another lucky student will have the privilege of spending his or her summer break in the castle, should he or she wish to do so. The lucky student will also have the castle library and grounds at their disposal. Let me just hint out that it is a very good opportunity to have brilliant literature and resources in aiding with your projects—the first settlement in Peidmond City. Remember, the more detailed, the better! Mr. Harway will explain more on this topic. You all have about two weeks at hand. Please be equipped by then." Mr. Bishop informed us and with a clipped smile, walked out of the class.

Everybody turned to face Mr. Harway.

I supposed everyone was interested in spending their summer at Castle Dovelore. I mean, I sure was.

"Okay, guys, the student for the scholarship will be chosen by their grades. So you guys better be wishing you did that homework well."

"What about the student who gets to spend their summer break there?" I asked, truly curious. I wanted that library's resources.

Mr. Harway smiled. "Planning on being that student, Ms. Anderson?"

Diandra snorted beside me. I turned to glare at her.

"The books and the library do sound tempting, sir," I mumbled back, smiling slightly.

Plus, I needed to find out about that man who jumped to his death. Mr. Harway nodded and seemed contented with my answer.

"The student will be chosen by Mr. Wilhem."

This seemed to grab all the girls' attention. Kendall, the school player, instantly shot her hand up. "Mr. Harway, will you please tell us something about Mr. Wilhem. I mean, we should get to know who our host will be, right?"

Ugh. These girls.

Mr. Harway looked at her with a slight frown before continuing.

"Mr. Wilhem is a twenty-four-year-old multi-billionaire entrepreneur and owner of a whole lot of corporate businesses. He also, apparently, holds the title of dukedom inherited from his father. Also, he is British obviously and just freshly graduated from Oxford."

"Woah!"

I clamped a hand over my mouth as I realized I had said that out loud.

"Any particular interest in Mr. Wilhem, Ms. Anderson?" Mr. Harway asked me, cocking an eyebrow up.

The class Barbie dolls snickered at his question causing my blush to deepen.

"I—"

"It's alright, Ms. Anderson. I'm sure half of the students thought Mr. Wilhem as a fifty-two-year-old man with a large belly and a broken nose."

I nodded. Thankfully, he did not press me to answer. It was the truth. I had in fact thought of Mr. Wilhem to be old. And here he was…so young?

I wonder how this duke happens to look like…

"Probably scrawny and *eek*!" Marley giggled from beside me.

I face palmed myself. "I said that out loud, didn't I?"

Marley giggled. "Yes, you did."

***

Thanking Matthew for the ride home, I walked into the kitchen with the intention of going back to the swing. I didn't know why I was going there because it was obvious Bryce wasn't going to come anymore nor did I want him to. But he had still managed to terrorize most of my thoughts all throughout the day. It was only natural I suppose. He had become a friend in the last couple of days.

And I knew that even though I missed him and he had become a friend, he was taken. So I gave myself a month to fully forget him and move on with one of my fictional lovers, hoping wholeheartedly that would work.

Slipping out into the pack patio, I made my way into the beautiful bench surrounded by the roses. The swing seemed inviting, but I really just wanted to be under the roses. They were beautiful.

The wooden bench seemed harsh against my skin as I sat on it. The cushions, however, provided the softness I needed. Easing myself into the bench, I lay on my side with my eyes on the swing.

Secretly, I was waiting. Maybe he wanted to explain. I shook my head. I was being pathetic.

But still, I waited and waited and waited.

He never showed. What did show, however, was sleep.

So with the last hope gone, I let my eyes close. A quick nap would do no harm…Besides, the roof over the seat was covered with glass, so no problem.

This bench isn't bad after all was my last thought as I finally let myself go.

CHAPTER FIVE

My feelings sunk as Caroline faked the Big O. Why couldn't she just get herself seen by a gynecologist? I mean, Simon was remarkable! Heck, I had a Big O here just by reading it, and she didn't! Obviously, there was something insanely wrong here!

I shook my head as I read on. The feeling that Simon knew about her faking the Big O lingered in my mind, and I knew that Caroline would have to face it sometime, or she was never going to get the orgasm that had been stripped from her.

As the chapter ended, the reminder that I had homework to do and the luxury of reading another chapter only after I finished my homework sunk into my head. Letting out a soft sigh, I placed my little doggy-ear bookmark on the page and closed the book, placing it on the window bench beside me.

The day was a dark one, and it was quite cold. I watched as the rain continued to pour over the dark forest. The windows were open, and the cold breeze occasionally blew in, heavily flowing the drapes over my face. I smiled as the light white drapes caressed my cheeks and retreated to its original place.

It was also slightly foggy. The mountains at a far distance were barely visible as the slow mist flowed through towards the castle, the rain and the dark glow giving it a even more mystical vibe.

I scanned through the windows, which was my habit, trying to find any form of life inside there—maids, valets or whatever the fancy rich people had in castles—but stopped at the fourth-floor balcony.

The man who usually stood there and always caught my eye stood there on the balcony. His blue shirt shined distinctively. His features were blurry, but I was certain that he was staring at me just as I, him.

I often caught the man standing there, and he often caught me looking at the castle. I supposed it was awkward looking at each other from such a great distance so often.

I wonder what he did there in the castle. Maybe I should wave. After all, we had been staring buddies for nearly a week.

Lifting my right hand, I waved at him unsurely; a small smile graced my lips. What for? I had no idea. It wasn't as if the man could see me smiling from there. Heck, I couldn't even see his face! How would he see me smile?

The man just stood there, and I felt like an idiot, placed my arm back onto my lap, and looked down embarrassed.

God, Theia! That man must be thinking you're such an idiot! Make a run for it woman!

My face burning with embarrassment, I quickly lifted my gaze towards the window to close it when I saw the man still standing there. He was waving back.

A short laugh left my lips as I instantly waved back happily and closed the window, walking towards my study table. That man saw me wave. He had waved back!

I wondered if the man knew of the other guy who jumped off the balcony that night. I thought as I sat on the chair and grabbed my textbooks. Art canvas, pastels, and paint rested just by my feet, and I looked at them awkwardly.

My hands were itching to grab hold of them and just get on with it, but I had homework to do first. *Oh, the pain of being a student!*

It had been a week since I'd last seen Bryce, two days since the stalker incident, and due to a storm, it was announced that Rosenberg High would be closed for the day. Although I had completed and packed most of my assignments, I only realized this morning that Math and Biology were still pending and due tomorrow.

As for the stalker, there had not been any visible signs of anyone being in my room, other than the open windows every morning. But being as forgetful as ever, I could never seem to remember if I had, in fact, closed the window the previous night. After all, I was not one to close windows especially when there was barely any solid ground beyond it.

Suddenly, a ping sounded from my phone, bringing me out of my thoughts, and I placed the pen down, picked my cell phone and unlocking it.

From: Dada

Pumpkin,

I am taking your mother on a date tonight, so we will be late. There is cash inside the linen drawer in the kitchen. Please order yourself some pizza. Lock the doors and windows if you feel unsafe and keep Mom or me on speed dial! Be good!

Love,

Dad

I grinned as I typed back a reply. Tonight, the house was all mine!

Placing the cellphone back, I got busy with calculus. It couldn't find the Y to its X itself now, could it?

I rolled my eyes at the stupid thought.

Of course, it couldn't.

***

Walking out of the bathroom, I caught sight of my reflection in the mirror and cringed.

Staring back at me was a wet cat.

Shaking my head, I ran towards the closet. My tummy was twisting and turning, and the fried chicken and fries from KFC that rested on the kitchen island wouldn't finish itself.

Hastily, I got dressed, gathering my hair on one side, grabbing onto my cellphone, and trotting downstairs.

The heavenly scent of the fried chicken drifted from the kitchen into the hallway as I rounded towards it, smiling because I had food in my sight.

I grabbed onto a plate when a ping rang through the kitchen, and I instantly walked towards the island and picked up my phone.

From: Cas-Cas

Owen asked me out today. I don't know what to say! Should I say yes or should I say no? OMG! I have been crushing on him since junior year! I should say yes! But he's a player...Maybe I should say no. HELP ME OUT WOMAN!

- A VERY DESPERATE CAS! X

I flinched. That Owen was bad news!

To: Cas-Cas

It's truly up to you. But I don't really want you dating him. He is a disgusting idiot, and I would rather choose you to go out with Leo. Before you say something, yes, Leo. He has a crush on you since sophomore year, Cas. It's about time! Besides, he is a hunk and a math wiz! How could you want more?

- Hopeful Thi x

"She should really just ask Leo out," I mumbled as I placed the phone back on the island and glanced up.

My heartbeat just somehow stopped.

"What the hell?" I whispered as I stared, shocked at the man sitting on the swing in the rain and glancing down at his lap as his hands held onto the ropes.

My body froze when I realized who it was—Bryce.

I hesitated. Taking a step forward, I stopped. He had a girlfriend, but then he was getting cold...But...but then...

I shook my head and turned away. Holding my breath as I tried to admit, I missed him.

As if that had been the missing key, I blinked back my tears and quickly moved towards the back door, rushing outside. Picking up an umbrella from the stand, I slipped my feet into a pair of flip-flops and walked out in the rain.

I should go back! But is he okay? Why the hell isn't he looking up? Is he? No, shut up, Thi!

"Bryce?" I asked softly as I stood in front him. Instantly, his head lifted, and his eyes met mine. His clenched jaw immediately relaxed and smiled sadly.

"Hi," he said quietly, still sitting on the swing calmly.

What's happening?

"Hi," I replied, cocking an eyebrow upwards and looking at him questioningly.

"Hi." He repeated, still looking quite unreadable. His blue eyes peered into my boring light brown eyes.

I sighed. *I couldn't stand it.*

"Let's get you inside. Come on," I murmured as I grasped onto one of his hand, the rain tickling my skin as each cold droplet touched and slid down my bare arm.

Bryce stared at my hand holding his before he let out a chuckle.

"Letting a *stranger* in, Theia? That's not a very smart thing to do." Bryce smirked, standing up.

I flinched back with guilt and grief. I let go of his hand I looked away while he continued to tower me by good inches. I couldn't even reach up to his chin properly.

Bryce's taunting smirk deepened as he looked at me staring at him, pulling me out my shocked state. My face turned into a scowl.

Fine then, you rude man! I thought as I regarded him with a sudden hardness.

I mean, I am not the one well on my way to getting a bad cold or anything. He is!

"Maybe I'm not being very smart right now, but I'd rather not let a man sit outside in the rain for God knows what reason. I'm going in. You can follow if you want to. In case you don't, goodbye, Bryce," I snapped back and without a second look at him, marched my way to the door all the while cussing at myself for being such an idiot! I should never have gone out.

Sighing sadly as I reached the patio door, I placed the umbrella beside the door and pushed it open. Getting in, I turned around to close the door but gasped when my face collided with a hard chest.

I think I just broke my nose.

Strong hands immediately grabbed onto my shoulder and pulled me forward, rescuing me from falling on my ass and embarrassing myself.

I mumbled a quick "thank you" before moving out of his grasp.

Damn, his touch for electrocuting me in the sweetest ways!

"I'll get you some dry clothes although I'm not sure if it will fit you. My dad isn't as huge as you are," I mumbled and quickly shot upstairs but not before nodding shyly at Bryce's thanks.

Rummaging through Dad's clothes, I thanked God he was on the bulky side when I finally found a gray t-shirt and deep blue sweatpants.

Walking downstairs, I came to a stop. A very shirtless Bryce stood by the kitchen island, glaring in the direction of my iPhone, which was blaring my ringtone around the room.

How had I not hear it?

I slowly moved towards Bryce, my cheeks probably the color of blood as I tried my hardest to ignore the bulging of his muscles and how wonderfully formed they were.

"Here." I handed him the clothes and kept my eyes on my iPhone.

`Alex calling...`

Damn it! What does he want!

Sighing, I grabbed the phone and pressed "accept," not noticing that Bryce had not moved an inch, and his jaws clenched in a death grip.

"Hello," I mumbled into the iPhone. *This boy better have a good re—*

"Two minutes, just two minutes! That's all I ask," Alex said, and the scowl on my face deepened.

Ugh! Fine!

"Okay, start!"

I thought I heard a low growl behind me and upon turning, smashed my nose into a warm wall again.

As if noticing who the "wall" was, I tilted my head upwards. Bryce looked pissed; in fact, he looked livid. As if sensing my eyes on him, he looked at me.

"You're so scary," I whispered at him before getting my attention back on the phone.

"I'm sorry for whatever happened that day! I'm sorry I didn't tell you about Diandra! It's just that…I wanted to break up with…Okay, listen. I'm sorry, okay! I just want to be friends if you let me! Matt and the guys are avoiding me now!"

I stared at the now dark screen, effectively ignoring the tiny growls emitting from a certain man who I supposed had throat issues.

I really wasn't one for fighting forever. So I sighed as I mumbled back a small reply, "Okay. See you in school tomorrow! Bye, Alex!" and disconnected the call after hearing a happy "thanks" and "bye."

Placing the phone back onto the island, I turned around again. This time, Bryce wasn't behind me.

I shrugged and picked out another plate. I guessed Bryce would like some chicken and fries too. Bringing out a can of cola, I took a sip, placed it on the island, and turned around only to be pulled towards a hard chest. Thankfully, this time, my nose got spared.

"Oomph!" I groaned as my cheek slammed against a hard chest. "What is it with you and me slamming against you?"

My eyes drifted towards the sweatpants, and I instantly blushed. The sweatpants clutched his hips deliciously, too deliciously. My gaze moved upwards slowly, and I noticed the absence of the t-shirt.

"What happened to the shirt?" I questioned him, and Bryce smiled sheepishly at me. He nervously ran a hand through his hair, leaving me suddenly wishing I could do the same.

"Well…I wore it, but then I moved my hands and…it ripped."

"Oh," I mumbled dumbly as I grasped the can of cola again and took a long sip, avoiding the feeling of having Bryce's intense gaze on me. For the fifth time, I silently reminded myself that he had a girlfriend.

Thi, breathe! Breathe!

"So…er…Chicken and fries?"

Bryce smiled and nodded before he grabbed the plates and the can of cola. He took a long sip lightly, closing his eyes for a second.

Damn, maybe he likes cola a lot.

Grabbing onto the bag, I led him towards the living room and plopped down on the seat. Bryce settled down beside me.

Well, this was going to be interesting! For my sake, though, I wished he would just leave.

***

"So, why were you on my swing again?" I asked Bryce as I dipped a particularly beautiful-looking French fry into the sweet and sour sauce and plopped it into my mouth, running the tip of my tongue around my lip to wipe the sauce away.

I noticed Bryce catch that, and his eyes instantly darkened.

Oh my God, Was he? Oh no, wait, but if he really did get affected by a lip lick…and if he kisses me? But his girlfriend? Theia, you are going to die for this!

"I wanted to meet you."

I froze. "So you waited outside in the rain?" I mumbled back and glanced at Bryce who sat beside me, munching on his fried chicken, his eyes glued to the TV screen. But I knew he was paying attention. His back was too stiff not to.

"I really wanted to meet you."

I sighed. There was no winning like this.

"Why?" I asked him, honestly curious why he would take such a big step to meet me.

He turned towards me, and our eyes locked for a second or two before his returned to the TV screen.

"Bec—"

Just then, a very loud ping rang out from the direction of my phone.

I looked down at my empty plate before I grabbed the bags and moved towards the kitchen as Bryce popped the last bit of chicken into his mouth and moved behind me. Quickly doing the dishes, I made my way towards my phone, slightly conscious of Bryce sitting on the sofa watching some random contestant singing on The Voice.

I grabbed my phone and smiled. My folks were really missing me today.

From: Matty

Elo? (Do I sound British enough?) Come over tonight if you can. I shall have Cookies and milk! - Matt

From: Matty

I also have Christmas pudding ice-cream ;) (I know you want it!) - Again, Matt

From: Cas-Cas

Guess what…I just asked Leo out. HE SAID YES! OH MY GOD! OH MY GOD! - A very ecstatic Cas!

From: Blond
Thank you for the second chance, Thi! I won't mess it up! - Alex

From: Ley
Elo, baby ;) I am bringing our art project ideas tomorrow…Think of some ideas too, aye? BTW, we need a sleepover soon! - Marley xx

From: Private Number
Smiling over a text from your 'boyfriend,' Theia?

My eyes widened as I read the most recent message from an unknown number.

I quickly turned around searching the house for someone spying on me when my gaze fell on Bryce, his cellphone in his hands. He looked at me with his jaws clenched.

Why does he look like he has his panties in a twist? Oh God, why do his clenched jaws have my panties twisting?

I shook my head. *Girlfriend.*

"How did you get my number?" I hissed as I walked towards him cautiously.

He looked like he was about to explode.

"I have my ways."

My frown deepened. I stood in front of him, clutching my cellphone while he sat on the sofa treating me now with silent indifference. In the back of my mind, I thought I deserved a little bit of that. I had been so rude to him that day after all, but I couldn't let him know that.

"What kind of ways? Why did you even want to meet me? Are you the one who yelled at Alex over the phone?"

He remained silent, and that pissed me off.

"Well?" I growled, and my teeth clenched in irritation.

"You want to know why, Theia?" His now dark blue eyes challenged me as he leaned forward, looking very intimidating.

"Yes," I retorted stubbornly, folding my arms against my chest.

Suddenly, his arms shot forward, grabbed mine, and pulled me down on top of him as his lips touched mine.

I could tell his arms were slipping around my waist and grasping into it like his life depended on it, but those were all hazy. The only thing I could focus on was his lips moving against mine, nipping as he ran his tongue along my bottom lip as if asking for entrance. His hand found my bottom, and a jumbled shriek ripped out of my throat when he landed his big hand swiftly on my butt with speed and force that left my senses hazy for a second or two.

As if seeing it as an opportunity, his tongue instantly dipped into my mouth, twirled around mine, and took full possession of my senses. I couldn't decide. Common sense told me to move away because he was clearly in a complicated relationship, but everything else told me to stay.

"I don't know what I said wrong the last time. You literally just cut me off. But I had been thinking, and I reckon it was because of the *maybe*." Bryce let out a low unreal growl as he deepened our kiss, his fingers now gracing my naked belly.

I flinched his acknowledgment and immediately tried to move away. How could someone have a serious conversation when their body kept singing and sighing, and their brain couldn't operate?

As if sensing that I wanted to move away, his grip on my bare waist tightened, and he pulled me close. A whimper of excitement left my lips as I forgot all rational thoughts and moved closer to him.

Damn it, Theia! Bad, Theia! Bad!

A groan left his lips, and he broke our kiss, immediately leaving hot trails of kisses on my jaw and neck, paying particular interest to a spot that made me moan every time his lips touched it.

"You, I came for you because when I said maybe and it's complicated, I meant that I haven't asked you out yet." He growled low as he brought his lips back to mine.

I couldn't breathe. The secret place between my thighs was crying out for something I had only read in storybooks about, and although I suddenly wanted it as badly as one could, it shocked me that I barely knew Bryce. How could we possibly kiss if I don't even know his last name?

"B-Bryce, no, please." I sighed as he nibbled on my sweet spot. He paused and lifted his eyes up to meet mine.

Gone were the bright blue orbs. His eyes were darker in a sense that they almost looked gray.

I felt my cheeks heat up as I looked down at my legs, still around him. God, I was so embarrassed!

"Theia?" Bryce murmured slowly as he placed a finger under my chin and tilted my head to face him.

"I barely know your last name and then this. I feel like an idiot," I whispered, my eyes wide and hazy with unshed tears.

He must be thinking I'm a young idiot! That I'm a…bitch.

I cringed at the thought, and a traitor tear spilled down onto my cheek. Bryce grimaced as he watched me, placed his thumb against my cheek, and wiped the tear away.

I noticed I was still straddling him and instantly tried to move away, but Bryce's firm grip on my waist stopped me.

"There is nothing to feel embarrassed about, Theia. You're beautiful, kind, and very smart. But best of all, you're mine. Or…I hope you will be! We've known each other for two weeks. But then we still have so much time to get to know each other, so don't think like you don't know me. You will," Bryce mumbled softly as he looked straight into my eyes, not once breaking eye contact.

I sighed and found myself nodding.

Was I actually saying yes to be his?

A small smile graced Bryce's lips as he leaned in and placed a soft kiss on my forehead.

"Good," he mumbled softly as his warm breath fanned against my cheeks where he placed another soft kiss.

"I have to go now," he muttered, his arms sliding around me as he pulled me in for a hug. My face smacked against his naked shoulder, and I immediately blushed.

"Thi?"

"Huh, yeah?"

"I said it's getting dark. I have to go now."

Dear God, please don't make him a serial killer. Actually, make him a good guy, please! Amen.

I sent a silent prayer upwards and nodded into Bryce's embrace.

"What are you going to do all night?" Bryce suddenly asked me.

He wanted to know. What will I do?

I thought over Matthew's text, then Marley's…*Hmm!*

"Well, Matt called me over for a movie. He actually lives next door. And then I have to think up ideas for an art project," I answered and kept a steady look on his expression which was turning slightly grim.

"Matt is a friend?" Bryce asked, his voice dangerously low.

"Most definitely," I answered, my voice confident.

"Okay, just…don't let him touch you."

I rolled my eyes and pulled out of Bryce's grip. Damn, he was heavy! Bryce chuckled as he got up.

"You're so tall," I grumbled. Thank God for not adding the "stomping foot" bit afterward. Bryce chuckled again before he placed both hands on my waist and just like it was nothing, lifted me up until my face was level with his. My feet automatically wrapped around his waist, and pulling me against him, he placed a playful kiss on the tip of my nose.

"I wouldn't have it another way, love."

Gah! How can he know all the right things to say?

I rolled my eyes at him, and Bryce silently chuckled before walking towards the back door.

"Where do you live?" I grimaced and turned my gaze to the thick layer of the forest.

The rain had stopped as we walked outside. It was growing dark. The sun was just about sinking, and the bats were coming out to play. *Ugh! I hated bats!*

I could feel Bryce still under me, but he kept walking towards the patio with me clinging to him.

"I live just beyond the forest," he muttered, sounding guarded.

"But the forest goes on for miles," I mumbled back, trying to study his expression.

He nodded at me. "Yes, it does."

"Then why do you go around prancing through the forests? Don't you know there are wolves in there?"

Bryce looked at me with a curious expression.

"Are you scared of wolves, Theia?"

I frowned. "No…I quite like them but not when they would like you as a meal," I answered, shifting in his hold so I could properly hook my legs around him.

Bryce looked at me for a while before he broke down laughing, his deep voice ringing out in the evening loud and beautiful. I rolled my eyes; he was laughing at me after all.

"I assure you, love. The last thing wolves would want is me."

"But isn't it getting a bit too dark for you to make your way through the woods?"

"Don't worry, love. I know my way through the woods," Bryce muttered, his breath fanning my forehead as I studied a scar on his chest. "Look at me," he murmured, his voice barely above a whisper.

Feeling a little on the shy side, I lifted my gaze to his and smiled when I realized how adorable he looked. His face was set in a soft wispy expression, and it made him look like a kid. I held back a small gasp as I noticed his eyes zero on my lips before he leaned in slowly and planted his lips on mine.

This kiss was different. It was warm, soft, and sweet unlike the one before, which was raw but passionate. To be honest, I liked both equally. Bryce nibbled on my bottom lip before pulling it lightly and then breaking the kiss. We stood there for a second or two. I sighed as I relished in his closeness. It felt like I needed a guy I barely knew. And by the way he was acting, maybe he needed me too? Was this how it was in real life? Clumsy and irrational yet the most rational thing ever?

I sighed contently as I held onto Bryce, my face resting on his shoulder.

"I have to go, love," Bryce murmured softly for what felt like the third time that day, yet he made no move to let go, so I nodded.

"Okay," I said softly and looked at the ground.

As if he caught onto my unspoken indication, Bryce slowly let go, and I slid onto the ground. A shiver ran through my skin as my bare feet touched the wet grass, and I smiled at the feel of it.

Everything was always so pretty after it rained.

Arms reached out and pulled me close. "I'll see you soon, okay?"

I nodded as I hugged Bryce back. "Okay."

He broke our hug and moved towards the forest. I stood still as I watched him enter the dark, dense trees. As he disappeared into the darkness, he turned around and gave me a wave. I smiled and waved back at him.

I'd see him soon was the last thought I had as I turned around and walked towards the house.

***

The persistent sounds of chimes stirred me from my sleep as I reached for my phone to turn off the darn alarm. Every night, I set up the alarm thinking it would be a great idea, and every morning, I groaned. Why did I do this to myself? Smacking the phone against my pillow, I literally slithered out of bed and onto the floor. I really did not want to go to school…But my assignments needed submission, and the flawless attendance record wasn't going to keep on going flawlessly by itself now, would it?

Just then, someone knocked on my door, and I yelled out a weak, "I'm up. I'm up," before crawling towards the bathroom.

The door shot open, and I instantly shot my head towards the person standing just inside my bedroom, looking at me with wide eyes.

"What are you doing?" Matthew exclaimed, clearly trying to hold on his laughter. He seemed ready for school in his unusual style of buttoned-down plain white shirt and black jeans with black Supra, and then there were those nerd glasses of his.

I rolled my eyes. Was he dumb? Did he not see I was crawling my way to the bathroom? And what was he doing here so early?

"Can't you see? I'm going to the bathroom. Why are you here so early, anyway?" I asked him as I turned my face towards the bathroom door and continued to crawl towards it.

"It's eight, Thi. We are nearly late." Matthew chuckled, unable to contain his laughter as it flowed out in strings just when I stopped crawling, got up, and instantly ran into the bathroom. *Damn! I was never late!*

I marched out of the shower into my room wrapped up in a towel when a sudden thud caught my attention, and I turned around to face a very red faced, wide-eyed Matthew.

A shriek escaped my lips, and I made a run towards the closet and once in, bolted the door shut.

"S-Sorry!" I heard Matthew mumble against the door, and I nodded before realizing he could not even see me.

Dear Theia, you are an idiot! Love, You.

"It's okay. You just scared me. That's all!" I called out before walking towards the floor-length mirror that was installed on the free wall.

A gasp left my lips as I stared at the bruise on the base of my neck. *My sweet spot!* The love bite shined proudly in its maroon splendor, showing off that the carrier had actually had some "fumble" time. Goodness!

I ended up going over to Matthew's last night. The idiot played *The Exorcist*, thinking it would be okay and he could handle it. But halfway through, both of us was on the verge of pissing our pants. Someone had to call quits. I was glad he did.

Coming home past ten, I had made him drop me home and was actually grateful when I found Dad and Mom already in and worried. Naturally, Dad had to drop Matthew back to his place. I swear that boy needed to grow some when it came to horror movies.

Sighing, I decided to just let my hair down. The love bite was pretty deep maroon and quite apparent, but hopefully, with my long hair open, I could conceal it long enough for it to fade.

After slipping on my undies, I grabbed a pair of dark jeans and pulled it on, quickly slipped into a white and blue striped tank top and black leather jacket. It was quite chilly today. Smiling at my reflection contently, I opened the door to walk outside when a yellow scarf caught my eye, and without a second thought, I wrapped it around my neck.

Great! I have protection now!

"Let's go, Matty boy!" I called out as I picked up my packed backpack lying beside the closet door and walked towards the doorway without a second glance around the room.

"Coming," Matthew called from behind me, and I briefly turned towards him to smile before starting to walk away again.

***

"She will come and get you." A warm breath fanned my ears, and I instantly stilled. My hand still in my locker, holding my biology textbook.

This was insane! There could be no ghosts in a hallway full of students! Still a bit shaky, I turned around and immediately moved back against the locker.

"Shit, Matthew! That was not funny." I hissed, giving the hysterical Matthew the best death glare I could conjure.

"Scared, little Theia," Matt teased as he gloated in his success.

I rolled my eyes and turned to take my biology book out before closing the locker shut.

"Let's just go to Biology class, moron."

Matthew's smug grin widened as he followed me into class, and I was sure, by the end of the day, I was going to kick his ass. Or...I could get back at him. *Oh, good one, Thi!*

***

"So what about the sleepover?" Marley asked as we placed our lunch trays on the table and slid beside Matthew and his friends, Connor, Jeff, and Keith. Alex, like always, was at Diandra's table. His arms placed around her shoulders.

I smiled. They actually did look great together. Alex and Diandra were made for each other! It was strange, though, how Matt's buddies from both Football and Math Group could mingle together so nicely.

Jeff was the *mathlete* of the three, but he looked anything but that. With windswept black hair and fairly pale skin, he totally defied his stereotype of a skinny kid wearing checkered shirts and had no social skills. Quite on the contrary, Jeff had proper broad shoulders and a pretty good body.

Then there was Connor. Now, however well Jeff managed to defy his stereotype, Connor was quite the opposite. In fact, he was the definition of a how a high school jock would look like. With a bulky form and sun-kissed blond hair, a tan any pale girl could die for, and a badass player attitude—Connor had it.

Then came Keith, holding the position of a striker in his team totally described his personality—striking. He too had a jet-black hair that managed to shine that would make the girls in Dove advertisements jealous. What was striking about him, though, were his amazing blue eyes, and there was his personality. He was unlike any other. And apparently, the only one with enough common sense in his team to play football and not play girls.

"You guys are having a sleepover?" Connor asked, his gaze on Matthew. The grin on his face was actually making me quite suspicious!

"Yes." I nodded, still looking at the boys with narrow, suspicious eyes.

"Awesome! We're having a sleepover," Connor exclaimed quite loudly, and I think about half of the cafeteria heard.

"No, you're not!" Marley protested instantly. Her hand smacked the plastic of the cafeteria table.

Jeff chuckled as he put his hands up in retreat. Keith, however, grinned at Marley and gave her a small wink, surprising both Marley and I. I looked at Marley to see her blushing. Grinning, I turned my attention back to Connor.

"No, it's a girls' sleepover. No boys allowed! Can you not have your own sleepover?" I blurted, looking at Matthew and silently begging him to agree.

Matthew grinned at me and shrugged lazily, not at all taking my side. Well, it wasn't going to happen, anyway. "No boys allowed" was the fundamental law of sleepovers.

"Can you not use English like you are from 1880 Britain?" Connor countered, and I grimaced. I couldn't help it. I read those books all the time!

"Shut up, Con-Con," I grumbled as I shoved in a spoonful of soup into my mouth. Damn, it was hot!

"Don't call him, Con-Con! It actually sounds cute, which he is not!" Marley whined as she bit into her burger.

I giggled. It was true. Connor looked anything but cute.

Just then, the siren went off at the end of lunch, and the boys, Marley, and I quickly scrambled to our feet and marched towards art class.

***

"Guess what we are going to paint today, guys?" our teacher whose name was too hard to remember asked us. Her sweet smile painted on her face by angels. I had never seen her pissed off. She was always smiling.

"Those boring cups and bottles?" a deep voice spoke up from the further back of the class.

Curiosity got the best of me, and I turned towards the voice but stopped dead in my position as I stared at him. Our eyes met.

The boy had shoulder-length jet-black hair. Truth be told, he looked dangerous. Now, I wasn't much for being judgmental, but I was surprised he hadn't sworn at me by now considering I was actually staring at him quite offensively.

"What?" he called out loudly, his voice almost threatening. My eyes widened as I realized he actually yelled at me.

"Shit!" I mumbled embarrassed as I quickly turned to face our art teacher.

She smiled at me softly before moving her gaze behind me, probably at dangerous dude whose name I didn't know. "No, Rome. We are going to paint each other."

She turned her attention to everyone and smiled. "I know you all are sorted into partners, but this bit is something I do every year with my students. So, a selected number of ladies will be called out as muses. The rest of you, ladies and lads, will hold the responsibility of tracing their essence onto your canvases. The names are as follows—"

My insides fluttered with excitement. This was going to be great! I didn't really care whether I was selected as a painter or a muse. I would be happy to be both since this project actually seemed exciting.

"—Heather Johenson, Amelia Brooks, Marlene Smith, Vannessa Jule, Sarah Louis, and Theia Anderson. Make your way up here, ladies! Now, the rest of you, please choose your muse. And remember, it should be someone who intrigues you, not only by personality but also by looks. I want to see that on the canvas. Oh, and, guys, this will contribute twenty-five percent towards your final grades and GPA. Let us begin!"

"We're friggin, muses!" Marley whispered as we both walked up to stand beside the rest of the girls who were either grinning or shy. However, some, like Marley and I, were incredibly excited! Art was our passion after all!

As we stood before the rest of the class, I did a slow class sweep, trying to gauge how each of the kids still sitting actually were. Arts class was small, considering that people in Rosenberg High ignored their artistic sides or aimed towards music classes instead.

I glanced towards Joshua, who smiled at me. I smiled back. He seemed nice. Behind him sat Kenny. I could picture him making me switch positions a million times before he finally decided on a perfect position and pose. That guy took being a perfectionist to a whole new level.

On the far corner sat Emegin, the cool kid. He grinned as he felt my gaze on him, and I blushed instantly. He was kind of cute with those dimples and all. And actually, I wouldn't mind him trying to paint me. He was pretty good at it!

Beside him sat Laila aka the chick who rocks goth. Her straight dark hair fell over her face, hiding most of her eyes and right cheek as she slumped against the table, and her eyes were equally analyzing a good enough candidate for her capability. I wondered how she would be if I became her muse.

My gaze shifts to the front of the class. Just in front of me sat Lionel. I smiled at him, and his eyes widened a fraction before he smiled back. I actually liked the guy. His nerd glasses made his beautiful gray eyes shine bigger, and his finger-combed red hair seemed adorable. What topped it all though was that he was incredibly talented!

In fact, everyone in the class was incredibly talented. That was the best thing about art class. We all appreciated art, and although most girls leaned more towards watercolors because let's face it, it's beautiful, we all tried and were well versed in everything from paint to pencils and pastels. Ms. Swein, I think, made sure of that.

And then my eyes found the person I was trying desperately to avoid—the guy whose name I couldn't remember although Ms. Swein just mentioned it a few minutes ago. I think it was Greece?

His dark eyes were already piercing through me as I glanced at him and almost instantly bit back a gasp. He looked like I was food, or maybe he just wanted to cut me up and feed me to the dogs. The bottom line was he scared the heck out of me, and I would rather partner up with Kenny than him!

Just as quickly as I glanced at him, I looked away, but I could still feel his intense gaze on me. What was wrong with him?

"Okay, let's start!" Ms. Swein exclaimed excitedly. "Let's start with Emigen! Emigen, who do you pick as your muse?"

Emigen smiled, as he clearly looked amongst us girls standing in front of the class.

"I pick Marlene," he called out, sounding quite confident. I could see where he was going, actually. Marley had this amazing innocent look about her. It was only natural the bad boy would try to capture it.

I snickered when I heard Marley groan under her breath as she moved towards Emigen and grabbed a seat on the other side of him. I guess she didn't like him!

"Okay! Next up is Kenny!" Ms. Swein called out excitedly, clapping her hands together as her whole body buzzed with happiness. How could someone be so happy all the time?

It didn't take Kenny a second before he announced his muse, Sarah. Unlike Marley, Sarah seemed quite excited to be paired up with Kenny. At least, someone was happy about being paired with Ken.

"Lionel." Ms. Swein smiled as she indicated who pick next.

Lionel's eyes landed on me, and I smiled softly. I wouldn't mind pairing with him. He looked like a sweetheart. "T-Theia," he murmured, his face turning a little deeper shade of red. The lad was shy.

Suddenly, a hand slammed against a desk loudly causing all the girls in class to gasp and jump in their places. Everyone immediately looked towards the source of the loud noise. The guy whose name I couldn't remember stood glaring at Lionel. His fists clenched on top the desk as he quite obviously did nothing to control his temper. What had happened to him?

"Do you have a problem, Rome?" Ms. Swein questioned him, her voice stern. Oh, so his name was Rome. His glare moved towards her.

"Theia is my muse." He growled loudly, suddenly moving forward before moving back again as if thinking better of it.

I could only stare just as the other students in the class. I watched Lionel flinch under Rome's glare.

"Well, Lionel has already picked Theia. You may pick someone else," Ms. Swein replied, her posture impeccably straight just like my posture would be whenever I was usually nervous.

"No. Lionel can pick someone else. Theia is my muse!" Rome growled, this time, louder as he took a step forward and the veins on his hands and neck becoming more prominent.

That's when I had enough. I was my own person, and he could not just behave like this. Even though out of nowhere, he decided to make me his muse right after yelling at me!

"Lionel picked me first. I'm his muse," I spoke up for the first time since the argument started, and everyone's wide eyes moved towards me, seeming to widen more out of fear.

Were they afraid of me or afraid for me?

I looked at Lionel, who seemed scared out of his pants. He caught my eye and gave me a pleading look as if telling me not to continue this. I frowned. There was no way I was going to let this scary guy win.

"No, he didn't, did you, Lionel?"

I gasped as I stepped back out of instinct. Rome was now standing in front of me.

"Mr. Naight, you cannot force someone," Ms. Swein warned him from behind me, her voice a bit shaky. I guess everyone was scared of Rome.

"Did you, Lionel?" Rome repeated, ignoring Ms. S and his voice steely.

"I-I pick H-Heather," Lionel mumbled. His looked at the floor.

Meanwhile, I glared at Rome who stood in front of me looking quite indifferent to the wide-eyed students and the slightly fuming teacher.

"Good boy," Rome said, his demeanor still indifferent. I gasped as he pulled my hand and started walking towards his desk. I looked back at Lionel. He had a sad smile on his face as he looked back with Heather sitting quietly beside him.

With all the strength I could muster, I broke away from Rome's grip and walked towards Lionel. I bent down and hugged him.

"I'm sorry, man," I mumbled and with a shaky smile, walked back to the now fuming Rome, who sat in his seat.

I rolled my eyes as I took a place beside him and instantly my eyes met with Marley's. Frowning, she mouthed, "He likes you." But she talked sense. Either he liked me, or he wanted to kill me.

"Joshua and Liala, pick your muse please" Ms. Swein spoke, her voice seemingly clipped. Someone was getting detention soon.

Joshua yelled out almost instantly, "Amelia!"

The small fallout was forgotten almost immediately. Everyone seemed to giggle as Amelia walked towards a grinning Joshua and Vanessa towards Laila. Everyone knew Joshua had a crush on Amelia. I think even Amelia knew.

"Alright, class! So since this is art, I will not give you a set time to submit it. After all, we all need our time zones when we feel inspired the most. But you will have to submit this at the beginning of the last month of school so I can grade your work. Artists, you and your muse will work on this project at home, in a park, wherever you are comfortable, but not in class unless I give you permission to do so. You have all picked your own muses, and I expect no bitter ends. Are we clear?" Ms. Swein asked.

"Yes, Ms. Sveen," everyone replied, and I bit my tongue out of shock.

"Oh, so her name is Ms. Sveen!" I mumbled to myself, mortified at the thought of actually yelling out *Swein* and getting laughed at by the whole class.

"Do you have a free class after this?" Rome suddenly spoke up beside me, and I instantly stiffened. Something about him yelled out *dangerous*, and I sure wasn't going to poke my head in that section.

"Maybe you shouldn't paint when you're so angry," I mumbled back, my voice barely above a whisper, but I guess he heard because he turned towards me. I could feel him looking at me with his cold eyes.

"Do you have free classes?" Rome repeated icily. Gone was the restraint holding back his anger.

I sighed. How was I going to get an A in this project if all Mr. I'm-going-to-smash-your-head and I did was fight?

Sighing, I closed my eyes for a brief motion repeating the mantra "Be calm" repeatedly.

When I felt the tension flow out of me, I opened my eyes and smiled at Rome whose eyes widened at my change in behavior.

If there were one place I would not mind having him, it was at home. There was no way I was going anywhere alien with him. He could be Jeff the Killer for all I know!

"I don't have free class after this, but how about we go to my place? It has a great view."

Rome did not reply, so I just shrugged it off and continued coloring on my sketchpad.

"You do know that's lame, right?" a deep, slightly husky voice sneered almost against my ear causing me to pull away.

I narrowed my eyes at Rome. "Shut up, moron! Never, I repeat, never call Beauty and the Beast lame! Adam and Belle are life!"

"Now, who the heck is Adam?" Rome exclaimed, seeming suddenly frustrated as he whirled his hands around in the air like a crazy person.

I stared at him. He couldn't be serious.

"Y…oh, never mind. I will just make you watch it," I replied before moving back to coloring.

Adam came first.

CHAPTER SIX

The last bell went off, indicating the end of the day, and I quickly made my way towards the parking lot. The slow tingle of hope for Bryce coming overstayed at the back of my mind as I walked further away from the school building.

"Anderson, wait!" a voice called up from behind me, and I turned around to see none other than Matthew running towards me. I smiled as I watched a dozen girls sigh dreamily when Matt passed them.

"What's up, Jefferson?" I chuckled, putting an arm around Matthew as we continued walking towards his jeep. He was my ride after all.

"Heard you caught Rome's eye in art class," he drawled out slowly as if cautious of not hitting a sore spot.

I groaned. "Ugh! Yes! That boy makes me so mad! Who is he, anyway?"

Matthew chuckled as he walked beside me. "Roman Naight, the only child of Alistair Naight, the great Roman tycoon, sole heir to his father's many incredibly successful companies, professional painter, a black belter in karate, and a total lady killer."

I flinched at the lady killer part.

"I knew he resembled Jeff the Killer for a reason!" I cried out, actually alarmed. "In case he kills me, you have the full permission to open that box I keep under my bed all the time."

Matthew suddenly stopped dead in his tracks and turned around to look at me concerned before he burst out in hysterics.

"Jeff the Killer doesn't exist, Thi! God, you're so cute!" Matthew chuckled as he pinched my cheeks.

This is so not fair. I was eighteen for god's sake!

"Yes, he does. And I hate chu," I grumbled, rubbing my slightly sore cheeks. He didn't have to pinch so hard.

"I love you too, Pump—"

"Theia," the dark slightly husky voice I had learned to be scared of called, causing both Matthew and me to instantly turn around, startled.

How could someone creep up on someone so quietly while they were walking?

"What the hell?" I hissed. "Do you get paid to scare people like that?"

"We're going to your place now for the project?" Rome questioned me, seeming irritated, totally ignoring my question.

Project? Today? What the? No! But the credits…ugh.

"Okay," I mumbled before looking towards Matthew with a guilty smile.

Matthew chuckled, seeing my expression and gave me a little sideways hug. *Best guy best friend ever!*

"See ya later, Thi," he called out as he raised a hand to wave before nodding at Roman and then getting into his jeep.

I turned towards Jeff the Killer, folding my arms in front. "Well?"

His eyes narrowed at me before he grabbed my arm and started pulling me towards a black Audi R8. *Damn it, he had the car I wanted!* I tore my eyes away from my baby for a bit. Everybody else was staring.

"Damn it, Rome, everyone is staring! Let go!" I hissed, making sure to glue my eyes on the beauty that was in front of me.

"Let them stare," Rome muttered back indifferently as we reached the car, and he opened the door and motioned me to get in.

As quick as I could, I placed my butt on the seat and pulled on the seatbelt before looking at Rome who was already seated in the driver's seat!

How the hell is he so fast?

As I stared at him, he turned towards me and lifted an eyebrow up. "Well?"

Oh! Yeah! He doesn't know the way…

"548 Woodslane Drive."

"Do I look like a cab driver to you?" Rome growled suddenly, making me jump in my seat.

"Take a left here," I mumbled quietly before waiting for the next to give him directions. I could feel Rome's eyes on me, but all I could think about was whether Bryce would show up. Maybe Rome and I could paint in the backyard so if he would come, I'd see him. I smiled. That seemed like a good idea.

"Look, Theia, I know I've been a bit harsh, and well, I'll try to be more civil for the project's sake. Okay?" Roman grumbled as if telling me that he was sorry even though he had not said it like saying it would actually burn his tongue. That made me frown. Why did he make a fuss over having me as a muse when he could barely tolerate me?

It's official. He hates you. This is his ultimate revenge. He's a psycho.

"Why did you fuss over having me as your muse?" I blurted out almost suddenly.

"Because I wanted to paint you."

I looked at him. He was looking straight at the road. *Liar!*

"Why did you want to paint me?"

His thick dark eyebrows dipped down as he frowned. "Because you're beautiful," he replied, his tone sour. I knew he hated saying it. Still, I grinned.

"Thanks. You're beautiful too!" I chirped happily, my face glowing from the compliment.

Growing, Mom had always told me, "When a man compliments you, hold your tongue because he may be lying. He may only be saying that to get into your pants or your best friends.

But at the end of the day, a woman deserves compliments. And guess what? You are beautiful."

"I still don't like you," Rome muttered, his frown deepening as he drove down the road.

Sliding in the key, I unlocked the door and walked in, Rome trailing behind me with his canvas and paint bag.

"So this is my home," I declared, smiling slightly as I walked into the living room.

"Oh! You're back, miss!"

I whirled around almost falling on my ass, shocked.

"Who are you?" I asked, startled, holding a palm to my chest.

The slightly elderly woman in front of me turned a shade red.

"I-I'm sorry, miss. I'm Agnus, and this is also Lilly. Mrs. Anderson appointed us maids o-only for today."

Her frightened demeanor made me frown. I looked at Agnus. She looked everything one would expect a great middle-aged mother figure to look like, but her scared blue eyes weren't staring at me with fright. No, she was staring at what was behind me.

I followed her gaze. She was looking at Rome. What was weird was that Rome was glaring at her. *What's his deal?*

Shrugging off the weird vibe going around, my eyes focused on the slightly young-looking girl now standing beside Agnus. I smiled. She must be Lilly.

I walked towards the women, still smiling, and took them by surprise as I hugged them both. "We're all going to be good friends. Thank you for applying to work here."

Both women smiled at me genuinely, their eyes now twinkling with warmth.

"I'll go and make you and your guest some warm chocolate. I also baked some cookies." Agnus smiled warmly as she turned around and sped towards the kitchen. Lilly gave me a soft smile before she too walked after Agnus.

Without turning around, I moved towards the stairs. Rome caught my drift and followed after. Walking towards my bedroom at the end of the hallway, I reached out, opened the elaborately designed doors, and walked in. Finally, I was home.

I supposed Agnus or Lilly had opened the curtains because the castle against the dark pine trees seemed to be on full display as the opened windows allowed the cool afternoon breeze to dance into the rooms, lifting the curtains.

"So this is my room." I smiled as I turned around and found Rome looking at the view with wide eyes.

"It's beautiful, isn't it?" I mumbled, smiling as I looked at the castle fondly. I wondered how my house would look like from one of those towers.

"Yes, it is."

I shrugged the bag off my shoulder and plugged my iPhone and iPod in before sitting on the bed.

Finally breaking out of his stare, Rome's gaze met mine. "We need to bond."

Those four words shocked me so much that my jaws really did fall slack towards the ground as I stared at Roman wide-eyed.

Jeff the Killer just told me that we needed to bond? Theia Anderson, you have officially lost it!

"I need to know what inspires you. I need to paint you, you know. I need to view you in light." Rome continued as I carried on staring at him. The scowl on his face showed his apparent irritation.

"What light do you see me in now?" I asked before I could stop, instantly wanting to face palm myself. Sometimes I just didn't know when to stop.

The tiny beauty mark just above Rome's mouth twitched as his expression turned to that of anger.

Wrong move, Thi!

As if sensing my alarm, Rome slowly turned towards me and stopped where I could see his dark eyes peering into mine with a good amount of detail.

"Golden, you're golden, Theia."

***

I watched as the vines that had begun to surround the ropes of the swing started to show signs of bloom, September flowers.

"So…" I drawled slowly as I turned towards Rome, who seemed to be sketching something on his sketchpad.

Almost immediately, his eyes left the pad and moved towards me. "Don't move," he mumbled as he started to gracefully move his pencil along the pad again.

I blushed realizing that while I was busy gawking at the woods and swing, he was actually sketching me.

I fiddled around with the brown shirt I had worn after the shower; I didn't forget to hide the love bite with a bit of concealer. The last thing I needed was being teased by this chump.

I was glad I had showered. I just could not stand not showering soon after school. It was slightly not normal, but hey, it kept me clean and smelling like roses while my friend, the angry young man here, smelled like sweat and raw power. I guess the raw power part was permanent.

"So…how come you're so mean?" I asked, trying my hardest not to move. This was getting harder by the minute!

"I said don't move!" Rome growled as he placed his fingers on my chin and moved it further towards the swing.

"Well, aren't you nice?" I retorted sarcastically, rubbing the tender skin of the spot he had just gripped.

"I try," Rome replied almost immediately, sounding very indifferent. It took me everything not to turn around and smack him on the head.

"Let me see!" I yelled as I leaned towards Rome trying to get a better look of the sketch pad, but he quickly shut close the pad and shoved it into his bag. "I hate you!" I grumbled, getting up off the bench and doing a little stretch.

It was getting pretty dark as we walked through the patio door. As I turned to close the door, I glanced at the swing once more.

Bryce did not come.

I followed Rome as he led his way towards my bedroom and grabbed onto the canvases resting against mine. Straightening up, he looked towards the window, now showing the castle with lights on around most of the ground, first floor, and the Eastern tower.

He turned towards me and attempted to deliver a faint smile to which I smiled back. An attempt was better than none.

"I'll see you tomorrow then," I mumbled as we walked out of my room and down the stairs.

He nodded and continued to walk. And walking behind him, I continued to wonder, *Who is Roman Naight? How is the condition of his soul? His heart? Why is he so cold? What could have made him this way?*

All sorts of questions bubbled around my mind as I continued following Rome towards the front door. The amount of time in which he had familiarized himself with most of my house was actually quite scary.

As he put his stuff in the back seat, walked around, and got into his car, he spared me one last glance, a soft, awkward smile and a small wave before he pulled out of the driveway and onto the road.

I turned towards the front door, only one thought in my head—bed.

The next day went by the same way—a day well spent in school, having fun with the boys and Marley during lunch, and then enduring Roman's mood swings during art class.

The next day ended the same way. Bryce didn't show.

I shrugged it off at first. Maybe he was busy? He had said he would come back soon. He didn't say the next day. I supposed he was just doing something else.

That night, I stared at my cellphone wondering if I should message him or not. I didn't want to sound clingy. That was the last thing I wanted him to think. I couldn't just message him. I didn't message him.

I figured he would just come by tomorrow. The weather had been pretty bad, anyway. So I shrugged it off.

***

A Thursday found me lying down on my bed, my back against the soft mattress and Marley beside me.

She moved my hair aside and looked at the slightly fading love bite Bryce had given me nearly two weeks ago.

Yes, two weeks ago. It had been two weeks since he showed up that rainy afternoon and fled into the woods. I had thought the love bite would last a week at most, but then again, I had also thought Bryce would come back around. Turns out, I was wrong on both parts. The bruise was too dark to fade so quick…and Bryce never came.

"He's a jerk! I can't believe you never told me," Marley muttered coldly as she regarded the bruise with sad eyes.

I sighed, touching the slightly less dark love bite that refused to leave. I didn't know what to think. He had not even called, not even replied to the message I had sent on the fourth day.

"Oh, I know that face of yours! Forget it. He isn't as innocent as you want to see him. In fact, I think he was one of those college boys, always making bets with each other about wooing girls around the neighborhood," Marley said as she placed my hair back against the love bite.

I stiffened. She was making sense. Why else would some hot hunk pop up from the woods and into my backyard?

As realization struck, I shot up and slumping forward, closed my eyes. I refused to cry. He never liked me. I was just a simple conquest. I was just an idiotic, simple conquest.

Letting out a small sob, I buried my face in my hands. I made a fool of myself! Bryce must be thinking of me as a desperate virgin and laughing over it with his friends!

"Shush! Remember, Thi, the best revenge is to be indifferent towards the pain. Smile. It will kill him. His existence doesn't matter…Everyone makes mistakes. Hey, I mean, I kissed

Mr. Phelps once!" Marley mumbled softly, her arms now around me, holding me to her.

I shot my head towards her. My eyes were wide with shock. "You what?" I shrieked, my voice a bit raspy.

Marley giggled. "I'm kidding! Although, I wouldn't mind,"

A small smile introduced itself on my lips. I shook my head. Maybe she was right.

"One day, I will be over it. One day, I will look at it and laugh." I consoled myself as I wiped away the stray tears with Marley's arms still around me.

"You should paint him, though, to remind yourself of the man who gave you your first heartbreak. And when you're finally over him, you should burn the painting to ashes!"

I looked at Marley, surprised because her idea seemed brilliant! Maybe it was missing his face or remembering those brilliant blue eyes that crushed my soul.

I smiled, and Marley looked at me confused.

"What's up with you?" he asked, slightly alarmed.

My smile widened. "I'm going to do it!"

Marley could only look at me surprised as only a smile could lighten the mood.

Maybe Marley was right after all…I'd smile. Maybe it would kill him when he saw me happy.

"I'm proud of you." She smiled once her initial shock at my sudden change of mood faded, and she pulled me in for a hug. I hugged her back.

A knock had sounded on the bedroom door before it flung open, and Dad strode in.

"Hey, sweetie, do Marley and you want some pizza?" he asked, his expression turning troubled as he looked at me.

"Are you okay?" Dad said softly before he strode towards me and pulled me in for a hug. As much as I felt like breaking down and crying, I couldn't, so I clenched my eyes shut and hugged my dad back.

"I'm fine, Dad. Marley and I were just watching *Letters to Juliet*," I mumbled, keeping my head buried against his chest.

A smile slipped onto my lips as Dad chuckled, seemingly relieved.

"Oh, good! Wouldn't want to hurt some lad now, would we?"

I giggled. "We wouldn't." I agreed, moving out of his embrace, and smiled at him.

Dad smiled at me comfortingly before turning around and walking out the door. I watched him close the door. If only Dad knew the real reason for these tears…

"Let's get this sleepover started!" Marley squealed, jumping on my bed as I giggled looking at her hair flying around everywhere.

"Let's get this sleepover started!" I agreed, getting onto the bed and starting to jump with her.

I already felt better as if a load had been taken off my chest. My mind felt lighter than it had in days. Maybe it was because of actually telling someone about Bryce or the experience of sharing the humiliation I felt every time I thought of being played. Maybe it was the feeling of being hugged and told it was alright after all.

Well, whatever it was, I was glad I shared it with Marley even though I hadn't gone up and told her straight that there was a guy who came by around my backyard twice, which I liked because he was beautiful and he seemed nice. No, she had seen the love bite while I was sitting on the window-side bench. I almost cried when she started going on about how I had a boyfriend and how I didn't tell her like everything was great…It wasn't.

I told her the truth. And I was glad I had.

"Wanna watch *Letters to Juliet* for real now?" Marley asked, fiddling with my laptop.

I nodded, placing a pillow beside hers and lying on my tummy.

"Get ready to cry your heart out, Ley," I declared excitedly as the movie started loading on Netflix.

Sure to my word, by half time into the movie, both Marley and I were crying rivers.

The sounds of the wind rattling trees floated through the air as I lay in bed wide awake. The whole household was probably asleep, well, except me.

I turned towards Marley, who was sound asleep before turning my gaze back towards the ceiling.

We had a class visit tomorrow to the Castle of Dovelore, but I just couldn't sleep.

What Marley had said earlier in the night popped up in my mind again.

"You should paint him, though…"

"You should paint him, though…"

"You should paint him, though…"

I sighed as I glanced towards the window, looking at the lit castle. I finally made my choice. I was going to paint him.

"Not again, damn it," I muttered darkly as I flung the canvas away. Thankfully, though, it landed on the other piles of canvases perfectly.

Letting out an exhausted sigh, I placed the paintbrush back on the pallet.

I just could not get the shades of his eyes correct! It was either too bright or too dull or too light or too dark! Damn it, why was it so hard to replicate perfection?

I glanced towards Marley, who was still quite asleep. I smiled. At least, one of us wasn't having a crisis here.

Stealing a glimpse at my wristwatch, I grimaced. It was nearly one. But I couldn't stop now. I picked up a new canvas and a new brush and dipped it into the blues.

I was going to paint Bryce tonight.

CHAPTER SEVEN

"You actually painted him!"

A loud groan escaped my lips as a huge load leaped on me.

"Can't...breathe!" I croaked and smacked the person on top of me repeatedly.

"Ouch, you hit like a man! Stop it!" Marley shrieked again, this time, out of pain as a pair of hands gripped onto my frantic ones.

What was she doing?

"God!" I groaned as I finally opened my eyes and gave Marley a glare.

She, however, seemed oblivious of my apparent irritation as she squealed when she saw me awake and rushed towards the canvas currently resting on the easel. The funny thing was the rest of the paintings had turned out to be too precious to lose and so now rested against the wall.

Marley stopped short in front of the portrait. I could practically see her mouth hanging open as she stared at the man on the canvas. I sighed as I got out of bed, padded my way over, and came to a halt beside her.

"He's beautiful," she whispered, her eyes wide open, and her mouth, just as I predicted, hanging open.

A sad smile graced my lips as I touched the side of his jaw lightly.

"Yes, he is." *Yes, he is.*

Soon, Marley's gaze moved along the other paintings, and she swayed slightly as she moved towards them. I stood frozen in my place as I watched her stare at each one piece after piece. It wasn't only because of Bryce, though. I wasn't that confident about my painting skills as well. Marley was only the fourth person to see me paint after Casey, Mom, and Dad. Others, however, saw me sketch.

Marley suddenly startled me when she turned towards me; her next words took me by surprise. "It will be fun burning this up once you're finally over him."

I smiled sadly. *Oh, Marley…if I get over him.*

Painting him all night had done nothing but remind me of him. I sighed. It was hardly fair. A startled squeal escaped my lips as I was suddenly pulled towards the bathroom.

"Go get ready, woman! We have school in an hour, and you look like you've been through the haunted woods. When did you sleep anyway?"

The door shut on my face, and I rolled my eyes before I turned around and picked up my brush.

"5:15 AM," I replied before shoving my brush into my mouth.

***

Wrapping my fluffy navy blue towel against my body, I walked out of the bathroom only to get shoved out of the way as a frantic Marley rushed in.

"God, you bathe like you have all the time in the world!" She complained, flustered as she slammed the door shut.

I glanced towards the digital watch perched upon my bedside table.

Oh! 8:15 AM…I guess I took more than what I usually take. Oh well!

I walked towards my closet and immediately closed the door. For a second, I wondered what Casey was doing back home. The second passed, and I let it go. Today was an exciting day. The thought of exploring Dovelore Castle had me completely shaking with excitement.

I quickly willed up enough courage to open the door, just as Marley walked out of the bathroom. Unlike me, she was fully dressed.

She did a once-over as she looked at me, causing a little laugh to ripple out of me. "It's me."

Smiling, she walked towards me and placed her flat iron in my hands. "Straighten it." She smiled as she quickly started picking at her gel eyeliner and on the first attempt, made a perfect wing.

Finally, after a minute, I clamped the flat iron against a small portion of my hair and pulled the straightener down, quickly. It left behind strands of perfectly straight brown hair, which I knew would turn wavy soon; it was only a matter of minutes.

***

"Don't you look beautiful?" Matthew exclaimed as Marley, and I walked downstairs and into the kitchen.

Marley looked at me as if asking what Matt was doing eating scrambled eggs and toast in my kitchen.

"Apparently, he lives here during mornings," I muttered before we took the chairs beside him, helping ourselves with some toast and scrambled eggs ourselves.

"Oh, Mr. and Mrs. A said that they had to run early and that they left you some cash on the fridge. They will be home by eight." Matthew informed me before he stole a big gulp of my iced coffee. Honestly, this boy was never going to learn.

"Paws off my coffee, Jefferson." I warned him as I swatted his arm away. Instantly, he reached for Marley's, who—no shock there—let him gulp down her coffee happily.

I rolled my eyes at her and made a little heart with my fingers to which she grimaced.

"Okay, let's go!" Matthew exclaimed happily as he plopped in the last of his toast into his mouth and moved towards the sink where I was currently doing the dishes.

I grabbed his mug and plate and quickly scrubbed and rinsed them, placing them aside. Moving towards the refrigerator, I got onto my tiptoe, picked up the three-hundred-dollar bills, and shoved them into my backpack my month's allowance.

"Let's go, guys. A castle awaits!"

***

Naturally, since this was a school trip we all had to travel in the bus.

So here we were, boarding the bus, I quickly made it to the middle seats and plopped down near the window. Marley sat beside me. But before Matthew could take a seat next to her, Rome slumped down instead and looked at me with a small smirk on his face.

He had been doing that a lot lately. It seemed like he was surrounding me. He was literally everywhere. In my head, I had begun calling him Rommy the bodyguard.

I narrowed my eyes at him, but he simply shrugged and went on saying, "I want the window seat." A giggle left Marley's lips while I cocked at eyebrow up, and his brows furrowed.

"What?" he asked.

Marley beside me giggled again before she spoke, "You could have just said that you wanted to sit beside Thi."

Matt, who had now settled on the empty seat in front of ours, turned around and looked at Rome shocked. They stared at each other silently, their expressions changing slightly from time to time before Matthew looked towards me and smiled softly and his warm brown eyes friendly and caring.

What's just happened between the two?

I smiled back at him and turned towards Marley, who simply shrugged before I glanced at Rome, who was now looking expectedly at me.

"You're not getting the window seat," I mumbled back, teasing him.

Rome's eyes narrowed at me before he turned around and looked somewhere else, still looking dead angry. I sighed.

Typical Roman—

It was becoming common now whenever his temper took a hundred eighty degrees turn within seconds. He was just extremely short-tempered and unnaturally strong.

I, after all, only had my latest experience with it earlier this week.

Rome had been over for our "once every two days" bonding session, and after waiting for Bryce for a week and three days, I had begun to see it as how it was. Naturally, I had been devastated. Roman had caught on to that, and as soon as he could not endure my bland replies anymore, he grasped my arm, and after informing Mom about where it was he wanted to take me, he pushed me into his car and drove on.

I had started as we arrived at Nando's. Roman hated Nando's. I keep guessing that's just because he had never tried it.

As he parked in an empty lot, he turned towards me and smiled. He got out, walked over to my side, opened the door, and helped me out by the hand.

We both had a good serve each: grilled chicken and peri-peri chips. It's safe to say that by the end of the night, Roman fell in love with Nando's, and well, I was smiling again.

We only just walked out when these boys bumped into me.

The next thing I knew, Roman had exploded, and Hulk emerged from his body. And as for the boys? Well, all the boys lay on the driveway, groaning in pain as blood dripped out of their open wounds.

I shivered as the sight of those bloodied boys flashed before my eyes again. I called for the ambulance, but Roman wouldn't let me help them anymore.

It turned out that in those two weeks of waiting and painting, Romanov had become…nicer. Granted he smiled and even occasionally joked with me, he became sort of friend who just didn't act like a friend all the time. He was too blunt and rude for that, anyways.

Shaking my head as I smiled, I glanced back at Rome. He still looked pissed as he looked at the scenery we drove by.

"I think you should just let him take the seat," Marley leaned and whispered in my ear, her voice concerned.

Sighing, I nodded. I really didn't want to ruin anyone's day at the castle. Marley smiled softly at me as I leaned in and placed an arm on Rome's. He instantly turned to face me, his eyes dark and stormy.

I smiled, tightened my hold on his arm, and pulled lightly towards me.

He got the memo. Glancing towards my grip on his arm as I tugged on it once again, he sighed and stood up. Before Marley and I shifted, he moved in to sit beside me.

I smiled as his mood lightened considerably. Maybe today was going to be a good day after all!

***

"Oh my god, it's beautiful!" Marley exclaimed as I stared in wonderment at the marvel we were now driving into, each second bringing us so much closer than it had been just a second ago.

There it was—the beauty I had stared at for weeks and had woven fairy tales and romances about, the object of my fascination—Dovelore Castle.

Its prim and pristine entryway seemed beautifully carved, looking just as beautiful if not better than the castle itself. The castle seemed inviting. Its beauty was now ten times more up close than when I looked at it from as far as my home.

As the bus slowed and came to a halt, a very elegantly dressed man, who rather looked like he was nearing his early fifties with his slightly graying hair, walked out and towards us.

"I'm so excited!" I squealed as we moved out of the bus in a line with Marley.

"Good morning, all. I am Finley Buckwood, and I will be your tour guide for today. Master Wilhem is very pleased to have you all here for a tour. You may see him by the end of our tour when he will announce the name of the scholar and the lucky student who will get to stay here for his or her holidays. Now, let us begin," he said as he turned and made his way towards the entrance of the castle, teachers and us, students, in tow.

His deep Yorkshire accent was still noticeable when he sprouted a few words, "Dovelore Castle was built by the sixteenth Duke of Devonshire, Alexander Wilhem, in the mid-eighteen hundred. The construction was completed in April 1884. It was built here in America rather than in England where the duke originally resided because he needed a place away from the hustle and bustle for his children, Maryen and Alexander, after his wife, Lilian, died in a tragic accident."

I listened intently as Mr. Buckwood continued to lay out the colorful yet slightly dark history of this castle while staring at every furniture perfectly placed around spaces which complimented them. The old taste in things still lingered around the walls of the castle and furniture, yet it seemed very modern. All in all, though, the new duke must have a great taste.

Suddenly, a hand slipped into mine, and I turned to face Marley. Looking around with wild wonder, her mouth was literally ajar. "It's so beautiful," she murmured excitedly as she turned around to face me and her eyes twinkling. "I am so daydreaming about marrying a prince and living here with him!"

I giggled but immediately quietened down when Mr. Bishop sent a very stern look my way.

"Let's listen to the handsome old man talk," I whispered to Marley and moved closer to him. He was now talking about the current owner.

"The current owner, Master Alexander, has taken care for the castle incredibly well after graduating from college a few years ago. Being extremely rich, together with the inheritance he attained through his father, he made renovations around the whole castle and castle grounds. The castle was redesigned and equipped to make it comfortable for this age. However, some places around the castle have been left untouched when it concerns designing, like the fifth and sixth floor, the west wing and the library. We will proceed to the fifth floor and library, but the sixth wing is out of bounds, so that shall be excluded in our tour," Mr. Buckwood said, his deep voice ringing throughout the hall as he led us into a grand hallway.

I stilled as I felt a pressure on my lower belly, causing Marley to turn around and look at me quizzically.

Shit.

I motioned towards my skirt, and her eyes widened with realization. A grin found its way to her mouth. I needed to pee.

Still frowning, I let go of her hand and moved towards Mr. Harway, who was seemingly talking to Diandra. As I neared him, I coughed slightly, causing him to glance at me, and smile.

"Ah yes, Ms. Anderson, how may I help you?" His dark green eyes were twinkling as he grinned down at me.

Diandra seemed to have stiffened beside him and was now glaring at me.

What's up with her?

I shifted on my feet as I fiddled around with my hair. God, this was so embarrassing.

"Sir, do you know where the washroom is?" I mumbled, feeling my face heat up as a chuckle left his lips. I could practically feel Diandra sneering at me.

"Here." He handed me a pamphlet. "There's a map there. It helps you move around. Go on, Ms. Anderson."

Nodding thanks, I turned around glanced at the map. The pressure on my lower belly reminded me of how urgent this was.

"Fuck my life!" I groaned as I stared at the map for the hundredth time. I officially hated maps. Glancing around the empty hallway, I groaned in frustration. This was no good! I was lost.

I was just about to turn around and retrace my steps when I saw an elderly woman, wearing a plain black dress moving out of a room on the further end of the hallway, holding clothes in her hand. But before I could call out for her, she was gone.

A bedroom, I thought as I walked towards it. Maybe someone inside could help me?

My bladder was killing me now! I was on the verge of twisting my feet to hold the pee in. Reaching the door in a desperate run, I knocked on it urgently. When no one answered, I knocked again. Surely, there was someone there

"Who's there?" a gruff sleepy voice called out, male and purely irritated.

"Sir, if you could please open the door?" I requested pleadingly. This was a matter of life or wet floor!

I stiffened as a deep growl ringed out around the hallway, the source: the man in the room. Suddenly, the door swung open, and instantly, I started shivering out of fright. This was not good. What if this man would throw me out?

Minutes passed, and the man was silent. I couldn't take it anymore. I needed to pee!

"Could you show me the way to the loo?" I mumbled hurriedly, my eyes still glued to the floor. The man remained silent. I couldn't dare glance at him. But I could feel his stare on my face.

Finally, the man spoke, "Come in. It's the door on the left."

Immediately, I rushed into the room. "Thank you!" I called out before walking into the bathroom and shutting the door.

Deed done, I pulled my underwear and slowly stumbled over to the hand basin and opened the faucet. I glanced myself in the mirror as I washed and dried my hand. My hair seemed to be in place. My face seemed to be fine.

Smiling contently, I nodded at myself in the mirror and walked out.

Glancing around in curiosity as I entered the room, I realized it was not a bedroom but an office. My wandering gaze drifted along the shelves to the man standing and staring at me. I supposed I needed to say my thanks. I stilled. My breath hitched in my throat.

Standing there on the edge of a table was Bryce.

CHAPTER EIGHT

A soft breeze blew into the room from the open window, and I glanced at it for a second, seriously contemplating if I should just make a jump for it.

I glanced at Bryce again and shuddered with disgust as the fact that he was actually smirking registered in my head.

He was laughing at me.

As I watched Bryce smirk, all of the hurt I felt the past two weeks rushed back—waiting by the patio, sitting on the swing until the first signs of darkness came, staring at my phone, waiting for a call or a text, wondering if I should text him instead, and sending him a text but never getting a reply.

I could practically feel my heart building up a wall around it. I still felt for him badly, but looking at him standing there and smirking at me, not an ounce of guilt on his face, made me determined not to fall into his arms again.

So I did the only thing I could do. I painted on a poker face and turned towards the door, however, not failing to notice the fall in Bryce's smirk before I did.

"Theia?"

I shivered as his deep husky voice called out my name but kept walking towards the door. If I stopped now, I would never be able to walk away.

Each step I took made me feel bolder and more confident. A smile touched my lips as I reached out and grasped onto the doorknob, turning it.

You're winning, Thi!

I could only hear the sudden rustle of sweatpants before an arm slipped around my waist, turned me around, and pushed me against the wall. A whole lot of weight crushed me into it. I couldn't even push him away. He had my hands held against his, rendering me completely helpless.

Bryce's warm breath fanned the side of my cheeks as I managed to keep my eyes fixed on the small amount of wooden floor visible to my view. I refused to look anywhere near his naked chest.

"Why are you mad?" Bryce mumbled warmly, placing a ghost of a kiss on my cheek.

You lied. That's why, you jerk! You lied and then you left.

I remained silent and kept my posture stiff. I continued to stare at the floor.

Bryce placed a kiss on my cheek again. He seemed to sigh contently. "God, I missed you so much,"

My view became blurry as he pushed my hair away, exposing the fading bruise just on the base of my neck.

I had forgotten to hide it with foundation. *Dammit.*

"You're not hiding it," he whispered, sounding a little surprised before placing a soft kiss on the same spot.

I remained stiff, but my facade was crumbling. I could not hold much longer. I needed to escape.

"Why aren't you talking to me?" Bryce mumbled, moving back to get a proper look at me.

I raised my gaze to his. His expression changed from soft to that of concerned as he looked at me.

"What's wrong?" he asked, his voice holding a bit of steely edge in them.

The atmosphere around the room suddenly turned tense as he looked at me as if looking for a wound. I barely managed to hide the whisper of a smile that threatened to form on my lips.

"Why aren't you replying?" I flinched at Bryce's sudden growl. His fist banged the wall just beside my head.

I returned my gaze to the floor. It was much safer.

"Look at me, damn it!"

Bryce held my chin with his thumb and tilted my head so I looked at him.

"Let me go."

It was more a request than an order, but I thanked God that I didn't stutter. The last thing I wanted to show him was a weakness.

Bryce's eyes widened before he clenched his jaw and landed his fist on the brick wall once more.

"What did I do wrong?" he asked coldly.

The sound of the door lock resonated around the room. Bryce removed his hands from mine and moved away, the key in his hand.

With one last look in my direction, he moved towards the bathroom, got in, and shut the door.

As if I were a ticking time bomb and my time were up, a whimper fell from my lips as I bit back a sob, the cursed tears already slipping down my cheeks.

Why did this have to be so damn hard? Bryce was guilty! He disappeared for God's sake! Somehow, saying it in my mind made it all seem trivial, but I knew it wasn't. It may sound petty when spoken out loud, but someone who went through it knew the pain—the pain of being promised love and being left deserted. It's like a husband kissing his wife at the doorway and promising he would return home early but never show up…then hearing he was in fact in the same town but in a different house…with a new life. It sucked.

I could feel goosebumps rising along my arm. The cool breeze from the window felt icy on my now blotchy, warm face.

The sound of the door being pulled open alerted me of Bryce's return, and I quickly wiped away any signs of tears before fixing my gaze on the floor again.

As much as I felt like making a run for it and jumping off the first-floor window, I knew better. It would only cause me more embarrassment and pain.

"Let's go," Bryce muttered, his voice steely as he grabbed hold of my arm with one hand and with the other, unlocked the door and marched out, pulling me behind him. He was now dressed in a suit.

Where is he even taking me?

"Leave me!" I hissed, tugging on my hand. I was no damsel in distress. Bryce's head snapped towards me.

"What the hell is your deal?" He hissed back.

Suddenly, it felt like there wasn't enough room around us. Bryce's nose brushed mine, and his eyes glared into my brown orbs.

"My fucking problem is that you won't quit getting up in my personal space!" I snapped back, pushing him back with my free hand. "Move away!"

"No!"

A startled yelp escaped my lips as my back hit the wall again, and Bryce's lips landed on mine. His kiss was urgent like he thought this moment would just disappear…and yet somehow it felt like he was trying. He was pleading. But whether it was to be kissed back or to entertain his lie, his fake feelings for me, I wasn't sure.

Bryce nibbled on my lower lip. His arms were now tightly wounded around my waist. He intended no escape. As much as I wanted to do both, to kiss him back and forget how I felt for the past fourteen days, I did neither.

Placing both palms flat against his chest, I pushed as hard as I could.

There was no moving him. After all, I was tiny compared to him. But I couldn't give up. I was about to break and kiss him back, but I couldn't do that to myself. I couldn't feel rejected again. It hurt.

So I tried once more. I pushed. And this time, I succeeded.

Bryce moved back, but his arms were still around me as he stared at me, looking helpless and pissed.

I didn't get why he couldn't just leave me alone, spare me. I mean, wasn't there some other girl to act upon as a conquest? I cringed when the thought of him with some other girl hurt a lot more than I was hurting right now.

Only when a traitorous tear slipped down onto my cheeks did I realize I had finally crumbled. Cursing inwardly, I reached a hand to wipe it away, but Bryce quickly grabbed my hand before I could.

He grabbed my chin with his finger and tilted it until I stood looking at him, the tear now slipping down my jaw and falling to its fate, the wooden floor.

Bryce seemed to change from pissed off to downright furious in a matter of seconds as his eyes narrowed on my face.

"What happened?" His voice was low and deadly.

"Nothing," I mumbled back, biting onto my lower lip, cussing myself for quivering seeing him so angry.

"Nothing? Nothing! You're cry—"

"Master Wilhem, please let go of the girl!" A soft voice pleaded loudly, but I couldn't look away from Bryce's face.

It wasn't his face staring back at me because this Bryce had dark eyes instead of blue. I blinked. How was that even possible? This Bryce couldn't exist.

Our eye contact broke as Bryce turned towards the woman who was staring at the scene before her with terror.

"It's okay, Melly. She's mine," Bryce muttered gruffly, his arms tightening around me.

Melly's eyes softened at that, and she nodded happily before she turned towards me and whispered, "She truly is a beauty just like Madam had predicted," and then turned around and walked away.

What was that about?

I could feel Bryce's stare at me, so I turned towards him, barely escaping from brushing our noses. He was that close.

His eyes were still dark. That one prominent vein running up his forehead was now ready to bulge out of his skin.

"Your eyes," I whispered, temporarily forgetting why it was that I was not talking to him.

Bryce stiffened. "That happens when I'm mad or…"

I lifted an eyebrow up. "Or?"

"Aroused."

Flashes of memories I had tried hard to avoid for the past days came rushing back. I nodded and turned away, not looking at him anymore.

Just hug him, Theia. You know you want to desperately. Maybe he has a reason. Maybe he has a very good explanation. Just ask him! a tiny voice whispered in my head. She made sense. I did want to, but I couldn't. He would just hurt me.

He played you. He doesn't like you. He doesn't even want you! He looks like God, and you expect him to give you his time for affections? No, Theia, he thinks you're an easy fuck. That's all you're good for according to him, another voice spoke up, sounding much surer of herself as if she knew she was right. She made more sense.

"Why are you mad at me?" Bryce suddenly grumbled, dipping his face into my neck and placing a warm kiss on the base.

"Master Wilhem, it is time. The students are waiting," a deep, gruff male voice spoke up awkwardly from behind Bryce.

And that's when it hit me. Everyone was addressing him as Master Wilhem. He was being called because the students were waiting where I was supposed to be waiting.

Oh my God, Bryce is…Alexander Wilhem? That means…He lied to me!

"Oh God, Thi! You're such a fool!" I scolded myself loudly as I tried to push him away once more, but he wouldn't budge.

I turned to look for help when my eyes met the middle-aged man who was staring at us, his eyes wide as if he couldn't believe what he was seeing.

I couldn't take it anymore. I exploded.

"You're Alexander Wilhem! The Alexander Wilhem! So you lied to me again! Your name isn't even Bryce! Oh my God, can you just let go already? And stop nipping at my neck for God's sake!" I yelled all the while trying to push him away with all my might.

He moved away and looked at me with regret.

Yes, you jerk! You should regret! Just like I regret the day I set eyes on your blue ones!

"I'm sorry," he mumbled, looking at the floor, but didn't let me go. "I'm sorry for whatever it is that I've done. Please don't be mad at me."

From the side of my eyes, I could feel the man's eyes widen. Clearly, he wasn't accustomed to seeing Br—Alexander saying sorry. I sighed. "You lied to me and then left. And now, you expect me to forgive you? Listen, Bryce—Alexander, whoever you are, just leave me alone, okay? Please."

He moved closer as if to hold me again, but I stopped him. That's when his eyes travelled to the hands I had in front of us. His eyes had narrowed before it turned into a glare.

"You're engaged." He seethed.

"What?" I exclaimed.

I glanced towards my grandma's engagement ring. Apparently, today, I had worn it on the left hand rather than my usual right.

Bryce—Alexander, whoever he was, was clearly misinterpreting this.

"N—"

"Save it!" Bryce snapped. I stared stunned at the sudden change in his mood.

Without another word, he grasped onto my hand and pulled me forward as he stormed down the hall. The man behind us still stood on his spot, staring as if unbelieving what just occurred in front of his eyes.

I could understand his plight. After all, even I couldn't believe what had just happened.

***

Bryce took a turn around another hall, and that was when I saw my classmates. Mr. Bishop looked at me alarmed as Bryce proceeded towards them. In fact, everyone became extremely quiet.

On my part, I was humiliated.

My eyes found Marley's as she looked at me frantically. I guess she was shocked to see that my Bryce was actually Alexander Wilhem.

I wanted to rush to her and weep my eyes out, but I couldn't. Bryce didn't seem to want to let go of my hand anytime soon.

Matthew stood beside Marley, but unlike her, he had a soft smile on his face as if he understood what was happening. What exactly was happening?

I did a room sweep when I finally found Rome standing on the corner of the room and looking as deadly as Bryce did. His eyes found mine, and I grimaced. He was that crazy kind of mad again.

"Ladies and gentlemen, may I present to you Alexander Bryce Wilhem," Mr. Buckwood announced happily when finally, Bryce stopped and stood in front of the whole crowd. I stole a glance towards him. His rage was now masked. His face was blank.

He produced a small smile as he looked around the room. His eyes hardened as he gazed at Roman but then lightened when he smiled slightly at the boy standing in front of him.

"Hi, guys, I hope all of you had an eventful time today? Okay, so I know, all of you are excited at what I am about to announce. I want those who would not get either the scholarship or the invitation to stay at the castle to know that there are more opportunities in life. You just have to wait for them, and when you get the one that belongs to you, you grasp them—"

Bryce's hold on my arm tightened slightly before he continued.

"The student who will get the scholarship will receive a letter at the end of the year. I wish you all the best of luck. However, the invite is to be extended to Ms. Anderson here, who I happened to have stumbled upon when she had gotten lost. There is one last part of this tour that is yet to be completed, the library visit. Now, the library is extremely large. There are many extremely valuable books and literature there. Hence, there will be two groups for this tour. Mr. Harway, could you please distribute the students into two groups accordingly?"

While I stood gaping at him, his grip on my arm never loosened. He had just announced that I was to stay over at the castle! I looked around for Marley, but she was being ushered away. I caught sight of Matthew as he still stood in the room, smiling softly at me. I groaned under my breath, wildly wondering why he was even smiling. I couldn't bring myself to glance at Rome, though. I could practically feel his icy stare. Over the past days, I had realized how to calm that crazy anger of his, but as much as I wanted to move and give him a hug, Bryce's grip on my arm still had me restrained.

I watched as Mr. Bishop and Mr. Buckwood led the small group down the hall and turned towards the left. The rest of the class now stood in front us, their heads bowing low, everyone except Roman. *What the heck is happening?*

The bowing stopped, and everyone looked back at us. I could see Diandra glaring in my direction. Alex, like most of the people in the crowd, though, stood staring at us.

I felt as Bryce left my arm and moved behind me. *Thank God!*

A loud gasp left my lips when Bryce reached for my hair and moved it away from my neck, exposing the lightening bruise.

Loud gasps were heard around the room as people stared at my neck and then at Bryce before most of them broke into grins. Some, however, stood looking at me like Rome and Diandra.

Mr. Harway's eyes met mine as I looked around frantically. And he smiled warmly at me before silencing the apparently happy students. What the hell was even going on?

I turned round to demand why Bryce had shown everybody the bruise and why everyone had bowed, but when I turned, I stared at an empty spot behind me. Bryce was nowhere to be found.

"We need to get out of here," a deep voice muttered beside me. His voice sounded urgent.

I turned and bumped nose first into a hard chest. Instantly, an arm went around my waist.

"Let's get you out of here, Thi."

Glancing up at Rome, I nodded. I really did need to get away.

I didn't know why he wanted to help me. Hell, I was hoping he did it for the friendship we had developed in the days since we got paired for the project. But since he was helping me, I was going to take it. So, when he clasped his hand onto mine and dragged me towards what I believed to be the entrance, I followed.

***

We managed to escape. I had no clue how Rome just happened to have his car parked in the garage unless he lived there. But it was there, and we had fled.

The fact that Rome had, in fact, traveled to the castle on the bus, yet his car parked in the private garage seemed remarkably strange to me. How could it be there unless, like I said, he lived there?

Still confused and ever so curious, I glanced towards Roman, who was currently driving me home. His lips were set in a thin line, and his eyes were narrowed as if he was in deep thought or pissed.

"How come your car was parked in the garage?"

I saw as Roman stiffened for a second, and his grip on the wheel tightened so much that his knuckles turned white. I wasn't scared of him anymore, though. I just wanted to know.

"Because I live there," he replied.

I stared at him.

"Excuse me! You live where?" I exclaimed, smacking my palm against my thighs in response.

Roman's knuckles turned a shade whiter. "I live in the castle. Alexander is my first cousin from my mother's side,"

I sat stunned in the car while he remained quiet as he drove towards home.

Another turn and I would be there.

I really couldn't wait to be there.

The fact that Roman Naight was Bryce's cousin was information my brain was refusing to accept. It just could not be.

Roman took a turn before driving into my driveway. He parked the car just beyond the gateway and looked down at his palm, silent. I remained silent as well. How was I supposed to converse with him now? He hadn't known, but surely, he couldn't know anything. Suddenly, his strong arms reached and pulled me towards him, startling me as I landed against his chest, and he hugged me. Strangely, I hugged back.

"Sorry. You know, it calms me down. Listen, Theia, everything will be all right, okay? I know everything that happened back there must have seemed crazy to you, and I know that you and I didn't start off great. I kind of hate you still sometimes, but I like you. You're the only person who stood up to my bullshit, Just trust me," Roman whispered as he hugged me, placed a soft kiss on the side of my head, and slowly let me go.

I nodded meekly and unlocked the door to get out. I really did need to clear my head. Today was just too much to process, but at least, Roman didn't hate me that much anymore. At least, that was progress.

As I opened the front door and got in, I turned around and gave Roman a soft smile and a wave. He waved back.

I closed the door and made my way to my room.

***

"Theia, dear, would you like something to drink?" Agnus's voice spoke out softly, and I raised my gaze towards her before smiling softly and nodding. She smiled back and proceeded towards the kitchen, leaving me to complete the task at hand.

Unlocking my bedroom door, I walked in.

On my way home, while in Rome's car, I imagined walking into my room, leaping onto my bed, pulling the covers up high, so they covered me whole, and just sleeping the day away.

But nothing of that sort happened in actuality. For when I opened the door and walked in, I was welcomed by the view of Bryce sitting on my bed and glaring daggers at the floor.

My eyes widened as I realized how ballistic he looked, so I decided to do the one thing I could think of. He had not seen me, and if I were to escape, I would, so I decided to do just that. I turned towards the door. I slowly opened it and took a step towards freedom.

"Escaping will not help, Theia. I will always find you…Always."

I nearly had a heart attack. Bryce's sudden warning caught me off guard. But the deadly tone of his voice forewarned me that he was extremely angry right now and that messing with him would do no good.

So releasing a deep sigh, I turned towards the room and closed the door. There was no need to get poor Agnus and Lilly into this.

But how did he get here so fast?

"What do you want?" I muttered cautiously, shifting further into the room, and terrified that Bryce would move from his position and ruin everything for me. I didn't want to give in.

For the first time in five minutes of standing in front of Bryce, he finally lifted up his head and looked at me. I nearly gasped at the look on his face. He looked livid.

"Escaped with your fiancé, I see," Bryce sneered, getting up on his two feet. His eyes are as dark as nightfall. "And you smell just like him."

He took a step forward, and unconsciously, I took one back. I frowned. *What was he even talking about? What fiancé?*

"What the hell are you even talking about?" I snapped, folding my arms in front of me. His eyes went straight to my arms. He glared.

I looked down curious, and my eyes widened with realization. He was talking about my grandma's ring again.

I didn't even get time to register what happened next, but my breath rushed off me as, in a matter of seconds, Bryce whisked me into his arms and onto the bed, slamming me underneath him.

"You're engaged to my fucking cousin, Roman! For fuck's sake, don't lie to my face! I can smell him all over you!" Bryce hissed, anger lacing his eyes as his fingers found my grandma's ring and began tugging it off.

"What the hell are you doing?" I screamed, trying to push him away. He was clearly losing it! I mean, I was the one who was supposed to be mad here, not him!

"Removing the damned ring! I told you, you are mi—" Bryce growled, but I cut him off. At this point, I was as mad as he was.

"Yours? Yeah, yeah, whatever! You have no right to tell me that after avoiding me for two weeks! And as for the ring, it's my grandma's for God's sake! I wear it because it reminds me I have a piece of her! I am not engaged! But you know what? Rome is hot! And heck if he proposed, I would say ye—"

I couldn't even complete my sentence because the next thing I knew was that Bryce's lips had slammed against mine. Moving over me instantly, he began nipping, nibbling, teasing me into weakness. I could barely feel my feet. Bryce ran his tongue along my bottom lip as if asking for entrance. I clenched my mouth shut. I wasn't going to kiss him if he didn't explain everything.

"Kiss me back! Show me that you're mine!" Bryce growled as he pulled back slightly, his lips still brushing mine.

"There will be no kissing until you explain, maybe not even after that!" I snapped back, pressing my head further into the mattress away from him.

We glared into each other's eyes; each one of our glares was steely. We were both waiting to see who lost.

"Kiss me! Prove it! Prove you're mine!"

My gaze didn't falter.

"Explain!" I retorted.

"I don't even know what you fucking even want me to explain! Just tell me what you want me to explain, and I will do it for God's sake!" Bryce roared, slamming his fist on the bed just beside my head.

I stared at him wide-eyed. Bryce was officially scaring me.

Maybe you should calm him down a little first, the tiny voice spoke up inside of my head. And after thinking it through, I nearly nodded. It was right. I needed to be calm. Bryce surely wasn't going to get calm anytime soon.

I looked at him. His eyes still held crazed anger as well as a little bit of fierceness. But what surprised me was that it was almost animalistic, or maybe it was just raw.

"You disappeared for two weeks. You didn't text, didn't call, and when I suddenly bump into you, you act like nothing is wrong."

Although I had initially planned to yell, to fight it actually came out as barely a whisper. I was losing. He had me pinned. I was the weak one.

Bryce stared at me for a minute or two before pulling out his cellphone from his back pocket and handing it over to me.

"Messages…Yours," he muttered gruffly. And yet somehow, his tone was now softer.

I was actually the first person on the list. Biting on my lip nervously, I tapped on the thread.

Wednesday:

7:45 PM
Tell me if that Matthew flirts with you okay? You're mine. But have fun! I'll see you soon - B

11:55 PM
Goodnight love. - B

Thursday:

8:10 AM
Rise and shine, beautiful. Have a great day! I'll see you today, okay? By the swing. Take care. - B

PS: That Matthew didn't flirt with you, did he? I tried calling. You didn't pick up. Is everything okay?

1:02 PM
Why are you not replying? Theia are you okay?

Okay, maybe you're in class. Look, babe, I can't make it today. This big important meeting came up in Los Angeles. Will leave in a few hours. I'll be back in two weeks tops!

Don't be too mad. I'll miss you! - B

11:00 PM
Just landed. Are you mad at me? - B

2:30 AM
Good night, Theia.

Friday:

10:45 PM
Had such a tiring day at work. Why aren't you replying, though?

I'm sorry if I'm not giving you space.

- B

Sunday:

9:34 PM
From: Theia
Hey, er...it's been ages...Are you okay? I kinda miss you. Message back. - Thi

To: Theia
Hey! I've been trying to message and call you all week. Have you not received any? I miss you too, Theia. I was actually worried you were mad. How are you? - B

Monday:

10:02 AM
I'll be back by next week Friday.

Wednesday:

8:00 AM
Fine.

Saturday:
3:03 AM
TOK 2 ME! I LO—

I stared at the last message. In fact, I stared at all of them. He had messaged me. He had called. So why had I not gotten any? How could this be?

Frowning, I placed his phone aside and grabbed hold of mine. There was nothing.

The realization that Bryce was in fact still on top of me struck me when he moved his weight so he could look into my phone. I glanced at him and froze when our eyes met. He had actually been looking at me. His eyes were still dark and brooding. His lips were set in a thin line. I smiled.

"Someone got my number blocked for your cellphone. I checked," Bryce muttered.

But I didn't hear. I couldn't. All that kept swimming around my head was the fact that he hadn't left. He hadn't played. I was not a conquest. I didn't give it a second thought. At that moment, there was no need. So I flung my arms around Bryce's neck and pulled him closer. I kissed him. He froze but only for a second before he kissed me back urgently and breathtakingly. It was a kiss unlike any other, not that I had received many, but still, it was breathtaking. Better than those sweet emotional kisses shared by the hero and heroine in the climax of movies.

A little moan left my lips as Bryce grasped my thighs and pulled them apart, settling himself between me.

His kiss turned urgent. He ran his tongue along my lower lip, and I parted my lips, giving him entrance. Immediately, he dipped his tongue into my mouth, causing another muffled moan to leave my lips as I moved my hips under him.

An animalistic growl left Bryce's lips as he grabbed my hips to hold me in place. "Stop," he growled, kissing his way through my jaw onto my neck.

I was panting now. I could hardly breathe.

Immediately, Bryce's hands grabbed onto my hips again and held it tight, disabling me from moving. "Dammit, Theia, if you want me to take you hard right now, then repeat that again! I swear to God!"

I shivered and hooked my legs around Bryce's hips, careful not to grind against it. As much as I wanted it and needed it, I knew I wasn't ready. I just couldn't do it. It wasn't the right time.

"In your last message, did you mean to say you love me?" I whispered, smiling up at Bryce as I placed a soft kiss on his chin.

"No," Bryce muttered darkly, frowning at me.

I smirked.

"Really?" I whispered teasingly.

Bryce groaned, his arms tightening on my hands that he now held above my head.

"Theia!" He warned.

"Really, Bryce?" I repeated this time and kissed his jaw.

"Well?"

He groaned. "You don't play fair, Kitten."

"I know." I grinned, freeing my arm from his grasp and instantly pushing it into his shirt. I sighed as I felt his warm skin against my palm. Lord, how I had missed it!

"Well?" I asked again, rubbing circles on his back.

"You talk too much." Bryce suddenly chuckled as he dipped his lips onto my neck and placed an open-mouthed kiss there.

"You're not fair either," I grumbled, retrieving my hands from underneath his shirt and turning towards something else, anything else but him.

"I know." Bryce chuckled again and tilting my face towards him, pressing his lips onto mine.

***

"Well, who do you think it was?" I mumbled, sipping on the cup of hot chocolate Agnus had brought me earlier.

It had been quite funny. She had knocked while Bryce was actually revisiting the love bite on my neck he so famously showed everybody, calling out to me sweetly like she always did. I panicked. And Bryce, well, continued his sweet torture. Needless to say, it had taken quite a bit of effort to actually get Bryce to hide and open the door, but I had managed.

It had been quite strange, really. Agnus had walked into the room and instantly froze before she looked right at me, smiled and continued towards the study table to place the mug of hot chocolate and cookies on it. After that, she had simply turned around and walked out the door, handing a final large smile my way.

I had been relieved when I had flicked the door lock and turned towards my room only to see that Bryce was now munching on one of the cookies, settled in bed, looking very amused. Eyeing him, I moved to the bed and grabbed the last cookie left on the saucer, finally figuring out why he had looked so happy. I sent him a glare. That cookie stealer!

"I'm not sure. They informed me that it had been you. But that couldn't have been you because you were in school at the exact time the supposed Theia Anderson called to request my number be blocked from her cellphone."

A shudder ran down my spine. Someone was actually trying to create rifts between Bryce and me.

"Do you have any suspicions?" I asked, moving my legs upwards so I could rest my head on it as I sat against the headboard of the bed. Bryce moved a little closer and pulled me near him. I rested my head against his chest.

"A lot too, but don't worry about that right now. We will find him or her soon," Bryce murmured against my forehand and placed a tiny kiss there.

I nodded contently. This was great. Everything was better now, well, almost…But the one thing that refused to leave my mind was why Bryce had shown my schoolmates the love bite, and why they bowed down to him.

Maybe…I should just ask him, I thought to myself and nodded inwardly. *I should.*

"Bryce?"

"Hmm…"

I sighed. Hopefully, he wouldn't shut me off and actually answer.

"Why did those people bow down to you? And why did you show them the hickey like that?" I mumbled cautiously, turning around to look at him for a second before pecking his chin and leaning against his chest again. That way, there were fewer chances of him getting mad. But he stiffened, nonetheless.

And then with a loud sigh, he finally replied, "I don't know why they bowed down…I suppose they tried to mock me or kid around. And as for showing them the love bite, I admit I just wanted everyone to know that you are mine."

"But what if they think of me as a…bitch?"

The question had come out of nowhere. But it really did bother me. What if my whole school thought I was a slut? What if Matthew thought I was a bitch? He hadn't even called!

"Why are you even thinking about that Matthew?" Bryce suddenly asked, seeming irritated.

I grimaced. "I said that out loud, didn't I?"

"Answer my question," Bryce snapped, seeming more irritated than he had a few seconds ago.

"Well, aren't you a jealous one?" I grinned. "Alright, alright," I muttered when I turned around to see that Bryce looked a little mad.

"He is my best friend, and I actually love him a lo—"

I rolled my eyes as Bryce growled and pulled me into his lap.

That's some good growling. I wonder where he learned to growl like that, I thought, trying to get comfortable on his lap.

"Oh, shush! I meant it in the best friend way. You should really have a big board nailed on your chest saying, *Caution: Extremely Possessive Male Coming Through.*"

I actually melted when Bryce burst out laughing. His deep rich laughter rumbled out of his chest, vibrating on my back as he held me around my waist.

"I think I'd rather have the board saying, *Caution: Extremely Possessive Alpha Male Coming Through.*"

"Tsk, tsk, alpha male? Where? I see no alpha male!" I asked, mock-looking around.

"Don't test me, love," Bryce whispered into my ear. I shivered. The heat on my cheeks was now extremely apparent, and I knew very well that I could resemble a ripe tomato.

"I need to go shower!" I yelled, shooting out of his lap, and running towards the bathroom. Finally reaching the bathroom, I quickly turned, and without a second glance at Bryce, I locked the door.

***

Just open the damn door and make a run for it, Anderson! Either that or stay here for the rest of the night or until he leaves. Up to you.

I groaned as I banged my head against the bathroom door. I had been standing and staring at the door for ten minutes now, and between the chilly weather and lack of clothes, I was dying.

Just do it, Thi!

"Dash it all!" I grumbled, and with a final tug to secure my towel, I opened the door and stepped out of the bathroom and into my bedroom.

The cold feeling that had seemed to surround the room screamed out that Bryce was now gone, and there was no one here besides me. The window had been left open, and the soft breeze, just like every other night, didn't fail to blow in the cool breeze. Smiling slightly, I padded my way to the closet.

Bryce must have gone to the castle. Must have needed a bath himself. I consoled myself.

Doing all the other essentials, I finally moved out of the closet and into my bedroom.

The day had been a great one although I admit initially, it had been bad. After all, the misunderstandings had been cleared. Everything seemed so much better.

"Theia, aren't you going to have dinner? Come down for dinner, darling. Dad's not home yet, and I'm lonely!" Mom called out suddenly, and I sighed slightly before replying, "Coming, Mom!"

***

With dinner well eaten and a cup of warm chocolate devoured, I padded my way into my room a happy girl.

"Good night, Mom!" I called out before closing the door and locking it.

I smiled as I heard a faint reply.

"Home sweet home!" I smiled and kissed my pillow lovingly as I slipped into bed and cuddled with my blanket.

"Can I get a kiss too?" a low tone whispered as arms reached out, wrapped itself around my waist, and pulled me flush into a hard chest. I smiled.

"You're back already?" I mumbled, placing an arm on his.

Bryce chuckled, moved my hair away, and placed a slow, sweet kiss on my back.

"You look good in your knickers," Bryce murmured, slipping his arms down my belly and curling his fingers around my panty's waistband. I stilled and instantly grabbed hold of his arm.

"Bryce," I whispered breathlessly, holding onto his arm tight.

Slowly, Bryce moved his arms away and slipped them once again around my waist.

"Sleep, love," Bryce mumbled, placing a kiss on the side of my forehead. I smiled.

"Only after you tell me how you got up here," I replied.

I could feel Bryce scowling, but since I could barely see him, I was fine.

"Through the window. I'm good at jumping and climbing," he muttered, and sensing his sudden anger, I turned to kiss him, but before he could kiss back, I moved away, took his bottom lip between my teeth and gave it a tug.

"Good night," I mumbled dreamily. Sleep was already beginning to knock on my door.

He planted a small kiss on my forehead instead and whispered, "Good night, babe."

CHAPTER NINE

A storm was coming. Branches swayed swiftly as if to witness the upcoming danger.

Well, maybe I exaggerated a bit.

But the storm really was in the forecast, and the branches really were swaying with the fast pace of the Saturday morning breeze.

I walked out of the bathroom, looked at the dull, grey day outside and smiled before returning to bed to lie beside the big bulk of a man who seemed fast asleep. It was only six in the morning, anyway.

A smile made its way on my lips as I watched Bryce sleep, the scars on his chest shining silver against the tan of his skin.

Wonder what caused it?

He looked so peaceful sleeping. Sighing happily, I ran a finger on the edges of a light scar just above his eyebrow before leaning in and placing a kiss on the tip of his nose. Instantly, his arm wrapped around me and pulled me closer. I smiled and closed my eyes, letting sleep once more take over.

***

There was something wet moving around my neck. It was tickling me, then caused a little bit of pain and then pleasure.

I frowned, the heaviness leaving my eyes as clear thoughts began to formulate itself in my head. Just then the pain in my neck increased a bit, and I nearly jumped upright in bed from shock. My eyes wide-open, I directed it towards Bryce and frowned. He was clearly having a field day with my neck. I smacked the largeness of his arm resting on my tummy, and he looked up at me curiously.

"Yes?" Bryce asked casually.

He is going around nipping and biting my neck, and he doesn't know what's bothering me?

Scowling at him, I moved a bit when my attention shifted to something entirely different, something completely raw and very male, and something that was currently poking me on the side of my thigh.

"Wh-what? It's poking me!" I stuttered.

"Mmm," Bryce hummed as he suddenly moved over me and with a wicked grin, lowered himself on me, and rubbed the huge bulge against my pelvis.

A throaty moan escaped me as I clutched onto his biceps, and he buried his nose into the crook of my neck, placing soft kisses on it as if he had all the time in the world for this one particular thing.

Bryce suddenly moved back and looked at me seriously, his eyes now dark, almost the color of midnight blue.

"You're so beautiful," he whispered before slowly leaning in, never breaking eye contact, and placing his lips on mine.

A dreamy sigh left me as Bryce's fingers found their way to my naked belly, and he started running wonderful tiny circles around it as he kissed me. Pulling and nipping on my lips, his tongue dipped into my mouth, completely diminishing any bit of resistance. I couldn't help but let out a low moan as his fingers moved upwards and edged the swells of my breast.

"Theia Anderson, open the door this instant!"

A growl ripped out of Bryce's chest. *Shit! Marley!*

"Bryce, go hide please!" I whispered, trying my best not to choke on the excessive amount of breathing I was doing or at least, trying.

"No, stupid human should know not to disturb us early in the morning!"

I stiffened and turned towards him. "And what are you exactly? Count Dracula? Just go and hide please!"

As if I had never spoken Bryce simply moved to lie on his back, brought his hands behind his head, and closed his eyes.

I rolled mine.

"Bryce!"

I sighed as I gave up and moved towards the floor-length mirror, fixed my hair, managing to look as decent as someone could with three dark hickies on their neck, and walked towards the door.

"Thei—Oh my Go—Hmmm!"

I sighed, my hand still covering Marley's mouth. I pulled her into the room, pushing the door close behind me. Marley's eyes widened as she looked towards the bed before turning to me, bewildered. *I guess she saw Bryce.* I sighed again.

"Look, if I let you go, you won't scream, alright?" I asked pleadingly, still holding her against me.

She glared towards the bed, a whimper leaving her lips as she turned to look at me again.

"Okay?"

She nodded. Her head bobbed up and down with my hand. Nervously, I turned to look towards the bed and saw Bryce sitting on it, still shirtless, leaning against the headboard. He grinned cheekily at me, and I rolled my eyes before turning back towards Marley and smiling.

"Okay," I mumbled softly as I removed my palm slowly away from her lips.

I stared wide-eyed as she marched towards Bryce angrily.

"You! Why are you back? Haven't you hurt her enough?" Marley hissed as she pointed a finger at Bryce accusingly.

Bryce, on the other hand, stayed still. His eyes were now directed to mine.

"Hurt?" he asked Marley. His gaze, however, never broke from mine.

"Yes, hurt! Do you have any idea how much it hurt her when suddenly you just disappeared? How much she cried? Oh, but, of course, you don't because here you are preparing to hurt her again. Leave her alone! She doesn't need you! She's going to get over you, and she's going to burn all of those portraits of you that she has painte—"

"Portraits? What portraits?"

I could feel a blush heating its way up to my cheeks. Well, damn it, this was embarrassing.

"Oh, she pai—"

I cut off Marley before she blew it all out.

"There is no portrait! She's just trying to intimidate you," I spoke up quickly, walking over to Marley, moving an arm against hers and pinching her slightly. "Right, Marley?"

Marley looked at me pained.

I handed her a lopsided smile, and she sighed. "Right, but that doesn't tell me why you are with this jerk again! I mean, honestly, the majority of the male population in our high school would love to be with you! Why him?"

Shit.

Marley and I both stiffened as the unquestionable growl sounded around the room. It was only when Marley started to stare behind me did I look back, only to gasp at Bryce, who sat on the bed shaking with rage, glaring at the floor. The veins on his temple, neck, and arms had started to show badly as if begging to be released. He looked lethal. I froze. This was definitely not human behavior.

"D-do we run?" Marley whispered, sounding as freaked out as I was.

I frowned and shook my head. He wouldn't hurt us. He was just angry, extremely jealous, and possessive…and exhibited actions and behavior not entirely human. But still…it felt like he wouldn't hurt us.

"Well, then, do something! He looks like a sociopath!" she whispered.

I turned to look at her desperately. "What do I do?"

She sighed, giving me a little push towards the still fuming Bryce's direction. "You're the girlfriend. Do something! God, men are so possessive!"

I hesitated, looking at Bryce when the pulsating vein on his forehead caught my eye.

Oh, crap.

Gulping down the intimidation, I took a slow step towards him and stopped. When he did not say anything, I continued to move towards him. Getting into the bed, I shuffled towards him and was instantly pulled into a hard chest, his face against the crook of my neck. I smiled softly as he breathed hard.

"You're mine," he whispered so softly I had thought it was just the wind for a second, but he repeated himself a moment later, his grip on me tightening.

"Woah, he is so possessive."

I turned towards Marley and smiled. "I guess," I mumbled, suddenly blushing with the realization of how intimate our embrace might look and with my best friend witnessing it.

"So…Theia, can I talk to you in private?" Marley finally spoke after a moment of silence, suddenly sounding nervously curious.

"Sure." I smiled, dropping my arms off Bryce's shoulders and trying to move back. Before I knew it, I was pulled back into a warm hard chest, and two powerful arms slid around my waist, holding me captive.

"No," Bryce growled against my ear, causing me to sigh at his aggressiveness. The ping in the back of my mind began buzzing again, and I pushed it down.

"Chill," I whispered back.

Looking over at Marley, I motioned her over to the bed. Once she sat down, I sighed before mumbling out what had happened. Marley stared shell-shocked as I told her about the calls, text messages, and someone blocked Bryce's number, pretending to be me.

"So someone is trying to separate you from *the* Alexander Bryce Wilhem? Why am I not surprised?"

"When I find whoever it is, I am going to make sure he regrets ever trying!" Bryce growled against my ear, and I smiled softly, the lights going off in my head again.

Yep, he really is possessive.

***

Letting the towel loosen around me as I moved, I padded my way into the closet, leaving the door ajar.

After spending half of the morning with Marley and Bryce, Marley had finally left two hours ago after picking up a dress from my closet. Apparently, she had a date with Keith. I was happy. I always knew he had a thing for her.

Bryce left just after Marley had, though. He used the window much to my astonishment. I could only stare while he swung onto a tree and vanished.

I couldn't stop panicking until he called and let me know he was fine. Frankly, I had strong suspicions which worked alongside radioactive spiders and the living dead or maybe…maybe he actually was Superman?

Curiosity still buzzing in me, I let the towel drop to the rug and picked out a black pair of panties and bra. Smiling softly at the sweater I currently had my eyes on, I casually moved towards it when a low growl caught my attention. I froze instantly.

Bryce.

"You are so beautiful,"

The warmth of his breath fanned against my temples as he placed his hands on my shoulder and turned me around to face him. His finger found my chin slowly before he titled my head up until my eyes met his. I shivered. Gone were the ocean pools; midnight blue was back. Bryce smiled at me mysteriously before moving down, his warm breath hitting against my chest and belly as his arms found my thighs. A surprised squeal escaped my lips when Bryce hoisted me up, and my legs automatically twined around his waist. Groaning lowly, Bryce pressed a kiss on the soft skin of my ear, making me shiver from the sensation.

How can he affect me like this?

It felt like having a dozen tiny lines of electricity jolting around the part of my skin he decided to touch.

"Theia?" I smiled. My name sounded so beautiful when he whispered it. "I'm so glad you're mine," Bryce whispered, pressing another soft kiss on my chin.

"And."

He smiled. "And I'm yours."

"Good!" I beamed, leaning closer and placing my lips on him only long enough to get him riled up before pulling away.

His frustrated growl only made me giggle out loud.

"You're so cheeky." Bryce groaned, his head slightly pulled back as he regarded me with amusement in his eyes.

I smiled at him shyly, only just remembering my state of undress. "C-can you let go now? I need to dress."

Bryce sighed but complied.

Once let down onto the floor, I quickly slipped into a navy blue skirt and the cream crop sweater I had been eyeing. I moved over to the tiny vanity I had placed in the closet and unclipped my hair, letting my hair fall down in perfect waves. It was rare, but I loved it when that happened, so I quickly sprayed my hair with hairspray and turned around only to stop. Before me was Bryce looking at all of his portraits with a strange look in his eyes as if he sensed I was looking. He turned towards me.

"You painted me," he spoke, his statement sounding more like a question.

I nodded. "I guess I did."

"You made me look ten times nicer," Bryce muttered as he made his way to me, his eyes holding that warm emotion.

"I painted you through my eyes. That's how I see you, and you're just as beautiful on the canvas as you are in real life, Bryce." Once Bryce was at a holding distance, I pulled him closer before slipping my arms around his waist, holding him close.

Bryce sighed. I smiled. I guess he needed it.

"I want to take you out today."

"And we're not out yet because?"

Bryce pulled back and holding my hand, led me out of the closet and into the bedroom. "Because I want to do it the proper way, Theia. I am…older than you…and I really don't want your father to have any objections against our relationship, you know?"

I didn't know what to say, actually. It was true that he was older than me with a big difference of six years. But that didn't matter, really! It didn't matter to me.

Dad was home today; even Mom was too. And since Agnus and Lilly lived down at the cottage on our property, I was sure they were in as well.

Suddenly, the thought of Bryce formally introducing himself to my parents made me a bit woozy. Was this moving a little too quickly? Quite possibly, but what was I to expect? Somehow, what Bryce said made sense. A formal introduction would seem nicer compared to playing hide and seek with my folks. Besides, in my household, boyfriends were expected to be shown before dating and not three months after. I was already cracking the surface of that rule.

Tilting my head to the side unconsciously, I gazed at Bryce, who himself was staring at me, waiting for an answer. I smiled and nodded. Instantly, his grin returned.

"Give me five minutes! I will be at your front door," Bryce murmured smoothly before leaping out of the window again.

I blinked.

Kryptonite? Radioactive waste? Highly classified science experiment? Demo—okay, enough.

Picking up my cellphone, I saw that there were three unread text messages before I shoved it into my bag and proceeded to do the same with my iPod.

The five minutes were coming closer, and with much agitation, I ran a hand through my hair as I slipped on my flats and swinging the bag from my shoulder, walked out and down the stairs into the living room.

Dad was plopped on the sofa, feet placed above the other on the coffee table in front of him as he read a novel I would never bother myself with. Mom, on the other hand, seemed to be doing the exact same thing her husband was doing. Boring stuff.

I coughed a little awkwardly, causing both the adults to look my way. Immediate smiles broke on their faces.

"Hey, honey, how's it going?" Mom asked, smiling as she closed the book and placed it on her lap.

A little tense, I padded my way to the couch across them and sat down.

"Mom, Dad, I—I have a boyfriend."

Silence.

"Ahem, aren't you going to say something? Ask me something?" I asked Mom, nervously avoiding Dad's gaze.

Dad cleared his throat while a smile lit up on Mom's face. My nerves eased up a bit.

"Who is he? What's his name? Does he go to school with you? What does his dad do? Since when have you two been dating? I don't want to become a granddad just yet, Theia Ander—"

The doorbell rang just then, cutting Dad's fit, but instead of sighing with relief, I tensed up even more.

"That must be him. Dad, please be nice. Ma, don't let Dad ruin this, please…I really like him." I pleaded urgently, looking in the direction of the door.

"Is there something we should know before you open that door, Thi?" Mom asked softly.

I sighed.

"He…He's twenty-four."

Dad froze. Mom, however, smiled at me assuringly. "Go open the door, sweetie,"

Nodding, I got up and moved towards the front door.

This is it. Dad will kill Bryce. Bryce will kill everyone, ugh.

I stared at the closed door for a second or two, sighed, and then opened the door.

Bryce smiled at me smoothly, pulling me closer for a hug, which was kind of hard, since I only just touched his shoulders.

"I'm scared," I whispered against his chest.

"Don't be, love. Everything is under control."

After a hesitant pause, I nodded before moving out of his embrace and closing the door. We walked towards the living room.

My dad, now, sat on the sofa, a regal look on his face as he looked at Bryce with curious warning eyes. Mom, however, looked like she had just seen an angel. I nearly giggled as she looked at me and mouthed an "Oh my God!"

Mom down, Dad to go.

Bryce, seemingly too calm, took a seat on the couch across my parents and slowly pulled me to sit beside him—a gesture my dad didn't miss. He frowned.

"I'll go get us some coffee," Mom chirped kindly before walking away in the direction of the kitchen.

Both Bryce's and my gaze shifted towards Dad.

"You intend on dating my daughter?"

Bryce shifted, pulling me closer, but smiled. "Yes…sir."

Dad's frown deepened. My hopes fell

"Can I have a private discussion with you, Mr…"

"Alexander Wilhem, and sure, sir." Bryce smiled.

The air around the living room seemed heavy. I turned towards Dad only to see his gaze widen.

Oh yeah, I forgot Bryce was a billionaire. Oh well!

"Y-you're the ki—"

Wait, what?

"With all due respect, Mr. Anderson, may I suggest we speak privately?" Bryce muttered, still sounding impeccably calm.

Dad glanced at me, his eyes still wide before he looked at Bryce and nodded. "Sure."

***

"Where is your father, sweetie?"

I glanced up to see Mom, placing a tray of steaming coffees on the table before straightening up and looking around.

It had been fifteen minutes since they had left. I knew; I had been counting.

I shrugged. "Probably in the study. He and Bryce decided to speak privately."

It irritated me that I didn't know what was actually going on between Dad and Bryce. I mean, it was about me as well! Clearly, I should also be included in this discussion of theirs. As if on cue, Bryce and Dad both strode into the room, Bryce towering my father by good inches, both their faces lit with humor and their eyes twinkling with a good mood.

I wondered what had caused the change. I suppose so did Mom because I caught her looking at Dad with disbelief as both the man resumed their original places. Bryce's hand found mine before entwining our fingers. I smiled softly at Dad when I caught him looking at us with a warm smile. Mom, on the other hand, seeing Dad's change in demeanor, smiled at Bryce warmly before offering him a cup of coffee and then doing the same with Dad.

I didn't drink hot coffee.

"So I suppose you boys are on good terms now?" Mom asked them. She, however, looked at Dad as she spoke.

Dad grimaced before glancing back at her. "We are men, dear."

"Well, of course, you are, honey," Mom cooed, leaning in to place a neat peck on Dad's cheek, who grew slightly red afterward.

"Alexander has told me that he intends to take you out on a date today?" Dad smiled, taking a sip of his coffee.

"Yes," I mumbled back, clearly not aware of what else to say. All these changes were really shocking.

"Be back home by twelve, Theia," Dad spoke in an authoritative voice, and although I heard Bryce growl a little from beside me, I ignored him and nodded at my dad, smiling.

Mom giggled beside Dad, putting her cup down. "Oh and sweetie, be safe if you know what I mean."

"Honey!"

"Mom!"

Well, there she goes embarrassing me.

CHAPTER TEN

Golden leaves blew down from branches as they swirled around in the air above of us before landing near our feet. The day was still grey. The sun was doing a great job hiding away, and the clouds were doing a great job helping.

I sighed happily as I turned towards the trees. It had been raining a while ago. The narrow wet road stood witness to that. But it was calm now. It seemed like it would be a while before the rain would grace us again.

As we continued to stroll down the path, my gaze wandered and stopped at the bed of white daffodils we were slowly approaching. Wild and untamed, they were harbored by the partially dead trees under dying branches and slightly browning leaves. The grass, however, looked as green as they came in this part of the area.

"This part of the park was not opened to public until 1993," Bryce spoke out, and I tilted my head up to smile at him.

"It's beautiful," I said, grasping onto Bryce's arm tightly before leaning in closer to him as we continued to stroll.

We strolled around in peaceful silence for quite some time before Bryce unexpectedly stopped and turned. I gasped in surprise as the grip on my arm tightened, and I was pulled in for a hug.

"Did I ever tell you how I felt when I saw you by the swing?"

I smiled. "I don't recall so no."

"I thought you were the most beautiful girl I have seen in my entire existence." I felt him place a small kiss on my hair before he continued, "I actually stared at you for quite some time before deciding to wake you up, selfishly regretted it the rest of the night."

"Why were you acting so mysterious and Italian, really?" I cocked an eyebrow up at him as I played with his t-shirt.

"Well, I made a blind throw. I didn't exactly want you to understand what I was saying. But then I wanted to say it all the more," he replied, chuckling.

"Funny." I rolled my eyes, smacking his back lightly.

Bryce's deep chuckle rang out around the mostly empty park, and I tilted my head upward only to smile at the sight of his brightly lit face. His bright blue eyes showed me the depths of the bright blue sea. He crossed his eyes towards his nose, and the soft brown spot of his iris showed itself, making my breath hitch in my throat.

"You're so pretty."

A gasp ripped out of my lips as soon as I realized that I had said that out loud, and my palms instantly found my shocked, gaping mouth. Bryce, on the other hand, only shuddered slightly before replying, "I believe the word you were looking for was *sexy*."

Oh, wow! But yes…but wow…

Despite his obvious confidence, I couldn't lie. It was the truth. No one could deny. Bryce was sexy, so I took the easy way.

"Hmm."

Bryce turned towards me.

"You don't think so?"

"Nope."

He frowned. "If not sexy, then what?"

I smirked. "Pretty like a princess!"

I couldn't help stifling the giggle that erupted out of me as Bryce moved back to look at me properly before, in one swift moment, taking me in his arms and twirling me around.

In our little haze, we almost didn't notice the guy standing behind a thick tree trunk and watching us with a firmly placed glare.

He walked out of the shadows, and my laughter died slightly when his expression registered in my brain, slightly diminishing being high of our little moment.

"R-Roman, what are you doing here? We didn't see you!" I rasped out, surprised as Bryce turned towards him with a blank face before placing me down onto the ground again.

Roman stood in front of us. His blazing gaze settled on Bryce for a minute before returning to mine. He was that crazy kind mad again.

"I was just passing by," Roman gritted out. I noticed his fist clenched against the dark jeans he had worn today.

I jumped suddenly when a deep growl rumbled against my back, piercing through the quiet air around us.

"Stop staring at her!" Bryce growled again. His arms slid around my waist before holding me tightly against him.

Roman's glare deepened, but he didn't look away.

"You're going to hurt her."

"No, I'm not. She's mine!"

Roman growled now, taking a few stances towards us before backing up again just like he always did when he was on the brink of utter destruction. "You know what I mean! Just tell her!"

This had to end. I sighed. Looking back at Bryce, I poked his side with my free arm to get his attention before motioning him to let me go. Reluctantly, he did. I turned to face him.

"Let me talk to him?"

"No."

This is so difficult!

"Please?"

"No!"

Impossible! Think, Thi!

"I'll admit you're sexy?"

I could have said, *Oh, thank God*, when a small smile broke on Bryce's lip, and even though reluctantly, he nodded.

Mouthing thanks, I turned towards Roman and with a hesitant step, began walking towards him.

All the while, my recently made friend, Rome, stood his ground and stared, his expression fuming, yet his were eyes blank.

Why is he so angry?

As I finally stood in front of him, I sighed, fisting my shaky hands beside my skirt. I didn't want to turn around and look at Bryce. I didn't want to see where the small bursts of growls were coming from.

"He will hurt you, Thi." Roman suddenly snarled, and I shuddered from the viciousness of the growl that ripped out from behind me afterwards.

Do it, moron! You both may hate each other, but he's your friend.

A soft sigh left my lips as I finally mustered enough courage to tilt my head up and look at Roman. He, on the other hand, stood watching me sternly. Taking a step forward into his personal space, I let my shoes slightly touch his before putting out my hand and wrapping it around his neck. Instantly, his arms went around my waist to hold me tight.

I ignored the growl coming from Bryce, instantly feeling guilty but not knowing why. I was just comforting Roman.

"I really, really like him," I whispered softly as Roman breathed into my hair.

"How can you know? It's barely been a month. You barely even know Alex."

I sighed. "It…I don't know, Rome. It feels like there is this thing that's pulling me towards him."

Roman slumped against me, his breathing returning back to normal.

"I won't let him hurt you." He promised. "I don't care if you're his or he's k—" he paused for a second "—I will kill him."

K?

Shaking the curiosity away, I chuckled and nodded. "Okay, deal. But, now, it is time to make peace."

I grabbed hold of his arm and turned towards Bryce. It took everything in me not to shudder when I saw just how livid Bryce looked.

"You shouldn't touch me right now," Roman whispered beside me, regarding Bryce with equally angry eyes.

My gaze still on Bryce, I nodded, immediately letting go of Rome's hand, and started walking towards Bryce who pulled me into his arms as soon as I was at arm's reach.

"Mine," he growled, his tone menacing.

I rolled my eyes. "You and your brother need to make peace."

"Cousin." Roman quickly butted in, but I ignored him.

Bryce snarled at Roman again. "No."

"Please?"

"N—"

"Stop being clouded by jealousy. You guys know this is the right thing to do!" I snapped at the both of them before they could bluntly refuse me again.

I felt Bryce sigh against me as he let go and moved back before extending his arm towards Rome. Rome glanced at me, and I nodded, smiling. He gripped Bryce's hand and gave it a good shake.

"I must leave now," Roman spoke, eyeing me as he smiled softly.

I nodded. "Okay! I'll talk to you later, okay?"

"Yeah, later." He agreed before turning around and disappearing into the woods again.

Strange…

"Why did he take the wood's route?" I asked Bryce, turning to face him.

He shrugged. "Roman prefers the atmosphere in the woods. It's peaceful."

I giggled. "Well, I guess so do you, since, you know, you come and go by the woods often as well. And there is that monkey-man aspect t—Did you just roll your eyes at me, mister?" He did it again. "That's it! You're going to give me a piggyback ride!" I yelled.

Bryce's arms instantly went under my legs, hooking them around himself securely while he chuckled.

God, his torso…

"You're just something else, Theia Anderson."

***

Some antibiotic inhibitors that could be involved at different protein synthesis steps are:

Diphtheria toxin. This inhibitor inactivates EF-2 and thus, prevents the translocation.

Clindamycin and erythromycin, which blocks (due to irreversible binding) to a site within the 50S sub-unit of the ribosome. It is in this way that it inhibits the translocation.

And lastly, ricin (from castor beans) is a very potent toxin that exerts its effects by removing an adenine from 28S rRNA, thus inhibiting the function of eukaryotic ribosomes.

"Finally!" I mumbled, exhausted as I put the pen down and rubbed gently on my sore fingers. "What was I thinking? Thinking it would be better to write rather than type this damned essay!"

Now, don't get me wrong, I loved biology. I just hated those lengthy essays Mrs. Jenson never forgot to hand out whenever we started a new topic.

Flipping close the book, I got out of the seat and marched towards the kitchen. It didn't take me long enough to avoid seeing my dad kissing Mom smack on her lips as if he were a starved man.

I don't know about him being starved or not, Theia, but you sure are scarred for life.

"Alright, break it up, people! PG-13 in front of the kid, please!" I yelled, opening the fridge and getting out my leftover pizza. *Yes! Dad didn't manage to find them!*

"Hey! Where did you get that pizza from?" Dad exclaimed, eyeing my beautiful pizza with yearning.

I smirked and bringing the plate to my chest, rubbed it like it was a lamp. "My precious."

"Theia." Mom scowled at me, and I rolled my eyes before handing my dad a big piece and doing the same with her.

"Thank you," Dad mumbled, his mouth packed with pizza. Did I forget to mention my dad loved pizza?

"All good, old man." I giggled as I moved towards the living room and plopping in front of the TV, switched the channel to *Glee*. Too busy staring at Kevin McHale, who I had a crush since his NLT days, I didn't notice my dad sit beside me.

"So, Alexander Bryce Wilhem, aye?" I was so caught up watching the beauty that is Kevin. "Thi?"

"Hmm…Hey!" I glared at Dad. "Turn the TV back on, Dad! Please!"

He chuckled, shaking his head. "There is a re-run tomorrow. Right now, I need to talk to you."

I sat there looking at Dad expectantly, hoping I looked calm on the outside. I felt anything but that on the inside, though. What if he didn't like Bryce?

"Alexander Wilhem. How do you feel about him?"

I frowned. "Dad, I like him a lot…a lot. Th-the…it feels like there is this rope, and it's pulling me towards him. I've never felt this way before, you know. I…" My voice died down. This was the part I was afraid to admit.

"Go on." Dad encouraged, a soft smile on his lips.

I sighed. "It feels like…maybe one day, I could l-love him."

Dad nodded, surprising me. "Theia, I want you to know that that's normal. Okay? And your mother and I approve."

He approves!

A smile broke on my lips, and before he could prepare himself, I leaped into Dad's arms. "Thank you, Dad! I love you so much!"

Dad chuckled merrily as he rubbed my back. "I know, darling. But, Theia, there is something else I want to have a talk about."

"Sure, Dad." I smiled and moved back to sit.

"Theia, there are things we think we know about this world, the things that we deem normal or usual. But, dove, one must keep their mind open to new things. Things and facts that are new to us may, in fact, be even older or more superior."

I frowned. "I-I don't know what you're trying to tell me, Dad."

He smiled at me lovingly, his hand soothing down my hair warmly. "I just want you to know that if you ever come across a situation that isn't deemed normal by human standards. Don't run away. Keep an open mind, Thi. The unknown is a dangerous thing, Theia, but it is also the most beautiful."

Still slightly confused, I managed to nod at my dad as he smiled at me warmly, got up and turned towards the stairs, declaring that he was off to bed but not before reminding me to be in bed before twelve.

Situation that isn't deemed normal?

Shaking away the thought, I looked towards the clock and sighed. 11:20 PM.

"Guess, it's time for bed," I mumbled to myself as I made my way to the kitchen, placing the dishes in the sink, and began to scrub and rinse them.

The sound of the storm outside made me smile. Even after hours since its beginning, the rain was still pouring down as heavily as ever. I could imagine the trees slightly wavering in their places, pushed and pulled by the strong forces of the wind. The storm started yesterday just after I came back home from the date although it did seem like only minutes ago, actually.

Still smiling contentedly, I wiped my hands and moved towards the stairs. Walking in, I turned and closed my bedroom door shut. Just then, what sounded like a pebble hit my window with a good amount of force, and I froze.

Oh my God, Jeff the Killer?

No, Thi, don't move towards the window! That's what it wants! a tiny voice in my head pleaded as my feet automatically moved towards the window.

I gasped when I saw Bryce gripping onto the bare wall with his hands while the other was fishing in his pocket, soon retrieving a pebble. He turned, and our eyes met. I immediately slid open the window and a gush of wind blew on my face, bringing with it the bone-chilling rain. Bryce jumped into the room on all fours.

Still quiet, I closed the window shut and grabbed hold of his hand, pulling him towards the bathroom. He needed a warm shower if he wanted to stay out of bed and not sick with a cold or flu! He let me lead him, following me slowly.

Walking into the bathroom, I turned the shower on before pushing him in. I turned towards the door.

"Where are you going?" Bryce immediately called out.

I stopped in my tracks and turned.

"There is a bloody storm going around, and you're hanging on my home's wall! How can you even do that? And I thought you told me to stay in because of the storm! That applies to you too. Just—just shower and let me go and see if you had the sense to bring clothes in that bag of yours."

A low growl sounded through the bathroom, but he nodded. I closed the bathroom door, shut the window, grabbed hold of the bag still lying on the floor, and pulled out its contents. Okay, I shouldn't have done that. His boxers were the first thing that popped out. My face heated. I quickly placed the pair of boxes on the bed and pulled out a pair of navy blue sweatpants and a white t-shirt before placing them on top of the boxers. Just then, warm wet arms slipped around my waist and pulled me back against a wall.

"Wasn't that a little too early?" I said, the sensations running along my belly and arm too overpowering.

"I had already bathed before coming over," Bryce mumbled back, his voice low and husky.

It was then that I noticed something fairly large and hard poking me on my lower back. I frowned and then gasped, my breath hitching in my throat.

"Bryce! You-you're naked!" I whispered, wishing my heart could slow down with the excessive beating. It was hurting my chest.

He brought a hand to my hair and moved it to one side, leaning down and dipping his nose into the crook of my neck. He let out a contented sigh.

"I missed you."

CHAPTER ELEVEN

A giggle left my lips as Bryce snuggled closer into me, his heavy arm wrapped around my waist as he drew lazy circles on my cotton tank top.

"Tomorrow's Monday," I commented randomly and turned my eyes on the Christmas lights placed in jars on my bedside stand. They looked so pretty.

"Aren't you a smart one?" Bryce replied, his tone carrying slight sarcasm. I couldn't help but frown.

"Shut up!" I mumbled, smacking his arms lightly while he chuckled and pulled me closer against him, his naked chest touching my bare shoulders. I was thankful he agreed to at least put on the boxers. The rest of the articles of clothing I removed from his bag now rested where I had obtained it from.

"Can we play twenty-one questions?" I asked, turning slightly to look at him. It was obvious that neither one of us were sleepy, and although I could feel his reason of sleeplessness pressing up against my butt, I, on the other hand, was beyond excited to have the man I thought to be the human replica of Adonis lay beside me, whispering soft compliments.

Smirking, I looked towards the ceiling and laughed mentally.

"Sure." Bryce chuckled, turning me so I could face him now. I, however, turned again so that my back rested against the soft mattress of my bed.

"You start," I said enthusiastically.

Bryce breathed in, and though I was not looking at him, I was sure he had his thinking face on. "Okay…Oh, wow, I got nothing."

I gasped and shot upright in bed. He didn't have anything to ask me. Nothing he wanted to know. Did he even want to know me?

"You have nothing you want to ask me? Nothing?"

Bryce grimaced. "Well, there isn't much—there isn't much to know anymore."

I stared at him wide-eyed. *What?*

"What do you mean?"

He sighed and pulled my hand, making me lie on my back again.

"I know everything there is to know about you," Bryce murmured. He changed positions so that he could loom over me. I gulped. "I know you, Theia," he whispered, his lips now only a pencil's width away.

"How?"

His lips landed on mine.

Bryce bit on my lower lip, slightly licking on it before pushing his tongue into my mouth. My tongue instantly massaged against his. I couldn't hold off the moan that left my lips as my arms went around his shoulder and pulled him closer. How had we gone from twenty-one questions to kissing?

It seemed like forever when I finally managed to settle back to reality. We couldn't put off knowing each other like this all the time. I was serious. I needed to know if he was too.

"Bryce," I said, pulling my lips away from his, and quickly turned my face so that his lips landed on my cheeks instead. That didn't deter him, though. He only continued to place warm wet kisses all over my neck, biting and nipping on occasional spots. I sighed. It was no use telling him to quit it. He would just growl and continue as if I had never spoken.

A soft sigh left my lips again as I felt him trace his tongue over a heated bit of skin. "Bryce! I thought we were playing twen— Bryce, please."

Bryce paused for a second before placing a soft kiss on my neck and moved over to snuggle with me again.

"Theia Anderson, born on the ninth of March 1995, you grew up in California and went to school there until you moved to Peidmond a month ago. Your favorite colors are gray and navy blue—two very complimenting colors if you ask me. You love pizza, French fries, and grilled chicken together. You love pie morc than cake. Your favorite ice cream flavor is cookie dough. You're in love with books and with *me*—with me more, though. You prefer rain over the sun. You're crazy and yet compassionate—" he moved closer, his lips touching my ear before he whispered "—and you also look extremely sexy in lingerie."

Lingerie.

I gulped. "H-h-have you b-been stalking me?"

Bryce had stiffened a little before he turned to face me. I didn't turn towards him.

"Maybe," he whispered, picking up my hand and entwining his fingers with mine.

"What! You stalked me?" I shrieked out in surprise, turning to face him.

"Not literally. I just...Don't you want to know anything about me?" He scolded suddenly, frowning at me. My startled stare turned soft as I realized he was right in a sense. *Well, wrong...*I did want to know about him.

"You're so strange," I mumbled, turning so I could snuggle against his chest.

"Er...So, tell me about your family? Where you grew up and all?"

Bryce stiffened again. *Why does he stiffen so much?*

"I was born in London. That was twenty-four years ago, though, in case, you're curious. My birthday is on the fourth of February. I studied and graduated from high school, after that from

Oxford, well before my peers, and jumped into new businesses, and well, here I am,"

I frowned. "You didn't tell me anything personal…"

"Personal?"

"Yeah, you know like your likes and quirks and all those tiny details."

He sighed. "Oh yes. Well, ask away…"

"Well, what's your favorite color?" I asked, settling better against him.

"Black."

I grinned. "Food? Song? Movie? Food? Drink? When was the first time you kissed a girl? Do you have any embarrass—"

"Okay, hold on there!" Bryce all but yelled, putting his palm against my lips. "Okay, let's get through this one by one. My favorite food would have to be good roasted lamb shank or ribs, actually; anything from Stevie Wonder; I don't have time to watch movies; I was thirteen; and my most embarrassing memory is too embarrassing to tell."

"You don't watch movies? How can you not watch movies? Tell me that was a lie! " I exclaimed after a brief second of shock, grasping onto his shoulders. "Tell me!"

"Will you calm down?" Bryce almost yelled, gripping my shoulders roughly and jolting me forward so that I smacked against his chest. I groaned in pain as my nose stung slightly. It made me cringe. I hoped I had not broken it.

"That hurt," I grumbled, rubbing the pad of my index finger and thumb against the tip of my nose.

Bryce only chuckled and pushed closer to the bed until his face was aligned with mine. He smiled at me softly, and before I could ask him what he was doing, he reached out and placed a soft kiss on the tip of my nose. Pulling back, Bryce smiled. His warm eyes were glowing against the string lights. I smiled back.

"For a bulky big man, you're kind of adorable, you know?"

***

"Do you know?"

"Do you know?"

That's it! I shot my head towards Marley and glared at her. "How many times are you going to say that and just trail off? I don't know, obviously. Are you going to tell me or not?"

She giggled a bit, and I only frowned.

"So the square root of forty-nine is seven. Therefore, the x is seven. Everyone got how we got x? Theia?"

Oh shit. Sending a final glare towards a snickering Marley, I turned towards Mr. Phelps. "Yes, sir."

He looked at me for a second before nodding and turning towards the board again.

Instantly, a brief breath of relief rushed out of my lips, and I settled into my chair again. That was close.

"So…do you know?"

I shot a glare towards Marley again and she pulled her hands up in surrender before continuing.

"Dolphins are the horniest things ever!"

What the hell? I flinched.

"Don't you dare continue, Ley, or else, I am going to kick your non-existent balls!" I hissed, my head nearly against my desk as I tried to make my threat as low as possible.

"And why are you threatening Marlene about kicking her balls, Ms. Anderson?" came a deep voice just beside my desk. A fit of giggles and chuckles rang around the room, and I couldn't help but bang my head against the desk once before looking up at Mr. Phelps.

"Well?" He urged with a mischievous twinkle in his eyes.

Why that man?

"I-I…I'd rather not say, sir."

He grinned. "Oh, really?"

Damn him for being so intimidating!

I gulped. "Yes, really, sir."

"Meet me after the class, Ms. Anderson and you too, Ms. Smith."

I nodded. I'm sure, besides me, Marley did too. "Yes, sir," we both chorused together. The rest of the class snickered.

***

"It's all those dolphins' fault!" Marley yelled beside me. I almost giggled…almost.

"Sure! Apparently, the dolphins who so nicely managed to whine out, 'Do you know?' all through half of the class!" I yelled back, standing beside her as we watched Mr. Phelps sorting out quiz papers and placing them into his bag too patiently. Finally, he turned and smiled at us.

"Ah, yes, ladies! You do both know that you two can get detention for disturbing my class, don't you?"

We both nodded.

He smiled. "But because I'm such an amazing teacher, I'm letting you both off this one time. However, please do discuss the breeding patterns of dolphins at home if you wish. Nat Geo is a wonderful place."

Both Marley and I could do nothing more than to stare at Mr. Phelps with gaping mouths. He only smirked harder. Finally, as if Marley found her senses, she murmured a quick, "Yes, sir," before dragging me out of the class and into the hallway.

"We shall not speak of this to anyone," I whispered, still rushing behind Marley.

"Agreed," she replied, looking back, and slightly nodded at me before looking back ahead and rushing towards the cafeteria.

"I'm starving!" I groaned to myself as I took a seat beside Matthew. Glancing at him, I remembered how he had reacted that day during the trip.

He, on the other hand, seemed busy munching on his burger. I rolled my eyes. *Typical Matthew.* I nudged his arm.

"Yes, Theia?" He acknowledged me, still proceeding to bite a huge chunk of the burger.

I glanced at all the boys around the table: Connor, Keith, Jeff, and Matthew.

"Why did you all bow down?"

They stiffened. I suppose they knew exactly what I was talking about, but Marley, being at the table, only complicated things.

Marley frowned. "Bow? Where?"

I shrugged. My attempt at being calm on the outside was wearing thin. On the inside, I was freaking out. *What am I going to tell her?*

"Keith, Jeff, and I went over to Matts, so we decided to bug Thi a little, you know, since she's his neighbor,"

"Oh God, you boys are so typical," she replied, rolling her eyes. She picked up her sandwich and plopped it into her mouth.

I giggled nervously. "Yeah…"

Maybe you should ask them later…

"Anyone miss me?" I smiled at the tone of the voice, uncaring and bored. The person placed his tray on the table and then proceeded to sit beside me.

"Of course not, dude. Why would we miss you?" Keith replied, looking at Roman with humor.

"Shut up. I was asking Theia specifically," Rome retorted, and I almost burst out laughing.

These two could never stop. It always seemed to me that Keith and Roman rarely ever saw eye to eye, and their opposite natures but strong personalities often made them clash. Many times, it's a good entertainment seeing them have an argument.

"Stop it, you two." I smacked Rome's arms lightly while looking at Keith intimidatingly. Well, at least, I hoped it would be intimidating.

Matthew's arms were wrapped around my shoulder, and he pulled me towards him, causing me to yelp in surprise.

"Say…can I borrow your fruit juice?" he whispered.

Oh…So his aim is set once again.

I rolled my eyes and moving back into place, picked up the bottle, and placed it in front of him. I was actually quite sure I could literally feel his happiness.

***

"Are you going home now?"

I turned in the direction of the voice but smiled when I saw Roman walking behind me.

"Yes, I suppose so."

"You did a great job hiding those love bites, you know."

I froze. "W-what?"

The tips of Rome's lips lifted for a minute before dropping down into a thin line again.

"We, the men in our family, were very passionate about our girls. We're also quite dominant. Love bites are what come first. And then…"

He trailed off, getting out a green apple from God knows where and taking a juicy bite of it. Little bits of juice trailed down from the sides of his lips. I, however, only managed to nod. The heat on my face was actually becoming quite unbearable.

"Let's go then." Rome chuckled suddenly, his arm around my shoulders as he moved me towards the love of my life—his car.

"What? Where?" I managed to exclaim just as he pushed me onto the passenger's seat and pulled the seatbelt into position.

"I have to drop you home," he murmured, his tone serious. He pushed the key into the ignition, started the car in a fluid turn, and the engine rumbled to life.

The rest of the car ride seemed boring mainly because Rome refused to speak or let my various valuable questions go unanswered. Well, that was until he decided to break the silence.

"The staying period starts next Friday."

I lifted my eyes from my twirling fingers to him. He, however, kept his gaze on the road.

I sighed. "Yes, it does."

He nodded then turned towards me slightly for a second. "So you're coming over to the castle?"

"I suppose I am," I answered, slightly confused why he was even asking. "The library seems to be a great feature, and then there is Bryce and you and everyone else."

He nodded again, but I could see his knuckles turning to a whiter shade.

"Keep an open mind, Theia."

"What do you mean?"

"You'll know when the time is right." Roman sighed, his gaze on me for a second.

I frowned. Why was everybody telling me to keep an open mind? Just then, he turned into my driveway and parked just behind my dad's spare car. I turned towards him, leaned in and gave him a quick hug. "Thanks for the ride, Rome."

He smiled and nodded again. "No problem. See you in class tomorrow."

Walking into my home, I quickly closed the front door and made my way to the kitchen.

Better get something to munch while I unwind, I thought to myself as I opened the fridge and pulled out a packet of chips and a can of orange juice, holding them close as I made my way upstairs.

"Do you want me to fix up something real quick, honey?"

I halted in my steps and turned around. Agnus looked at me with a soft smile on her face.

"No thanks, Agy. I think I'm all set with chips and juice for now, anyways." She nodded warmly before walking towards the kitchen. I frowned.

I wonder where Lilly is…

I found Lilly loitering around the first floor, a bucket in one hand and a white cloth in another. She instantly sent a warm smile my way to which I replied softly before opening my bedroom's door and moving in.

Weird.

I sighed happily as I placed the bag of chips and still chilled orange juice on top of the study table before moving towards my shower. I felt mucky and sweaty anyway.

Just as I was about to open the door and move in, a ping sounded from my jean pocket, and I instantly felt through my pants, slipping my cellphone out of one of the side pockets. I clicked on the newly received message. It was from Bryce. I frowned. There were only four words on my screen, four words that still managed to send a cold chill down my spine.

```
We need to talk.
```

CHAPTER TWELVE

`Sure, what's up? - T`

My fingers started tapping on the screen nervously after pressing *send*. I couldn't help but have a bad feeling about this. Something wasn't right.

The sudden ping from my phone grabbed my attention almost too suddenly, and the thud that sounded around the room in return paired with the intense pain on the side of my thigh enveloped me. I groaned as I lay on the floor for a bit. It was never peachy falling off the bed.

Waiting for the pain to subside, I stared at the wall, breathing and trying to calm myself, but fear still floated around.

What if he wanted to break up? What could be so serious?

Realizing that the pain was less intense, I finally started to get back on my feet. The sharp pain flowing down my leg made me wince in pain, but I managed to plop myself on the bed. My eyes fell on the cellphone that had remained intact and safe despite its fall from the edge of the bed, and I quickly grabbed it. I took a shaky breath. The pain in my leg really was getting bad.

Will it bruise?

Someone knocked on the door suddenly, and I turned my head towards it before calling out a very shaky, "Come in."

"You should be more careful, Theia." Agnus's worried motherly tone floated around the room as she swept into the room with what looked like a bowl containing an ice pack. She placed it on the bed in front of me and sighed. "Well, take off those skinny jeans and let me assess your bruise. I'm sure there is one by the sound of the thud I heard. It must be pretty bad."

Grimacing, I nodded. Maybe she was right. It was always better to ice rather than bruise. After shifting awkwardly on the bed, with very wobbly legs, I stood up. It hurt like hell.

As quickly as I could, I slipped out of my jeans and looked at the side of my thigh, only to wince by the already slightly purple bruise forming. I always did bruise up pretty quickly. What was worse was how it looked. The bruise looked horrendous.

"Oh, that's a bad one but not the worst I've seen. You will be all well and done in a few weeks. Just don't pressure it much. Here," Agnus spoke warmly, extending the ice pack towards me.

I smiled and nodded my thanks before slowly grabbing the pack and pressing it onto the bruise. I winced. That hurt more.

"Call me if you need anything, dearie," Agnus called out softly before she walked out of the room and closed the door behind her.

I eyed my cellphone again. Sighing, I picked it up again and quickly tapped onto the unread message.

`I'll be there soon. Keep your window open. - B`

Shit. I glanced at the sickly darkening bruise on my leg and then at the message again. I sighed and looked back at my bruise, then the window. I shook my head and let out a shallow breath before slipping out of bed and walking towards the window slowly.

My plan was pretty simple: open the window, rush into bed as fast as I could and get under the cover, hide my state of undress and bruise from Bryce, act like I wasn't scared he would dump me, and ask him to pass me that potato chips before he leaves.

But what if he is already here?

I held my breath as I padded my way towards the window and almost broke into a relieved laugh when I reached it. He wasn't there. Sliding the window open, I quickly made my way to my bed, ignoring my leg painfully resisting against any movement, and slipped into bed and underneath my covers.

My eyes found the cellphone as another ping sounded from it, and I quickly grabbed it and tapped on it.

`On my way - B`

I had no sooner just put my phone away when Bryce nearly leaped into my room. I stared at him. He smiled as he walked in, and all the while, I practiced my reply speech for his breakup statement.

If I did give a speech…If he did break up…

Wait for it, Anderson…It may as well be coming soon! Wait for it.

"Hey."

Hey?

"Hey." I smiled, slightly guarded as I clutched onto the blanket wrapped around my lower body.

Bryce stopped as he reached the edge of my bed and sat on it. He leaned in and placed a gentle kiss on my lips before placing another on my cheek. I sighed, feeling the usual emotions that envelope me whenever he held me—love and protection.

"You wanted to talk about something?" I said, my heart instantly starting to beat faster with nervousness when I see Bryce's smile falter a bit.

Bryce looked away as he nodded, suddenly looking solemn. "I wanted to know if there is someone you think is behaving suspiciously around you, a girl, perhaps, or a boy. They have retrieved the recording for the call, the company records, all customer care calls and so forth for legal purposes, just in case…Do you want to give it an ear?"

The breath I didn't know I was holding immediately rushed out from between my lips as I slumped back against the headboard.

"Oh thank God, I was scared!" I blurted out, sounding as relieved as I felt.

The warm expression on Bryce's face almost instantly vanished before a smirk took its place as if he knew exactly why I was scared.

I shivered.

"Scared, huh?" Bryce's grin widened, and he leaned into me, pressing his lips onto mine for a second. "I wonder what for?"

I frowned. The idiot was teasing me. "Shut up."

Bryce only chuckled as he leaned in again and placed a soft kiss on my lips for a minute longer than what would be called chaste.

"You're so cute."

At the sound of amusement on his voice, I rolled my eyes and smartly moved back to lean against the headboard.

"Okay! So getting back on the topic of things, I mean, the only girls that hate me are the ones that are jealous because they want you or Diandra…but I'm not so sure about her. For the boys, that Mr. Bishop is a menace."

Bryce and I stared into each other's eyes after my sudden exclamation about the loon, Bishop, before he threw his head back and let out the sexiest laugh I'd ever heard.

"Shut up," I muttered bitterly, trying to ignore my lips' sudden twitching, which was purely a random occurrence when Bryce's eyes zeroed on them, and he stopped laughing. His eyes suddenly a strange midnight blue.

The tone of Bryce's ringtone filled the room suddenly, and I almost let out a raspy sigh of relief.

Bryce's attention redirected towards the blaring iPhone in his hands. He let out a low growl before accepting it. I tuned out from their conversation and concentrated on the well-concealed ice pack that was beginning to numb my thigh. I really needed to get that away from me. It was starting to hurt. My hands itching to just grab and push the pack away, I almost jumped when Bryce cleared his throat, grabbing my attention once again.

"Listen, I need to go, love. I'll be back tonight, okay?" he mumbled apologetically, and I nodded, smiling a little. He was adorable when he wasn't all dominating and possessive.

"Okay."

"Okay." He smiled back, and this time, I leaned in to place a small kiss on his lips, once again ignoring my protesting leg.

Only when Bryce had jumped out of the window—God knows how he could always do that—did I finally grab hold of the ice pack and place it on the stand beside my bed.

"You need a bath, Theia," I mumbled to myself as I looked towards the bathroom door. After a minute of deciding, I finally got out of bed—put aside that I couldn't help but groan out of pain occasionally—before moving towards the door and into the bathroom.

I sighed contently as I opened the bathroom door and moved out into my room. My leg was still numb, and that helped me move around a bit. Plus, the warm water did wonders soothing tense muscles.

"What's that on your thigh?"

I froze. *Shit! Why is he even back?*

In an instant, warm arms were wrapped around my back and underneath my legs before hurling me against a hard chest. Bryce placed me on the bed slowly before pushing the edge of towel up. Warily, I finally mustered up enough courage and glanced at him, only to flinch at the cold fury burning through his now almost black orbs. It wasn't hard to see Bryce was livid. Bryce's anger was impeccably destructive. I flinched again as Bryce's fingers probed around the now sickening purple bruise on the side of my thigh.

"S-stop it," I managed to mutter, cursing myself for stuttering, but damn it, I was nervous.

"How did you get this?"

His tone wasn't agitated. It wasn't furious. But the underlying storm in his dark, calm tone was all the more evident with his wild livid eyes shooting straight into mine.

"I fell o-off the bed," I mumbled, the knowledge that my cheeks were now stained crimson all the more embarrassing.

"Are you sure, Theia?" Again, he spoke with the same dark, calm tone.

It was strange that I wanted him to yell at me or at least be angry and not pretend to be calm. Somehow, it scared me more than if he would openly be angry. I almost laughed at the irony of that.

"Yes."

He growled, now eyeing my bruise. He glanced at the ice pack and then leaned to pick it up, gingerly placing it back on the spot. I immediately wanted to swat it away, but his warning growl as I stretched to grab it echoed around the room. Sighing angrily, I moved back into bed, my towel still wrapped around me.

No good. This needs to go.

"I'm in my towel, you know."

Bryce directed his gaze to me and titled an eyebrow up, regarding me with a blank expression. "Yes, so?"

Ouch.

"I'm naked underneath it. The towel's wet. Hypothermia?"

"Don't you think you're exaggerating it a bit?"

"Well, if you were in my body, you would know!" I retorted stubbornly and then instantly blushed as the realization of what it could be hit me. *Crap, Theia, you've done it this time!*

I gulped as Bryce placed the ice pack back in the bowl on the bedside table and turned towards me, his eyes now a shade darker than midnight blue. What was strange was that specs of golden were now beginning to show, and I almost held my breath as I witnessed the wonder of it. How could he do it?

Pulling my blanket on top of me, he grasped onto my now loose towel and pulled it away from my body, unwrapping it and separating it away from me and towards him.

"You have no idea how much I want to be in you." He leaned closer and nipped on my bottom lip. "Wait, sorry, love. I missed out *body*."

Shit...

"Bry—"

"I love it when you say my middle name," Bryce said softly before his lips landed on mine, his lips warm and strong against my slightly chilly yet supple ones. I sighed, my hands now gripping his shirt as I pulled him closer. And then suddenly, the pain in my leg was forgotten. The bruise was forgotten and the culprit behind Bryce's and my miscommunication forgotten.

The rush of having him above me with only a thin material to separate my skin from his made my mind all the fuzzier. I shivered as my hands found solace against his warm torso. My fingers slipped past his shirt, caressing each scar I could feel as they made their way towards his chest.

"Theia."

"Hmm."

"What are you doing?" Bryce's voice sounded more and more strained as my fingers continued to caress him. I couldn't stop. What was wrong with me?

My fingers slipped past his belly button, and he let out a loud growl, his fingers now digging into my waist while he landed open-mouthed kisses all over my neck.

"Feeling you…can I?"

A low moan left my lips as Bryce dipped his tongue on the soft spot on my neck in reply and licked at the skin that had just been bitten a little harshly.

As if automatically responding to the rush of liquid surging between my thighs and Bryce's lips working its way on me, my hands slipped into his jeans, and he froze. He breathed heavily as he seemed to wait for my fingers to reach their destination. I held my breath, my eyes still closed as I thought about it.

Did I want to?

I sighed, shivering slightly by the urge to just reach out and grasp it. Yes. Yes, I wanted to.

Still holding my breath, I softly moved my fingers deeper into his jeans and almost fainted as they came into contact with the thick, long length.

On top of me, Bryce growled. His whole body tensed, but he didn't move. It looked like he couldn't even breathe.

"Bryce," I whispered, leaning towards him. My eyes still closed, I placed a kiss blindly on his lips before moving my hands all the way in and wrapping itself around his shaft. I pumped once, twice, and then an unearthly growl rang around the room as Bryce jerked his hips against my hands, his thick shaft running against the hold of my hand.

"Take it off," Bryce growled against my breast, and I immediately unbuckled and opened his jeans, pushing it down enough to bring his large shaft out.

It's huge! It's…whoa…this is happening…This is really happening!

I sighed as he nipped against my neck, his growls and groans becoming more and more animalistic as he continued to jerk off with my hand. I tried to test my waters. Moving my thumb over to the tip of his cock, I rubbed the pre-cum around it before bringing the hand that was grasping his shoulder to grope his balls. I could feel him shuddering, shivering, and his dick twitching against my palm with each longer, deeper stroke.

His peak was coming, and I felt it. A growl escaped Bryce's lips as he continued placing open-mouthed kisses against my neck. My back arched into him, the dizzying ache in between my thighs slightly distracting. My strokes increased in pace when suddenly his thrusting stopped. He froze and then shuddered violently. I froze too. I could feel something warm land on the sheets above my tummy, and I smiled softly, finally opening my eyes.

I felt accomplished. Bryce's reactions, his uncensored groans, it made me feel better.

I smiled as I watched Bryce above me. His eyes were still closed tight as he continued to shudder from the aftermath of the orgasm. His eyes opened slowly as the high, subdued, and I almost screamed. His eyes were golden. His eyes were shining golden!

Superm…Kryp…Kryp…Vampi…W-werewolf? N-no!

Finally not being able to hold it in, I let out a scream, shutting my eye. Maybe I was being delusional. He stiffened, and I slowly opened my eyes again. *Blue—*

I sighed in relief as I cussed at myself for being an idiot. Of course, his eyes weren't golden, right?

I smiled at him slightly, and a speck of gold flashed through his eyes. I froze.

What if it was real?

Suddenly, Bryce moved up, out of bed, removed all of his clothes, and without a backward glance, walked into the bathroom. The sound of the door shutting caught my attention.

He locked the door…

Pushing aside the thoughts about his golden eyes, whatever it was, I pulled the sheets up into a ball and then grasped onto the towel that now laid on the floor. I wrapped the towel around me and moved towards the closet.

Be strong. Be strong! Chanting my mantra over and over again, I finally walked out of my closet dressed, my hair up in a messy ponytail. What did I feel about what had just transpired between Bryce and me? I mean, the intimate bits were okay. He was my boyfriend, but his eyes? And then, how did he feel about this? I stopped when I saw Bryce on my bed, looking quite brood-worthy.

"Hey," I murmured as I stepped in between his legs, looking down at him with warm curiosity.

Mutant…ET…Werewolf…Werewolf?

Bryce looked up at me, and I smiled warmly at him, managing to push aside the "mental" thoughts for a bit. I was starting to feel like I was finally going mental actually even considering such ridiculous reasoning behind his golden eyes and incredible strength and the inhuman growls. *Crap.*

"Hi," he murmured back. He dropped his head at his feet.

I frowned. "What's wrong?"

"Nothing."

"Sure, and I'm Kim Kardashian."

His lips curled upwards slightly, and I almost grinned in victory. "I have to admit I don't really mind having Kim Karda—ow!"

"You're mine."

Getting possessive, Theia.

Bryce's groan turned into a grin, and he pulled me into his lap. I shrieked as my chest connected with his face.

"Broke a nose?" I giggled, moving back a little to evaluate his pretty face and settle down in a comfortable position when Bryce's face darkened. Getting up with me in his arms, he placed me on the bed with him on the other side. I couldn't help but notice the distance he was keeping now.

The silence carried on for a few minutes like a thick fog before I decided to break it. He needed to tell me why he was acting so strangely.

"Why did you do that?"

"Do what?"

So he wants to take the oblivious route…

"Since when did you just put me on my side of the bed and not even cuddle? Since when do you just march towards the bathroom after—after—and lock the door?"

Bryce sighed. "You're getting this wrong. I'm sorry if I've hurt you. I—I just think you should know what you're getting into before we—you know…"

I frowned. "And what am I getting into?"

"Soon, Thi, I'll tell you soon. Please."

I sighed. *Maybe I needed to cut him some slack?*

"Okay." I nodded.

Bryce chuckled slightly and moved closer to put his hands around me. "Any more questions, your majesty, or can we go to sleep?"

"One more," I spoke up.

"Sure, love."

I took a deep breath and then counted till ten.

"Why do your eyes turn golden?"

CHAPTER THIRTEEN

The silence of the night seemed eerie against Bryce's sharp intake of breath. I almost regretted asking him the question. But it was done. And I had asked. So now all I could do was wait for his reply.

It had seemed like hours before his shocked eyes darted from mine to something behind me. Or maybe it was nothing in particular. I couldn't tell. He moved away, not looking at me anymore as if deep in thought, before getting out of bed and stopping to stand beside the window and stared into the night…in the direction of the beautifully lit castle—his castle.

"You caught that, didn't you?"

I sighed. "Yes."

He turned towards me. His expression grave. "My eyes…they're different."

I rolled my eyes. "I can tell. A-are you not human?"

Bryce's eyes widened a fraction, and I could only hold my breath, waiting for him to say yes. *Yes, Theia, I'm an alien.* I almost braced myself for that, almost planned out how I would react. But all that came was a pearl of hysterical laughter.

Bryce watched me with his eyes twinkling as he continued to laugh, breathing deeply in between laugh spurts. He finally stopped when I began to glare at him. He laughed so much it almost seemed fake.

"I assure you, Theia, I'm human and not a God-sent angel."

Strangely, where I should have been feeling relieved, I felt a tinge of irritation. Maybe it wasn't surprising at all because I was far from blind, and my senses hadn't run highway. I was painfully aware of the walls built up behind his laughter. Bryce had lied. And that hurt. I bit back a "liar" quite convincingly well, to my standards anyway, smiled and replied with a soft, "Okay."

I'd find out the truth. No more lies. Bryce would have to learn.

As if contented with my response, Bryce beamed and marched towards me, pulling me against his chest, and just like always, the only thing I managed to do was cling to his shirt so that I wouldn't fall to the floor like mush.

"I like you a lot!" I froze. *Had I said that? Oh, crap, Theia!*

I moved back, panic-stricken as I watched a wide-eyed Bryce stare at me. I swallowed hard but looked away.

You're officially an idiot.

"I…er…I'll just…" I stepped back to move away. *Need space to recover…recover lost sanity and a mouth filter.*

"No." I froze as Bryce growled and immediately pulled me back against his chest. "I like you too…a lot."

As if Bryce had read my mind, he pulled back to look at me and repeated, softly, "I like you a lot."

I smiled, hooked my arms around his neck, and pulled him down, smashing his lips with mine for a peck before breaking the kiss. I giggled at his slight pout. "Good, you better!"

Now all I had to do was find out what you're hiding, Bryce…

***

Flipping the page of the book that laid open on my lap, I leaned into the trunk of the fairly large tree and bit into an apple.

The day was a dull one, and unlike the others, I absolutely loved this weather. Maybe that was why I was currently leaning against a fairly large maple tree, away from the rest of the bustling students.

I sighed and snapped the book shut. I couldn't concentrate, anyway. All that kept floating around my head was Bryce's golden eyes. I let out a low groan. *What is he hiding?*

"And what are you doing here all alone?"

I almost jumped on my spot at the sudden sound of intrusion. Looking up, I saw Matthew gazing at me amusedly.

Maybe I could use a little company, I thought as I patted the ground beside me, and he immediately sunk down beside me, our arms touching as we both looked onwards.

Maybe Matt could help me out…

"Well?"

"I've been thinking…"

That got his attention. Matthew turned toward me. He seemed to have caught onto my sullen tone, his expression worried.

"Is everything okay?" Matthew asked, his finger tilting my chin so that I would look at him.

Was it?

I shook my head. "Not quite."

"What happened?"

I looked at him, making eye contact I kept it. His warm reddish-brown eyes twinkled as he looked at me. Not breaking eye contact, I managed to answer, "I think Bryce is not normal as in not human."

Just then, a warm spark shot through his eyes, and I almost bit back a gasp as I moved in closer to look at his eyes. He turned away almost immediately. *Matthew was too?*

"I can't quite help you there, Thi. But all I ask is to keep an open mind about Bryce. Don't run," Matthew mumbled, looking back to gaze at me. *Warm brown eyes. Normal.*

With a small smile my way, he quickly got up and brushed the leaves off his jeans. Looking back, he extended a hand towards me, and I, still being confused, took it. We walked towards the school in silence when I was suddenly pulled against a warm chest.

I knew who it was, so I just leaned in and held onto Roman with my dear life.

"I see you're happy to see me." He chuckled, rubbing the pad of his thumb against my cheeks before smiling a little and moving back.

I rolled my eyes. "You wish. Where were you half the day anyway?"

"I know you want me." Roman winked but continued when I glared, "I'm going to Rome for a week. Dad called…a little business transaction. I just came to say goodbye and if you wanted me to get you something."

I giggled. "Just get your ass back."

Rome mock-gasped as he moved away in shock. "You only want my ass back? Did you hear that, Matthew? Our little Theia seems to have a thing for my ass!"

Matthew chuckled as he moved away slightly as if scared I would smack him. "I think Thi has herself a little ass fetish."

I gasped. "I don't!" I exclaimed, looking at the two laughing boys. I narrowed my eyes. I would get them someday.

Finally, when their loud laughter seemed to cease, I pulled Rome in for a hug again, his arms almost instantly slipping around me as I held him. "Get back soon. I won't miss you at all."

He sighed against me, his arms tightening on his hold. "I'll be back soon. I'll miss you too, Thi."

I smiled as he moved back and turned towards the door. Only stopping when he opened it, he turned back and gave me a small wave. I waved back smiling.

"Well, then, he's gone. Now, no one will protect your coffees from me! Bwahaha!" Matthew laughed maniacally as his arms slid around my shoulder and turned us towards the cafeteria.

I almost groaned. I'd build a damn fort before letting him steal my coffee.

***

Leo and I had a fight today. I think it was because his older brother hits on me. Tell me how to fix this! I want Leo, not Cole! - AverySadCasey

I almost banged my head against the desk as I read the message. I clearly didn't understand why Cole would not just give up. Cass wanted Leo! Leo was hot. They both were hot, but Leo held much more substance! Plus, what the hell happened to bro code?

March over to his house. Stand outside his window. Sing to him. - I'mPatheticAtThis Theia

Almost instantly, my phone pinged, and I stared at the reply.

Which song? - ImpatientCasey

Wait…What? She's serious?

"Arms" by Christina Perri? - Theia

It doesn't fit. He runs I don't - CaseyCatastrophe

How about "Never Let Me Go" by The Click Five - OptimisticTheia

Omg, that's a good one! I'm off to his! Guitar and the whole shebang! Wish me luck! - Casey

All the best, babe. Rock your man's world ;) - Thi

A smile touching my lips, I placed my phone on my bed and made my way out of my room. I found that the bruise on my thigh hurt a lot less after I woke up today and that helped a lot with walking around school. It also helped a lot with marching to and from the kitchen. Not being able I grab snacks, now, that could have been a problem.

The skies glowed purple outside as the setting sun finally settled against the mountains in the west. It seemed unreal to see the sky this shade of purple, but I smiled at the beauty of it. Seeing the note from Mom that I had already read a while ago, I picked it up and dropped it into the bin. Mom and Dad would be late, one of Mom's usual surprise dates. I could feel a blush touch my cheeks as I went over a particular line from the note.

P.S. Bryce is welcome while we are away. Use protection!

"Ugh…Mom!" I groaned out loud, shaking my head as I tried to rid the images that popped into my head. She was crazy!

I mean, I did want to—do it with Bryce—but it just seemed too fast. I wanted to wait.

Just then, a shrill cry rang out through the cold evening air, and I froze, my head whipping towards the woods immediately. The cry rang around again. Somehow, I couldn't help but rush to the door, slide it open, and run towards the woods. The scream seemed to be coming from in there.

Another scream sounded through the woods as I whipped my head around in every direction, trying to gauge which direction it was coming from. It sounded like a boy, merely a teenager from the sound of his scream. Whoever he was, he sounded like he was in really bad pain! Another scream. *Right.*

"Hello? Where are you? I can help you!" I called out, moving towards the right. I cursed not bringing a torch with me. It really was darker in the woods than out. I cursed myself for even coming. This was what those heroines did in every scary movie.

I stopped when I realized the screaming had stopped. I frowned then gasped. Did something happen to the kid?

"Where are you? I want to help you, kid!"

Silence.

"Crap!" I muttered, reaching for my pockets. Maybe I should call the police.

I almost smacked myself in the face when I realized I had left my phone at home. *Stupid!* Just then, a twig broke somewhere, and I froze. My heart suddenly beat frantically. There were wolves in the woods. Looking around, I tried to gauge which direction I had walked from when another twig broke, and a small warning growl sounded through the air.

I stood frozen. My eyes went wide as two red eyes shined through the darkness from between two trees. I turned to look for an escape, and another growl erupted around me.

The cold night air seemed to sting around my warm face. It was only then did I realize that I was crying. The silent but absolute fact sunk in with every sweeping second—I was probably going to die tonight.

It moved towards me, walking into the moonlight, its fur gray and teeth white. It growled once again. Their stances calculated like the predator it was, his eyes cautious, treating me like the prey I was.

I cried harder. I sniffled. I couldn't die…I didn't want to! I wouldn't…I wouldn't. So building up the remaining courage I had, I ran. I ran as if my life depended on it because it did. I ran as if this was the last day of my life because it could be.

I almost faltered when a deep growl emitted from behind me, and I heard the wolf running towards me, towards its kill.

The paths seemed little to non-existent to my eyes because of the ever increasing darkness in the woods. The growing night didn't seem to help.

The wolf behind me howled as if in the rush of a hunt. I almost broke down knowing that I was the prey and very soon, the wolf's whole pack would be joining their brother on the hunt after me.

I almost sighed when an idea popped into my head, but just when I thought I saw a shimmer of hope—the large tree that looked climbable—I tripped.

The rocks scraped against my hand as I tried to save myself from the impact of the fall, but I knew I had lost.

A growl sounded from behind me, and a tear fell down my cheek; this was it. I looked up towards my last hope but almost bit back a scream when I saw a large light brown wolf standing in front of me, its snout just inches from my face.

This is it…

A tear escaped my cheek once again, and the wolf whimpered. I frowned. *Why wasn't it killing me yet?*

It moved closer, and I almost yelped, moving away immediately. It whimpered again and lowered its head. What it did next caught me by surprise. It slumped down on the ground in front of me.

I could only stare as it lifted its head and looked at me. Its warm brown eyes seemed so familiar. I couldn't help doing the craziest thing ever. I reached out and placed my hand on its head, patting it. Surprisingly, it seemed to purr in reply. *Wolves purr?*

Why is it so docile?

I looked into its eyes again when a warm spark shot through its eye, and I gasped. I knew who its eyes reminded me of.

"Matthew," I whispered.

CHAPTER FOURTEEN

The trees seemed to whisper his name with me as I stared at the wolf lying before me, his warm brown eyes looking at me with warmth in them and the hostility absent from its gaze, so unlike wild animals.

"Matthew," I whispered again, almost uncertain of what I was doing, what I actually wanted out of this. Could I actually come to terms with the fact that I thought this wolf could, in fact, be my best friend? That werewolves could exist...did exist?

I shuddered. "I-I know it's you." I stuttered, cautiously reaching out to caress him behind his ears. He closed his eyes and leaned closer, dropping his head lightly before looking back at me, as if that gesture was to a nod.

"C-can you turn back into a human?"

I stared silently as the wolf got up and moved behind a thick tree. I waited. Digging my heel against the slightly wet soil, I realized I had forgotten to wear shoes before rushing out of the house. The sight of my arms and legs bruised, scratched, and slightly slashed from the sharp stones proved to serve as a witness to the fact that tonight actually happened. That was in case I woke up tomorrow and decided to question the sanity in this and me.

Just then, the sounds of twigs breaking sounded behind me and I bit my lip to prevent me from screaming out bloody murder when a half-naked Matthew moved out from behind the dark bushes.

It was then I realized. It was true. Werewolves did, in fact, exist.

I suppose my plight was obvious to point out because Matthew almost hurriedly put his hands in front of him in submission while moving closer almost at a pace of a tropical turtle.

"Don't be afraid. I know I have a lot of explaining to do."

I nodded, and he moved closer almost regarding me with utmost care before lowering down beside me.

"S-so I was right, right? Werewolves exist…Y-you and…Bryce. Who else and how? I thought all this was great in books and all…But in real life?"

Matthew stared at me. I frowned.

"What?" I asked him, my frown deepening when a soft smile spread across his face.

"You're more accepting of this situation than I would have thought you would be."

I smiled weakly. "I suppose *Twilight* and *The Vampire Diaries* helped a little. Besides, what choice do I have other than to be accepting? I can't run, can I?"

Mathew nodded, the corners of his lips lifting in a soft gesture. "I suppose not. He wouldn't let you leave."

I froze. The momentum of the situation hit in a matter of few deadly seconds, shaking me inside out. Bryce was a werewolf—and by the looks of the castle, a very important one at that.

"He's alpha." Matthew informed me, answering my unvoiced question, but I didn't hear. The buzz from all the emotions flaring around me was quite overwhelming. All I wanted to do was hold Matthew and cry. Why exactly? I didn't know.

I looked at him, my gaze a little confused. "He's what?"

This time, though, Matthew seemed to hesitate. He looked around the dark woods and then back at me. He frowned and then got up shaking his head. "I've been a dick of a friend, sitting here and chatting with you when you're bloody and bruised. Let's get you home, Theia."

I shook my head, refusing to grasp onto his extended arm. "He is a what, Matthew?"

Matthew sighed. "It is not in my position to tell you."

"Oh, shut up! You're my best friend! You are in every position to tell me! Besides, you already did tell me! What's bad in saying it again then? P-please, please just tell me." By the end of the outburst, my voice was barely a hoarse whisper. I didn't even mind that I was practically pleading. I couldn't take it anymore. Everything seemed so overwhelming. I needed answers.

I expected Matthew to answer, but being how he was, he only lowered himself and in one fluid motion, scooped me up in his arms, my scratched bloody arms and legs splattering red over his chest, neck, and arms.

"I'm sorry," I mumbled, my voice breaking in between as the events of the past few hours finally caught up with me. I broke down in his arms, forgetting completely that just a few minutes ago I was worrying bloodying him.

To hell with blood right now. I needed answers, and no one was giving it to me.

Matt sighed against me. His silence cut through me. Why couldn't he tell me?

"If I tell you, you must not let Bryce know that you know until he is comfortable in telling you this himself, okay?"

My eyes shot up towards Matthew, gleaming with victory. He was going to tell me!

I nodded almost vigorously. "Okay. I promise."

He nodded in reply.

"Well, you see, Theia, Bryce is the alpha king."

What?

He sighed, pulling me up suddenly, making me jump in his arms before continuing with the walk.

"This is going to be difficult," he muttered, stepping over a smaller sized rock as he followed an invisible path only he seemed to know about.

"Okay, so in every wolf pack there is an alpha as the leader of the pack, and then there is a second in command, the beta, and a third, the delta. While the alpha leads the pack, the beta and delta assist him, the beta being more strategic and an all-rounder while the delta usually the commander of warrior wolves. I am the delta. There are the pack members, or weres, who hold normal positions. And well, then there is the most important member, the luna, which, in this case, is you."

I opened my mouth to say something, but Matthew only continued talking.

"Alpha Alexander, however, is royal. Now, there are a lot of packs around the States, a lot of alphas and betas and deltas. They, however, are common weres. Royals are different. Alpha Alexander is the alpha of all alphas, the king so to speak. Every pack in the States comes down to him. There are other royals, other kings. They all are cousins in a way. After all, they are quite distinguishable than us, even me being delta of all deltas."

As much as all this was freaking me out, I couldn't help but want to know more as Matthew continued to walk us out of the woods, his stride seemingly faster than before but his face calm, so I just gave into the curiosity. I asked him questions.

"What exactly do you mean when you say that royals are different? And what's a luna? And how am I it when I'm human! How many people are weres here?"

Matthew let out a low chuckle at my questions, his chest giving out a low rumble. "Well…I have a feeling I am going to get myself killed telling you all this…" He sighed, sobering up. "Royals are lycanthropes, Theia. They are more powerful. They hold more speed, strength, and more. And with Alpha Alexander as king, that increases a notch there as well. As for you, Luna, since you have watched *Twilight*, this will be easier. Alpha Alexander was imprinted in you. In other terms, you are his mate, short for soulmate. I'd answer you if you have any more questions, but we are at the edge of the woods, and Alpha Alexander is beyond livid, trying to control himself from exposing his truth to you and freaking you out. For my sake and yours, Thi, please pretend you know nothing."

It was true. I could see the light glowing from the direction we were walking in, so I only nodded in response to my best friend's whispered request. He seemed to catch that because his grip around me tightened and he leaned in to whisper a few helpful tips, "Alex is on the brink of going frenzy although he has consumed wolfsbane to make him weak. But its effects will probably deplete as soon as he sees you, so if he grabs you and lashes out on someone else, hold him, kiss him, control him. He will only listen to you. If he cuddles you, let him. If he seems like an over protective prick, for tonight, let him be that. If he…gets touchy and needy, well, you take care of that however you want to. Okay? Okay. All the best, love!"

"Okay," I whispered back meekly, and Matt pressed a small kiss to my temple just before he stepped out of the edge of the trees and into my backyard. With the light illuminating from the patio, it was clear to see that Bryce was sitting on the patio steps, his head down and his shoulders slouched as if he was extremely tired. Two bulky men were standing on each of his sides, holding him. But as quickly as Matthew walked out of the woods with me, they stepped as far away from Bryce as they could.

I sighed as I watched him, my soulmate, a lycanthrope, not human but mine.

This is not right, Theia. This is not normal. Wake up! You're dreaming! A tiny voice urged me from somewhere inside my brain, sounding frightened, and scared of everything. I swallowed hard as I considered the sanity of my situation. Could this really be real?

Can't you see, Theia? This is real. Bryce has been made for you. You have been made for Bryce. So what if he is werewolf or lycanthrope or whatever? Does it really matter as long as he is Bryce? This tiny voice seemed surer, more adamant about its decisions. It sounded more right. I almost nodded in submission. It was true. This was real. I had to live with it, with him.

Bryce seemed to have sensed my presence because, in a matter of seconds, I was ripped out of Matthews's arms and cradled in Bryce's. He growled as he held onto me and immediately dipped his nose into my neck. Matthew and the men were now standing a good distance away. I realized that the two bulky men standing beside Matt were Connor and Emigen. My eyes widened as our gazes connected, and they smiled. *Them too?*

Bryce's low growls were starting to tire me a little, and his ever increasing grip on me wasn't helping exactly, so I used Matthew's advice and moved my lips near his ears and whispered soothingly, "I'm okay. I'm here."

Bryce growled again, only this time, it seemed lighter as he continued to hide his face in my neck. "Can't lose you," he murmured lazily, his fingers rubbing tiny circles on my back. I almost cried.

"You won't. I'm here," I cooed softly, sinking my fingers in his hair before pressing a dirty peck on his temple.

I felt as Bryce nodded, and when he lifted his head to look at the three boys, I turn to look at them again.

"Thank you," Bryce said appreciatively, his hands tightening around me as he pulled me closer against his chest.

All three boys nodded with small smiles before they turned and moved towards the fence on the sides of the yard, jumping over it as if it was nothing.

I didn't even have time to stare at them in wonderment. I was rushed into the house, and the back door had closed after me. How Bryce had managed that was truly beyond me.

"Hi?" I mumbled slowly. The silence was a killer.

"You're bleeding," Bryce growled in reply, pulling me closer as we made our way up the stairs.

I tilted my head to look at him and almost gasped at how his features had changed. From his clenched jaw to the blazing midnight blue eyes, I could tell he was holding off those golden flecks with everything he had.

"Bryce, I think you need to—"

"Don't you dare tell me to calm down."

I sighed. "Okay."

Pulling him closer still, I dangled from him by my arms as he opened my bedroom door and then marched towards the bathroom. Slowly, he settled me on the edge of the bathtub and started turning on the hot water. Almost immediately, the bathroom started to turn foggy.

"What are you doing?" I gasped as I placed my hand on him, stopping him from pulling off my top any further.

"Shut up and let me do this, Theia." He growled, tugging on my shirt, but I managed to keep my hands on his, stopping him from leaving me half bare.

"Bu—"

"Just stop resisting," Bryce spoke through gritted teeth, and in one swift movement, I sat on the edge of the bathtub half-bare. But he didn't stop there because, with a few more tugs, he managed to strip me bare of any clothes, well, all except my knickers. I blushed as I kept my hand across my chest, covering my breasts as Bryce picked me up and gently placed me in the tub full of hot water.

He just stood there.

"Can you…get out please?" I mumbled, looking down at the white dreamy foams, trying to hide the blush that was beginning to form on my cheeks.

"No," Bryce snapped at me harshly before marching towards the loo, closing the lid and sitting down on it. He looked at me sternly as if daring me to kick him out of the bathroom. I sighed. There was nothing I could do. Bryce would have to stay.

***

The feel of having a hard stare on you while you're bathing, completely naked, is unraveling.

It felt like I was coming undone just sitting there, washing away the blood and dirt with only soapy bubbles to hide what was meant to be hidden. The irony of things was that nothing was hidden anymore. There was no use of feeling undone. Bryce had already caused my undoing. It was already done. So all I could do while sitting in the tub surrounded by soothing warm water was to actually wash myself, which was quite difficult seeing Bryce's searing gaze on me while he sat on the closed lid of the toilet.

I sighed as I brought the sponge up to my neck and rubbed off the dirt. The silence was almost deafening. It was only when I brought my leg from under the water to rest it on the edge of the tub did Bryce let out a warning growl, moving slightly in his seat. I glanced at him in surprise and quickly scrubbed the dirt from my feet put it back under the water.

"If I were you, I would hurry up a little. I'm losing my patience. I'm sure you don't want me in that tub with you now, do you?"

I shuddered. Couldn't he just go out already? "C-can you please move out so I can sh-shower? Please?"

I didn't dare break eye contact as I said that. His darkening gaze hovered over my slightly chilled exposed skin before he stood up and briskly walked out of the bathroom, placing my towel on the vanity. I sighed as I got out of the bathtub and unclogged it, letting the foamy water run out and then rinsed it with the running water before stepping into the shower.

Closing my eyes as the warm water ran over some of the cuts, burning a little, I tried to shut out the pain and sighed when I succeeded. The wounds were barely important right now. What was important was the fact that I had learned only a few hours ago that werewolves existed, and Bryce was the king. I was his mate, his only mate. *That made me qu—*

I shook my head, shuddering at the impact of the new revelation.

What now?

This doesn't change anything, Theia. Well, it does. He is still your Bryce. And hey, now, you know this means something to him, and you mean something to him. At least, you know that you and Bryce are solid, not just a phase. Smile, Theia, face the music. So what if he can be classified as a beast?

You always did like Beauty and the Beast, didn't you? Well, he's yours, your Adam. Be his Belle, a tiny voice piped up in my head, urgent and commanding.

I smiled. Sometimes the voice at the back of my head was such a genius.

Running a hand over my tummy, I rinsed off the last of the foam and soap before turning off the shower, wiping myself dry, wrapping myself in the towel and with a more confident mind, walking out into the bedroom.

I closed the bathroom door and turned around only to let out a shrill scream.

"Bryce, put me down!" I yelped as he picked me up bridal style and started walking towards the bed.

"I need to tend to the wounds."

I shook my head. "No, it will be fine. Forget about it please."

"No!"

I looked up to glare at Bryce. "I don't want any tending to, and you will not force me!"

He snapped his head towards me, and I nearly shivered at his expression.

"Don't test my patience right now, Theia. Just get the damn—"

I pouted, looking at him with soft eyes. If being straightforward didn't work, hopefully, this would.

Tightening my hold around his neck, I pulled close and buried my face in the crook of his neck. Gently, I pressed a soft kiss at the base of it and couldn't help but sigh happily. "Please don't…I don't really like those creams. They burn. Besides, you already poured Detol into the tub, didn't you? Can't I just get dressed and go to bed? Please, babe."

I could feel as Bryce sighed against me and without a reply my way, marched towards the closet.

I stared expectantly at Bryce, waiting for him to say something and walk out of the room but frowned when he started rummaging through my doors, pulling out a navy blue pair of knickers and a soft thin white tank top, before handing it my way and taking a seat on the high vanity chair.

I sighed, ignoring the heat on my cheeks. He was very difficult tonight. I stole a glance at him and stopped. His gaze was locked on mine. My blush deepened. A shiver ran down my spine as I quickly looked down at my feet, my toes buried in the fluffy white rug. I had to be smart about this.

I let my towel stay before bending over and hooking both feet into my panty, pulling it up to my thigh and successfully in its place. It didn't take looking at Bryce to know that he had an amused look on his face. I couldn't help but smile at my own intelligent idea.

"You do know there is no way you can wear a shirt without letting go of the towel, don't you?"

Blushing, I rolled my eyes. Men could be so stupid sometimes. *Wait and watch.* I mentally snickered at Bryce as I ensured that my towel was wrapped around me properly before picking up the tank top and slipping it on from over the top, grinning. My back still facing Bryce, I finally let the towel go and pulled it from under the top before marching towards the towel hanger.

Padding my way back into the room, I couldn't help but snicker at Bryce. His expression, however, pulled into a frown. Not a minute into walking towards my bed, Bryce reached me in two long strides and picked me up in his arms. Again, I stayed silent, remembering Matt's cautious advice.

Bryce placed me on the bed just as I stifled a small yawn and blinked back the haziness that had begun to form in front of my eyes, my eyelids dropping lower and lower by the minute. Who knew running around the woods from a wolf, then getting saved by another wolf, who just happened to be my best friend, and finding out my boyfriend was my soulmate and the alpha king could be so exhausting? Nope, no one could know. Suppose their imaginations stopped at the "running from a wolf" bit.

"You should sleep, love," Bryce murmured softly against my ear as he wrapped himself around me, engulfing me completely. Normally, I would feel suffocated, but tonight, I let it slip. Matt had said to let him do whatever he pleased. Suddenly, a sharp pain erupted from my ankle, and I pulled my feet away from Bryce with a yelp.

"I'm sorry! I'm sorry!" Bryce exclaimed, freaking out as he pulled me closer. I shook my head, my eyes shut as I tried to assure him and push out the pain at the same time.

"It's okay…It's okay. Shush," I whispered soothingly as I tried to calm him down, placing a soft kiss on the corner of his lips.

Breaking the kiss, I smiled into the embrace as I rested my head against Bryce's chest, my lips touching the smoothness of his neck.

"Goodnight, Alex," I whispered sleepily, swinging an arm around his waist as I finally let myself go, smiling at the last words I heard before sleep took me.

"I love you, Theia."

***

Wet.

My sleep broke, and I bit back a groan as consciousness floated itself back to me. There it was again. Something wet touched my ankle. Creeping my eye open a fraction, I realized it was still night, the moon's glow served proof enough.

Just then, a shadow moved on the bed, its true form quite blurry in the dark room. The only thing that gave away what is was, though, was the pair of glowing golden eyes.

Fuck. All the haziness left in that one moment. The glowing golden iris. Bryce.

I held my breath as the shadow held onto my leg and lowering itself, ran a wet pad of muscle along the soreness of my soles. I watched almost frozen as a strong gust of wind blew into the room, bringing forward the light curtains as it danced around in the darkness, letting the moonlight shine through and exposing

Bryce completely. My breath hitched in my throat, and Bryce almost immediately stopped and turned towards me. His golden eyes glowed in my direction as his dark fur-covered figure came closer. I stilled.

Was he suspicious? No, no, no…

Immediately, I clamped my eyes shut, moving my head to my side as I let out a soft sleepy moan, hoping he would buy it. I couldn't help but press my lips tightly in shock when a hairy claw grabbed at my arm, and Bryce began licking the wounds on my palm and arm. I shuddered as he moved away and another gust of air hit me, hitting the wetness around my bruises and wounds.

Bryce must have noticed me shiver because before I knew it, the hairs contacting my legs turned into smooth skin and a very muscular leg wounded itself around me, an equally heavy arm slipping around my waist. My heart beating a mile a minute, I finally mustered enough courage to turn my head towards Bryce and open my eyes a fraction once more.

Golden eyes glowed back at me.

I closed my eyes and sighed as Bryce twirled a loose strand of hair behind my ear, pressing a soft kiss on my lips. Sleep seemed to be making its way back to me.

"I love you, mate."

I hummed in reply as the last remnants of consciousness floated away.

Smiling, I snuggled closer to Bryce, not at all noticing that I had just replied to Bryce's confession. I replied when I should have pretended to be asleep.

CHAPTER FIFTEEN

Mmm...This feels good!

A soft contented moan left my lips as I buried myself into the comfort of my bed. It strangely felt solid against my cheeks. I snuggled in close. Smiling against the comforting hardness of my bed, I slowly opened my eyes only to gasp and move back. Bryce's bright fiery ice-blue eyes stared at me, his lips pressed into a thin line. I frowned as I moved closer, my fingers touched the corner of his lips and slowly but surely, pulled them up into a smile.

What's wrong with him?

I frowned looking at him, an eyebrow titled up. He titled his eyebrow up as well in reply, and I couldn't help but smile. Bryce was really cute.

I should really brush before he decides to smack a smooth across my lips or something, I thought suddenly and made a move to rush out of bed, almost letting out a victory cry when I successfully got out and into the bathroom. Bryce had not pulled me back today. I wondered, Should I take that as a good thing or bad?

***

Placing my brush back in its little stand, I wiped my face with a towel. The impact of things kept rushing back. The funny thing was that although I looked calm and collected about it, on the inside, I was freaking out. I couldn't help but think of how I was going to handle this. How was I supposed to handle this?

I turned towards the door and stared at it; beyond it was a werewolf, not entirely human but a part wolf. He was a king no less, the werewolf king. I took a step back. This was not happening. This could not be happening!

"Dammit!" I growled, reaching out my fingers and pulling out my hair in frustration. How was I supposed to handle this? Could I even handle this? What would Cas or Marley do? I scoffed as I thought what my two best friends would do.

Marley would probably faint dead, and Cas? Yeah, Cas would be all up for it. I could practically hear her saying, "Were-sex, dude! Imagine the sex!"

A shiver ran down my spine, and I immediately shook the images starting to bloom in my mind. Not good, Thi, not good!

I looked back at the door and slumped my shoulders in surrender. It was heart over mind here. I supposed it always would be.

I mean, sure, he was a werewolf. He was a king, but he was still the same guy I fell for. He was still my boyfriend. And the fact that we were soul mates, that solidified things. Wasn't that what all girls wanted—solidification? A concrete guarantee that the boy they were investing so much in was actually "the one?"

A smile produced itself on my lips, and I squared my shoulders. It was time to face the beat. I was his beauty, and he, my beast. My smile broadened.

Opening the bathroom door, I strode into the room with a bright smile on but instantly stopped when I saw a brooding Bryce sitting on the edge of the bed, his shoulders slumped and his head hanging low. A frown slipped its way on my expression.

"Bryce? Hey, you okay?" I mumbled softly as I reached him and sunk down on my knees. I sunk my fingers into his hair.

Bryce immediately shot up, his face now inches away from me. My breath hitched in my throat. "What happened, babe?" I asked softly, trying to ignore the steely gaze he had managed to fix on me.

"How did you find out?"

Silence.

I watched Bryce with wide eyes, frozen in my spot. He stared at me straight in the eyes as he waited for my answer.

I tried to figure out coherent words to hand his way but cussed myself when I realized I could not think of a single way to admit that I knew. So I took the easy way out, well, at least for some time. I denied.

"What? Know what?" I laughed shakily, cursing myself again for picking the harder way. How could I tell him now?

Bryce stared at me. His gaze was still steely, and I almost whimpered at the lack of warmth in them.

Liar!

Shut up! I growled at myself.

Bryce's eyes still seemed emotionless as he finally let out a small sigh and pulled me closer. His hands slipped around my waist and he hid his face in the crook of my neck, his warm lips touching my soft spot. I shivered as he pressed a kiss there before pulling away and walking towards the window.

He turned towards me. I frowned. Why is he avoiding eye contact?

"I have a bit of work to do. You're not going to school today, so I'll be back here in an hour, okay?"

I narrowed my eyes at the "not going to school today" bit but nodded, anyway.

Why couldn't I go to school? I had noticed that my wounds were gone, not the slightest trace of them, really. I realized that that was the result of Bryce licking them last night. Then why couldn't I go?

Noticing that Bryce was gone, I made a mental note to ask Matt more about this wolf bit in school as I marched right back into the bathroom and took a shower.

I was absolutely fine, and I didn't see any need not to go to school. Therefore, I was going. Bryce and his over-possessiveness would have to take the backseat for a bit.

Quickly, I picked my backpack and thanked the heavens for not getting any homework yesterday. It was extremely rare to go a day without homework in Rosenberg High.

"Theia, come back here, young lady! At least, take this sandwich for a bite on the way," Mom yelled as I rushed downstairs and towards the front door. I froze and then with a huge blinding smile, turned towards my dad who was still seated on the island high-chair, gulping down his extra strong black coffee. My nose scrunched up as the strong smell of the coffee hit my nose. How he could drink that every morning was beyond me.

"Daddy," I called sweetly, walking towards him and clutching on his shirt. Dad let out a chuckle and stepped off the chair.

"I know what you're going to ask, so let's go. I can drop you off in the way."

Smiling brightly, I jumped into his arms and placed a sloppy kiss on his cheeks. "Thanks, Dad! I love you so much!"

"Hey, I'm still here you know!" Mom grumbled, giggling just afterward as I latched myself to her and placed a kiss on her cheeks as well. "Love you, Ma," I mumbled softly in our hug.

"Alright, ladies. Theia, let's go!" Dad spoke up as he kissed Mom on her lips and pulled away, walking towards the front door.

I turned back and giggled at my mom's dreamy expression before running after my dad. Those two really needed a second-time honeymoon trip. My eyes widened as a lightbulb lit itself up above my head. Now, I knew what to get them for their anniversary, which was in four weeks to be precise.

***

By the time we arrived, I had the places and hotels picked and the entire trip planned.

"Thanks, Dad," I said as I turned towards him and placed a soft kiss on his cheeks.

He chuckled as I moved out of the car. "No problem, honey. Be back home by seven, alright?"

I laughed. "No problem."

Waving at him, I turned around and walked towards the entrance of the school. Now, if I could only find Matthew…

"Where the hell is he?" I grumbled to myself as I marched around the hallway and glanced towards his locker. It had been fifteen minutes, and I had one round around the school. Matthew, however, was nowhere in sight.

I rounded around the corridor when the bell rang, and I groaned.

Maybe I will see him in class? I consoled myself before turning towards homeroom.

Homeroom ended, and I found out Matthew was actually absent. Marley could not help but gush over how adorable Keith was when he got mad. I, on the other hand, couldn't help but wonder if he too was a werewolf. I shook the thoughts out of my mind as we went to English class.

"Oh, there's Keith!" Marley whispered excitedly as we walked in, and I pushed her slightly towards him when he motioned her to sit beside him.

"You sure?" Marley whispered softly, turning towards me.

I smiled. "Heck, yes. Go on now!"

Marley let out a giggle as she pulled me into a hug. "I love you, Thi."

"I know. I love myself too." I winked back. She rolled her eyes and made her way to her boyfriend. In turn, I faced the rest of the class, hoping to find an empty seat and only found one beside a familiar redhead sitting in the corner right of the room, his head down as he continued to doodle something in his book.

"Hi, Lionel." I greeted happily as I took a seat beside him.

I frowned as he stilled and shot his head up, his eyes widening in horror and regret.

Hmm, what's he regretful about?

"You alright, mate?" I asked as I watched him fidget in his seat. He gulped visibly before looking back into his book, moving his head a bit in a nod before he did so.

What's up with him?

I sighed as I shrugged and picked out Hamlet, placing it neatly on the desk in front of me.

***

"If you could, would you save Polonius from his untimely death, Ms. Anderson?"

My head shot up from the play at hand, and I frowned in confusion. What?

"He's asking if you would save Polonius from dying," a whisper sounded from beside me, and I turned towards a slightly less fidgety Lionel to smile in thanks.

I looked back at a waiting Mr. Phelps and answered, "No, I would not."

Mr. Phelps lips quivered up in a sign of amusement. "And why not, Ms. Anderson?"

"Polonius was a rat. He was disloyal and extremely corrupt. He didn't even leave his daughter out of the mind games he devised against Hamlet. The man was vindictive without any reason and sneaking his way behind the curtains, spying on what Hamlet had to say to his mother/aunt was uncalled for. When one does something he knows may lead to damage, one should be ready to face the pain. Polonius did. I wouldn't change a thing."

Mr. Phelps nodded, his face lit up with a warm smile. Just then, the bell rang off, and Mr. Phelps started yelling about a three-page essay describing whether Hamlet's nature to contemplate and think things through was of use or not.

Finally after jotting down the assignment in my notebook, I shoved the contents in my bag and turned towards the door. I sadly noticed that Lionel had been the first to march out of the class when the bell had rung. It hurt a bit. I had considered him a friend.

I shrugged and smiled a little. Maybe he was having some personal issues.

Pulling on my bag tightly, I pushed past the chatting people as I walked out of the room.

"Aaah!"

"I'm sorry! Please don't yell!" a desperate voice whimpered as I was pushed against the wall. Meanwhile, I couldn't help but pant, slumped against the wall and my palm over my breast. I looked up and almost calmed down a notch when my eyes locked on soft blue ones.

"Lionel, you scared me!" I gasped out as I tried to regain control over my breath.

Lionel's cheeks turned pink, and he dropped his head to look down at his shoes.

I frowned and moved closer. "Hey, what's up? You okay?"

Lionel lifted his head up to look at me and smiled. He nodded, but then sadness seeped into his eyes again. "I-it was me."

What?

My eyebrows scrunched together. I considered what he actually meant. "I'm sorry. I'm not sure I quite understand," I mumbled apologetically, smiling sadly at Lionel.

He gulped and nodded. I thought he would turn around and leave, but he continued. "It-it was me…yesterday." By the end of his confession, his words broke, and he dropped his head again, his shoulders slumped.

I could only stare at the grown boy standing in front of me and a dozen other students passing by giving us weird looks.

The wolf was him, Theia! Lionel is a were! He wanted you for dinner yesterday! I moved a couple of steps back but stopped when Lionel looked up, and a tear slipped down his cheeks. He was crying?

Of course, he is crying, you idiot! Maybe he was out of control last night. You're fine, and he is saying sorry! Cut him some slack! a bossy voice sounded from the back of my head, and I almost nodded in understanding. Lionel seemed sorry. He was my friend. I walked towards him again and pushing my hands between his torso and arms, pulled him for a hug.

"It's okay, alright?" I murmured soothingly as I rubbed his back. Lionel slumped against me, his arms going around my shoulders. He hugged me back.

"I'm so sorry, Theia. It-it was my f-first time. You see, I'm a late bloomer. That's why e-everyone b-bullied me. They thought I would never…"

He couldn't continue, and I didn't force him. I only nodded as I continued rubbing soothingly on his back, telling him that it was okay.

It was only when I heard a loud, almost animalistic growl did I realize that everyone around us had gone quiet. Lionel let go quickly, and I moved back just in time to see a livid Bryce storming towards us with a worried looking Principal Williams beside him.

Bryce looked deadly. He looked like he wanted blood. I looked towards Principal Williams for help but then realized that he was actually clearing away the gawking students.

"Shit, man," a geeky-looking junior gawked at me just as I heard a crunch of breaking bones. I shot my head towards a fallen Lionel, holding his jaw, and a raging Bryce readying his fist for another collision.

"Bryce, let Lionel go! Bryce!" I screamed as I rushed towards him, grasped onto his raised arm, and tried to pull him back.

Bryce snapped his head towards me and glared. "I told you to stay home!"

I whimpered but continued to pull him towards me. He needed to let Lionel go. "L-let him go!"

"P-please, Alpha."

Both Bryce and me turned towards the boy on the floor still holding his jaw in pain. Bryce only growled louder and attempted to pound him once again. But somehow, I had known it would come, and just in time, I managed to fling my arms around Bryce and press myself against him. Immediately, almost as if a reflex action, he bent and buried his face in the crook of my neck. He visibly calmed a little.

I looked at Lionel with an apologetic look, and he shook his head, smiling a little. I motioned him to leave, and he nodded, getting up and taking a step towards freedom.

It all happened in a second, but before I knew it, Bryce had Lionel's neck around his grip and Lionel against the wall, his feet nowhere near the floor. "Listen, close, pup, she's mine! Keep your claws away if you value your life. Next time, I will kill you. Understand?"

Lionel gulped visibly and nodded as much as he could. Bryce let him go and turned towards me. Oh shit. I let out a shrill scream when Bryce flung me over his shoulder and proceeded to march towards the door, nodding at Principal Williams as he passed him.

"You're in a lot of trouble, little Theia."

"Let me go! I can walk, you know?"

"No!"

"What? I said le—Hey, Where are you taking me?" I screamed as Bryce opened his Jeep's door and dumped me into the front seat.

Banging the door shut, Bryce made his way to the driver's seat and got in. He drove us out of the parking lot. Meanwhile, all I could do was gawk at the brooding man beside me, ignoring me as if I barely even existed.

"Are you going to tell me where we are going?"

Silence.

"You know hitting Lionel was wrong, right? The poor guy didn't even have a chance!

"Bryce?

"Alexander Bryce Wilhelm, I am talking to you!

"Fine, I won't talk to you anymore too!"

Waiting for a reply seemed hopeless, so with a frustrated sigh, I slumped back against the seat and looked at the streetlights we kept on passing. It was only when we reached a spot where I could see the castle that I realized where we were heading—Dovelore Castle.

CHAPTER SIXTEEN

It was a gloomy day today, but despite the dullness, Dovlore Castle still stood proud and tall, shining brightly against the little light it did have kindly bestowed upon it. I supposed it was about to rain soon, anyway.

An annoyed huff caught my attention, but I looked defiantly ahead, refusing to even look at an exasperated Bryce standing outside and holding open the car's door. I refused to get out. If he wanted to play dirty, I would play dirty too!

It failed to pass me, though, how childish we were both behaving, and I almost shook my head in disappointment at my own behavior. But this was a repercussion to his childish behavior. So surely, it couldn't be as disappointing as his was.

I could hear as Bryce finally shuffled his feet in annoyance before taking a deep breath and leaning in towards me. Naturally, I moved farther away, not that it stopped him. Bryce only leaned further in, slipping his arm under my thighs and another around my back, picked me up in his arms and shut the door almost with unnatural fluid ease behind him.

My eyes narrowed. I looked at him, huffed out a breath, and muttered complaints under my breath. His jaw seemed to tighten under my gaze, and I almost stopped when I realized that being a werewolf meant he would have advanced hearing.

I supposed Bryce had enough of my ranting because, with a livid growl, he moved quicker, almost too quickly, because everything else seemed blurry. Before I knew it, I was thrown over a bed, and Bryce stood still, behind a now locked door, his hand still on the key.

"I know you know."

I froze. *Shit. Not now, I'm not ready!*

Almost ready to take the "deny it" way out of it, I stopped when Bryce turned almost frighteningly fast towards me. His eyes were now golden. I couldn't help but let a cuss go under my breath. The moment I just realized I had been running from was finally here. And I was cornered.

"When did you find out, little Theia?" Bryce drawled calmly, but his tone held the promise of anything but calmness as he stalked his way towards me like a predator.

No, Bryce wouldn't kill me. He's supposed to be my soul mate, I thought and a little color came back on my pale, frightened face.

"Answer me!" Bryce suddenly growled, and I whimpered, pressing myself into the bed a little more. Slowly mustering up enough courage, I looked up at a pissed Bryce who had only just a second ago been standing by the bed and now, had me pressed against the bed.

My eyes found his golden ones and widened at the realization of how beautiful they actually were, almost like pools of liquid gold.

Just then, Bryce growled in warning, and my eyes snapped towards his lips. His canines seemed to have slipped from under his lips and were partially in view for all to see.

"I suppose I've always known you could not be human to get into my room through the window like you do." I looked up at him. His eyes were now narrowed, focused on my face. I quickly refocused my gaze on his chest.

"And then yesterday, Matthew had to save me from Lionel. So I…I found out about him. And well, I figured if he is one…so are you. A-and when I woke up later that night, you were licking my wounds…So, you know…er…yeah."

The room was dead silent as neither one of us uttered a word. It seemed like ages before I finally grew tired of the silence and glanced at Bryce. I couldn't help but let out a small gasp as I realized just how close Bryce was, his nose just barely brushing mine. His steely golden eyes remained on mine as he finally spoke, Are you afraid of me?"

I froze, then quickly glanced at his chest.

"No. I don't fear you. I think it's more for this situation, really. I-I've only just imagined this kind of things in books and movies till yesterday...And...And to be suddenly thrust upon such a well-hidden fact is...scary. I'm in the unknown, you know. That's what scares me. Not you—well, except when you go around punching guys without any reason. That's when you scare me."

The silence built itself up again, but only this time, I felt like I had a sudden rush to say and keep on saying. Bryce, however, looked blank.

Sighing slightly, I glanced up at him. His eyes were filled with intense emotion. His lips were pressed into a thin line. Still, underneath him, I managed to free my hands and brought them to his face, and like earlier that morning, I eased up his lips into a smile.

"It's okay...I don't mind, you know. It doesn't change things," I murmured softly as I slowly ran the pad of my thumb over his lower lip.

"I'm a beast, Theia. Could you ever love a beast?"

Despite myself, I smiled.

"I already did."

The sharp intake of breath didn't escape my senses as Bryce tilted my head up to meet his gaze with mine.

"Y-you what?"

This time, I giggled.

"I love you."

"But I'm—"

I rolled my eyes. "Yes, I know. I know. You're a lycanthrope. You're not human. You're a beast, etcetera, etcetera.

But it doesn't matter, Bryce. So what if you're not completely human? You're still *you*. That doesn't change who you are. As for the beast bit, I'm fascinated, really. After falling for Adam, who was a beast himself and wishing I would find my own, I found you. All those fallen stars I had wished upon when I was six finally heard my prayers. About time, really."

Bryce growled, his grip on my chin tightening. "Who the fuck is Adam?"

I couldn't help but smile. "Ever heard of Disney's *Beauty and the Beast*? The beast's name was Adam."

Bryce scowled. His eyebrows furrowed together. His gaze was locked with mine. "You're mine."

It was almost a growl, like an order. But the vulnerability in its underlying tone didn't fail to get noticed as I smiled and pulled his head closer, my arms around his neck. I pulled his lips to mine. His lips were soft. The familiar warmth of it all was more comforting. His kissed me back gently, almost at an agonizing pace, and just when I thought he was going to pull away, he dipped his tongue into my ready mouth and pressed himself against me. A strangled groan left his lips as I let out a breathy moan and pulled him closer. My legs parted so he could settle against me better, or let me feel the dangerous hardness now pressing against my lower belly. I'd never know. My mind was too fuzzy to form any solid thoughts, anyway.

We both broke the kiss, panting for air. Almost immediately, Bryce pressed his face against my neck and started placing tiny kisses along it. His elongated canines slightly pinched the skin at places, causing a shiver to run down my skin. Placing an open-mouthed kiss on my sweet spot, Bryce finally moved up and instantly pulled me so that I had a leg flung over his legs and an arm around his waist. I blushed as I realized there was a large bulge on his pants. That must hurt.

Bryce let out a pained groan before he got up and made his way towards a door, not before muttering a painful "Need a cold shower" as he got in and slammed the door shut.

I smiled as I lay on the bed, my back against the mattress facing the white ceiling. I had a feeling my skirt was way above my waistline, and my top was slightly askew, but that didn't bother me right now. Everything was wonderful. Everything was fine.

I lay there for what felt like ages when the door to the bathroom pulled open and a towel-clad Bryce walked into the room only to stop short. His gaze snapped to mine. He let out a growl as he stormed his way to me. His lips formed a smirk. I frowned. *What is happening?*

"You're aroused, little mate."

Oh, shit.

Almost instantly, I tried to move out of bed and away from Bryce. There was no way he was going to tease me! Hell no!

The next second was a blur. Before I knew it, I was pushed against a wall, Bryce's warm breath fanning the side of my cheek before he descended his lips on my neck and his hand moved downward. A loud gasp escaped my lips as his fingers slipped past my panty and rubbed against the swollen nub. I moaned out loud. He stopped moving his fingers. Dammit, I was definitely not getting any sleep tonight.

"Fuck, you're so wet." Bryce groaned against my neck, and I moaned in reply, wanting him to move his fingers, wanting him to do something—anything! But he kept still, teasing me as his fingers remained just close to my nub but not close enough.

I growled in frustration as I felt my blush increase and tried to move away but got pushed against the wall again, and he flicked a finger across the swollen nub again. I hid my face against his shoulder, and he groaned as I placed a shy kiss on the base of his neck, pulling the skin between my teeth. A sudden sharp rap against the door brought us back to reality, and I almost gasped, blushing as I tried to move away again.

"Bryce, move!" I whispered, trying to push him away and his hand out of my panty. He growled and moved me against the wall again. His finger was now pressed against the swollen bud.

"Mine."

I nodded. "Yes, I know. Now, please, open the do—"

"Alexander Bryce Wilhem, you open the door right now, mister! I will not be disrespected like this! How dare you not introduce her to me? Open the door I say!"

"Fuck," Bryce muttered as he quickly removed his hand from my knickers and plopped his index and middle finger into his mouth, licking his fingers clean. Meanwhile, witnessing that, I only blushed a shade deeper.

"We need to get you cleaned. She'll know what we were up to, the minute she walks in." Bryce rushed as he pulled me towards the bathroom door, shoved a long t-shirt in my hand and walked towards the door.

I had only just stepped under the shower when I heard a distinctive "Where is she?" I blushed harder. The scene from earlier replayed itself in my head.

"Oh, God." I groaned as a blush found its way up my neck to my cheeks, and I shook my head, soaping myself, trying to avoid the thoughts of Bryce's long thick fingers against my lady parts. *God, Theia, get your head out of the gutter!*

Quickly rinsing off the lather, I wrapped a clean towel around me and walked out of the closed shower. After I wiped away the dampness, I groaned again as I slipped on the shirt. Bryce had forgotten to give me anything to wear underneath it. God, I felt practically naked. Sighing tiredly, I looked into the mirror and tried desperately to tame the waves I had foolishly decided to let flow today. At least, the shirt reached up to an inch above my knee. That would have to do.

A soft knock sounded on the bathroom door, and I shuddered from nervousness.

Who was that woman, anyway? I wondered as I padded my way towards the door and opened it a bit.

Bryce stuck his head in and grinned. "You look great in my shirt. Now, let's go! She's killing me."

I blushed and looked at my feet as he grabbed hold of my hand and pulled me out of the bathroom gently. In another second, I was pulled in for a warm hug.

"Oh, dear, it's so good to finally meet you! I'm Meryl, Alexander's aunt. But you can call me Meryl. Oh, good lord, Alex, she's a beauty! And she looks so innocent and naive. She will do you well! You're too big, bad, and dangerous for your own good! Oh, I'm so glad we're finally meeting! If it were for my nephew here, I would have never known. Thank God for Romanov. That boy always was a softie at heart. I see you've captured his heart too. I see why, though. You look like a jewel, one that needs guarding! Oh, dear me, I've been talking and talking and talking! Please say something! Or I may feel like you're crossed. I speak so much!"

Romanov? Roman's name is Romanov?

I blinked my wide eyes once or twice before a warm smile pulled itself on my lips. I liked her!

"Hi. I'm Theia. It's nice to meet you." I smiled warmly. I tried to move towards her when I noticed the strong arms circling my waist and holding me against a hard chest. Surprised, I tilted my head up to see Bryce's tight jaw. What was he pissed for?

"Oh, the pleasure is all mine, dear! Bryce seems to be very possessive, jealous even of your cousin, dear."

I snapped my head towards Bryce again. His jaw tightened. "She's—"

"I'm yours." I assured him before he could finish. He looked down at me, and his golden eyes morphed into his normal sea blue orbs. He nodded. And I smiled, leaning up to place a kiss on his jaw.

"Oh, sweet buttons, you two are so adorable!" Aunt Meryl cooed as she moved towards us with a wistful smile. Reaching for her bag, which I was sure was a designer, she pulled a black velvet box. She handed it to me.

"Take it. It's supposed to be passed down from generation to generation. From my great grandma to my ma, to Bryce's mom, but...Well, now, it's yours."

I looked back up at Bryce who had a sad smile on his face. He nodded looking at me, and I smiled softly before accepting the gift with a simple "Thank you."

"Oh, it's alright, dear." Meryl smiled. She then turned to Bryce, her eyes hard. "Well, help her wear it, boy!"

I couldn't help but bite back a giggle when Meryl winked at me as Bryce huffed and grasped the box from my hands. As the chain snaked around my neck, I couldn't help but feel a warm fuzz in my chest. Bryce's arms circled around my waist, and the warm fuzz grew more, making me let out a contented sigh.

Meryl, who had seemed to be studying me, smiled contentedly and nodded at Bryce before turning towards me again. "I must be gone now, dearie. Midday snacks await! Feel free to join me if you want to later, though I don't think Bryce will let you go anywhere till the full moon has come and gone."

I frowned. *Full moon? What's up with Bryce and the full moon?*

With a final wink and wave, Meryl stepped out of the room, closing the door behind her.

Bryce and I both stood still for some time, neither saying anything though both enjoying the comfort our embrace brought.

Finally, when I broke away, I turned towards Bryce.

"Bryce, what's the full moon got to do with us?"

CHAPTER SEVENTEEN

Bryce was just about to reply when a ringtone sounded from his pants pocket, and he immediately reached for it. Grasping it and giving it a look, Bryce turned towards me with a soft smile, and I nodded. It was probably important.

I stood there in the middle of the room as the sound of the door closing behind me echoed from the wall. I was looking nowhere in particular, but my mind seemed to be on overdrive. For one, the feeling of appreciation wouldn't leave. I seemed to be extremely thankful for how things had settled in so far, how smoothly things had gone. God knew how bad it could have been, how bad I could have reacted had I not have prior suspicions and a love for Jacob Black, Professor Lupin, and Adam. But I was not going to tell Bryce that. Who knew what he would kill in his jealous frenzy?

My gaze drifted towards the open window, and I found myself walking towards it slowly. The day outside did seem like a damp one. The clouds hung heavily in gray hues. I couldn't help but smile. This was my perfect kind of weather. If only it rained too, though. That would be great.

As if hearing my unvoiced wish, the clouds started pouring. The fresh smell of wet soil floating around the air reached my nostrils, and I smiled as I closed my eyes and leaned against the edge of the window.

"Hey." An arm slid around my waist as warm lips touched the skin of my neck. I shuddered and leaned against the familiar solid chest.

"Hey," I replied, smiling.

"So, where were we?"

I turned around with a wide grin. Well, this was a first. Bryce willingly offered to give me answers to my questions.

"I asked what the moon had anything to do with us," I said, putting my arms around his neck and pulling his huge form down. His arms around my waist tightened as he leaned in and kissed my chin.

"You're adorable. I had meant something else, but we could do this too," he murmured against my neck.

"Great! Let's begin then!" I announced, moving out of his embrace and placing myself nicely on the huge bed.

Bryce frowned as I moved out of his hold but quickly followed after, settling himself on the bed beside me. I turned towards him excitedly, and he groaned when he noticed the expectant look in my eye but continued.

"Before I begin, you must understand some things, okay?" Bryce began and then turned to look at me. I nodded in understanding, feeling slightly nervous about all this. Bryce continued, "You might have noticed…seeing as you have both seen Matthew and me in our…beast forms that we are different. There is a concrete theory behind it. You see, there are two types of wolves. Matthew happens to be a werewolf whereas I, a lycanthrope. Lycans and weres differ in a sense that we lycans are royal. We royals are stronger in every sense. And being lycans allows us to stand, more like…people unlike werewolves. Understandable so far?"

Once again, I nodded meekly. He was getting closer to the mate thing. I knew it. Why did I suddenly didn't want to hear it? Why was a suddenly so scared?

"Now, we all, both lycans and normal wolves are affected by the moon. Although we can change at will, our powers and strength increase during the full moon nights. And…well…since the full moon affects us all; it also affects our—fuck! It makes us want to mark our mates, okay. It'll make me want to mate with you. And that's bad because I fight every second to control myself from taking you. I'll go crazy, Theia, almost obsessive. And if I don't get you during the full moon this month or any month, I will kill anything and everything which stands in my way." I sat gaping at a pissed-off Bryce as he glared at the dark silk bed covers.

*Well shit…*a tiny voice choked out, and I gulped nervously, shuffling around with the pillow at hand.

"Say something." Bryce demanded, sounding exhausted. He turned to take my hands, but I quickly retrieved it, avoiding his eye as I moved away slightly. His eyes shot up to mine. I looked up, and my gaze faltered at the hurt in his eyes.

"Bryce, I—" I almost moved back to touch him, but before I could, Bryce was gone. All that was left of his presence were the lingering smell of his musky, mysteriously delicious smelling cologne and the swift, cold air that whipped across my face as he left.

"Way to go, Theia. You just hurt him!" I closed my eyes and tried to shut down my guilty conscience. I had just fidgeted away from Bryce, my soulmate. The look in his eyes kept swimming around mine, and I groaned as I sunk down against the mattress, a frustrated groan leaving my lips as I did so.

"Trouble in paradise, dearie?"

My head snapped towards a smiling Meryl standing by the door. Her comforting eyes bucked me closer to sharing my problems with her. I yielded.

"Yes," I finally said after looking at the off-white ceiling for some time. Meryl waited patiently for my reply as she settled herself on a comfortable spot on the edge of the bed.

Everything seemed so overwhelming, and it was all starting to catch up to me. I grimaced when a thin cold finger swept the tear off my cheeks and leaned back once again as if waiting for me to deliver another outburst or two.

I didn't.

Finally realizing I was not going to continue; she finally spoke up, "Scared because everything just seems too overwhelming, and the anxiety to lose your virginity to Bryce seems scary? Terrified and guilty because you hurt Bryce a lot?"

I sobbed harder and nodded. A comforting smile replaced itself across the thin line that had formed after Meryl had entered the room, and once again, she wiped the tears off my face.

"Breathe, dove, we are just like you folks but just a little different. You have nothing to be worried about there. As for your virginity, you're mated to the alpha king, dear. He must claim you…or someone else will. And that someone else wouldn't truly love you, never as much as Bryce. Now, moving on the topic of hurting Bryce, I admit he's extremely hurt and embarrassed. But go talk to him, dear, because he needs you. He needs your acceptance, your love. By the night of the last full moon, if you both don't mate, he will give into his beast. It will take him days to get back. He might even hurt himself. Think about it, Theia."

I sighed as a solemn looking Meryl moved out of the room after placing a ghost of a kiss on my forehead and a pat on my knee.

What am I going to do?

The sound of the drops of rain trickling down the window pane filled the room in an almost soothing manner, and I took a deep breath to calm myself before moving my gaze back on the ceiling.

What am I going to do?

Almost instantly, another voice replied, *Find him…*

My breath hitched in my throat. My eyes widened. I slapped my forehead as the frightful impact of things crossed my mind. I was eighteen, lawfully an adult. I was in love. Bryce was my soul mate. This was concrete, and we had to make love. What was I scared of?

The unknown…

I sighed and pressed my head further into the pillow, my eyes now shut tightly. It was true. I was scared. I couldn't deny that.

Another soft sigh escaped my lips, and I concentrated on the soothing sounds of the rain instead. The calm never came. Instead, another bit of thought that had been floating around my head etched itself in my brain in big bold letters.

Take a chance.

A light bulb lit up, and I shot up in bed, my tear-stained, blotchy face stinging from the heat. I could almost feel a headache coming up as I made me way out of the bedroom. I needed to find him.

Corridor after corridor, I tried to memorize the directions I was taking, this time, determined not to end up getting lost, but I couldn't find Bryce anywhere.

Finally, exhausted, I hunched over, my hands grasping onto my knees as I tried to catch my breath from all the rushing and running. It was no good. I would never find him in this cursed castle. I stopped panting when I heard a distant footfall, and determining which direction it was coming from, I made a mad dash towards freedom and hopefully, Bryce.

A slightly middle-aged woman seemed to have been dusting what seemed like a row of portraits. I rushed forward, almost desperately.

"Excuse me!"

The lady's head turned towards me in a surprised manner, but she smiled warmly when she saw me better. A small smile lit up on my lips. She could help me.

"Yes, dear?" she asked, her dusting finally at a pause. She looked at me with warm concern.

"Have you seen Bryce? Please, can you lead me to him!"

The woman's expression softened further until a sad tone seeped in. She shook her head. "I'm afraid Master Wilhem left, dear. Jumped off the fourth-floor balcony, he did—" she stopped when she noticed my horrified expression and quickly clarified "—

oh, don't worry, dear! Master does that a lot. He does! He will be back before nightfall. You are to stay the night?"

He left…

A thousand thoughts kept swarming around my head as I shook it distractedly and without asking for directions, turned around and started walking away, no idea where I was headed.

"Ow!"

Gravity was winning; my butt was going to meet its fate. I was going to fall flat on my ass. I hadn't even managed to see which wall I had collided with headfirst when a strong warm pair of arms slid around me, quickly pulling me. The person saved my backside from what could have been gruesome demise. I frowned as the person still held me. His nose was now buried in my free brown locks.

"I heard," the man spoke up, loosening his grip on my waist as he let his hands fall to his sides and moved away. I knew the voice immediately.

"Romanov," I sang, giggling, remembering the name Meryl had called him.

His eyes furrowed irritatingly, his lips thinning until it looked like he had none. "Don't call me that. It makes me sound old!"

I snorted. "It makes you sound sexy, you nutter."

Roman rolled his eyes and leaned forward to grasp onto my hand before he turned and started moving forward across the hallway.

"I heard about what happened."

I frowned. "Heard what?"

Roman continued leading us both towards a location I was still to find out. "About the Lionel incident. If Bryce hadn't broken his bones over and over again, I would have given him a piece of my mind too."

I gasped. "He did what?"

Rome chuckled and stopped, turning towards a door. He opened it and ushered me in.

"Don't worry. We, lycans and weres, have speedy healing qualities. It took him four hours, at least, to fully recover, though. After all, he had just newly shifted."

I glanced at him, stopping my wide-eyed inspection of the library halfway. "So, you're a lycan, aren't you? Like you walk on two instead of four?"

Roman smiled, his brown eyes now shining golden. "That would be correct, love."

I nodded, returning my attention back to the millions of books that happened to sit cozily on millions of shelves. Each shelf reached the ceiling two stories up the floor. Stairs and ladders were ready to aid in finding one of the many worlds hidden beneath the old worn pages. My insides tingled as I looked around. And in a quick second, I decided that the library was my favorite part of the castle. No doubt.

Bryce…

My shoulders slumped suddenly as the thought of Bryce flashed across my mind. *Where could he be?*

***

"So weren't you supposed to come next week?" I asked Roman, trying to break the tense silence that had settled between us as I leaned against my bed's headboard.

After convincing Roman to drive me over, as he barely had any jet-lag, I had finally told him everything that had happened earlier that day, and he had told me how Bryce had returned to the castle after I had slept and he had beaten Lionel to the brink of death. I found that extremely wrong and managed to make a note of being extra nice to Lionel. The guy deserved it.

"Yes, I was. But the National Beta Meeting ended earlier than we expected, and here I am." Roman motioned to himself happily as he shrunk beside me.

Smiling, I was just about to pull my sass on him when I noticed a look of irritation pass him, and he quickly got out of bed, turning towards me almost apologetically. "I need to get to the castle, Thi. Beta duties. I'll see you soon, okay?"

I smiled and nodded, waddling over the bed on my knees. I moved towards Roman to give him a good hug before yelling out, "Later," as he ran and jumped out of the window in a graceful motion as if it was no work at all.

Once Roman was gone, the silence of the room now caught up to me, and I slumped back against the headboard. Explaining things to Rome had made it easier. I knew now what I wanted. It was easier to accept, to process. Bryce was the one. And the next time we met, I would apologize and tell him yes.

***

A frosty gust of wind broke past the curtains and hit my naked feet with full force. I gasped and shot up in bed.

Crap.

One of the first things I realized was that I had over-napped and it was now turning dark. I hated complete darkness. So as quickly as I could, I reached for the switch and turned the string lights on.

That was when I took notice of the presence that stood beside the window, still, tall, and in the shadows.

I gulped down nervously and turned towards the door, but before I could even contemplate on an escape plan, the figure had moved out of the shadows and into the light, his face pulled up in a blank manner, his eyes looking as if it were desperately trying to get the spark it usually had.

"Bryce?" I asked, getting out of the bed and moving towards him. He took a step forward, and my palm touched his chest, almost as an assurance that it was actually him. "I'm sorry," I whispered, slipping my arms around his waist as I buried my face against his chest. I had heard a sigh before he lowered himself and his arms wrapped around my waist.

Picking me up in his arms, he moved towards the bed and placed me there. I smiled at the same expressionless Bryce who only leaned in and placed a small kiss on my forehead before turning around and moving towards the window. I frowned.

"Bryce?"

He stopped with his arm on the open window frame. "You might want to go to sleep, Theia. I'm returning to the castle. Some work to do. Good night."

I could only stare at the empty space Bryce had just been occupying.

What the hell had just happened?

CHAPTER EIGHTEEN

Waking up the next morning wasn't as difficult as I had hoped it would be, considering I had barely slept at all the previous night. Yes, it hadn't been difficult at all.

The alarm rang at its assigned time, and I rose from my spot on the bed and made my way into the bathroom quite gingerly. I suppose the lack of sleep had, in turn, caused such a sour mood. I only frowned harder as I dressed myself up, noticing the dark circles under my eyes.

Picking up the English and history essays that were not due until a couple of days, I placed them into my backpack and strode out of the room. I would make an early submission for those two assignments. At least, one good thing came from my lack of sleep.

I grimaced and almost bit my tongue to hold off a scream as I lost footing while walking down the stairs. Luckily, my hand grabbed onto the banister, and I saved myself from premature death.

Bryce's odd behavior still bothered me. I could not tell why he was behaving that way. I knew it was no use thinking about it. I wouldn't find an answer, anyway. After all, I hadn't found any all night, but I couldn't help but have a definite feeling that things were going to change now. The Bryce who had visited me yesterday was not *my* Bryce. Something was wrong. And God save me, I had to fix it.

I jumped off the last steps of the stairs and marched into the kitchen only to stop dead.

Instead of Matthew, Bryce was the one sitting on the high bar stool today and drinking what smelled like a cup of warm coffee. With his cup already inches away from his lips, he stopped for a second as he noticed my presence but continued as if he hadn't.

I frowned at that too but moved further into the kitchen, ignoring him as much as he ignored me. Bryce still did not acknowledge my presence. A soft sigh left my lips, and I decided to just jump headfirst into it. The need to know what was bothering him seemed higher than my self-respect right now.

"Are you mad about something?" I mumbled, biting my lip as I finally turned around and lifted my gaze to his.

His dark gaze stayed on me for a second before it slipped away. "No. Good morning, love."

My frown deepened, and I moved closer to him. I pulled his dark gray shirt forward, and he got off the chair to face me.

"Don't lie to me. Why are you here? And why are you mad at me?"

Bryce sighed and met my gaze. His arms slowly moved around my waist, and with a light tug on his part, he slammed me against him. I could only stare at him wide-eyed as he regarded me with his stormy ones.

He leaned forward, and I could almost taste his lips on mine when his arms suddenly loosened against my waist and placed a small peck on my forehead before moving away and taking a seat on the high chair again.

I grit my teeth as the heat on my cheeks increased. That was embarrassing. Letting out a shaky breath, I turned towards Bryce, his strong back facing me. Eyeing the granola bars placed in a bowl on the kitchen island, I made a grab for a couple before turning around and moving towards the door. If Bryce wanted to be difficult, so be it.

I was just making my way down the driveway when a hand gripped my arm and pulled me to a stop.

"I'm driving you."

Yeah, right, you are!

"It's fine…babe. I'm fine," I snapped back as sweetly as I could, making a move to get away from him. His grip only tightened.

"Don't make me carry you to the car, Theia, because I can, and you can fucking bet I will!"

I froze. And when Bryce pulled me forward to his Jeep. I let him.

* * *

"Look, Bryce, I need to talk to you about yesterday."

There, I said it. After mustering up courage almost all throughout the ride from home to school, I finally said it.

Bryce stopped the car in an empty parking space and turned towards me. I almost bit my lip off at the foreboding look on his face.

I sighed nervously and placed a hand on his, intertwining my fingers with his and bringing his palm over to my lap. His eyes darted towards the palm resting on my lap to me. His jaw hardened.

"I—"

The sound of his ringtone filled the car, and I almost bit back a frustrated cuss.

Bryce removed the iPhone from his pocket and instantly smiled with his eyes on the screen.

"I knew you would call as soon as you'd wake up." Bryce chuckled. He looked happier than he had since yesterday. He laughed out loud at something the person on the other side said and almost cheekily replied, "I miss you too, beautiful. You know I would give everything to keep you with me, don't you, love? No, you're the prettiest girl I know. I'll come by today, okay?"

I stared at Bryce. My eyesight was blurry. And when a tear finally slid down my cheeks, I turned and opened the door as numbly and softly as I could, then ran.

Shit, shit, shit, shit, shit!

Hurriedly wiping the reckless tears running over my face, I kept on walking in the direction of the library.

You know I would give everything to keep you with me…

I quickened my pace as the dark doors of the school library came into view but failed to notice the equally hurrying Diandra moving from a corridor. Only when we both collided and my head snapped towards the person already murmuring sorry, I noticed an unsettled Diandra standing in front of me. Her troubled expression turned into a smug one as she realized my state of emotion. I almost cussed out loud again.

"Well, well, well…Look at what the dead duck dragged in, little Miss Queen Luna." Diandra sneered as she folded her arms in front of her.

I really wasn't in the mood for playing. Between being confused about Bryce's new behavior to him flirting on the phone right in front of me as if I didn't exist was troubling enough. The last thing I needed was a stuck up plastic woman putting me down.

"Fuck off!" I snapped and tried to move past her when her hand shot towards mine and grabbed it, halting me mid-step.

"Finally found out what a playboy of a mate you have? Well, congratulations, better now than later. I think it's suiting, honestly. A whore mated to a player, a match made in heaven. Next time, leave my boyfriend alone, bitch! Maybe karma will be nicer to you!"

I sobbed just as Diandra let go and pranced away looking like she had won a battle. I quickly moved towards the library, the stabbing pain in my chest now making itself well-known.

When I reached the furthermost corner of the library, "the dark bend," I slumped over a chair I had placed here previously and cried, muffling my voice as much as I could with my hands.

"H-how could he?"

"Theia?"

I froze. *Oh no…*

"Oh my God, Theia!" Marley bent down on her knees in front of me, tilting her head so that she could see my face.

I couldn't help it. I shot out of my chair and into her arms, pulling her close as I sobbed into her white t-shirt.

"Oh my God, what happened? They're looking for you!" Marley asked, her tone bewildered. She grasped onto my shoulders and softly pushed me away. I raised my teary, red-rimmed gaze and locked it with hers.

"You tell me now, Theia Anderson! I want to know who I have to kill!"

I couldn't help but chuckle in between my hiccups and crying.

"Talk to me. Please?" Her soft tone was soothing. I nodded.

***

"What a fucking jerk?" Marley almost yelled out loud! Her hands curled into a fist.

I nodded, fresh tears streaming down my cheeks. Turns out, Marley knew about werewolves and lycans. She was Keith's mate and all. So when I tried to modify the story, she told me to cut the crap and tell her as it was. I did.

"Okay, enough of the crying. What we need to do is give you a girl's day out, and you're staying at my place tonight! No excuses."

My eyes widened as I stared at her, wiping the tears off my now blotchy face.

"But how—"

"Well, you need to sneak out, how else?" a stern voice spoke up for the first time from behind both Marley and me, and I let out a shocked gasp, our heads snapping in the direction the voice came from.

"Mrs. Priscort." Marley gasped and her grasp on my arm tightened.

The stern look on Mrs. Priscort's face softened, and she looked almost kind when she replied, "I suggest you both take the back route, though, dearies. King Wilhem is creating an uproar around the school."

A minute or two passed, and neither Marley nor I moved an inch. We both sat, staring at the usually stern slender woman, her graying hair complementing her sky-blue eyes and her half-moon spectacles always reminding us of Professor Dumbledore. The horror she usually put students through, now, seemed dead and gone. Almost as if the overly strict, hard-mouthed, and short-tempered Mrs. Priscort was another Mrs. Priscort altogether.

"Well, don't just sit there staring at me! They are going to search the library in a few! I suggest you girls flee before they do. Here—" She shoved a can towards me. "Spray it over yourselves before you leave. Covers your scents."

My eyes widened, and I almost gasped at Mrs. Priscort before a cold spray hit my neck almost knocking me back in shock.

"Dammit, Marley, that is not funny!" I groaned as I glared at her and got up from our position on the floor.

Marley sprayed herself over and quickly pulled a surprised Mrs. Priscort in for a hug.

"Thank you, ma'am. You are my new favorite person!" Mrs. Priscort smiled, patting Marley's back before I hugged her too.

"Now, off you go, ladies. Move along before a livid king walks in and kidnaps his own mate, a mate he has hurt without a care. You deserve some time off!"

Mrs. P spoke softly as she ushered us from the corner and out of the library, directing us towards the back exit.

"The world is full of surprises," Marley mumbled under her breath, still in high of the shock. I nodded, moving as quickly as she was, sprinting actually, around the school grounds and towards the parking lot where Marley had parked her car.

***

"Let's get out of here," Marley said, looking at me warmly as she drove out of the school grounds and down the road.

Our drive downtown consisted of an hour worth of things we could do. Marley very smartly avoided bringing Bryce up, and I was almost thankful for that. The last thing I needed was to be constantly reminded of someone I was stuck with for life, someone who turned out to be so fake.

I quickly rubbed at my eyes as tears started to accumulate again. *Dammit, Theia! How are you going to survive this when you're a puddle of a mess!*

I almost wished I could go back to being as strong as I was when Bryce had gone missing for two weeks. I had been able to pick myself up then. *This*, this seemed different…Maybe it was because Bryce had knowingly hurt me this time.

A sigh left my lips as I turned towards the window on my side. The less I thought about Bryce, the better.

"Let's go then."

"Huh?" I turned towards Marley, confused.

She rolled her eyes, opened the door, and got out. I sighed before following suit.

"Where're we going?" I asked Marley as we entered a mall.

"Shopping." I tried to respond, but Ley stopped me. "You do know that Bryce would find you when you go home today, don't you? We need to get you clothes and a pair of bikini. We're going to the beach!"

I sighed and slumped behind her as we entered Forever 21.

An hour and a half later, we emerged from our last stop with bags filled with shorts, crop tops and tanks, dresses, a pair of bikini, and some lingerie.

"Nex—"

The mild sound of my ringtone sounded as I turned on my iPhone to call Dad and let him know where I was going to stay tonight. I had switched my cellphone off in fright after Mrs. Priscort informed us of a livid Bryce looking all over for me. "Good thing too." I breathed out loud. The ever increasing missed calls proved exactly how mad Bryce could be. Glancing down, I sighed as I accepted Dad's call. Well, here goes nothing…

"Theia, sweetie, where are you?" Dad's worried voice rushed out almost as soon as I accepted the call.

"I'm fine, Dad. I'm…You have to promise not to tell Bryce, okay? I'm going to be at Marley's, Dad. B-Bryce is…He has someone else," I replied, wiping the tears that were now sliding down my cheeks again.

There was a slight pause at his end before he replied, "I suggest you stay there for a day or two, Thi. I'll let Mom know so she doesn't worry. Let things cool down, yeah? I love you, kiddo!"

"I love you too, Dad. Thanks."

"Take care, pumpkin."

"I will, Daddy."

I slumped against the car seat as I placed my cellphone down, fully aware of a sad Marley looking at me with worry.

"Ready?" she asked me softly.

I lifted my gaze to the view of waves crashing against the shoreline, the golden sand shining under the heat of the sun. A soft smile broke on my lips. I nodded.

"Ready!"

***

"Aaah!" A huge wave crashed into my back, rocking me forward into the water again.

"Good! You deserved it!" Marley shouted back, laughing her ass off as she sat on the sand, making a very impressive-looking sand castle.

I giggled as an idea popped up in my mind. *Oh Ley, sweet Ley, you are in for so much trouble.* I grinned as I innocently waded out of the water and made a run for Marley as soon as my feet touched the slightly drier sand.

"Ay! *Gerrof* me, you!" Marley choked out loudly in between her fits of laughter as I sat on top of her, completely wetting her.

I was vaguely aware of the eyes that were trained on us, but after such a draining day, I was finally having a bit of fun. And I really didn't care.

The beach was far from empty. Couples and singles, even a few grandpas and grandmas, walked around and played in the water, having a carefree day. The beach seemed like a good idea after all.

"Dying here! Get off, so I can seek revenge!" Marley yelled and smacked my thighs. I laughed at her before sprinting towards the water as fast as I could.

"Oh, I'll get you, Theia Anderson!"

"Never—oops!"

"Gotcha! Daddy, *wuk*! I caught the *bwedgul*!"

I groaned as the five-year-old girl held onto my leg, her backside facing me as she straddled one of my thighs. She gripped my leg almost in a tight hug.

"Woah, sweetie! Good job! Now, let go of the lady! It's bad manners to knock her down, sweetie."

Still groaning, I glanced towards the source of the voice and almost had a jaw-drop moment when my gaze found a very tall, broad-shouldered man with blonde hair standing just beside me, his form fully shadowing me from the sun. His golden wedding band glistened in the sun. A wide smile formed on my lips. Suddenly, I had immense respect for this big, bulky man.

"Sorry, love. She tends to get a little frisky sometimes, my little Evangeline."

I smiled as I accepted his hand and pulled to my feet. The little girl stepped aside, letting her daddy pull me up.

"She so *pweety*, Daddy! She can be my new best *fwen*. Can we take a picture *wib* her?" Evangeline pleaded, fixing herself around my leg once again. I bent down and extended an arm towards her. She happily hopped on. Just then, Marley finally caught on to us, panting almost lightly.

"Sweet dumplings, I really need to start exercising more." She huffed before finally seeing Evangeline in my arms and Mister Dad beside me.

"Hey, could you be a sweetheart and take a pic of us?" Mister Dad asked Marley. "I'm Chris, by the way."

"Sure!" Marley giggled excitedly, taking Chris's cellphone and then snapping a picture or two as we posed.

"There you are, mate!" a dark brooding voice spoke up behind me, and I turned almost immediately out of curiosity.

Dark hair, hazel eyes, lean, putting off undeniable authority—great makings of a sweet serial killer.

"Oh, hey, mate. Sorry. Thanks." Chris beamed as Marley handed him his cellphone. I placed a tiny kiss on little Evangeline's forehead and passed her to her father.

"It was lovely meeting you, Evangeline. I hope to meet you here again someday," I spoke softly, smiling at the grinning kid who looked way smaller in her dad's big arms.

"Call me Angie or *pwincess. Eryone* else does! I'll meet you soon too, *missh*!"

"It's Theia. See you around, princess." I smiled, giving Chris and Angie a wave. I turned towards Marley, and we both made our way back to our spot.

"That hot blonde dude couldn't keep his eyes off you," Marley spoke up nonchalantly as we waded into the water.

"Oh, really? Well, good on him, then!" I giggled, splashing water on Marley, and for the next few minutes, we both broke out in giggles, playing splash like a bunch of ten-year-olds.

***

"You sure you folks won't mind, right?"

"For God's sake, Theia. No, they won't. In fact, they would be quite excited to have their little Marlene bring home a friend for the first time ever."

I gasped. "The first?"

Marley looked at her lap and nodded. "I wasn't exactly popular around school until you and the boys started talking to me…All the girls, they…"

My lips lifted in the corners as I glanced at Ley. The amount of humility she possessed was actually astounding. Even I could not be as humble and modest as she was. It wasn't entirely a bad thing, but I knew Marley was more than she gave herself credit for.

I nudged her slightly with my elbow, and when she looked up, I grinned. "Let's go meet your folks. I'm sure your parents will be excited to meet your best friend."

Marley grinned and pulled me in for a hug. "I love you, Thi."

I smiled as we broke away. "I *wub* you too, Ley-Ley."

"Ready?" she whispered as we stood outside the door of her modern-looking mansion.

I grinned and nodded.

"Okay!" she whispered before sliding in the key and letting us in.

"Ma! My best friend, Theia, is going to stay—"

"Best friend? Oh my goodness, she's beautiful! It's lovely to meet you, dear! I'm so happy you and little Ley became friends! Oh my, where are my manners! I'm Judy, dear, Judy Smith, but call me Judy! It's so—"

"Ma! Stop! You're embarrassing me!"

I stood wide-eyed and pink-cheeked beside an equally shocked and embarrassed Marley staring at the very pretty red-headed woman. Mrs. Smith looked every bit the prim and proper house maker she was—her red locks pulled up in an elegant bun and her simple yet classy green dress complimenting her warm green eyes.

Snapping out of my daze when a still slightly red Marley nudged me in the sides, I smiled at the bubbly older woman and extended an arm towards her.

"Hi. I'm Theia. I hope you don't mind me—."

"Of course not, dear! Oh, it's lovely to have you here! Although I must ask, on a school day?"

Both Marley and I grimaced.

"Well, you see, Ma…"

Mrs. Smith immediately frowned, taking both our hands in hers and pulled us to the nearest couch. "Tell me everything, young ladies, and be very honest!"

***

"What a jerk!" Mrs. Smith exclaimed, looking as appalled as she sounded when she practically yelled out her reaction.

"That's what I said!" Marley exclaimed outrageously, throwing her hands up in the air.

She turned towards me, her smile very motherly and warm.

"I think Marley and your dad are right, dear. Benny would agree too. You should stay here for a couple of days. The last thing you need is to face King Jerk-Alert after he hurt you so badly! The good thing is, though, he can't impose himself on us or hurt us because we are humans, and it's against the treaty."

She turned towards Marley. "I'm proud of you, dear. You did the right thing. Just don't let Keith know because he will be obligated to tell his king."

I couldn't help myself. I reached out and hugged Mrs. Smith. I supposed Marley had the same idea because she jumped in the same second too.

"Thank you, Mrs. Smith," I murmured softly as we broke our little group hug.

Mrs. Smith smiled. "Judy, dear. And off you girls go, take a shower! You both smell like seaweed! I've baked some cookies. I'll bring them up in a few, okay."

"Thanks, Ma!" Marley yelled as she let us upstairs, both of us giggling from getting sand all over prim and proper Mrs. Smith. "You first," Marley spoke out as we both put down the shopping bags.

"Oh my God, you have a friggin balcony!" I squealed, rushing past her light pink breezy curtains and stood with my arms bracing the railings. The view was great with the sea shimmering silver against the midday sun, the roofs of the other mansions flowing downhill, suiting the view wonderfully.

"I'm so jealous," I muttered, grinning as I padded my way back into the room and walked over to a door Marley pointed, throwing a towel in my direction.

"Well, you bet your knickers, you should be! I get to play Romeo and Juliet."

I rolled my eyes. "They both died, Ley."

"Tsk, tsk, tsk, no, Theia. They both died in *love*."

It had been an hour before we had both bathed and dressed up. Both our tanned bodies ached slightly from all the running around at the beach earlier. Dinner at Smith Manson was truly a delight. Mr. Smith was an incredibly learned doctor with an extreme sense of humor. Him agreeing to me staying over seemed like a blessing, and before I knew it, dinner and the dishes were both well and done.

Now, here we were, sitting in Marley's room as she flicked around DVD cases, trying to find a good movie to watch.

"No, I refuse!" I exclaimed in protest, grabbing hold of the movie case.

"It's a great movie, Thi! And besides, Ryan Gosling is hot!" Marley cried out, making a leap towards the case.

"No!" I slumped back, actually devastated as Marley held up the case in victory.

"I think I've cried enough today, Ley," I muttered sadly, moving my hands over my eyes in a pathetic attempt of hiding the tears.

"Don't think about him, Thi," Marley almost whispered, softly as she pulled me in for a hug, rubbing her hands on my back soothingly.

"I can't help it. I mean, I was fine all day…But now…Here…What am I supposed to do, Ley? How am I supposed to cope when the person who is made for me, only me, is in love with someone else? I…I feel so suffocated! And…I don't know how to break free."

"Shhh, it's alright, Thi. It's all right. Everything will be fine one day. I promise!" Marley mumbled soothingly.

"I just want to run away."

Marley stared at me, her sad eyes, now, wide and frightened. She scowled and then shook her head, grabbing onto the remote control she quickly placed the disk in and sat back beside me.

"You—"

Taylor Swift's voice blared around the room, mixing with the sounds of the TV, and Marley and I grew tense. She glanced at her cellphone and then snapped her head towards mine, mouthing, "It's Keith. Be quiet!"

I nodded and gulped nervously.

Somehow, I felt like Keith was calling for something more than just talking to his mate.

"Babe?"

My eyes widened when I heard Keith's voice over the loudspeaker. I almost fell off the bed in fright.

"Hey! I'm sorry. I didn't come to school today. Lady problems!" Marley rushed, faking a giggle quite wonderfully.

I gulped. In my nervous state, I picked up a handful of chips and stuffed them in my mouth.

"Oh, I hope you're resting, Ley. Do you want me to stop by?"

Marley's eyes widened as we stared at each other. "No! I mean, no. I really don't want to kick your ass. My temper is very questionable right now. I think I might just sleep."

There was a bit of silence from Keith before he finally replied, "You sure?"

"Uh-huh," Marley replied quite easily.

I shoved another handful of chips into my mouth, my mind trying its best to block thoughts of Bryce.

"Okay," Keith replied almost hesitantly before continuing, "Babe, have you…er…seen Theia by any chance?"

I gulped down the munched potato chips, looking away from Marley's gaze.

"No, is something wrong?"

"Oh…Yo—" A loud growl sounded from the other end of the phone.

"Where's Theia, Marlene?"

My heart stopped. I closed my eyes and bit on my lip—Bryce.

"You tell me! I barely got out of the room all day! And she hasn't replied to my text from last night!"

"If you're hiding—"

"Why would I hide her?" Marley laughed sarcastically. She didn't seem the least bit intimidated by Bryce. I bit my lip harder.

"Fine!"

"I'm sorry, babe. King Alexander is really worried because Theia ran off this morning. We can't find her anywhere. He's gone full beast, ruining the courtyard. The full moon is close, and he is going crazier than usual. I need to go. We need to tie him up with wolfsbane. Will you come to school tomorrow?"

There was a second of silence before I heard Marley sigh and reply, "Yes, I'm coming to school tomorrow. I love you. Please take care, okay?"

Keith sighed in relief on the other end. His tone sounded happier when he replied, "I love you too, baby girl! I'll see you in school tomorrow. Good night."

I love you, Theia. I smiled sadly, letting one traitor tear slip by.

"Good night."

"Thi—"

I looked up at her. My eyes were blurry from all the tears threatening to flow out. I shook my head, willing a few drops to slide down my cheeks, and quickly wiped them away.

"Let's just watch the movie, Ley."

CHAPTER NINETEEN

"Theia! Theia, get up. I'm going to school!"

What the hell? I swatted the hands shaking me vigorously away before moving up to a sitting position. My eyes were still squinting and trying to make off all the light suddenly being bombarded on me.

"Turn off the bloody lights please," I protested, covering my eyebrows and trying to shield the light away.

"Theia, I can't do that! That's the sun! I'm going to school, where Bryce would probably be. Want to wish your best friend all the best or something for going to the wolf's turf?"

My eyes immediately shot open, and I jumped backward. "Don't do it!"

"She must go to school, Theia."

I turned to face Judy, her face pulled up into a bright, comforting smile.

"I need to cut off chances of you being with me, Thi. By being present in school, I will strengthen the fact that I was indeed sick yesterday and not with you."

I sighed and nodded, staring at both the women as one sent me a soft smile before walking out of the room, and the other picked up her backpack and padded her way to the door.

"Be safe. Do not turn on your cellphone, or they will locate you. I hope your GPS isn't turned on."

"Don't worry, it isn't. Thank you, Ley. This means so much to me. You know that, don't you?"

She nodded and smiled at me sadly. "After what you went through, you deserve a bit of a break."

I smiled and moved back into bed when she closed the door behind her. I had barely been able to sleep at all last night, and now that sleep was visiting me, I really wasn't going to let it just go.

***

"Theia, it's for you."

I turned from my math assignment towards Mrs. Smith and glanced at the cellphone she was extending towards me.

"Marley?" I asked softly.

She smiled and nodded sadly. I gulped down the sudden bile that had just risen. This was nerve-wracking.

As quickly as I could, I took the phone from Mrs. Smith and placed it against my ears.

"Hello?"

"Theia, Bryce is going crazy!" Marley whispered, sounding a mixture between panicked and excited.

My heart beat faster.

"W-what?"

"Yes, he's going crazy! He just walked into class today and then glared at me for a good minute before storming out!"

My eyes widened, and I gulped down nervously again. "He knows," I whispered, my heart beating at a rate I didn't think was capable or normal.

"Nah. It's nearly one. We didn't have any art class today. He would have been there if he knew. That happened in the morning. Matthew says he didn't leave your room at all last night, that he patrolled around your yard. Keith's worried he is going to hurt someone, or worst, himself and Rome, yeah…It's better not to even mention him. He is that bad." Marley giggled. The excitement in her voice seeped through the cellphone and towards me, but I shook my head. The ache in my heart seemed worse than it had been yesterday.

"I just don't want him to get hurt or hurt anyone because of me, Ley. I don't know why he can't just go to that woman he was so in love with. I'm gone now, aren't I? He's free now, isn't he? Why is he so selfish?" A tear slipped down my cheeks and onto the page of the book as I waited for Marley to reply. My breath hitched in my throat when I heard him.

"Who are you talking to?"

I froze. His voice sounded like home. But then, with how he behaved yesterday, it made me cry even more.

"My mother! Who are you? Private calls minister?"

A low growl emitted from somewhere around Marley's side. "Why do I have a feeling you're lying, Marley?"

"Why would I be lying? You're the one who hurt Theia so much she had to get away! Don't make this my fault, somehow. It's obvious it was you who did something wrong. She's gone! You won't get her back! Now, go sulk over what an amazing girl you have lost!"

I flinched when what sounded like a fist against a wall reached my ears. *What was going on there?*

"You will learn to respect your king!"

I heard Marley scoff. "You're no king of mine. I haven't mated with Keith, and you can't demand me to respect you when you least deserve it till then! Good day, King!" Marley sneered as I heard footfalls. I held my breath as I waited for her to start speaking again.

"That cheating scumbag pisses me off so bad! I'm going to the last class, and then I'll meet you at home, okay?"

Still numb over what just happened, I nodded then realized that she couldn't see me. Sighing, I muttered back a weak reply, "Okay, I'll see you here."

"What was it?" Mrs. Smith asked when she saw the look on my face.

I looked at her, my eyes wide with fear. I didn't want to see Bryce so soon. I just didn't.

"I think he knows," I whispered, looking at her with wide eyes. "I think he knows, but Marley told him to go away. I heard."

A proud look showed on Mrs. Smith's face, and she grinned down at me as I handed her cellphone back, murmuring a soft "thank you" with it.

"I'm glad she did. I was hoping for it too. Hopefully, I can give him a piece of my mind too!"

"He's—"

"Dangerous?" Mrs. Smith asked, her lips pulled up in a smirk. "Oh, honey, so is a woman scorned!"

I smiled. I suppose she was right…

Hell hath no fury like a woman scorned.

***

"Oh my God!" Marley exclaimed as soon as she set foot into the house. Her excited eyes found mine, and she laughed as she rushed her way to me.

"Oh my God, you won't believe what happened!"

I stared at her. A tiny smile of my own formed because of her bright ones. "What happened?"

"Alex finally dumped Diandra!"

My mouth hung open. "What! Why?"

Marley slightly grimaced at that. "Well, she finally gave in to pressure. She had your scent all over her yesterday. She supposedly refused to say if she had seen you. But today, after Bryce directly questioned her in front of all of us, she finally gave in and started to giggle over how pathetic you looked when she collided with you, all red-eyed, crying like crazy, blotchy face, the true ugly self you are—"

I grimaced and slumped in my seat. Ley caught my expression and moved towards me, engulfing me in a hug. "Hey, that's what she said! It's not true at all. She also said she was happy that you looked so broken and lost. It made her week. That's what you got for trying to steal her boyfriend. So Alex ripped the locket she had given him and handed it over to her and said how just because his mate had died didn't mean that he would ruin his life tolerating what a bitch she is! He stormed out. But not before looking at Bryce straight in the eye and saying, 'I hope you know how lucky you were to get her.' You should have seen Bryce. He looked completely broken. I kind of felt bad for him."

I couldn't do anything but stare at her while she recited the whole thing word by word. The inevitable feeling of a warm sense of sadness and appreciation towards Alex for speaking for me like that crept into my mind, and I promised myself to thank him later.

Marley reached forward and wiped a loose tear that I didn't even know had fallen, away. "It's okay. Don't cry. It'll be fine, okay?"

I nodded and moved in closer to give her a small hug.

"Do you have enough clothes?"

"Why?" I asked, suddenly curious.

"Mrs. Anderson called today; she suggested you stay here a couple of days until everything is settled a bit. Your dad is thinking of sending you back to California."

I looked down at my palms.

Do I have to run away like this without facing him? Is it even right to just leave without even hearing his side of the story?

What side? The side where he treated you so awkwardly and then flirted with someone else in front of you? He doesn't respect you. Surely, to have a mate in one's life is a necessity, but to love them is a choice…

No. I shook my head. I was going way over my head.

I was not going to go back without facing him. I would not tolerate him being with someone else while wanting to have me for himself. I would leave but not without giving him a proper goodbye. I would leave but on my terms.

Right now, though, I needed to keep a distance. I needed to sort this out. I needed to plan everything.

I looked up at Marley and nodded. "I have enough clothing and enough cash to buy more. I think Dad's right. I'm not going to tolerate being a third wheel. I will leave but not to California—well, maybe until I end school."

She looked at me sadly. "I understand. I don't want you to go, but I know you have to. I understand."

I smiled at her softly and closed my homework. Grabbing onto my stuff with one hand, I grasped onto her arm with another.

"Let's go watch that *Notebook* movie again. I'm ready to face the hotness known as Ryan Gosling. I promise I will pay attention tonight," I said, giggling slightly as I pulled her upstairs.

It was completely unfair of me to push my pain onto my best friend. The least I could do was try not to become a zombie that I felt like and do some girly things with her. Yes, I suppose it was time to start collecting memories. Maybe I should collect pictures?

***

I felt like shit. I was sure my top was wet from all the tears I had cried for the past two hours and six minutes.

"Pass me some more tissues please." I sobbed, not even trying to hold it in anymore because Marley was as bad as I was if not worse.

"Oh God, I had forgotten how bad that movie was! It stabbed me in my heart, Thi!" Marley hiccupped as she passed me the tissue box, took out some for herself, and proceeded to wipe off the freshly fallen tears.

"It's safe to say I'm never watching it again. But, Ley, that's how love is supposed to be. I wish…" I couldn't continue because I fell into another fit of sobs.

"Okay, get up!" Marley suddenly ordered as she got up from her position on the floor and extended her arms towards me.

"We're dancing to the first K-Pop song that's going to come on MTV Asia," she declared determinedly, pulling me up on my feet and switching the TV on again, only this time, switching it to MTV Asia.

"Oh my God, Ley, stop! Ha-ha," I squealed as she suddenly started twirling me around when "Fantastic Baby" by Big Bang came on.

By the end of the song, we were both panting from dancing like we were professional hip-hop dancers and completely mucking around her room. I lay on the floor, trying to catch my breath as Marley crawled her way towards me.

"You should go shower, woman. You stink." She giggled as she fell flat on her back beside me and positioned herself just as I did, with my arms and legs wide apart.

I rolled my eyes but giggled when I replied, "Talking about yourself, Ley?"

Ley only laughed more.

A smile seemed to have permanently etched itself on my lips as I got up to sit on the floor. I looked at Ley. "I think you're right, man. I do smell."

"Make a move then, soldier!" Marley mock-saluted me, still lying on the floor on her back. That only made us fall into another fit of laughter.

***

After pulling my cotton short shorts over my underwear, I slipped on a white cotton tank. My gaze found my reflection on the mirror, and I stopped slightly, my brown eyes large and red-rimmed. My face was flushed. I sighed.

That movie did a good number on me, I thought, shaking my head as I ran a comb through my hair. *That Bryce did a good number on you too, Theia.*

I stiffened but ignored the small voice in the back of my head. It wasn't helping.

Placing the hairbrush down on the vanity, my gaze landed on the clear doorway to the balcony. I smiled as I thought of fresh air and the smell of wet soil as it felt like rain was approaching. *Maybe a tiny stroll outside on the balcony would do me good.*

I moved towards the door. Still smiling, I slid open the door and moved out and rested my palm against the railing. It was a dark night. I supposed it was because of the impending rain. Thankfully, though, the night seemed quiet enough to close my eyes and breathe in a few breaths of peace.

My breath hitched as a memory bubbled up, and Bryce's face popped up, his hand on mine, holding me to the swing—the first time we met. Desperate to get that image away, I immediately snapped my eyes open. A single drop of tear slid down my cheek almost instantly.

"Sometimes it lasts in love. Sometimes it hurts instead," I whispered but laughed midway as a few more strands of tears made their way down. I was ridiculous, standing there singing a line from Adele's song.

I closed my eyes and breathed one last breath of the night air, the smell of wet soil, and the woods and turned towards the door.

Wait.

I froze and immediately spun around, searching the wood clearing.

I thought I saw…

I shook my head but stopped again when two bright yellow orbs glowered at me from the darkness. I stood frozen as the figure moved closer. Another tear slipped down my cheeks.

Don't cry, dammit! Don't cry!

I almost held my breath as I realized that I was actually shaking with fright.

Not now…Please, not now! I'm not ready! The two yellow orbs came closer, and then became three, then four, and then a dozen. I almost fainted of relief. *Fireflies…*

A small smile lit my face just as a gust of chilly wind hit my cheeks, sending my hair in disarray. Still smiling, I quickly tucked my hair behind my ears and turned around to quickly move into the room, sliding the door shut behind me.

"What were you smoking?" Ley asked as I padded my way towards her, my palms closed, holding a few fireflies that I had managed to catch.

"Here." I giggled. Standing in front of her, I pulled my palms away slowly. Three fireflies carefully settled on my fingers.

Marley's eyes widened as she watched the tiny torches moving around my palm, and she almost touched them when a huge crash sounded from the balcony door. The fireflies fled. Marley let out a loud scream as she looked towards the door. I stared at her wide-eyed, scared to look back as her gaze snapped between what was behind me.

"Come here, Theia!"

I froze instantly, my eyes widening, a rush of chills ran down my spine.

Bryce.

You know I would give everything to keep you with me, don't you, love?

"N-no," I stuttered. I needed to get my courage. I needed to face him. I was not going to be a third wheel.

I flinched as Bryce growled loudly, and the sound of glass breaking reached my ears again. I turned quickly on impulse. This needed to stop. I caught sight of him. Gone was my Bryce. This was his beast, his lycan. He stood just outside the balcony door, shattered glasses surrounding the once secure door. His canines were bared as he moved forward slightly. His dark hairy arms were outstretched as if to receive me into a hug, his only recently bleeding fists now healing.

I heard Marley whimper behind me as I unconsciously took a step towards Bryce. I gasped when I realized what I was about to do. *Shit.*

"Move back," Marley whispered, and I nodded, taking a step back. But it didn't last long because before I knew it, Bryce had stormed over to me and flung me over his shoulder, his dark fur brushing against my skin.

"Bryce, let me go!" I almost screamed, landing a few punches on his back. He only growled louder as he proceeded towards the balcony door.

I lifted myself up a little and looked at the startled, scared Smith family as they all looked at me with tears in their eyes. Marley wiped a tear away and mouthed an "I'm sorry." I only shook mine and sent back a "No, I'm sorry."

As Bryce brushed past the broken door, glasses dug past his bulky form, red immediately following its trail. I almost reached out to touch the wound when Bryce moved towards the railing. With the night air hitting my bare legs and arms, I shivered.

"Bryce, let go! I don't want to go with you!" I smacked his back again, harder this time.

"Shut up if you want everyone around us to survive, Theia, or I swear to God, I will slaughter each and every one of them!"

I held my breath as Bryce climbed on the railing with me still in his arms and jumped into the night, off the first floor.

CHAPTER TWENTY

The fall seemed effortless as we reached the ground smoothly. My head bobbed a bit, and I couldn't help but punch his back again.

"Let me go! I don't want to get kidnapped by you! Just let me go, okay?" I yelled as I squirmed in his hold. His claws on my thighs tightened, and I squirmed even more at the discomfort.

We just reached the edge of the woods when a slightly mad deranged Roman rushed forward. He moved around to face me when Bryce growled lowly in warning.

"Back off. cousin. She's mine."

I scoffed and punched him in the back again. Who the hell gave him the right to claim me when he already had a girlfriend? "Actually, I am Theia, not *mine*. And I missed you too, Rome."

A deadly growl ripped out of Bryce's throat, and I let out a startled scream as I got pushed against the trunk of a large tree. *Shit.* I stared into Bryce's glowing angry golden eyes.

"Let her go, brother! She doesn't need to be treated like this! You cannot possibility want to mark her after kidnapping her and that too against a tree—" Roman stopped immediately as Bryce turned towards him and snarled. Bryce seemed to be mulling over what he had said. "Calmly think it over. You both need to have a calm talk over this. Do not do something you will regret in the future, cousin."

With a last soft look in my direction and his gaze assuring and warm, Roman turned and fled into the woods. Bryce growled angrily, and I snapped my head towards him. His snout nearly grazed my jaw as he continued to push me against the tree, his sharp canines bared for all to see. Truthfully speaking, I was a bit scared. His claws were starting to impale me, but I don't think he took notice in his rage.

"You left me!" He growled, his canines nipping at my jaw lightly. His grip has now loosened itself around my waist. I almost thanked him for that.

Instead, I glared at him. "When I leave you, you will know."

His gaze darkened, and he growled loudly. An owl hooted somewhere in the distance. His arms tightened around my waist, and he pulled me closer.

"You will never leave me again!"

I couldn't even give him a proper reply before he hoisted me up on his shoulders again and ran at a speed I knew was not capable by human standards. Heck, even wolves couldn't run that fast.

Everything seemed like a blur as he ran, his claws gripping my thighs. He adjusted me over to his front, making me wrap my legs around his waist as he pushed my face against his chest and leaped up, latching onto a trunk of a tree. He growled as I whimpered at the impact but didn't stop for a second before he leaped again, this time, landing on solid ground.

"You can look now."

I almost flinched at his dark tone. His mere voice was doing a pretty good job at conveying how livid he was. I heard rain just beginning to pour down, and I nearly cried out loud. I supposed there was no escaping tonight. Hearing his command, I quickly unwrapped my arms and legs around him, but his claws tightened around my thighs. He pulled me against him again. I snapped my gaze to his and glared at him.

His snout was closer to me than what I would find comfortable, and his canines were displayed ferociously. The only place I could gain comfort was from his golden eyes that were now harboring specs of blue. *So beautiful…*

He gazed into my eyes as I reached out to touch him, almost wanting to know that what was happening and what was standing in front of me was real.

"You're the prettiest girl I know. I'll come by today, okay?" My eyes hardened, and I recoiled my hand back against my chest. *That ass!* I turned my attention to the walls behind him.

"Let me go," I said, my voice just as hard as my eyes. *The nerve of the guy to act as if nothing ever happened! Why I oughta shove a chopstick up his ass?*

"And what if I said no?" Bryce suddenly broke the silence. His claws retracted as well-maintained nails took its place, the hair all over him almost vanishing as rough skin managed to replace it. I glanced at him out of curiosity and stopped dead to stare at his blue eyes. Bryce was back.

I looked away. "Let me go, Bryce."

"Shut up! Shut up, shut up, shut up! W-why do you fucking have to say that over and over and fucking over again? I'm not letting you go. I am never letting you go! You're mine, and it will be my last day on earth when you leave me."

I stared at Bryce wide-eyed while he continued to heave in fury, literally shaking in anger. I noticed then that he was now towering over me, and I was now under him on the bed. Only then did I notice that an angry monster in between his leg was furiously poking me against my tummy. I flinched when Bryce caught my gaze's direction and growled in warning.

Surprised by the sudden sound, my eyes snapped to his, and his hips launched forward automatically. He groaned and dipped his face against my neck.

"Why did you just…run? It wasn't what you think it was…back in the car."

I stiffened, and Bryce seemed to notice. His eyes lifted to meet mine.

"Then what was it, Bryce? What was it if it wasn't you behaving very awkwardly with me, keeping me at arm's length and flirting with some girl over the phone right there in front of me? I'm not going to be a third wheel! I'm not going to be here just because you need your mate to survive and be strong but with someone else. I'm finishing high school, and then I'm leaving. I won't ever look back. You can be happy. Now, please let me go!"

I was thankful not one single tear dropped out of my eyes, and although everything was blurry and I really just needed to blink the tears away, I refused to show weakness. So instead, I turned away, presenting Bryce with my profile as the tears rolled down discretely.

"It's not what you think, Theia. I could never—I would—Theia, it's always going to be you. No one else. Believe me!"

I looked back at him, suddenly not caring if he saw my tears. "Prove it then."

His eyes hardened, and he moved away, his gaze darkening "Well, don't mind if I do." He growled back and began pulling a pair of navy blue sweatpants and a white shirt on.

"No, Momma, I wanna see Uncle Alex! Uncle Alex! No, Momma, *pweez*!"

Bryce moved towards the large door but then suddenly stopped and turned towards me, gesturing that I follow him. "You want proof, don't you?"

I only stared for a short second before getting out and scrambling after him. He pulled open the door and marched outside before I could even reach his side, so I hesitated and stopped by the door. *Was I wrong to presume things?*

My attention was piqued again when the little girl's squeal sounded around the hallway, reaching Bryce's room too. *Be calm, Thi. Let's see how he proves you wrong.* I heaved out a large sigh and quickly counted till ten before moving towards the door a little and slipping out of the room.

"Why *didn* you come over yesterday, Uncle Alex? Daddy and I were waiting all afternoon! You *tol* me on the phone you would in the *mownin*. You lied, Uncle Alex. You—you said lying is bad. Do I get to take away your candies now?"

I froze.

"Evangeline?"

The little girl currently hanging off of Bryce's waist turned her attention towards me sharply. Instantly, a very large smile formed on her lips as she quickly ripped herself off Bryce's embrace and ran towards me.

"Thi!" She jumped as I caught her midway and brought her tiny frame against mine for a hug. Evangeline turned towards her Mom who was regarding me with a warm, excited expression.

"Momma! She's the girl Daddy and I met at the beach! She's my best friend! Uncle *Dewek*! Uncle *Dewek* said she looked f-fit! Yes, fit!" Evangeline turned towards me. Her excited expression was contagious. "Uncle *Dewek* said you look fit, Thi." She frowned slightly. "What does fit mean, Thi? A-and *wahwo yew* doing in Uncle Alex's *woom*?"

I stiffened and then glanced at a livid Bryce. His gaze found mine, and he quickly moved over to us.

"Alex's mate! Thanks for having us, Theia?"

My mouth opened and then shut by itself as I looked at Chris standing there and looking at me with a big smile, his arms now wounding around his wife.

"Theia, this is my wife, Emily. Emily, she's the girl our Evangeline decided to stalk and knock down at the beach yesterday!" He glanced back at me, a large grin lighting up his face. "She snapped loads of pictures. And when you were running away from your friend, she dropped my iPhone flat against the sand and rushed in to knock you down."

I looked down at the slightly sorry Evangeline in my arms. She looked down as she continued to hug me, her arms around my neck. I smiled and then softly smoothened her blonde locks behind her ear.

"Well, I'm sure Evangeline and I could go visit the beach again soon. Aye, Eva?"

Her excited eyes snapped to mine, and she nodded enthusiastically. "*Ofcwos*! *Tamowo*?"

I shook my head. "I have school tomorrow, love."

She nodded, still excited. "Saturday?"

I grinned and nodded. "Saturday"

"Evangeline said Derek thinks Theia's fit. Is it true?" Bryce suddenly growled out, his low voice foreboding.

Chris's expression turned guarded instantly. He glanced at me and then at Bryce. A knowing look spread on his face, and he immediately shook his head. "He didn't mean it, Bryce. You know Derek never means things like those."

Bryce's expression only darkened. "That's the thing. I know Derek. He never notices women. And when he does…"

Bryce snapped his head towards mine. Just then, Evangeline tugged my top, and I let her down, allowing her to rush back to her slightly scared mother. I smiled at her, but she only mouthed a "Calm him down," gesturing to Bryce with her eyes before she excused herself. And with a final soft smile my way, she walked away with a sleepy Evangeline in hand.

I finally glanced towards Bryce, his gaze still on me.

"Can you show me those pictures, Chris?" he spoke, not once leaving my gaze.

I frowned and glanced at Chris. He frowned as well.

"I deleted most of them, man. Only the ones Eva made me promise I wouldn't delete until we printed it out and got it up in her little scrapbook."

"May I see them?"

I frowned as his eyes hardened on mine. *What is he doing?*

"Sure, man." Chris moved towards Bryce and then looked at me and smiled. "Come on over and check 'em out, Theia."

Ignoring Bryce's eyes on me, I smiled at Chris and moved forward to stand between the two men.

Chris shuffled over to his gallery, and I all but gasped at the picture of me moving out of the water with a creepy smile on my face. I knew it to be the time when I was sneaking towards Ley, but what I had clearly missed were the guys behind me bluntly looking as I passed. Chris slid over to the next picture. In this, I was sitting on top of a laughing Marley, a couple of grandpas and grandmas staring at us with wide eyes while, again, the younger generation stared, girls with amused grins and boys with smirks. I unconsciously shook my head, smiling at the memory. He then switched to the next picture. This one, I smiled at widely. I was standing by Chris, who was almost towering over me, with Evangeline hooked on my hips. We were all grinning widely. I gasped when I suddenly noticed the bunny ears Evangeline was making behind my head with her arm. Chris seemed to catch that too and laughed. "That's my girl."

"Derek shouldn't get his hands on this, Chris." Bryce almost spat icily before turning around and storming right back into the room.

I glanced back at Chris apologetically. He stood there, looking towards Bryce's direction, a smile playing on his lips.

"Haven't mated yet?"

My jaw fell to the floor. I gasped at his bold question. "What?"

He shrugged, the smile still intact as he looked down at me.

"Because he would have killed Derek if you were both mated. Territorial tendencies only increase in intensity after mating with your mate. For all wolves, I almost feel sorry you got a royal. We're worse. You should go before he loses his temper thinking you've run away."

I glanced towards the bedroom door, worried.

My head shot towards him, wide-eyed, and I nodded.

"Thank you for showing us the pictures," I mumbled, genuinely thankful.

Chris only shook his head, a chuckle breaking past his lips.

"I only made things worse. You'll see. I apologize, though. One just does not listen to Alexander. I advise you to be patient tonight. Good night, Theia. I'll see you in the morning."

I stood staring at him as Chris walked away and rounding around a hallway, disappeared from sight.

What was he talking about? With a deep sigh, I turned towards the bedroom door.

Why didn't you come over yesterday, Uncle Alex? My back straightened, and my eyes widened. Evangeline was the girl Bryce was talking to? I shook my head and walked back towards the bedroom door.

But what if it was? I froze my mind reeling with possibilities. *What if it was, Theia?* Had I blown this one out of proportion? I looked towards the door, my mind on the man that was beyond it. Could he have been talking to Evangeline?

I sighed, shook my head and continued to slip into the room. The room was now partially dark. The only lights illuminating it were the table lamps. A shudder ran down my spine when I noticed a hunched Bryce sitting on the bed, his head dropped low, and his fingers curled together on his lap. He looked up as I closed the door. Bryce's eyes solely stuck on mine.

"Do you believe me now?" he asked tentatively in a clipped voice.

I didn't answer immediately, looking away on purpose. *What was I supposed to say? It wasn't tangible proof. Did I really want to risk this?* A little voice in me kept urging me to just leap onto his lap and tell him I believed him, but the part of me that still bore the wounds from yesterday always managed to hold me back.

"Theia." I looked up. "Do you believe me now?"

A knock sounded throughout the room, and both Bryce and I instantly turned towards the door. It creaked open only minutes later, Matthew's and Roman's heads sticking in. I frowned in confusion. Behind me, Bryce immediately let out a warning growl and leaped up in front of me.

"Now is not a great time, boys. I'm tired and extremely pissed off, and if you so much as breathe down on my mate, I will rip out your heads from your neck. How many fucking times do I have to say it? She's mine! And I won't share! So get the hell out of our room."

Woah!

Heads still sticking in, Roman turned towards Matthew. "What an ungrateful dick."

Matthew chuckled and nodded. "What an ungrateful dirty dick. He hasn't showered since yesterday remember."

Bryce growled and was about to leap onto the boys when I quickly grabbed onto his arm His head shot back. Canines were bared and eyes shining golden. I gulped down a frightened whimper and turned towards the boys, motioning them in. Immediately, Bryce's arms wrapped around me. I sighed into his embrace and let him hold me. There was no reason to anger him anymore.

Matthew and Roman grinned at each other as they strode in. I was glad to see that Roman looked happier and healthier than he had only just a few hours ago. I suppose whatever they carried in that laptop of theirs really did have a good impact on their moods.

Matthew looked at me, his grin still intact. "I don't believe Bryce can ever cheat on you, Thi."

What? My eyes narrowed. Maybe it wasn't such a good idea to let them in. They were confusing the hell out of me. What were they even up to?

Bryce stiffened behind me, his arms holding me tighter than it did a minute ago as if he had picked up on my uneasiness. I leaned into him.

"What are you talking about?"

Rome's eyes dropped a bit, and his previous sadness seeped in, his expression slightly dead again. He regarded me with a heavy sigh. "Bryce can't cheat on you, Thi."

"And how can you say that?"

Matthew and Roman grinned again and turned the laptop towards us. What looked like security camera footage started playing.

I watched as Bryce walked down a store aisle when he suddenly stopped and started checking out boxes of what looked like dried fruit and nuts. I stared as he reached out, quite clearly, picked up a box and began reading its package. Just then a lady wearing a yellow dress rounded the corner and slowly made her way past the aisle, coming to a stop beside Bryce. It seemed like she wanted the nuts that were directly placed in front of Bryce. When she reached out to grab hold of it, Bryce immediately flinched and glared at the woman. The woman seemed to have gotten quite a fright because she immediately rushed off, the nuts and trolley forgotten.

My head snapped towards Bryce, a shocked expression on my face. He just looked down at me blankly.

"It's not over yet," Matthew called out cheerfully.

Sighing, I looked back on the screen.

This time, the camera focused on a woman who seemed to be drinking a glass of juice in the kitchen. She seemed young enough and extremely beautiful too. I immediately tensed up when Bryce walked into the kitchen wearing a white vest and a pair of dark blue jeans. He nodded a greeting at the woman before he grabbed the fridge door and pulled out a tray of pie. I smiled as he took four slices. Bryce smiled slightly in the screen as he moved towards the kitchen sink to wash his hands just as the woman turned to wash her glass. Bryce immediately flinched back, a look of disgust on his face as the lady came closer to him within nine inches and snarled at her. This time, the woman however only smiled and moved back, immediately easing Bryce's stance.

My frown deepened. *Why was he so defensive?*

Another footage rolled on the screen.

He was sitting in the library and a book in his hands. He quickly flipped the pages, a look of concentration on his face. A smirk found its way to my lips when Meryl slipped into the room slowly with a creepy smile on her lips as she walked towards Bryce, not making a single sound. She reached closer and closer but just as she was about to shout, "Boo," Bryce turned around quite sharply and let out a deadly growl. I immediately let out a whimper, closing my eyes in fright.

"Meryl, I'm sorry! It's just...It's just..."

"You don't do well amongst other women?" Meryl seemed to smile as she moved slowly around the large sofa and sat near Bryce.

I watched with interest as Bryce looked at her surprised.

"Yes," he replied and hesitated but then continued, "I don't know how, but other women, I do not find them attractive, just bland, not...colorful...well, other women who aren't Theia. They can barely stand beside me without me snarling at them. It's like my wolf doesn't want to have any other female around us except for Thi. Is-is this—"

"Normal?" Meryl cut him once again with a smile. "Your father was like this too, don't you remember? Something your mom appreciated wholeheartedly. I suppose it runs in the family. Having Theia as mate doesn't only mean that she is yours. It also means that you are hers. You both belong to each other. Do you find this trait not likable?"

My eyes widened with surprise when the Bryce in the camera smiled. He shook his head. "No. I might like the idea of belonging to her. And now, I feel less manly."

Roman and Matthew couldn't seem to hold it in as they both fell on the floor laughing. I chuckled slightly too. It was sweet how he said it.

"Get out!"

Everyone except for Bryce froze. Matthew and Roman immediately scurried up from the ground, grabbed the laptop and fled.

I couldn't help but yell out, "Thank you, guys!"

"Good night, Theia," they both yelled from the other side of the door. Bryce immediately walked towards the door and moved back. It all took about a second. Sometimes I felt extremely jealous of their abilities. He stood in front of me. His blank eyes were calculative, yet for a second, I actually thought his eyes warmed up.

I looked down at my feet. "You belong to me, huh?"

He didn't reply. I almost whimpered by the lack of reply.

What if he was mad at me?

Bryce caught me by surprise when he tilted my head upwards with his thumb and index finger. His thumb caressed my chin as I stared into those blue orbs, my breath slightly catching in my throat.

"What do you think?"

My breathing stopped. Time stopped.

"Hmm?" he mumbled again, his thumb caressing my lower lip and slightly parting it before moving over to caress my cheeks.

"I-I—"

Fuck, stop stuttering, Theia!

"Do you believe me now?"

I looked up to him. My face fell by his expression. Bryce stood in front of me, his eyes sad but a little hopeful. I blinked back the tears that were now threatening to fall down.

I couldn't help it any longer. Pushing aside everything running around my mind, I jumped on him, and my hands hooked around his neck as he quickly wrapped his arm around my waist.

"I'm sorry!" I sobbed as I kissed all over his face, framing his face with my palms. "You were distant and then…and then—"

"It's okay, love." Bryce breathed against my cheeks, placing a quick kiss on the spot.

I held him closer.

"Bed?" he asked softly. I nodded, pressing a kiss on the base of his neck. Bryce froze, and his breath hitched in his throat.

"Don't do that," he muttered as he walked over to the bed and laid me down softly. He moved away, but I quickly pulled him back.

"Do what?" I whispered back against his neck and then placed a soft kiss on the spot I had just a few minutes ago. Only this time, I nibbled lightly before I let go. "This?"

"Dammit, Theia, please!"

"Please, what?"

"Please stop!"

I looked at him. "You mean it?"

His gaze shot to mine.

"No." He groaned and leaning in, pressed his lips against minc. Passionatc, I supposcd that was thc only way I could dcscribc the kiss. The battle of dominance was lost the minute his tongue slipped between my lips. I pulled him closer to me, moaning as he deepened the kiss. We broke free to catch our breath, and Bryce let out a chuckle before leaning in, nipping on my bottom lip and pulling it teasingly as he broke away again.

He dipped his face into the crook of my neck and placed a soft kiss on my sweet spot. "I want to mark you so badly."

A soft, breezy sigh left my lips. "Then why don't you?"

Bryce groaned at my reply and nipped on my sweet spot, pulling it between his teeth. I clutched onto his shoulder as he ran the tip of his tongue along the hot throbbing spot before pulling it between his lips again and nipping on it lightly. He repeated this once again before pecking the slightly buzzy spot.

"It's not that easy."

"Are you going to tell me how so?" I wrapped my arms around him, his heavy weight feeling weirdly comforting on top of me.

Bryce sighed, turning us over, so I lay on top of him. I smiled at him softly caressing his cheeks.

"Not tonight. For now, this will have to do," he murmured, caressing my sweet spot.

"Bryce?" I mumbled in a small voice after a comforting moment of silence.

I knew there was a thin chance, but I still had to ask.

"Hmm."

I sighed. *Well, here I go.*

"Can I call Marley and my parents?"

"No!" He snapped immediately, shooting up in bed so that I sat straddling him, his arms now tightly wound around my waist. "No, I won't let you go! That girl tried to keep me from you, and your dad didn't cooperate at all!"

I sighed and pulled my face away a little so I could look at him. "Okay, okay, let's go to sleep tonight, but I want to talk to them tomorrow, Bryce. They only wanted what was best for me. I did need space to cope, and Marley helped me. You can't punish her for something she did for me."

"You didn't even seem sad."

My eyes widened. "What?"

"You don't even seem mad or upset in those pictures!" Bryce growled, his eyes lowered.

I frowned. "Would you rather—"

"I know! I know, okay. I know you've cried. I can see it in your face. I saw it tonight from the woods. It just fucking pisses me off that she can make you smile, and all I fucking do is make you cry all the time!"

I shook my head, slightly oblivious of the tears that managed to escape me as I tilted Bryce's face so he would look at me.

"Don't you ever say that again. It was my fault as well. I should have stayed and demanded an answer or gotten your side of the story too. I'm sorry. I didn't mean to hurt you so much."

He sighed.

"Come here," Bryce said as he wiped the tears off my cheeks.

We gazed at each other, his fingertips still lingering on my cheeks. I smiled slightly before grasping his t-shirt and pulling him forward, capturing his lips with mine.

CHAPTER TWENTY-ONE

I woke up to a heavy weight on my stomach. I tried to push it away, but it wouldn't budge. This was futile. Groaning tiredly, I tried to move, and my eyes slowly fluttered open, but I quickly shut them close because of the impeccable amount of light shining through the tall, wide windows.

"Mmm…"

I stiffened slightly as Bryce groaned, pressing his face closer against my neck. With the heavy feel of his head on my chest, I felt his warm breath against my neck. I sighed and wrapped an arm around him, turning my head towards the open window. The chilly breeze hit my skin strangely soothingly. I closed my eyes and smiled at the calmness it brought with each breeze.

A knock sounded around the room, and I felt Bryce climb closer to me.

"Bryce." He snuggled in closer. "Bryce!"

I winced slightly as his arms tightened around me. Three sharp raps on the door followed. I lifted my head up slightly then turned towards Bryce again.

"Bryce, wake up!" I yelled, grabbing his shoulders and trying to push him off now.

A low rumble erupted from his chest, and his eyes shot open, yellow, no blues.

"What's wrong?" he said, his tone sharp as he turned towards the door.

"Someone's at the door. Get up!" I murmured, trying to slowly push him off.

His head snapped to mine.

"Don't do that!"

"Can you not?"

"Not what?"

"Glare at me with those beautiful golden eyes. I have to admit, though, I love your blues better."

His lips pulled up slightly, and he leaned in, his eyes on mine.

This is your chance, Thi! Move it! I smirked at him, and confusion glazed his features. *Well, this is going to be easy.*

With a speed I could almost give myself an award for, I slipped out from under him and quickly rushed towards the sofa. I slumped on it, grinning.

"Don't do that too!" He growled as he stalked towards me. I rolled my eyes again and leaned back, tucking my legs underneath me.

"Say, where can I get clean and dressed? Considering I don't have my brush, my clothes—crap, I don't have anything here!"

My wide eyes shot up to Bryce's slightly amused ones. He slowly took a seat beside me, and I frowned at how easily he was ignoring the person on the other side of the door.

"He's given up," Bryce spoke up as if he had read my mind. He smirked when my eyes widened. "For now, that is."

"How do you know it was a he?" I blurted out, still staring at him with wide-eyed fascination. The werewolf world seemed to be getting more and more interesting day by day.

"Scent," Bryce muttered, grasping my hand with his overly large one and pulling me towards a white door. He pushed open the door and nudged me in.

Looking around the elegant looking bathroom, I smiled. I turned towards him.

"Thanks. Wait!" I was about to close the door but forgot to ask something. Pulling the door open, I asked Bryce, embarrassed slightly, "Brush and towel?"

"Top right corner of the bottom shelf."

"Thanks!" I smiled and turning around closed the door.

***

Dropping the wet toothbrush in the holder beside the faucet, I was on my way out the bathroom, slightly nervous, and upon realizing Bryce was not in the room, I made a mad dash towards the other door across the room.

The large brown leathered bag was hardly small enough to miss as it sat on the dark wooden floors. I seated myself, towel-clad on the little white seat just beside it and started rummaging through my bag. I flinched and shuddered when my fingers laced around a very interesting piece of undergarment I had sworn I would never slip my legs into. Bryce really did know how to narrow down his preference.

"God, there's nothing wearable here!" I groaned, smacking a palm against my forehead and dragging it down my face, an exasperated sigh releasing itself from my lips with the motion.

After another futile attempt at finding a decent-sized simple panty, I finally gave up. I fished out the most decent pair of black lingerie in the bag and slipped it on. Making a grasp for my tiny black shorts, I hurriedly shrugged it on too when my eyes caught a certain bluish-gray sweater set on top of a large white chair. I slowly made my way towards it. It felt all soft and warm against my fingers as I ran a slow line down its intricate patterns.

Would Bryce mind me wearing this? Bryce? Sweater? I hesitated for a second, staring at the sweater as I had pondered on the thought before the sweater won, and I put it on.

Finding my body lotion in the corner compartment of the bag, I quickly pulled it out and was just about to apply it on my legs when the sound of the door opening caught my attention. My attention was piqued, and I quickly ran my palms along my legs and arms before opening the closet door and walking out, my comb in my hand, hidden carefully behind my back.

"Aaah!"

"Fuck!"

I wriggled back against the floor, panting, away from the man currently lying on it, holding his head in his hand, covering the spot I hit with my comb. In my defense, I was merely protecting myself. Another man, his accomplice, was also on the floor holding his head in his hand but not from pain, instead, from undeniably loud laughter.

I watched the two men wide-eyed, still trying to control my wildly beating heart as I clutched my hands to my chest, panting from fright.

"Fuck, that hurt, Thi!" Matthew groaned in pain as he finally managed to look up at me. He reached his arms for me and tried to crawl closer. I gulped, still feeling startled before a little bit of the shock rushed cold, and I dragged my butt towards him, taking his hand away from his head and gently trying to probe for any swellings or lumps.

"You're such an idiot, Matt! You scared me!" I said, smacking his biceps before narrowing my eyes, scowling at Rome, who was still busy rolling on the floor having a laugh fest.

"Stop being a jerk, Romanov!"

His laughter immediately stopped, and he frowned at me.

"Don't call me that!"

I frowned at him harder. "Or what?"

Roman's frown turned into a smirk, and he moved forward. "Wouldn't you like to know?"

He added with a wink in the last second, and I almost rolled my eyes at his childishness.

"What are you guys here for, anyway?"

Rome smiled, turning towards Matthew, and Matthew smiled back almost creepily. *What are these two—*

"Oomph—Rome!"

"What?" Rome chuckled, holding me down on the floor, his arms around me as he held me in a bear hug. "I missed you! I was so worried!"

I wrapped my arms around him as I noticed the slight wavering of his tone before it turned into a whisper by the end. I supposed Matthew noticed the deeper turn the mood had taken and moved in to hug me too, pulling both Rome and me into the embrace.

"I missed you too, Theia. Don't ever run like that!" Matthew nuzzled his face in my hair. Chuckling, Matthew continued, "Anybody hungry? I know I am!"

Just on cue, my stomach rumbled, and I immediately let out a giggle. "I'm starving. I'm sure you all know that, though."

"Oh, we know." Rome chuckled, getting to his feet before extending his hands towards me.

I smiled at the boys as Matthew did the same. What is with these two idiots? Still smiling, I grabbed both their hands and let them help me to my feet. We walked out of the room, closing the door behind us, all three of us hand in hand, swinging our entwined arms as we walked towards our destination.

***

"Well, Mr. Phelps was asking about you in class yesterday. He said to pass you his get well soon wishes." Matthew chuckled as we walked the last step down the stairs into the living room. I giggled when Matthew wiggled his eyebrows suggestively and nudged him on his side.

A growl rang throughout the air, causing all three of us to come to a halt. My gaze shot up to meet a bulky middle-aged man. His glare was directly upon me. He launched forward, almost in a violent run, while I stood there, confused why he was behaving this way. It wasn't until Rome launched forward and pushed the man away did I break out of my shocked state.

The man snarled loudly as he quickly backed up and made a move towards me again.

"You wouldn't dare if you valued your life, pup," Rome muttered icily, his dark claws currently retracting from his nail beds quite visible as he stood in front of me, almost holding me captive in his shadow.

"She hurt my daughter. She made my daughter try to kill herself. I'm going to kill her! I'm going to rip her throat apart!"

I could only whimper as the man's eyes dead with hatred glared into mine.

"I don't know what you're talking about, sir," I whispered, immediately pulling away as he almost growled louder and pushed forward towards me with bruising force. For a second, I thought he would break past Roman's grip. Thankfully, he didn't.

"Diandra! You ruined my daughter's life! She doesn't want to live anymore! She wants to move away and go rogue!"

"Enough, Sethrium! You will be detained in the holding quarters until you learn to control yourself and respect your luna!" Matthew spat, just as Roman started dragging the scary snarling man away from me. Meanwhile, all I could do was watched teary-eyed at the defeated look in the man's eyes as he got pulled away. Had I really ruined Diandra's life?

"The kitchen is just beyond that corridor towards the left, okay? It's a private kitchen; that means the cooks won't be there. That's just for the alpha, his luna, and his guests. Eat something. And after finding out about this, Alpha will not be happy, so you might not want to add that to his list, aye?"

I nodded.

"Now go!" Matthew murmured softly, putting both his hands on my shoulder and turning me into the direction of where the kitchen was.

I sighed as I slowly padded my way there and almost gasped at all the modern appliances lined up. My low mood slightly lightened, and I stepped behind the kitchen counter, tapping my fingertips against the island's smooth surface, thinking of what to make for breakfast.

I smiled. A full-fledged English breakfast sounded great. I quickly made my way towards the refrigerator and pulled out the ingredients I needed to use. I wasn't one to eat bacon, but I supposed Bryce would've minded if his breakfast excluded that one important bit, so I gathered that packet in my hands too.

Quickly sauntering around the kitchen, I seasoned the sausages, mushrooms, and tomatoes with a little dab of salt and pepper before placing them on the already heated grill. The aroma from the tomatoes and sausages made my stomach grumble harder, and I almost giggled out loud as I quickly turned towards the next thing. I placed the pan of grilled black pudding and bacon away together with the sausages, mushrooms, and tomatoes and poured baked beans into another pan already warming on the stove.

I wonder if Bryce will like it…

"I didn't know I'd find you here."

My stirring stopped, the wooden spoon in my hand coming to a sudden halt. I immediately turned around, only to move back in reflex. Evangeline's Uncle Derek stared back at me, a small grin played on his lips as he stood just behind me, a little too close for comfort.

Breathe, Theia…He is just another guy who thinks you look good, just another guy.

"I don't think I know why you'd even want to find me," I replied, quickly composing myself as I turned back to the stirring.

"But isn't that what's exciting? The whole process of finding out?" Derek chuckled behind me. I could feel him step a little closer.

"I'm sorry. Did you want something?" I asked him as formal as I could, pretending that I had not heard what he said.

"Go out with me to dinner tonight?" Derek almost immediately blurted out, and I froze as his palms landed on my shoulder.

And for the second time that day, I was turned around by someone else; this time, however, to face a warm, hopeful looking Derek. But Derek wasn't what my eyes landed on when I turned around. Instead, my eyes fell and locked upon livid gold ones, standing by the kitchen entrance. I froze.

Bryce's eyes shot towards the palms that were still settled on my shoulders and then back towards me before they moved back towards the palms and then towards Derek. His white shirt looked stretched by his bulging muscles.

I could feel as Derek frowned and turned towards where was I looking at, although his hand made no indication of moving. I gaped at him ,bewildered. Was he inviting death?

"Alexander, my man, it's good to see you! I thank you for allowing us in your home's comforts till this meeting between the monarchs blow over. I really do not agree with what King Boiston is petitioning. Branding rogues as dangerous? Ridiculous! Well, I— Alex, are you all right?" Derek spoke loudly and passionately until he noticed the look on Bryce's face.

I sighed. This man was too dense for his own good. I shrugged his hands off my shoulders and stood still as Bryce started stalking his way to me all the while daring me to move an inch or to look away. I did not.

My arms slipped around his neck automatically as he wrapped an arm around my waist and with the other, quickly turned off the stove, saving the baked beans. He used his free arm to move a stray lock behind my ear before he smiled slightly, visibly calm now that he had me in his arms, and placed a soft, warm kiss on my forehead.

I smiled at him too.

Bryce turned towards a now slightly shaking Derek. I frowned at the expression on the latter's face. *Why was he so mad?*

"Am I to assume that she is your mate, then?"

I winced slightly as Bryce's grip on me tightened. "Derek, meet my mate, Theia." He turned towards me with a warm smile. "Babe, meet King Derek Mccgal"

My eyes widened. *King?*

"Hi," I mumbled slowly, deciding against extending my arm for a handshake.

Derek's bitter expression softened slightly, and Bryce's frown increased. "Hi," Derek murmured back slowly, almost softly, as he looked me directly in the eye. He turned towards Bryce and nodded. "I'm going to your lands a little. See you by noon."

I smiled slightly as Derek moved out of the kitchen and looked at Bryce to see his jaws set. As if sensing my eyes on him, Bryce looked down. And within a heartbeat, his lips crashed on mine. I clutched onto him as he pulled me up and placed me on the island, wrapping my legs around him. I could only moan as he deepened the kiss.

"Do you mind if I borrow the breakfast, considering you both prefer eating each other's faces instead?"

We both froze. Bryce groaned as he broke away and placed his forehead against mine, both of our breaths heavy and wild. I couldn't help it. I leaned in and placed a tiny kiss on his swollen pink lips. He groaned and pulled me closer.

"I must admit. I do want to become a grandma desperately. So please do continue, just not on the kitchen island for Lord's sake!" Meryl continued. Her tone was humorous.

I giggled as Bryce let out a growl before he placed a chaste kiss on my nose and pulled me down to my feet, still not letting me go then.

"Oh, thank God, they are done. I thought we would never be able to have breakfast," Matthew said as he and Roman marched into the kitchen, Chris, Emily, and Evangeline in tow.

Evangeline smiled brightly as she spotted Bryce and me with his arms still wrapped around me. She quickly rushed forward and jumped into my arms. She turned towards Bryce, her grin not even wavering once.

"You lied, Uncle Alex. You think Thi is the *pwettiest* girl you know, not me. I see it in the way you *wuk* at her. It's beautiful. Do you think I will *fain* my *pwince* one day?"

A slightly shocked Bryce finally moved towards the young girl, his face level to hers. He placed a kiss on her forehead.

"Of course, you will, princess. Of course, you will."

***

The wooden floors creaked underneath my feet as I followed Bryce to wherever he was leading me. The walls in this part of the castle looked to be renovated too although the original pieces of the castle were left displayed on the walls. The bricks were also exposed, no paint adorning them. The wooden planks were in their original brown shade. It was unclear if they were stained or not, but they looked beautiful, nonetheless.

Bryce opened the door and moved aside, motioning me to move in. I nodded and walked through the open doors, only to come to a stop.

"It's so beautiful," I murmured softly as I eyed the room.

Designed simply with cream and white furnishing and ornaments, the room seemed the epitome of modernized vintage. There was a living room, a bedroom, a bathroom, what seemed a door leading towards a closet, and finally, a glass door leading to a beautiful balcony.

I turned towards Bryce with a twinkle in my eye before settling in his arms. I sighed happily.

After the kitchen incident, we had all settled to having a nice morning breakfast. Surprisingly, my cooking had sufficed for the crowd of eight, and Roman declared his plans on making me his private cook. Matthew and Meryl didn't seem too behind with that idea. It was sad because Bryce had a meeting around noon and disappeared throughout the rest of the afternoon only to appear at about six, and I was busy lying in bed and reading a book I had found underneath his bed.

He smiled and leaned in to give me a peck on my lips, which turned out to be a full-fledged make-out session within minutes. His lips probably left a dozen red bruises all along my shoulder and cleavage, his hips grinding against mine, and the angry monster between his legs dominating each thought and sense. I gasped when Bryce slipped his hand underneath the sweater and run a thumb over my nipples; even more so when Bryce had broken free with a growl and immediately informed me that he had something to show me.

When I was told he would show me something, I assumed it would be my parents or Marley. But here we were inside what for me was the most enchanting room in the castle even though I had barely seen most of the rooms in the castle.

Why he showed me this, I still didn't know.

"This is your room, Theia. You will be sleeping here from tonight."

I froze in his arms.

"What?" I asked dumbly as I stared up at him wide-eyed.

Bryce sighed slowly and shook his head. Making a move towards the door, he turned towards me again.

"We can't sleep together. Lock the doors before you sleep, Theia. Open for no one."

I could only stand there wide eyed and watch him as he turned again and walked away.

What the hell had just happened?

CHAPTER TWENTY-TWO

Somewhere in the distance, the tower bells chimed. My eyes automatically moved towards the wall clock.

It was ten o'clock, exactly two hours after Bryce had left me here in the beautiful concrete room. I left the windows open. The hope of Bryce paying me a visit through the window just like he did back home was winning over the rationality of the fact that this was a castle and my house had barely two floors.

I sighed and slumped down in a fairly comfortable chair, pulling my legs up as I did. When Bryce had kidnapped me, proved his innocence, and cleared the misunderstanding, I assumed that everything would go back to how they were before he changed.

It was a shame to know that things were the same, and he was still distant. It frustrated me. It made me want to storm up to his room and demand an explanation although I was not sure how I was going to find it without getting lost. I rubbed my chin thoughtfully and leaned against the comfortable armrest. The chilly night breeze blew in effortlessly through the open balcony doors, dancing beautifully with the flimsy white drapes.

With the height of where the castle was situated, I was sure the lights shimmering in the far distance was that of the city. Modernization was slightly far, considering the vast amount of land the castle occupied. Still, the presence of the city lights in harmony with the clear night sky was soothing enough for me not to feel suffocated, alone in this room.

I glanced towards the door. My fingers now drumming an unconscious beat. I had not locked the door. I had left that open too in hopes that Bryce might return through there. But after waiting for two hours, I supposed it was clear he would not. Was I to sleep here every night and why? Why wouldn't Bryce let me go home?

A sigh left my lips again. It was obvious why. He was uncertain that I would stay. He was uncertain if I would run again. I almost didn't blame him. I supposed hiding away was a rash decision, but I knew that I would do it again if I could. Self-preservation came first. I admit I was scared of heartbreaks. I almost laughed at that. It was silly how I was scared of heartbreak, but here I was experiencing it again on a small scale and without the actual break. But I was indeed, experiencing it. The ache in my heart proved to that.

I leaned against the warm, comforting embrace of the armchair, my arms now tightly holding the large, thick blanket around me. I couldn't help but wonder why Bryce would turn away like that and be well on his way to ravishing me one moment and the next, move me to a room across the castle from his with an order to not let anyone in? I shook my head, trying to clear myself of the confusion.

"If you didn't want anyone with me at night, why not keep me with you? Why send me away?" I mumbled out loud, my words floating in thin air.

I sighed and closed my eyes. All this was so confusing. The need to go home and just sleep it off was actually taking over me, almost that I was suddenly craving the feel of my bed, the glowing string lights, my dad's warm embrace and even my mom's innuendo-filled jokes. Deep in thought, I didn't even notice as a tear slipped down my cheeks and hit the blanket below.

"Theia!" My head snapped up and immediately went to the door. The sudden sounds of hushed whispers hung around my room, echoing back at me from the brick walls as I sat there on the armchair and stared at the source of the argument, beyond the door.

"You're one to say—"

I didn't even know I was up and walking towards the door when a sudden crash sounded from the outside, and there was another round of muffled yells and growls. I reached the door, my heart thumping as I gripped the door with my slightly sweaty palms and twisted it lightly.

Should I do it?

"She doesn't des—"

I frowned.

"What's it about her—"

Yes, you should.

I pulled on the door lightly and peaked outside. Shadows marred the walls to my right. By the looks of it, one had his arms around the others neck.

"You're accusing me with baseless amount of reasoning, Delta!" The man snarled. I watched as the shadow holding the man around his neck leaned in.

Delta? Matthew? My heart started beating faster, the need to remove Matthew from danger now overwhelming.

"A reasoning you are only putting out as baseless because you know it's true, King Mccgal." Matthew spat back. I couldn't help but peek out of the door a bit more, still carefully enough not to be spotted.

Why is Matthew fighting with Derek?

A shudder ran down my spine as a heart-chilling laughter broke free from Derek's lips. I watched as his grip loosened around Matthew's neck, and he moved back, still laughing. He suddenly stopped and then glared at Matthew. All traces of humor vanishing from his good-looking features. The two man stood in the hallway illuminated by pale yellow lights, slightly reminding me of the medieval wall torches.

"It's quite foolish to tell me to stop having feelings for Theia when you, yourself, have such a large crush on the girl, not to mention that beta of yours shows to be a little too possessive over her for his own good too!"

My breath hitched in my throat. *A crush? Matthew? But how?*

My head snapped up when I heard a sudden crunching of bones, only to realize that Matthew was now the one smiling. His hands were now formed into fists. Derek's eyes darkened. He regarded Matthew with a glare.

"Yes. I love Theia. I don't care if she is spoken for. The sad thing here, though, is I can hug Theia. She trusts me. She adores me, but you are just another stranger to her. The sad thing here is that although I love her, I know I will find my mate someday, and I will love again." I watched wide eyed as Matthew confidently moved closer to a shaking Derek. "I know it's wrong. I don't make my moves on her. When will you learn that she belongs to Alex? She is not yours to begin with! Leave her alone, King Mccgal! This one is Bryce's. Get your own mate, instead!"

It all happened in a heartbeat. I couldn't even scream before Derek had changed halfway and slashed his claw across Matthew's face.

"You best learn your place, Delta. What I want is my concern. Mind your own fucking business." Derek spat venomously and turned around to stalk away.

I rushed out and towards a heaving and bloodied Matthew as soon as Derek stormed away from the scene. My eyes were blurry from the hot tears threatening to wash down my face. I proceeded to try and pick up a still limp Matthew. His eyes widened as he saw that it was me who was helping him up.

"Matthew, get up please!" I sobbed, trying to pull him up as hard as I could.

"Thi, you heard. I'm sorry." He groaned, pulling himself up as much as he could so he could lean on me. I pulled him towards my room.

"Stay here!" I ordered him, still sobbing as I sat him on the bed and rushed towards what Bryce said was a closet.

I walked out with two shirts, one I placed on the bed and the other I ripped into pieces. I rushed towards the bathroom and emerged with pieces of wet cloth, a bowl of water, and a first aid kit.

"Take off that shirt." I urged Matthew and moved towards the first aid kit.

The sound of fabric tearing up sounded throughout the room, and I quickly started wiping off the blood from his face, wincing when he winced and shuddering slightly as the deep gashes cleared away of blood. *This is all my fault.* Putting the cloth in the bowl, I quickly applied the antiseptic and sighed when the skin slowly started to heal itself in front of my eyes, the gashes turning near nonexistent as it healed.

"I'm sorry," Matthew murmured slowly, his voice as low as a whisper, and my eyes snapped to his.

"How?" I murmured back sadly as I handed him the button up t-shirt. I didn't even know what I wanted to know from him.

"I thought you'd know when I told you the type of girl I wanted as a girlfriend. But you didn't. And I realized just how little you notice about yourself. That made me like you more. It's just a crush. I know. Don't worry. I'll find my mate too someday. What are you doing here, though?"

I couldn't help it. I leaned in and hugged Matthew, sobbing against him. He patted my back comfortingly.

"You were stupid for going around warning a king, you know?"

Matthew breathed out a shaken breath, moving lower in bed as he closed his eyes, suddenly looking more tired than he ever had for the month.

"I know."

I sighed and moved away. Grabbing hold of the bowl, cloth, and first aid, I walked into the bathroom, threw the cloth and Matthew's ripped shirt into the bin, and washed and placed the bowl and first aid kit. I walked into the room again, changed and blood-free; I smiled when my gaze fell upon a snoring Matthew, his gash halfway healed.

The distant tower bells chimed again, and I sighed as I picked up a pillow and moved towards a sofa in the far corner of the room near the balcony door. It was eleven o'clock. I blew out a small breath and settled into the surprisingly warm sofa.

I suppose Bryce won't come tonight, after all, Theia.

***

"Theia!"

I jolted up to the angry sound of my name yelled out. The drowsiness that was dancing across my eyes only minutes ago was, now, nowhere to be found. I blinked and turned towards the door.

"Theia! Open the door!"

I quickly got up and moved towards the door, the knowledge of Matthew still lying out cold in my bed in the back of my head as I rushed towards the door.

Just as I was about to reach my destination, the large wooden doors burst open, both doors barely holding by their hinges. I stared open-mouthed at the heaving Bryce in the doorway. His eyes darkened as they landed on me. His jaws tightening, he started to storm towards me when he suddenly froze, his gaze now on something else. Bryce's canines slipped down, and he snarled. I noticed a helpless looking Meryl standing at the doorway, not willing herself to come forward.

"What the fuck is Matthew doing in your bed?"

I froze and then turned, only to stumble back as my face nearly collided with Bryce's. Behind him, Matthew still seemed knocked out, oblivious to the world and its chaos.

"Talk to me, dammit! What the fuck is he doing in your bed? In your room?"

My eyes settled on Bryce's as he jerked me forward, slamming me flush against his chest.

"I can't believe you would think something as stupid as what you are thinking when I'm standing in front of you showing off all the love bites you gave me, probably every male important enough has seen on me. If you would just stop trying to go all wolf mode, I would be able to explain it properly!"

Bryce's grip tightened on my arm.

"Don't tell me what to do, mate!" He snarled, leaning in so his canines stopped only inches away from my cheeks. "Now, before I decide to kill the bastard and chain you to my bed. Tell me what is Matthew doing here."

I blinked, then, grasped onto his arm and pulled him forward, forcing his grip to loosen and break away as he followed me into the bathroom. I picked up the ripped bloodied t-shirts and cloth and turned around to show them to Bryce. He frowned. His jaws still clenched as one arm still held onto my arm, refusing to let me go while the other pulled the cloth near his nose and took a whiff, dropping the cloth into the bin again. Not giving him time to say something, though, I pulled him out of the bathroom and back into the bedroom. I moved towards the large sofa and stopped.

Motioning towards the pillow and blanket, I mumbled, "I slept on the couch, by the way. His wounds are almost healed, and the scars are almost gone. I just don't know why he is so oblivious to the world."

Bryce turned towards the sleeping Matthew. His fists were still clenched. "How did he get hurt?"

I shrugged. I was not really a fan of his actions at the moment. Therefore, I was not going to fling myself into his arms and kiss him silly—like I secretly wished I could do.

"That's something you should ask him yourself."

Bryce's gaze snapped towards mine. He looked at me with stormy eyes. He looked away and nodded. "Alright, then." Without another word, he dropped my hands and marched out of the room.

I growled a dozen profanities under my breath as I turned away and made my way back to the sofa, completely unaware of the preppy old woman still standing by the door, regarding me with knowing eyes. Slumping back into the sofa, I hid my eyes with my hand. It was becoming extremely frustrating to witness and put up with Bryce's new behavior. He barely told me anything I wanted to know. And he always ran.

"Coward." I spat into the cold air. My fist thumped against the sofa quite violently as I banged my head against my pillow.

"You know, rage dulls down our senses especially when it is directed towards our mate. It helps our beasts, not harm them."

My breath hitched in my throat, and I shot up in the couch. Meryl moved further into the room and settled herself beside me on the sofa.

"It's eleven in the morning, by the way. The full moon is in a couple of days."

"And?"

"And Alexander is trying not to defile you against your apparent wishes. That's how this room comes into play. It keeps you in and away. And most importantly, it keeps him out."

"Great, what will the doors do now?" I scoffed, looking at the partially broken doors.

"That can be fixed, dear. But how about the tension between you and Bryce?"

I sighed. "I want it too. What if I don't mind being mated to the alpha king, anymore?"

"Difficult, dear. Alex believes you do not want to give yourself to him yet maybe because of his beast and his abnormality. You're pure. His beast will emerge to mark his mate during the mating. It's inevitable, and he thinks you might leave him because his beast might scare you if you knew."

What the fuck?

"He is being stupid! How can he not see that?"

"As the full moon nears, all rationality disappears. All that is left is his mate and the tenfold oncoming of obsessive possessiveness towards you. Since for him, you seemed to reject him, he will have to bind himself to keep himself away from you. Wolfsbane hurts like a bitch. But to him, he must. Elsewise, he will take you. It's the way we are born, dear."

"What should I do, Meryl? I don't know how to fix this! I didn't mean to—to reject him or anything. I was just scared!"

Meryl moved closer and pulled me in softly for a side hug, her hand rubbing smooth circles on my arm.

"That is something you must learn for yourself, dear. I cannot help you in that matter. But I may be able to help you in another. Come take a walk with me?"

I glanced at the hand she now had outstretched before me. Her long navy blue dress swished around her ankles as she got up from the sofa and stood in front of me. I turned towards a still knocked-out Matthew and then towards the long fingers outstretched towards me. Looking up at Meryl's warm smile, my very own curved up, I slipped my hand into hers. "Okay."

***

"You might love this section of the castle. It has always held a soft spot in my heart." Meryl gushed lovingly as she led me into a dark hallway and stopped in front of a large door. "My husband proposed here. Strange thing life is. I met him here. I also lost him here." Her suddenly sad eyes turned towards her feet, and I almost rushed forward to embrace her. She quickly looked back up and smiled. "That is why I am hoping to make this place happy again. After all…all's well that ends well. I want it to end well for this place, at least, before I return to London."

Meryl suddenly beamed brightly. The precious sadness on her face disappeared completely as she pushed the large doors forward, giving way for me to witness the magnificence of the large room. Books aligned along each wall in every corner of the room, aided by secured sliding ladders and stairs. It was only when my eyes left the high shelves and reached the ground did I notice the small group of people that were rushing towards me. One held me just as soon as my gaze landed on them.

It was Mom. She clutched me as she sobbed, shaking her head. Dad softly informed her that she was suffocating me. I watched Dad with sad, warm eyes, and when my gaze fell on

Marley and Mr. and Mrs. Smith, my smile brightened. It felt wonderful to get a chance to apologize to them and thank them.

"You scared us! Never do that again!" Mom grumbled as she finally let go of me and pushed Dad towards me. "Go on, Arthur. I know you want to cry too."

Dad turned a sour face towards Mom and grumbled out something that sounded like, "I'm a man!" under his breath before he pulled me in for a hug.

"We're going home, pumpkin, okay?" he whispered, and I nodded.

I probably knew I would not be able to go home. Bryce would not allow that. He would kill before he would allow that. But that didn't stop me from wanting. I wanted to go home. I wanted to sink my face into my pillow and bawl my head off or just sleep it all off.

I sighed as I pulled free of his hug. Maybe I just wanted to go home because I hoped things would go back to normal if I did. Or Bryce would jump through my window and smack me against his hard chest in bed while he slept, his strong fingers tickling me slightly as they would manage to sneak underneath the hem of my tank just like before.

"Hey." I chuckled as an eagerly awaiting Marley rushed forward with Mrs. Smith in tow. Both ladies trapped me in a hug, and we all giggled like little girls when we tried to break free, and Meryl muttered a teasing, "Awkward."

"I'm glad you're fine, Theia." Mr. Smith chuckled as he put his arms around Mrs. Smith's shoulder and pulled her against him.

"Glad I'm fine too, sir."

"What's wrong?" I asked Marley who I noticed was looking agitated and sad.

"Keith's mad at me. He hasn't talked to me ever since the jerk found you."

I slid my arms around the girl's shoulder and pulled her away from our conversing families. Meryl watched us with knowing eyes as she moved over to us.

"I've contained the dear boy in the room situated right beside the one we are currently occupying. You might want to hurry, though, Ms. Smith. Go there before the lad realizes there is no such book such as *The Levitations of Time*, which I have misplaced in the study."

Both Marley and I stared at Meryl with looks of fascination. The woman blushed and chuckled and waved us off. Moving towards our parents, she hurriedly added, "Go along, ladies, while I cater to your parents."

I nodded quickly and pulled a suddenly frightened Marley towards the library door and out into the darkened hallway. Our movements were as quick as we walked towards the door next to the library. Upon reaching it, I gingerly pushed it open. Sighing slightly, I removed her grasp from mine and pushed her into the light just in time for a busy Keith to freeze in mid-attempt of finding the book on the large table while I stood in the shadows.

Keith stood frozen in front of the large table. He moved his nose up and sniffed the air before a growl left his throat, causing Marley to let out a whimper. He turned around immediately, and I watched with a gaping mouth at his blurred movement before he stood in front of Marley and his yellow eyes glowed brightly.

"Why are you here?" Keith growled, moving Marley's hair to the side before dipping his head and pressing his lips on a mark I had missed for the past few days.

"For you," Marley mumbled, her voice cracking slightly and showing that she was, in fact, crying now.

I, however, watched the paw marks with wide eyes and almost yelped when Keith pulled Marley against him in one fluid movement and sunk his teeth in the same spot the mark was in.

As discreetly as I could, I pulled the door open and slipped out. Sinking against the now closed door, I let out a shaky breath I didn't even know I was holding. Keith had bitten Marley in front of me. He had bitten her, and she moaned instead of screaming. How was that even possible?

"Theia?"

I looked up instantly, shocked at being found like a deer caught in the headlights.

"What are you doing here?"

"Keith bit Marley. She—she…moaned."

Meryl let out a startling laugh and with a large grin, strode towards me and pulled me up. To be quite honest, I was slightly surprised at the amount of strength the elegantly aging woman still possessed.

"It doesn't hurt when your mate bites you, dear. It's supposed to be orgasmic, instead."

"Oh," I mumbled numbly, my mind still on the scene I had just witnessed, and let her pull me forward as she started to move away from the dark hallways and into a separate corridor instead.

"We should hurry, though. Your father is adamant about moving you back home, and Alexander is losing his calm. Any longer and he might severely hurt either your father or his office."

Just as she informed me of the torrid news, we reached a large dark door, and with a slight smile my way, Meryl pushed the door open. I hadn't even walked in before two strong arms had engulfed me between them and a very hard chest. We were so close that I had to step on his feet while he dipped his face in the crook of my neck.

The feel of his claws stretching out as I tried to free my arms from between his chest and mine notified me that he didn't like that particular action at all. But I continued to retrieve my hand, anyway, and when it finally broke free from its previous restraint, I slipped them around his neck and held onto him.

"You're not going anywhere. I won't let you, not now, not ever. You were made for me. And I don't share."

CHAPTER TWENTY-THREE

It's funny how sometimes you just want to run away, escape because that seems like the best thing to do; because that seems like the only thing to do. When in reality, it isn't?

Standing there pressed against a silently seething and pleading Bryce, I knew I should go with Mom and Dad. I knew I should go home, and damn it, I wanted so badly. But the cracking in Bryce's voice made my every thought falter. I didn't know how to fix this. I didn't know how to get things back to how they were a couple of weeks back.

I didn't know how to stay and endure this change.

So I just stood there. I just stood there, let Bryce growl and tighten his hold on me, and then nudged my face against his chest when my dad made a move for me. I was still thinking, granted though that it looked like I was burning holes at Bryce's chest because I was staring at his shirt really bad.

I sighed and tried to move back, but stopped instantly when Bryce let out a warning growl. Giving up, I sighed again and leaned into him. I closed my eyes. I really needed to focus. Bryce's rippling muscles moving against my waist were distracting.

"Funny how you don't want me gone, but you rarely stay as well. What are you running from?" I said lowly under my breath, but I knew he could hear me. Standing there and leaning in his embrace felt slightly embarrassing because my parents were just a few footsteps away.

Bryce froze as I whispered against his chest, my arms now clutching on his shirt. "Theia, let go. We're going home now, pumpkin."

I dropped my grip on Bryce's shirt and moved my head back to look at him, my favorite shade of blue pools now glowing golden. He looked back, ignoring my father altogether. But I knew better. A snarl kept showing itself on his lips. His canines were slipping out. Bryce was losing control to his beast. And although it looked like he was trying to control it, his beast seemed to be a very strong opponent.

"Mr. Anderson, I suggest we discuss this elsewhere. I'm sure you understand how fragile the situation is. Removing a soul mate from a male were is life-threatening. Removing a soul mate from the king were is suicide. He's maddeningly possessive when it comes to your daughter, please," a weirdly nervous-toned Meryl spoke up suddenly as if trying to mediate with my dad.

"Arthur, please, h-he won't hurt her. You know that. Let's just listen to Meryl." Mom softly soothed Dad. I could see from my peripheral viewpoint that she was holding onto his arm and pulling him towards the door.

I couldn't help but whimper slightly when I felt Dad give in. He stopped beside me and looked at me for a moment when Bryce's snarls got deadlier.

"Your things are in your bed, honey. I want you to come home."

"Yes, Daddy," I mumbled, my gaze now on Bryce's t-shirt again.

He suddenly moved forward, snarling at my dad, dragging me forward with him. I gasped at the sudden movement, and when the impact of things struck me, I quickly grabbed onto his t-shirt and pulled him back. My heart beating at a sickening pace, I quickly did the one thing I knew would calm Bryce down. Hooking my arms around his neck, I pulled him down and captured his lips on mine.

The door shut, and we filled the room with soft humming and moaning. This time, however, I pushed him back.

Growing up, I had always been adamant that there is a certain time for things—a certain time for studying, a certain time for raiding Netflix or a certain time for falling in love. Clearly, if anyone asked my seventeen-year-old self when she thought she would find love, I would have said at the age of twenty-six when I had become a criminal psychologist. Growing up, I had always viewed blossoming love around me with little to no interest. My statistics towards love occurring and blossoming till its last stage during the teen years seemed highly bleak.

But now here I was, standing before a man I loved, a man who was now regarding me with hooded eyes. My love was different, yes. My love was unconventional, yes. My love was unorthodox, yes. Yes, a year or two ago, I would have fit into the bleak statistics, but it was true. My love for Bryce was blossoming and reaching its last stages. I was completely defying my beliefs. Then again, flowers do wilt after its full bloom.

"Why'd you break away?"

I moved a little further, trying to create an arm's length distance between us. He let me. I looked up at him when I became comfortable enough standing there.

"No reason."

Bryce growled, and I shrunk back. "You've got to be fucking kidding me."

I frowned. Did he have to swear so much? "I'm doing neither, actually. I am not kidding you nor am I having sex with you. Your next question?"

"Stop being so difficult!" Bryce snarled at me as he stepped closer with just one long stride and perched me up against his hips. My legs were automatically wrapped around him to save myself from falling. He moved us towards his dark wooden table and quickly placed me there, his arms still pressing me around against him.

"Tomorrow's the last day of school before the break. You'll have to come here in the afternoon, anyway." His voice was nearly pleading as he dipped his nose into the crook of my neck, placing a soft kiss on my sweet spot. I tilted my head to give him better access just as he grazed his sharp teeth against the smoothness of my skin. I shuddered. My eyes closed as I tried to concentrate on what he was actually saying. Like I said, having Bryce's rippling muscles against my waist was distracting. Having his lips on my neck, the world didn't even exist.

"Then let me go home for tonight?" I mumbled pleadingly. His kisses stopped almost instantly. He moved back and looked at me angrily. Then suddenly, it changed. It went blank, no expression at all.

"It sucks," Bryce replied, carelessly shrugging and looking around the room with an intentional movement.

"What is?"

"That you're not going."

"I am!" I almost shouted back, suddenly feeling extremely agitated. It irritated me how Bryce kept avoiding the real problems, clearing up ways for tiny new ones just to keep my head occupied. All the tiny bubbles were now overcrowding my thoughts. I bloody didn't even know how to feel anymore!

His eyes narrowed at my fuming form, and he leaned forward. I didn't move, firm about keeping my stand.

"I will tie you to my bed if I have to. I will kill for you if I have to. Don't test me, love." Bryce hissed against my ears, each word delivered slowly and with extreme emphasis. I almost shivered at his tone.

"Oh, yeah? Well, you're a potato!" I retorted back almost instantly, nearly smacking my face the next second. *Did I have to be such an idiot when I least wanted to be? Potato? Seriously?*

I watched as the most uncanny thing occurred before my eyes, well, other than seeing Bryce transform. Bryce's gaze was now distant. He had stayed that way for a second before he came back. I watched him curiously as he blinked. His eyes were refocusing on me. His frown returned.

"You okay?" I blurted out, pressing my palm against his face out of reflex.

Bryce nodded, his palm upon mine.

"I have to stay away from you till the full moon passes. I-I don't want to force you into anything—"

Whoa! Where is this coming from?

"Bryce, it's okay. I want to—"

"No! You don't. You just don't want me using those fucking wolfsbane tonics. I won't force you, not this full moon. That's final!"

Is he mental? Crap, now, I feel even guiltier for my reaction that day!

"M-marking helps, right?"

Bryce's gaze shot to mine. He sighed and shook his head. "Royals mark when they mate, love. When we meet our mates, the need to lay our claim is almost painful. But we, royals, can only mark while mating. This way it ensures that we will mate with our soul mates and expand the lineage."

My eyes widened.

"Like-like…babies?" I whispered, watching him with huge wide eyes.

Bryce smiled, his thumb now making tiny patterns against the back of my palm. "Yes, babies."

I gulped and nodded. There would be no making babies for now, and that settled me enough for the time being.

"Oh, and by the way, Matthew is up."

A grin formed on my lips, and I looked towards the door. Bryce's eyes clouded with an unknown emotion, and he moved away, his stance a little slouched. My gaze instantly turned to him. I reached for his hands and laced my fingers with his.

"Bryce?"

He looked up at me. "Hmm."

"Kiss me, please?"

***

"I can't believe he invited us to stay at the castle for the weekend," Dad exclaimed disbelievingly as he slumped down on the comfortable sofa I occupied as a sleeping space yesterday.

After kissing Bryce, meeting Matthew and berating him against challenging a royal, bumping into Chris and Evangeline, bidding Mr. and Mrs. Smith goodbye, and promising Marley that she would see me in school tomorrow, I made my way into the trusted corridors of the first floor only to collide with a grinning Meryl and tortured-looking Bryce. I discovered that Meryl had in fact negotiated with Bryce on my behalf, and he had agreed on inviting my parents over to the castle for the weekend.

Needless to say, I was ecstatic and feeling appreciative. I slumped down on the sofa just beside Dad. Mom followed my action although she improvised with the lack of space and plopped her legs on our thighs.

"The handsome man is in love with our daughter. Of course, he would do anything to make her happy." Mom giggled slightly, which was not really out of her character, considering that she really didn't do half the things normal mothers did.

Dad huffed as he leaned against the comfortable cushions of the sofa. "Hmph! I didn't see him doing anything to make her happy when he had ripped her heart out just a few days ago!"

I sighed and leaned towards him with my head against his chest, his arms immediately wrapped around my shoulder. "He was talking to his niece, Dad. It was all really my fault. I picked self-preservation before actually giving him a chance to prove himself. I got scared of heartache, so I ran."

"Oh, honey," Mom mumbled lovingly and quickly changed her position to lean in and give me a hug. I hugged her back. Dad's grip on my shoulder tightened, and he leaned in to place a kiss on my temple.

I wiped away the loose tears that had escaped my eyes, finally able to hold my folks. Now, all I felt was embarrassed.

"Let's not talk about that, though! Let's talk about something else!"

"Oh, oh, I have something to tell you!" Mom exclaimed, jumping up and down in her seat. I could only giggle as Dad groaned and hid his face between his palms.

"Tell me."

"Casey called. She's hoping to visit with Angelo!"

My grin turned sour and bleak in just a matter of seconds. Angelo wasn't actually a guy. No, Angelo was actually Angelia, Casey's twin, well, fraternal twin. It was weird because while I loved Casey, Angelia just pissed me off.

One minute and two seconds Casey's senior, she looked everything but a girl. Actually, truth be told, I always thought she looked exactly like a boy, not that she minded, though.

Angelia first proclaimed that she was a boy and liked girls when she was as little as nine years old. Mr. Lolein saw it as a phase and discarded it. It was only when Angelia was twelve did she strongly made an announcement that she was a boy, and she didn't want to be a girl anymore, and that she wanted to marry me. That's part of what pisses me off, but that aside, Mr. and Mrs. Lolein refused.

So Angelia found another outlet. She joined soccer, rugby, boxing, martial arts, and swimming and everything a normal stereotypical person would classify as a "man's activity." She grew buff like a bull somehow. So, they sent her away to a boarding school.

She got tattoos, got her hair cut, and started dressing up like a man. She would also, countless times, try to approach me in the dark or in places. She would call me and leave sweet notes, and when she would be back in the neighborhood on the breaks, she would bash boys who would look at me.

Last I had heard of her was a week before moving. She was finally getting her transitioning surgeries done. So I supposed she was a "he" now. Casey knew about his slightly more than obsessive tendencies towards me. She couldn't do anything because she loved her brother. I couldn't do anything because he had been through so much already. Realizing you didn't want to be in the body you're in and getting denied the freedom to change things could be very emotional. So I had always tolerated her behavior. I supposed this obsession was partially my fault. I only hoped he wouldn't try anything here. Bryce had not lost his cool so far, well, except for Lionel, but I really didn't want to see him losing it anytime soon…or ever if that could be done.

Mom immediately read my face. She knew about the Angelo situation. Dad didn't, for obvious reasons.

"Honey, you don't mind having Angelo over, do you?" At this, Dad perked up, and I almost winced at what he was going to ask next.

"Why would she have a problem with Angelo?" Dad looked at me next. "Anything I ought to know, pumpkin?"

I shook my head. Dad's eyes widened behind me, and I looked back to see Mom shaking her head too. I sighed. "No, Dad, All's well."

Dad's eyes narrowed at us, but he quickly rolled his eyes and shook his head. "Women."

The door opened, and all three of us turned towards a smiling Meryl and a shy Evangeline gliding towards us.

"Here you are. Evangeline has been looking all over for you." Meryl beamed as she finally came to a stop before us, her gaze, however, on me.

I nudged an eyebrow up, looking at her with a suspicious look while Mom and Dad smiled. They both decidedly got up, and I followed after.

"Your Dad and I should be going now. Work tomorrow and all, love. We'll see you tomorrow afternoon, all right? Do you want something from home?" Mom smiled as she turned towards me and pulled me in for a hug.

Dad's arms came around both of us, and he placed a firm kiss on my forehead. "See you tomorrow, pumpkin. Take care and be good, okay."

"I love you, Dad," I mumbled, putting my hand on him as we all broke away. I turned to Mom. "Could you please pack me some clothes and my laptop and stuff. You know, for the break."

Mom's eyes sparkled as a grin lit up on her lips. "Of course, dear! I'll bring your things tomorrow."

She then leaned in to whisper into my ear, "I have a feeling you'd need your things here too."

My face heated up, and I turned to my dad who only tightened his grip on me.

"We should leave now, pumpkin. We'll see you tomorrow. Please call us if something goes wrong, okay?"

"Okay, Dad."

Mom pulled me in for a last hug before they turned towards Meryl, giving me a last wave, and moved out of the room behind her. Evangeline stood at the edge of the sofa, watching me with shy but excited eyes.

"Come here." I grinned, reaching for her arm and pulling her onto the sofa beside me.

She giggled as she plopped down on the sofa.

"Your daddy scares me. Is your daddy strict?"

"No, no, he isn't, but he sure is scary." Eva giggled, nodding. I smiled and pulled her into a side hug. "So what are we going to watch today?"

"Can we watch *Fifty...Fifty Shades*?" Eva immediately chirped up, looking extremely excited. A gasp escaped my lips before I could even stop myself. I looked at her, my mouth hanging open.

"No! You're too young to watch that movie. How about we watch *Harry Potter*? Draco is mine, though!" I tickled a giggling Evangeline. She nodded, still laughing like crazy as she wiggled under my tickling fingers.

"Okay, okay! I like Neville better, anyway! He likes plants!"

"The Weasley twins are mine!"

Both Evangeline and my head turned towards the still open doorway where a grinning Matthew and warm-looking Rome stood.

Matthew marched into the room, his grin increasing when he noticed both our bewildered expressions.

"What? I always had a secret thing for Fred and George." He mimicked an excited girly voice, his palms clutching to his heart in a mocking movement.

"Shut up you," I muttered, grinning despite myself. Evangeline nodded. "Yes! Shut up, Uncle Matt!"

Matthew scoffed as he grabbed the coffee table before us and placed it away. He grabbed the dozens of pillows on my bed before throwing them on the fluffy rug and plopping down on them. A grinning Roman moved towards me and out of nowhere, pulled me up for a hug.

"Hey," I murmured against his chest. My arms were around his waist.

"Hey." He sighed, his warm breath fanning my neck. "I'm glad everything's better. I won't let anyone hurt you anymore, promise."

"Good." He smiled, moving back and placing a soft kiss on my forehead before he ruffled a frowning Evangeline's hair and plopped down on the rugs beside Matthew.

"Uncle Rome, why do you hug Thi like that? Do you love her?"

Both Roman and Matthew froze and turned back to face me. I blushed, frowning because I really didn't want Roman to have feelings for me.

Matthew turned towards the TV again and started flipping through the movie case, trying to find the movie while Roman smiled and nodded. "Yes, Eva, I love Theia a lot. She didn't give up on me even when I was scary and very mean to her. She's my best friend. Don't you love her?"

Evangeline smiled brightly, nodding excitedly. "I love her too, Uncle Rome! She's my best friend too!"

I couldn't help but blush harder. My gaze, however, was on Matthew. Freshly finding out he had feelings for me, I really didn't want to all this to be awkward for him. I watched as his stance visibly relaxed, and he flipped the flaps of the movie case with much less force. He slipped out a DVD, crawled his way to the Blu-ray player, and then crawled back to his spot with the remote.

Roman got up and switched off the lights while I leaned in towards the side table and turned the string lights on.

"Don't you have anything to eat?" Mathew suddenly whispered just as Harry got locked in his cupboard room under the stairs.

"Pause it! I mean it! Don't you dare play it till I get back!"

Quickly jumping out of the sofa, I ran towards the tiny kitchen area and opened up the fridge. After grabbing a couple of bottles of soda and bottle of orange juice, I turned towards a cupboard and took a large bag of chips. Items in hand, I made a move to run back to the living room area when I stopped and turned back.

Chocolates!

Quickly opening the fridge again, I got four packets of Snickers before pushing back the refrigerator door shut with my butt. I quickly jogged towards a very guilty-looking group: Matt, Rome, and Eva.

Rolling my eyes, I placed myself in my spot again. "You, guys, played the movie didn't you?" I said, rolling my eyes again.

"No!" Evangeline piped up almost instantly, her head moving up and down as she denied my accusation. I smirked at her before handing her a packet of stickers. She accepted it almost instantly, grinning. "Thanks!"

"Here," I mumbled, passing the boys their bottles of soda and chips.

"Where's my chocolate?" Matthew pouted, looking at a happy Evangeline taking a bite on hers. I grinned and brought out their packets one by one.

"Aha! We knew you hid it there! Oh, what torture, Theia! Truly!"

The door creaked, opening barely to even register in our senses. Someone cleared their throat, catching all of our attention.

My eyes widened as they locked on Bryce's, and my breath hitched. He was, however, calm and collected, kept on moving, walking into the room, towards me.

He quickly leaned down and picked me up in his arms before settling down on the sofa himself with me still in his arms. Roman and Matthew both scoffed.

"Told you he wouldn't be able to stay away," Matthew mumbled to Rome, who only grinned.

"Hi," Bryce whispered against my ear, his palm slipping against my tummy.

"Shh, I'm watching Harry! Besides, little Draco is about to come!" I snapped at him lowly meanwhile opening my packet of Snickers as my eyes were glued on the red-haired boy who had been my ultimate crush. Thinking back now, I really didn't know what I was thinking. Percy Weasley was not as good-looking as I had always believed him to me. In fact, the twins beat him to a pulp!

I bit down on the chocolate, immediately closing my eyes as the combination of caramel, chocolate, and nuts engulfed my palate. *Damn it, this is good.* I opened my eyes again as the high rolled over, just in time to see Evangeline lean in to steal a fist full of potato chips from the boys. I grinned at the little monster. She really was a character. I almost felt like she was the little sister I never had.

Bringing the chocolate back towards my mouth again, I stopped instantly when Bryce's fingers found my chin, and my gaze caught him as he tilted my head towards. He leaned down slowly to nip on the side of my bottom lip. His tongue flicked on the skin of it.

"It tastes even better off your lips," Bryce whispered, grinning as he looked at me. At that moment, I was sure my ovaries had exploded.

Evangeline cleared her throat quite obviously, catching all four of our attention; she rolled her eyes at Bryce and me.

"Cooties!"

I couldn't help but blush harder when Bryce smirked, a proud paternal look gracing his features. He reached out and patted Eva's head. "Not when your mate kisses you, sweetie."

"Really?"

Bryce smiled. "Really."

Just then, a loud chiming ringtone I recognized as mine sounded around the room. I quickly moved towards the bed. Maybe it was Dad. He rarely called unless he had to. Although one thought seemed a little unsettling: how could my cellphone be on when I had clearly left it off? Frowning, I glanced at the screen and signed.

1 new message. Definitely Dad.

The frown still playing on my face, I tapped on the notification.

```
A thousand nights I've moaned it seems,
Your name leaves my lips each night.
A strange face graced my dreams,
A stranger I knew before a meet.
But now I know…It's you. It's you.
There's no escaping now…
You've run away a million times
But came back when I closed my eyes.
They're open now, and still, you're here.
I won't let you leave.
You're mine.
You're mine.
-S
```

I didn't even know I was shivering with fear until I realized my phone's screen kept moving. I took in a deep breath and deleted the message. The feeling it gave me was intense; almost so that I knew in the back of my head that it was the same person who tried to block Bryce's contact, faking to be me. But how concrete could that reasoning be? *Exactly, not much.* Well, at least, one thing was concrete. It was definitely not Dad.

With shaky hands, I placed my iPhone back and turned towards the living room only to bump face first into a hard breathing wall. My breath hitched in my throat as my eyes moved higher and locked onto livid golden ones.

"Bryce..."

CHAPTER TWENTY-FOUR

It's funny how sometimes when you least expect it, fear comes and bites you in your bum. Most of the times you escape it, and the other times, well, you'll just have to deal with it.

I couldn't help but think about the hopeless and countless amount of ways I could deal with my fears especially when Bryce stood in front of me looking like he could announce a blood bath any minute now. There was no doubt that he had read the text message. His expression said it all.

I was just slightly nervous about how he would react to me on deleting it like I had something to hide. I didn't. I supposed I was trying to be a coward. Things were going so well tonight, and I didn't want anything to ruin it. I thought removing it would get rid of it. Only later, looking at Bryce, I realized how foolish that was. Fear would always come and bite me in my ass. There was no running here. I was cornered.

"Why did you delete it?"

Nervously, I turned towards the still oblivious Evangeline who kept giggling at something Harry said and the two boys who seemed to be faking not paying attention. I knew they were listening. Their tense stances said so. Feeling a little better, I looked at Bryce again and moved towards him, wrapping my arms around his waist.

"I just thought it was a case of a wrong number. The sender was a private number as well."

I watched as his eyes narrowed, and he reached out his hands. Expectantly, I placed my phone on his open palm.

Bryce's frown deepened as he went through my phone. With a mad growl, he handed me back my cell and slipped his hand around my waist, steering me towards the awkwardly silent Roman and Matthew and a still oblivious Evangeline.

"Now, I want to promise you something," Bryce whispered, his arms sliding around me as he pulled me on his lap. "When I find whoever that is, I will break his hands, one by one, and then I will rip his head off. The whole fucking world needs to know that you belong to the king. You belong to me." His breath fanned the side of my neck, and I could tell he was trying his hardest to control himself. Gulping down nervously, I could do nothing but shudder at how fierce he sounded and nod.

***

"That was so much fun!" Evangeline chirped up and yawned.

"Sure was," I mumbled lovingly, holding her against me as she rested her head against my chest. It was funny how we were seated. I was still in Bryce's lap, his arms wrapped possessively around me while Evangeline had crawled on my lap an hour into the movie. He didn't seem to mind, though, which made me question his strength more.

"Did you see how Neville stood up to them? Neville's *bwave*! Even Dumbly thinks so!"

My eyes glided to Matthew when he returned from the kitchen, dusting his hands on his pants as he walked towards us. He smiled at a shrinking Evangeline and held out both his hands. "Come on, bug, we need to get you to your mom before she starts hunting for our head."

Roman nodded beside him but chuckled when Evangeline moved towards Matthew reluctantly while looking at me with pleading eyes.

"Go on. Emily must be worried, Eva." I smile softly at her, leaning forward to place a kiss on her cheeks before Matthew picked her up and straightened.

"Night, Thi." Rome reached down to hug me but stopped at Bryce's warning growl. His eyes widened, and he moved back, his head down. "Yes, Alpha. I apologize."

I frowned and then turned towards Bryce. "Stop it," I said and reaching out a hand towards Roman, pulled him down and into a brief hug. I knew I was pushing it, but Roman meant me no harm, and I really was not in the mood to go with Bryce's possessiveness.

I felt Roman stiffen before he quickly pulled away again, his head facing down. He quickly moved towards the door and out, followed by a blank-faced Matthew and an already sleeping Eva.

"What was that about?" I hissed, turning around to face Bryce.

The next thing that happened was a blur. One second, I was on Bryce's lap, twisting my head and glaring at him, and the next, I was pressed against the sofa, Bryce's large form looming over me.

"You know exactly what it was!" Bryce hissed, his eyes steely as he leaned in closer.

I gulped down nervously, and immediately, Bryce's eyes followed the motion. His nose dipped down against the softness of my neck.

"You make me want to mark you so badly. I'm fucking going crazy because of it! Tell me. What am I fucking supposed to do when all you do is tempt me?"

My breath hitched in my throat as Bryce nipped at my neck, planting a soft kiss on the heated skin as he let the skin go. "Mark me."

He froze and pulled away, looking at me with surprise. I felt myself turn deep red and switched to look at his t-shirt.

"You know I—" He groaned, his lips now pressing kisses on my collarbone.

"Can't till we make love. I know. Still, Mark me."

I heard as Bryce's breath hitched in his throat, and he leaned back, looking at me with hooded eyes. He stayed that way for a minute or two until I finally mustered enough courage and looked at him. I watched fascinated as his eyes darkened, but he didn't lean in.

Lean forward, Theia, and just do it! You know you want to.

I would be lying to myself if I said I didn't want him. I'd be lying if I said I didn't want this god of a man to take me because, heck, I did. I shed off a tiny bit of shyness in me and leaned forward to catch his lips with mine.

My hands trailed down his shirt as he nibbled down on my lips. I tugged on his shirt, and with another quick movement, he had his shirt off and his lips on mine again. The sound of fabric ripping flared around the room before warm, soft lips descended upon my breast, his moist tongue licked the tight bud while twirling its twin with his hand. Everything seemed hazy to me, everything except the feel of him doing things I had only read about in books.

He pushed me against the sofa again as his hard thickness rubbed between my thighs; I wrapped my legs around his waist and pulled him closer. A sharp pain shot across my lower back, and I jerked forward, pushing against his increasing length again. He stifled a groan, but I couldn't help wincing at the feeling of something sharp pressing against my back. It had to go. Bryce pressed his lips on mine again.

"Bryce…wait!" I gasped, disentangling my lips from his. The pain of the sharp object increased slightly as my back pressed against the sofa harder.

"I'm sorry—fuck!" Bryce growled as he shot backward. His back collided with the concrete walls far across the room. I stared wide-eyed at the fast-breathing, dark-eyed Bryce; the angry dent in his pants almost too large to concentrate on how broken and angry he looked.

I reached down and pulled out a small earring, almost immediately smiling as I realized who it belonged to. I moved to show it to Bryce, a sheepish grin on my face. But that faded when I realized there was no one in my room except me. Bryce was gone.

What the hell?

The grin was gone, and a frown replaced it. I reached out for my cell, quickly dialing Bryce's number. He picked up on the fourth ring.

"Hello?" I couldn't help but quiver as my voice broke, and I managed to stifle a sob. Why did he leave?

"Theia."

Gone was the soft tone of his voice. Instead, it was almost steely as if guarded and withheld. I couldn't help but get angrier by the minute. I was so sick of crying and trying to make him realize that I was here, that I was not going away, and I wanted to give him everything I could. But he always made this hard!

"Why did you go?" I muttered back. Although my tone was flat, I knew it was apparent that I was crying. Heck, I knew I was, but that didn't mean I was any less angry. I wanted to punch Bryce until he stopped hurting me.

In the distance, the tower clock chimed, and I looked towards the closed glass balcony door. The gibbous moon illuminated the night, and the city shined like stars dusting the ground—red, yellow, and blues.

"I'm not going to let you have pity sex with me."

"What the hell makes you think I would ever give myself to you without wanting the same thing you do? God, Bryce how can you be so dense sometimes? I hesitated the first time. We talked about this because I was scared. It was going to be my first time for god's sake! And then, you went around acting like you're doing the right thing, trying to push me away and all that crap. How hard is it to see that maybe the girl wants you too? How hard is it to just admit that maybe you should just have to give into what you need? But no, you always run and push me away! Why, dammit?"

There was a long silence from the other side of the line, and I almost rushed out to start searching for his room when he replied, "You hesitated. I told you. We won't mate until you're sure. Go to bed, Theia. Good night."

I stared at the phone, mouth gaping as the line went dead. How could he do this? How could he be a king and be such an idiot? Do alphas lose brain cells when it comes to mating?

Anger bubbled in me again as I turned towards my bed. I dialed Bryce's number again and placed my phone against my ear.

"The number you are trying to reach may be switched off."

"Fuck!" I let the phone bounce against the bed as I fell backward, slamming into it.

"Why did I have to get the most complicated alpha king? Why couldn't I just bloody get Scott or Derek and get it over with! Love is so complicated, dammit!"

My phone pinged loudly, and I almost jolted up in surprise. Its shrill tone broke the silence. I reached for my phone and cringed. A shudder ran down my spine.

Private Number. Please let it be just someone else…Please…

I hate that he gets to kiss your lips.
You're mine,
Not his.
I have proof.
I'll fight to the death.
(I will) rip his head.
You're mine.
You'll see,
One day.
I miss you. It's been so long since I've seen you. Can't wait till tomorrow. I'll be close.
Good night, Theia.
-S

"I don't even want to deal with this right now." I groaned, my arm coming to fall over my eyes as I placed my iPhone on the bed and turned away. My hands still on my eyes, I tried to think of something else, but when that didn't work, I resorted to counting sheep until my body finally gave into sleep.

***

"Theia, please tell me you're ready." I heard Rome groan from the other side of my door just as I walked out of the closet.

Waking up in the morning had been a tough act especially when my whole body rejected the idea of moving because each muscle in my body protested against it. Needless to say, I had stayed in bed for the next half an hour, only getting up when the need to pee reached a point where I couldn't stand it much longer. I needed a release.

And now, well, here I was, sighing every five seconds as I made my way towards the door. I couldn't help but pray silently to not see Bryce today especially not before school. I was still mad at him. With a final reach towards the door, I pulled it open before sliding out and shutting it.

"Let's go," Roman immediately said, grasping my hand as he pulled me towards the kitchen. I sighed for the nth time as I let him drag me along.

"You're hurting me, you know?" I muttered as we got closer to the kitchen. Roman only grunted in reply and continued pulling me behind him.

"You hurt me all the time. Do you see me complaining?"

I froze. *What the hell?*

"What did I do?" I blurted out and pulled his hand so he could stop.

Roman sighed as he stopped moving. He turned around to me with a blank look.

"You don't let me have a proper breakfast just like you're doing now. It's unfair."

I had no idea why I was feeling so emotional. I supposed it was the time of the month because I teared up and nodded, moving towards the kitchen and leaving behind a stunned Rome.

"You can't expect unmated wolves to stay away from her if you don't mate her, Alex. That just makes no sense! And then you just leave? Hell, what business do you even have to take care of so suddenly?"

My feet froze mid-stance, and all I could do was stare at a flustered looking Chris and a suited up Bryce. Both their eyes met mine. I, however, stuck to the man with dark hair. Bryce stared back. I stopped when I stood a step away from Bryce. His steely gaze did not once leave my angry ones.

"You're leaving?"

"Yes," he replied, not even blinking once as he continued to stare into my eyes.

My insides ached, but I nodded. Suddenly feeling a deep need for escape, I turned around, grabbed an apple from the fruit bowl, and moved towards the door.

It was only when I reached the door did I stop, a hand on the handle. I shook my head as a bitter, broken smile formed on my lips; a lone tear fell to the floor. "Coward."

It was less than a whisper, but I knew the whole room had heard. The hitching breaths that followed my bitter whisper had proved they did. I didn't stop, though. Pushing open the door, I marched into the hallway, determined to get to my room and grab hold of my important belongings. Nobody knew it yet. But I was going back home. I was not going to stay here if he was running away.

Maybe you should call Casey and call her over for a week or two. Even Angelo seems like a better idea than tolerating cold, empty walls.

The sound of the kitchen door echoed back from the cold stonewalls, and I faltered for a second before continuing to move away.

"I could drop you at school!"

I stopped and turned around almost hesitatingly. "Thanks, your highness, but no thanks. Have a good day."

The winds whipped past me, and I almost jolted back when my gaze met Derek, who now stood an inch away. His warm gaze solely pressed on me.

"You can call me Derek, you know?" he mumbled softly, glancing between his feet and me.

A small smile played on my lips, and I shook my head. "Thanks, Derek, but I'd rather not," I mumbled as I tried to move past him. He stepped forward, cutting my path again.

"I insist, please."

*And there goes your escape plan, moron…*I almost rolled my eyes at the small sarcastic voice in my head.

"Alright, thank you. But I need to get a book I forgot first."

A brilliant smile glimmered on Derek's face, and he motioned a hand as if to say, 'Ladies first.' I could only put up a tight smile and move along towards my room.

***

I almost smiled as Rosenberg High came into view, its cream building standing tall and proud against the gray hues of the sky.

"I suppose the clouds are feeling pretty Christian Grey today." A deep voice chuckled from beside me. My head whipped towards the amused voice, an automatic grin of my own placed on my lips.

"Why do you say that?"

Derek only grinned before he answered, "Well, they are fifty shades of grey today."

"Good one." I grinned back, almost forgetting for a moment that he probably just wanted to woo me for his own twisted reason even though he knew I was not his soul mate but his friend's.

His expression turned serious suddenly. He turned away to glare into oblivion. "I leave in the afternoon."

"Oh…"

Derek turned towards me. His gaze was still serious. "Do I get a goodbye hug?"

No! Don't do it, Theia! Your conscience demands you not to do it!

He looked at me expectantly, and after a few seconds, it was resolved. Leaning forward, I wrapped my arms around him and pulled him into a hug. "Goodbye, Derek."

I stiffened when I felt him press a kiss on my collarbone. My eyes widened when he pulled away. "Goodbye, Theia."

Run, dammit! I told you it was not safe!

As quickly as I could, I nodded dumbly and pulled out of the vehicle. Grasping my backpack tightly in my arms, I broke into a run and reached the school doors in record time. It was only then that I mustered enough courage to look back.

Derek still sat in the car looking at me. A small smile seemed to light up his lips, and he waved a goodbye before pulling out of the car park.

***

Dropping the math book on the table, I quickly fished out the assignments I had missed and began flipping through it, giving it a last minute check.

"Theia?"

My head shot up, and a genuine smile lit up on my face. "Blond!"

"Still stuck on Blond, huh?" Alex smirked as he walked around my row and slumped down on the seat before me.

"Never doubt it!" I grinned, my fingers reaching out for the assignments once again.

I watched as Alex's smirk loosened, and he showed a more serious expression. "Hey, look, Theia. I'm sorry about, well, you know…everything. I mean if there is any way I can make it up to you, just ask!"

Smiling at him warmly, I nodded. "Thank you for everything, for what you said to Bryce and well, everything. Thank you, Alex."

"There it is!" He suddenly grinned, leaning forward as he fluffed my hair.

"Hey, Stop that!" I shot out, moving backward at lightning speed as I tried to half-heartedly set my hair.

I sat watching the class fill up quite quickly, a small grin dancing on my lips when a pissed-off Roman marched into class. His gleaming eyes zeroed at mine, and he increased his pace, dropping down on the seat beside me when he reached me. Following him, a blank-faced Matthew marched into the room. He slumped down beside Alex and with a weary glance at me, began talking to him. I turned my attention to a still furious Roman as he sat glaring daggers at his desk. A frown slipped itself in place when I noticed his still bleeding but quickly healing fist as he kept on clenching and unclenching them.

What the hell has he done now?

My hand shot to grab his, and I brought it to my lap. His eyes darkened when I ran a finger along the quickly healing cuts. It didn't take much to see that the bruises and cuts were bad. *What had he done?*

"What happened?" I mumbled softly, trying to sound as calm as I could. I didn't let go of his hand.

Roman sighed as he slumped forward. His head hung low, he said something gibberish.

"What was that?"

He sighed again, nearing closer. "May have punched a wall or two."

"But why?" I cried out, holding his hands closer. "Why the hell would you do such a stupid thing?"

"I don't want to talk about it, Theia."

"Too bad. I want you to."

"Fuck. Just drop it, okay!"

"Is there a problem, Mr. Naight?"

Both our heads turned towards the front of the class, only then did I realize how loud Roman must have been. Everyone was looking at us with an unusual unshaded interest. My eyes met Mr. Phelps's angry ones, and I almost shrunk back into my seat, letting go of Rome's hand when I realized that's where his glare was directed.

"Sorry, sir," I mumbled quickly before picking at my textbook.

"Now that that is over. Could everyone hand in their assignments, please? I wasn't joking when I said it would be graded."

I grinned as I held my assignment. *Oh, the perks of being a nerd!*

***

The skies looked like they were about to weep any minute. The winds were starting to take their toll against me as I made my way towards the bus stop as quickly as I could.

The school had ended far too quickly, and naturally, the joy of finally having breaks could not be clouded by anything, not even the massive piles of assignments we had received to keep us "busy" during our breaks. I scoffed out loud at the thought of that. My eyes drifted towards the skies again when a strong hand rested on my shoulder, halting me.

"Theia?"

"Alex." I grinned, turning around to face the huffing, sweaty blond. He looked like he had a good run.

"Where are you going? Roman has been looking for you ever since the bell went."

Oh, crap.

Suddenly, a light bulb lit above my head, and I breathed a sigh of relief, looking at Alex with a hopeful expression.

"Could you please give me a lift home, Alex? I missed it, and I really want to just lie down in my bed."

Alex's brows furrowed with confusion as he scratched the back of his head. He seemed to think it over for a second or two before he grinned again and nodded. My heart immediately jumped at the prospect of being able to go home. But I knew I was avoiding the truth. And the truth was that when I'd be lying in the bed I missed so much right now, I'd be missing something else entirely.

I shook my head as I chased his stern face from the morning away and got into Alex's Jeep. When I turned back to the spot, a distressed Roman appeared, obviously looking around for me. I secured my seat belt, and Alex movedout of the car park and onto the street.

Guess you're finally going home, Thi.

CHAPTER TWENTY-FIVE

The sight of my dusky-colored home seemed welcoming and warm as I slid out of Alex's Jeep and turned around to shut the door. I leaned into the open window and smiled. "Thanks for the ride, Blonds. I appreciate it."

A pout settled on Alex's face when I said his nickname, but he grinned only a mere minute afterward, giving me a mock salute and a hearty "Anything for you, Thi." He shifted the gears into reverse and drove.

The winds picked up just as I turned towards my home. I merely smiled as I brushed it away gently and moved towards the door, unable to wait another second. Fishing out the keys from my bag, I quickly pushed it into the keyhole and twisted the door open.

Everything was the same. A broken smile flashed on my lips as I slowly passed the living room and made my way towards the kitchen where I could hear my mom cooking, her famous lasagna's aroma wafting through my senses, my mouth salivating.

Turning around the corner, a gasp escaped my lips when an arm pulled me back.

"Miss, what are you doing here? Aren't you supposed to be in the castle? His highness will be so very angry! Oh, no, miss, you must go back! I thought Mr. and Mrs. Anderson were supposed to spend the weekend at the castle."

I frowned at Agnus and shook my head. "Change of plans. I refuse to go back there if Bryce is going to be cowardly and run away from stupid misunderstanding! I feel like I'm the twenty-four-year-old one here, Agnus."

A small giggle left Agnus's lips, and she shook her head in humor. "Oh, yes, that does sound like Alexander. He loses his calm, cool-headed self whenever you are mentioned. Oh, you should have seen him the very first time he smelled you."

Smelled me? My nose scrunched up in an awkward way as I looked at Agnus with bewildered confusion. "Smelled…me? Like…a…Okay, sorry."

"No, dear—" Agnus shook her head, almost rippling in laughter. "His highness, or Master Alexander as we the maids call him, smelled your scent, his mate, from the castle the day you moved into this house. He did almost break Romanov's arms when he tried to stop Master Wilhem for a chat! And afterward, he was fuming thinking you had a boyfriend. It was a sight to see!"

I almost cried because it was so funny. I supposed I did because the tears milked out by intense laughter slipped down my cheeks as I noticed Agnus was doing the same.

***

It took us a while to calm down, but we got there. And when we did, Agnus continued to coax me into returning, her fear for her king greater than her understanding for my peace. I thought she couldn't help it. She knew his anger, and if she wished not to be at the blasting side of it because she was a housekeeper, it was right that I not blame her for trying to coax me into going back.

At the end of the day, although she had tried her best, I relented. After all, what was the purpose of going back to the castle when Bryce had fled? All matters put considered, it only seemed fitting I leave if he had left, too. I mean, it wasn't like it was permanent. I just needed to stay at home for a few weeks, maybe even have Casey over, before leaving for the castle. What harm could a week or two do, right?

Well, after the little chat with Agnus, I had merrily marched into the kitchen, leaving the slightly scared and understanding woman behind. My father was only just standing by the corner of the doorway, watching Mom cook. Mom, like always, had her iPod plugged in as she cooked. Her little head bobbed up and down to the beat, and her eyes occasionally closed as she pretended to waltz with an invisible partner. And while it took her a while to notice me, Dad and I found ourselves suddenly quite preoccupied with recording a secret video of her. Teasing Mom was always fun.

When all was said and done, and the fun had ended, things took a turn for the awkward.

And so after being berated about whether Bryce had hurt me while being pulled and pushed into hugs by both my parents, I finally managed to sufficiently lie that Bryce and I were great, and he just had some work to do in Italy. So I was here while he was gone because I missed home.

Well, it was not entirely a lie. I really was missing home, but the truth still stood that Bryce and I were not great. And I had no idea where he had so cowardly disappeared to.

Thankfully, though, Dad and Mom believed me, and after an amazing dinner, here I was in my room, lying on my bed and trying to ignore my phone as Roman's ID flashed on the screen.

Romanov calling…

I glanced at my phone slightly but immediately looked away as he continued to call. The slight trepidation in my chest made me feel like I was hiding in Marley's home again, and I felt like Bryce was going to get me any minute now. Only this time, I didn't know who would get me, and I really wasn't hiding. This was my home after all!

4 messages received

20 missed calls

A slight shiver ran down my back when I tapped onto the missed calls tab: fifteen missed calls from Bryce, three missed calls from Romanov, and two missed calls from Matthew.

I left the messages untouched. A sigh slipped from my lips as I switched back to looking at my faintly lit room. And when the slight tinge of sweat caught my senses, I quickly got up and marched towards the bathroom. A bath was in order, a much needed one at that.

***

I walked back into my room. Glancing towards the slightly rattling window, I padded my way towards it and pushed it open, breathing in the cool night breeze. An owl hooted somewhere in the distant forest, and I almost smiled at how loud it sounded in the silence. The moon seemed almost full, and I couldn't help but let a shiver pass me. I watched the moon as if looking at it connected me with Bryce. A slow pain settled into my chest. I missed him. I missed the Bryce that was mine, not the one who drove me away.

I found myself padding towards my bed quite furiously but only froze when I saw the screen.

Bryce calling…

My chest tightened as I slumped down into bed and pulled my iPhone towards me. My heart beating a mile a second, loud enough to be heard around my silent room, left me even more nervous. My eyes widened in alarm. I quickly unlocked my laptop and tapped on the first music file I encountered. Turning back towards the blaring phone, I tapped on the "Accept" button. My eyes widened as the song started to play. My free palm moved smacked my forehead. It just had to be a sad song! It was just then I realized no one was speaking from the other side of the line. I frowned and pressed the phone closer.

"Hello?"

It sounded more a question than a greeting, but I supposed it had to do. I missed him, and although I knew he was going to be mad, I also knew he was too far away to do anything. So I was slightly less scared of the possibility of partial abduction. Partial because no matter how reluctant and disagreeing I could be to him turning beast mode, throwing me over his shoulder, and jumping from a two-story building, I always wanted to go with him.

The silence on the other side broke. A controlled growl sounded through my cell, and I moved closer towards my headboard, tugging the sheets above my knees. "Go back home, Theia."

Despite myself, I couldn't help but let the slightly amused smile shine through, leaning against the headboard I eased out. "I am home, Bryce."

"Our home, dammit!"

The pure anger in his tone made me freeze for a second. The next, however, brought back the knowledge that he was in fact too far away to do anything. I relaxed a little, grinning again.

"We are yet to buy a home together, babe," I replied as sweetly and innocently as I could. It wasn't hard to grasp that he was referring to the castle as our home. Although it made my heart tingle, home was wherever my parents were, or wherever he was. And he wasn't in the castle. My parents, however, were here.

I listened as Bryce let out a growl, and the sound of something crashing and breaking in the background followed. He let in a deep breath as if to control himself before he spoke again. "The castle. Go back to the fucking castle, Theia!"

My smile disappeared, and I found myself blank faced when I muttered back my reply. The anger from the previous hours rushed back in such force that I suddenly felt like sobbing. "No. I'm staying here, since you've so kindly run off somewhere. Because you refused to acknowledge what I agreed to, I have decided to postpone my castle stay until two weeks into the break. My best friend and her brother wanted to visit, and I think I'm going to invite them over! You know I-I love you, but I won't let you toy me like this. I have feelings too, you know, and I can decide what they are for myself. I don't want you doing that for me and then pretending that staying away from me is the best thing because, let's get real, you know as much as I do that it hurts. Being away hurts. I—just good night, Bryce. I think I need some sleep, and you do too."

Nothing, just pure silence, so much so that I could almost hear the distant traffic sounds coming from his side of the line.

"G-good night, then," I mumbled, almost whispered into my cellphone. Bryce obviously didn't want to talk about more. So I supposed it was goodnight for tonight.

"I'm coming. And you better be ready for what you've asked for, Theia. Good night."

The line went dead.

I could only stare at the screen as it went dark.

He's coming back? From where? Didn't he leave? What the fuck?

The cell went off again, and my palm shot to grasp it, accepting the call without even looking at the screen. I was hoping it was Bryce. I needed to know where he was.

"Open your damn window!"

"Rome?"

"The window, Theia!"

My heart beat, pounding in my ears. I quickly padded my way towards the larger window and slid it open. Almost instantly, a fierce Roman jumped into my room. His eyes shined bronze. In the next minute, he pounced on me, pushing me onto time floor under him. He quickly started turning me over as if checking for an injury. When he found none, he relaxed a bit, moved back, and sat on the floor.

"He is coming."

I sighed and got up to sit beside him, rubbing a sore ankle as I did. "He didn't leave?"

Roman frowned and then shook his head. "Oh, he left. New York. He's coming."

"Well, then, I'll see him tomorrow or the next day I suppose."

Roman froze for a second, his gaze hazy and locked on my rugs. I continued to watch him as he came back, his gaze brightening considerably. He blinked and then turned towards me. "Tomorrow morning. He's taking a private jet here."

"I'm still not coming back to Dovlore. I want to stay here for a week or two. My best friend and her br—" Rome growled suddenly, barring his teeth at me. Shocked, I moved back but continued. "B-brother are com-coming over for the h-holidays, and I want to spend some t-time with them."

"Sorry. That growling bit was Bryce. I didn't know the connection was still open," Roman muttered, pressing the bridge of his nose as if trying to rid a headache.

"W-what?"

Rome's eyes shot to mine, the steely gaze almost melting into something warmer and more comforting. I froze as he moved forward until his hand slid along my shoulder, and he pulled me towards him. "All packs have a connection. Royals have a connection, too, where we can communicate mentally. Bryce, being the king, can communicate to anyone he wants to as long as the connection is strong and personal. A connection is like a mirror or a sieve. He can hear what's going on around me because I think about it. That is if I keep the connection open. It's complicated."

I blinked myself out of the haze and nodded slowly. I supposed that made sense.

"Can you hear what he is thinking right now?"

Roman's expression tightened, and he nodded, pinching the bridge of his nose again. "I'd rather not say."

My eyes widened. "Tell me?"

Rome shook his head and got up, dusting himself off as if out of habit. He reached out his hand, grasping mine, and he slowly pulled me up.

"Please." I repeated as he led me towards the bed and pushed on my shoulders gently so that I slumped onto it. He got to his knees in front of me.

"I punched the walls because I was angry. Alex behaves like he is saving you, but he is hurting you, instead. Sometimes…sometimes I wish you were my mate instead, Thi. I know I'm difficult and short-tempered, but I would treat you right. I'm sorry my cousin is such a mutt. I'm sorry I couldn't keep my promise. I let him hurt you. But I know if someone can fix him, you can."

Leaning in, Rome placed a ghost of a kiss on my forehead and before I could reply, moved towards the window and leaped out. I stared at the window, the smell of him still lingering in around the room, something spicy and something fresh.

Sometime, I wish you were my mate, Thi. A sigh left my lips as I leaned against the headboard, going further down so I sunk into bed. I tugged the covers over me.

"Fuck my life," I mumbled out sadly, watching the dark ceiling above me, the reflections from the string lights making it glow in certain places.

"You can."

"You can."

"You."

***

"Theia, come downstairs. Will you please?"

Oh, God, no, not this early! I don't want to go shopping! The thoughts of the last time Mom took me shopping early at nine in the morning ran through my mind, and I shuddered at the recollection of a dozen shades of lingerie I had been forced to bring back home. "Coming, Mom!"

I quickly walked out of the bathroom, freshly brushed but still wearing clothes from last night: Bryce's shirt and my boy-shorts. It didn't seem like much of a task to just go downstairs, so the need to dress up didn't seem important. A sigh left my lips as I watched myself in the mirror, my brown locks looking wavier than normal even when they were pulled up in a messy bun.

"Theia!" Mom's voice drifted into the room in a sing-song tune, and I almost scoffed at her habit of pretending to be an opera singer. I think it's important to put out the fact that my mother didn't know the M to music.

"Coming!" I yelled back, pushing away a rebellious lock of hair as I turned towards the door.

Sleep had visited me almost instantly after Rome had left last night. I suppose it had been a long and tiring day, and although

I had gone to sleep almost immediately after his departure, I had risen earlier than I was used to as well. I supposed it was because of the gnawing feeling in my tummy. Bryce could be here anytime today, but I knew I would continue with my plan. I would call Casey up and invite her over, anyway, and then spend time with her and Angelo.

"Oh, darling, there you are! Could you please help me get the table ready? Your dad must be getting up any minute now, and I really want to surprise him with a good hearty breakfast. Lord knows he will miss it when I am gone all of next week. Business in Cali is blooming!" Mom quickly rushed out as she placed another amazing smelling pancake on a plate, quickly pouring another perfectly round batter on the pan.

"Sure, Mom." I smiled and immediately started moving around the kitchen, setting to work at preparing the breakfast table.

I was only placing the packet of cereal when the doorbell went off, and my heart skipped a beat before switching to a maddening pace. I stared wide-eyed at the front door, a nervous look etched on my face, the milk carton almost on its way to slipping from my suddenly sweaty palms.

"Theia, darling could you please get the door?" Mom rushed out as she turned and bent towards the oven, pulling out what smelled like apple pie.

"Sure, Mom," I said, my feet already making its way towards the door. I stopped only when I held the crystal knob in my hand. I gulped back a nervous breath, without much thought, turned the knob, and pulled the door open.

Well, that's strange, I thought as I looked around the empty driveway. The doorbell rang, but how could there be no one here, though?

A frown etching itself on my face, I moved slowly into the driveway and almost jumped when a foreign voice spoke up from behind me.

"Remember me?" The voice seemed deep, deeper than what would seem normal seventeen-year-old guys have. His

Romanian accent reminded me of someone, but that could hardly be possible since I had yet to call them over. I turned towards the man in question sharply, almost falling back at his unearthly beauty—platinum blond hair which was shaved on his right side, lips as red as a cherry, and a lip ring to shine through the cherry. What caught my attention though were the stormy grayish-blue eyes. I froze, suddenly realizing who the tall man in front of me was.

"Angelo?" *No...fucking...way.*

"That's right! We're here! Let us rejoice!" another happy voice called out from behind me, and I got only moments to turn around before being tumbled down onto the pavement, my boy-shorts, I'm sure, visible to the world to see.

"Casey, too tight, can't breathe!" I managed to choke out as the platinum blond held me in a tight grip, her thick locks almost covering my face.

"Let her go, Cas." Angelo's voice drifted through the air. His now manly voice mixed with his knowing Romanian accent, courtesy of the boarding school, made him sound anything but the girl who I had known since my childhood. An accidental glance at his slightly dented jeans notified me that there was more to him now than what he had been as a girl.

I looked away, blushing when Angelo finally had enough, ripping Casey away from me. He pulled me up, his arms sliding around my waist.

I, on the other hand, wasn't even sure on how to react anymore. It had been a common occurrence when he had been a girl, and I hadn't paid much attention to his cuddling self. But now, that he held the whole male package, what was even considered correct, anymore?

After a minute or two of debating, I only shrugged and let his hand rest there, also making way for Casey when she decided to hug me again.

"Missed me?" Angelo whispered against my ear, his cold lip ring causing shivers to run through my hand as it touched my warm earlobes.

Don't know about you, but as much as a hunk he has transformed into, Bryce is still the man, the little voice in my head spoke up sarcastically, and I almost grinned at its remark even my subconscious had lost its heart to Bryce.

"I missed you both." I smiled, pulling both of them closer. It was safe to say that I had noticed a change in Angelo's height. He had grown six inches taller and was now well beyond one and a half heads taller than I was.

"Babe?"

I froze. *Oh, shit, no. Shoot me! Just shoot me, someone!*

Slowly, I managed to move out of the two embraces and turned towards the source of the voice. The knowledge that the voice seemed like the definition of controlled barely passed me when my eyes locked on Bryce's bright blue ones. I could already detect shades of gold twirling the sea blue iris.

"Bryce, these are my childhood best friends: Cassandra and Angelo. Guys, this is Bryce, my—.

"Her boyfriend." Bryce smiled as he reached me and pulled me smoothly into his arms while also smugly extending a hand towards Angelo.

I watched sighing as Angelo's smile disappeared and shriveled up to bleak expression as he reached towards and grasped Bryce's hand, giving it a firm shake.

I supposed he saw, too, how obviously pointless trying to rouse a fight with Bryce would be. No matter how much of a man Angelo looked like now, the truth still stood that Bryce would always end up being larger. Casey, on the other hand, stood still in blunt awe of Bryce. The only time she broke free of the haze was when Bryce waved an awkward hand in front of her face.

I leaned into Bryce's arms, feeling suddenly possessive over him. I felt guilty because that was my best friend, and I would never feel a need to be cautious of her, but I couldn't help it. Perhaps it was just primal instinct with this bond between mates thing. Bryce's arms tightened around my waist as I stood snuggly in front of him. He reached out a hand towards Casey, which she gleefully accepted. I couldn't help grinning when she turned towards me secretly and wiggled her eyebrows cheekily.

"Theia? Oh, dear lord if that Bryce has whisked her away to that castle of his again, I'm going to literally ground him!"

I turned towards Bryce wide-eyed and with flushed cheeks as Mom rushed out of the front door muttering to herself and looking slightly alarmed. She stopped when she saw us, her mouth slightly agape. Well, that was for a minute before she unleashed herself on Casey and Angelo, pulling them into the home with her, worrying over how they must be hungry, how long the flight that must have been and how she was glad they were here.

Bryce and I stood still in the driveway. The knowledge of not having any audience anymore was slightly agitating because the anger and pain all came rushing back. Frowning suddenly at how at ease I felt in his arms, I tried to move away.

"Don't," Bryce growled slowly, pulling me against him again. I shivered as he dipped low and snuggled his nose into my neck. "You're so tempting when you're possessive especially while wearing my shirt. Tell me…are you nude inside?"

"Perve." My hand grasped his just in time as it reached the edge of my shirt. When had he started talking like this?

Bryce chuckled against my neck, his warm breath fanning my sensitive skin. I almost did a did a double take when he suddenly nipped it before running his warm tongue over it. He repeated this action twice when he tugged on the skin more aggressively, nipping, biting, sucking, and licking until he seemed satisfied and pulled back to view his masterpiece. Meanwhile, I was a puddle against him. I could barely feel my legs.

"There. Now, he'll know whom you belong to. You need to get out of these too. As much as this turns me on, babe, I could have murdered the boy." Bryce growled, and I shivered as he tugged on the collar of my shirt.

"You're not even wearing a bra." He groaned shakily, nipping at my shoulder.

"Why are you so horny?"

I smacked a palm against my mouth as soon as I blurted out that question. Bryce only stilled before he rolled his hips into my back, his arousal bluntly obvious. I blushed when he replied, "I'm always horny when you're around me. I just don't make it obvious."

"So you're not running away anymore. We're mating?"

Bryce froze and moved away, coughing to clear his throat. I almost sobbed at the loss.

"I don't want your pity sex, Theia. I'll deal with it."

"Fine. Deal with it. Goodbye," I muttered, shrugging as I started to move towards the door, not even trying to hold the tears or hide the bruise on my neck. It was breaking my heart to say goodbye even though I knew that he was my soul mate. I just needed a break. All this whirlpool of emotions were really overwhelming me, and I didn't like it. I needed to get away for a second.

I didn't even stop when a growl rang out on the driveway or when I got roughly pulled against a hard chest. "Fine, babe. You can have it your way."

And then, he was gone. I almost thought I heard a whispered "for now," but the hurt of him actually agreeing to me was too much to actually ponder on that.

I lost minutes standing there and glaring at my creamy bare feet. It felt like hours. I fought myself over trying not to cry. The concept of crying suddenly disgusted me because that seemed like the only thing I kept doing nowadays. I was tired of feeling sad, tired of crying. I was tired of the brain-wrecking headaches that followed.

"Chubby?"

I glanced up to see a concerned Angelo standing and holding the open front door. His navy blue sweatshirt over his buttoned up white shirt only made him look more mystical. He made a move to walk over to me but stopped when his eyes landed on something. I blushed knowing exactly what it was. The anger on his face came and went just in a few seconds. I noticed that his fists were still clenched as he started to walk over again and upon reaching me, pulled open my messy bun, letting my hair fall over my shoulders. I could only watch dumbfounded as he then slid his arm around my shoulder and pulled me into the house.

"We need to get you fed," he muttered softly as he edged towards the kitchen. I found myself wondering once again, just as I had done on numerous other previous occasions, how easy it seemed for Angelo to memorize things so fast.

We walked into the room to find an enthusiastic Casey tucking into a pancake. My dad raised an eyebrow at me in question, and I only shook my head in reply. I knew he was wondering what was up, but that was the last thing I felt like talking about. Mom, however, quickly pulled me out of Angelo's grip and pushed me onto an empty chair beside her and Casey. I raised an eyebrow at her, but she only sheepishly shrugged back.

"So I heard Bryce lives in a castle. Is it true?" Casey suddenly asked, biting over her pancake.

I suddenly felt awkward, but I nodded and smiling softly replied, "Yes, it is."

"That is so cool. Does he have any brothers?" she replied, her eyes sparkling as she continued to feed herself.

A giggle slipped out of my lips seeing Dad's expression, but I shook my head. "He is the only child. But he does have a cousin, Roman."

"OMG, you must introduce us!" Casey immediately jumped in her seat, giggling.

"Sure, but what about Leo?" I mumbled back, amused at her enthusiasm.

"Oh, we broke up. Figures since he cheated on me," Casey muttered bitterly, her lips trembling slightly.

"You can't be sure about that, Cas! For all you know, Kira could be lying," Angelo suddenly snapped. My gaze went to his. He, on the other hand, was quite busy glaring at his sister.

"That's right, dear, I think you should talk to Leo," Mom said. Dad and I, however, continued to stuff our mouths with pie while nodding awkwardly.

Cass looked at me expectantly, but I shook my head. "They're right. You should talk to him."

Knowing she had lost, she finally nodded in defeat and moved onto the next topic. "Brian can't stop talking about you, you know? I think he's become a little obsessed."

"I did accept his request on Facebook, though," I muttered, stuffing more pie into my mouth. Mom patted my back, noticing my unhealthy amount of consumption.

"Yeah, we know. Actually, I think the whole school knows," Casey replied.

"Well, I'm done. Thanks for the breakfast, Mom." I smiled, gathered my plate and glass and moved over to the kitchen sink.

As quickly as I could, I washed my dishes and turned around to find both Cas and Angelo finishing and moving towards the sink. When they seemed done with their dishes, all three of us moved towards my room, dragging their luggage upstairs.

"Sweetie, Angelo and Cas can have the rooms beside yours," Mom called out as we made our way upstairs.

"Alright, thanks, Mom!"

"Yeah, thanks, Mrs. A!"

***

"Woah, that's some view!" Casey gasped as she took in the view from the large open glass windows.

I smiled as I took the view in, too. "Yeah. It is, isn't it?"

"Is that his castle?" Angelo drawled almost snidely as he slumped down on the bed.

I ignored the pang in my chest at the mention of Bryce again but quickly avoided it as I took a seat on the bed.

"Yes. That's his castle."

Angelo scoffed as he let himself fall flat against the bed. "Caught yourself your very first boyfriend and he just had to be a millionaire. I always knew you were special, Theia."

"You're mean, Angelo. Stop being jealous," Casey blurted out, rolling her eyes, and she took a seat on the bed.

Once again, I ignored his bitter words, and taking a deep breath, I switched the topic. "So, guys, what's the plan?"

"Shopping, sightseeing, movies, all that shebang, but for now, let's stay in. I'm kind of tired." Casey giggled as she turned towards Angelo and me, now lying on her side.

"Alright, alright." I giggled back and eased into the bed, lying flat beside Angelo.

The sound of the doorbell caught my attention, but I continued to lie down, my eyes closed. It seemed peaceful.

"Theia, Roman's here, dear!"

"Roman? Oh, it's my lucky day!" Casey almost shouted out excitedly as she shot out of bed, leaving me behind.

"She's…mental," I managed to blurt out, still looking at the open door wide-eyed.

"I always told you," Angelo murmured from beside me. I glanced towards him and quickly looked away.

"I should…you know, go." I quickly breathed out as I shot out of bed and rushed out the door and down the stairs.

I hadn't even stepped the last stair when a worried Rome started walking towards me. A wonder-struck Casey, who stood frozen beside me, watched almost in awe as Roman walked in front of me and stopped.

"Hey, Rome, this is my best friend, Casey." I grinned, knowing he was fully aware of the stunned girl beside me. I turned towards Casey, my grin widening at the blushing girl. "Casey, this is my one of my best guy friends, Rome."

"Hi," Casey murmured dreamily, and I almost let out a bark of laughter when Roman froze and took a sniff around the air, his gaze then directed towards Casey.

"Nice to meet you," he muttered back and managed a small smile before pulling me into a hug. "I'm so hot. Your friend's horny just looking at me. I don't know if I should be flattered or shocked."

This time, though, I did let out a bark of laughter, almost instantly frowning and smacking Roman on his arm. One glance at Casey showed that she was still oblivious to everything and was just as awestruck as she had been a few minutes ago.

"Shut up," I scolded Rome. He, however, gave me one of his rare grins.

"So he came?"

"Yes."

"Had a tiff?"

"Yes."

"Strange."

My eyes shot towards Rome's. *Strange?* "How so?"

Rome shrugged, his brows still furrowed together. "He seemed pretty happy, grinning and smirking."

I ignored the pang in my chest and shrugged. "I dunno."

Rome watched me curiously, and when I didn't falter in my expression, he nodded and pulled me into a hug before turning towards the door. "Call me if you need anything, okay? I don't know what he's up to, but if I find out, I'll let you know."

Turning towards Casey, he gave an amused smile, "Goodbye. Have a nice stay here at Peidmond."

I could only help but stifle giggles as Casey continued to let out dreamy sighs all the while Roman walked towards and out the front door.

***

"Christian's hotter!"

"No! His brother!"

"Christian!"

"Ladies, ladies, let's admit it! I'm hotter!"

Both Casey and I glared at a grinning Angelo.

"Shut up!" We both shouted at the same time.

Angelo put up his hand in defeat as he continued to grin. "Alright, alright, don't get your panties in a twist, aye!"

"Christian's hotter!" I declared in finality as I quickly got out of the bed and switched the TV off, yawning out tiredly as I marched towards the bathroom to brush.

The day had been filled with awkward conversations about Roman and Bryce, swimming and just lazing around, checking each other's Facebook out after Rome had left.

Naturally, getting a tan here didn't seem like a thing. So the sooner we got into the pool, the sooner we got out. It was barely summer, and that meant that it was chilly all day round on "bad days." Today was one of those bad days.

I could still hear as Angelo and Casey continued bickering. I, on the other hand, only shook my head and gurgled all the foam out, scrubbing and washing my face afterward. Finally fresh-faced and minty-breathed, I marched right back into the room and bounced in between the two siblings, leaning more on Casey's side as I finally let the comfort of my bed seep into my bones.

The breeze from the open windows only helped calm me more, but I couldn't help but miss a certain heavy weight of an arm on my waist. I sighed as I turned and chucked away thoughts about him for the fiftieth time today.

"Truth or dare?" Angelo suddenly murmured beside me. Both Casey and I turned our heads towards him, and he repeated himself.

"Truth," Casey replied, slightly amused but even more excited.

"What were you hiding under your bed last Wednesday?"

Casey groaned and muttered something that sounded like, "I knew it was going to be that question," before answering, "It was Leo. We…er…Yeah, well, we were making out. Okay, truth or dare, Theia?"

"Truth." I giggled, still not being able to get the image of Casey hiding a guy under her bed out of my head.

"Have you and Bryce had sex yet?"

My breath hitched, and I'm sure I looked like a deer caught in the headlights. "No," I murmured back slowly, and I could almost swear I heard a relieved sigh slip from beside me.

I turned towards Angelo. "Truth or dare?"

"The truth."

"Every time you used to have those bloodied knuckles when you'd be over for the holidays, how'd you get them? Were you participating in illegal fights?"

"No." Angelo chuckled, bringing his head closer to mine. He looked at me directly in the eye when he answered, "I wasn't participating in fight clubs because I was too busy giving every guy who dared have a crush on you a free plastic surgery."

"What the hell? Why?" Casey almost burst out from beside me.

Angelo, still looking into my eyes while I could only stare at him, replied, "Oh, I think you know exactly why. I think you've known exactly why for ages."

***

A groan left my lips as I tried to smack away the persistent hands pulling me. I just wanted to sleep, and all this pushing and pulling wasn't helping! A strong pair of arms shot towards my waist again and hurled me up in a quick motion.

As I felt myself being moved, I opened an eye and almost squeaked when the sight of a lit castle in the distance met my gaze. Both my friends were still asleep. The chilly night breeze smacked my face as it passed me and danced into the room.

I didn't really know when sleep had taken over, but I was sure it was somewhere between truth and dare and five questions—five because we know each other so well.

The strong arms around me tightened, and I looked up just in time to see a determined Bryce looking straight ahead.

What the hell is he doing here?

As if deciding how to act, Bryce took a forward all of a sudden, and a squeak escaped my lips. His eyes immediately met my own wide ones.

"So, you're awake," he drawled, a small grin surfacing on his lips. I don't know if it was the haziness from the sleep or the lack of illumination, but somehow, the grin seemed bitter.

"What the hell are you doing sneaking me out while I'm unconscious. I thought you agreed to goodbye!" I hissed, smacking a palm against the bulge of his bicep.

Bryce only seemed to grin more. He lowered his face beside mine before replying, "No. I believe I told you you could have it your way. I never said I will too. Right now, though, babe, I have it my way. And that's to have you in my bed, in my arms, not his."

The next second seemed like a rush as Bryce's grip on me tightened, and with me still on tow, Bryce jumped from my window into the dark woods.

CHAPTER TWENTY-SIX

The sound of a distant owl's hoot and then a familiar tower bell's chime alerted me that we were nearing the castle. I could do nothing but sigh in his arms as Bryce held me closer, leaping on a tree. How many times had we been here with him taking inhuman leaps and me on his shoulders? Clearly, I was not in a mood to do a head count, but it felt like one too many. I gritted my teeth together and shut my eyes tightly as a cold wind blew, and the violent shivers began. Everything just seemed like a large cycle of never-endings.

The quick click of a door opening alerted me that we finally reached the castle.

"We're here."

I was mad at Bryce—very, very mad. But as he dropped me onto the all too familiar black silk bed covers, I couldn't help but let a small smile show at how appreciative he looked as he stood at the foot of the bed, watching me.

"I like how you look in my bed."

*What an enigma…*I thought as I mentally rolled my eyes.

"Well, great because that's all you'll be doing for a while—looking. Now, tell me, why the abduction?"

Bryce let out a bitter chuckle, shaking his head slowly as he started making his way to where I was on the edge of the bed.

"You know, when I climbed through the window tonight, I thought I'd see my mate in her bed alone and asleep. Turns out, she was asleep. But alone?" He shook his head again. "That, she was not." His chuckle dimmed, and his lips pulled into a thin line, the coldness in the room suddenly matching the coldness in his gaze. "What I climbed through the window was my mate sleeping, but with her overly bubbly best friend and a man who happens to have the strangest of obsessions for her."

"Bryce, it's no."

"Not what I think?" Bryce let out a stiff chuckle, his cold eyes giving off a strange gleam. He leaned over me, resting a knee on the bed as he did and going lower with me as I tried to move back on reflex. "Then why were his arms around your waist, under your shirt? And why was one of his legs over yours? Clearly, it's obviously not what I think, Theia. It's obviously not the fact that you're letting a man who harbors affections for you entertain himself as he wishes!"

I knew at that moment that my mouth kept slowly opening then closing like a fish out of the water. But really, what was there to explain?

Bryce, however, seemed like he did not care for a reply because he immediately continued, "I have never tried to forcefully dominate you. I have never tried to go against what you wish for, intentionally, but gods forbid, I am too selfish when it comes to you being mine. I want you, Theia...your soul, your body, your heart, you. I want you." He leaned in low enough so that his warm breath touched the back of my ear. I could almost feel his lips on that particular skin. "And if I have to kill someone for it, for you, I will feel no remorse at all."

"Y-you're t-trying to scare me into sending b-back Cas and Angelo." I could do nothing but stutter back, my wide eyes peering into his, occasionally drifting towards the thin-lined smirk he was pulling off quite well.

Bryce only leaned in more, so that his lips brushed against my cheeks. "Am I, love?"

"Y-yes bu—" I was barely able to complete the sentence when his angry lips smacked onto mine. Quickly my retort turned into a breathy moan. *What were we fighting over, anyway?*

The room seemed to fill with electrical sparks. Even the open window was unable to diffuse the heavy warmth that hung over the air. I couldn't help but grasp onto Bryce's shoulders and pull him roughly against me, his denim-clad hips rubbing between my thighs. I let out another breathy moan at the sparks that shot through my body when he pulled back his hips and pushed it against my lower stomach again.

"You're mine, Theia. Don't you ever fucking forget it." Bryce growled as he pressed his lips against my neck, working their way down the thin line of my satin tank top and his tongue tracing the swell of my breast.

A gasp left my lips as his fingers traced the hem of my tank before slipping under it, slowly running the flat of his palm against my taut belly. Quickly finding its destination, his palm cupped my breast and gave it a slow squeeze.

"Bryce." I breathed shakily, arching my back to unconsciously give him more access.

Everything felt like it was sending a hundred volts of shock down my body. It seemed so sudden, but before I knew it, Bryce had pulled my tank over my head, and his shirt was nowhere to be seen. The chilly night breeze drifted into the room, and I watched as Bryce's gaze turned dark, his eyes frozen on my hardening nipples. As if unable to hold himself, he let out a strangled growl before pulling one of the hard buds into his mouth, sucking it with his teeth before softly flicking his tongue on it almost as if massaging it.

"You're so beautiful," he groaned, pulling back as he did.

I almost let out a whimper at losing the feel of his tongue on me when he suddenly pulled away, his eyes blazing with something deep. He moved back to sit on his knees beside the bed before he suddenly grasped me around my legs and pulled me towards him, quickly resting both my legs on each of his shoulders.

I watched with jaded eyes as he closed his eyes and inhaled, smiling slightly. His hands reached up to caress the flat of my stomach. He looked up to gaze at me and smirked triumphantly. "You're mine."

Oh, God, that was sexy, the tiny voice inside me screamed. Despite my racing heart and the gush of something wet that had probably soiled my panties down there, I managed to uphold a frown, only long enough to question him. "Who says?"

"I suppose you need some convincing, love," Bryce whispered as he chuckled, leaning forward and cheekily grazing my aching nipples with his taunting teeth. He moved back almost suddenly and almost in a heartbeat, resumed our earlier position. Only this time, he did so after pulling away my bottoms.

I shuddered with a newer sense of shyness and was just about to cover myself when Bryce held my hand with his, a warning growl emitting itself from deep within his chest.

"Never hide from me." He growled, slowly running his tongue along a tiny silver scar on my pelvic bone, which I had obtained by slamming on a sharp table's edge back in ninth grade. I had been quite a klutz then. "Your scars are beautiful, each and every one."

I felt tears brimming in my eyes at his soft-spoken admission, and before I could contain myself, I slipped my legs off of his shoulder, sunk my fingers into his hair, and pulled him forward, leaning towards him midway before catching his lips with mine. I gave my all into that kiss, all my love and adoration, silently praying that I was able to convey my feelings with it.

Finally fighting for our breaths, Bryce finally pulled away and chuckled immediately, shaking his head as if in disbelief. "You blow my mind, Theia. I think I'm going to end up neglecting my duties once you move in. I can see it. You and I in bed, naked, day after day, making mad love."

A giggle left my lips as I said mockingly, "What if I want to make sweet love?"

Bryce's eyes gleamed, and he moved back, resuming the same position for the third time tonight. His gaze met mine, and he smirked again, "I don't do sweet love."

My voice hitched in my throat as he pressed a slow, open-mouthed kiss on my left thigh, pulling it between his teeth as he repeated the same on the other side. His hands, however, held both my hands down, our fingers entwined together. I knew that he was teasing me, but the need for friction between my legs almost made me cry out in frustration.

"B-Bryce, please." The breathy plea sounded alien to my ears, and my eyes automatically widened when I figured it was me who had so wantonly begged Bryce to do some of the naughty things that were running through my mind.

Bryce chuckled as he pressed another kiss closer to my aching bundle of nerves. I moaned out quite loudly, my hips rubbing against him unconsciously. "Please what, babe?"

"I—ah—oh, God, Bryce!" I couldn't help but let out a scream as I felt his tongue touch the opening of my pussy and slowly lick its way up, applying pressure on my throbbing clit. I gasped as my hips shot towards his face and my fingers in his hair, pressing him against me.

It felt new. This feeling, this pressure, this pleasure, heck, I wanted it. I almost seemed to crave it so much that somehow holding Bryce's face against me didn't make me feel any less uncomfortable than when he growled at me before continuing his sweet torture over and over again, sending shivers down my spine.

Another loud moan left my lips and had me almost shot up in bed as Bryce suddenly plunged a thick, long finger into me. The sudden invasion had me clamping against him as I continued to shudder with the new sparks that were coursing through me now. His arm was pressed around my waist as he pushed me into the bed so that he could continue doing what he wanted. I could do nothing but release a string of moans, finally giving myself into all my senses, my toes curling as he nipped and then sucked on my clit while slowly pumping his finger into me, almost at an agonizing pace. I gasped as I felt the tension build inside of me. Bryce tightened his grip and pulled me towards him. I realized I had writhed away from him in the hazy clouds of passion.

"Stay put," he mumbled against my lower lips, lazily pulling and nibbling on one before returning to the tiny bundle of nerves, slowly sucking on it, his finger now pumping almost roughly against me.

The knot inside me was beginning to tighten, almost painfully, but there was still something missing as I twisted, turned, and clutched onto Bryce, moaning his name loudly again and again. He brought his hand to my stomach and with an almost lazy pace, finally reaching my breast, tweaking and pulling one of the nipples. He sucked on my clit a little harder, and that was all it had taken before the knot in me exploded, leaving me screaming and shaking against Bryce's neck as he moved back over me.

"Fuck. I need a cold shower."

My legs wrapped themselves around Bryce's hips as he made a move out of bed. I pulled him back.

"I-I could help." I breathed against him, still recovering from the orgasm. My palm reached to hook against his jeans waistband before slipping underneath it.

Bryce let out a groan as he quickly grasped my roaming hand, stopping me just in time as my fingers slipped against the monster. His cock throbbed at my touch, and Bryce let out another strangled groan. He pulled my hand away as he continued to lie on top of me, his face hidden in the crook of my neck.

"No. This was about you. I'll just…take a cold shower okay?"

We were back to square one again, but unlike the rest of the times, I was just going to let it go this time. The last couple of days, our relationship had been quite strained, and I really didn't want that anymore. If I had to let him have his way for a while, I suppose I would. I would respect his wishes and not push myself on him. I was not going to do that anymore.

"Alright." I nodded. "I'm next."

Bryce chuckled as he moved towards the edge of the bed. Turning quickly, he gave me a long breathtaking kiss before slipping out of bed and into the bathroom. I could only blush at the memories of what had just happened, a warm smile etching itself on my lips. I supposed it really isn't such a bad thing, this constant abduction.

***

A sleepy groan left my lips as the last few drops of sleep started to fade.

Feeling something slightly uncomfortable pressed up against my back, I tried to move but found myself unable to. Feeling slightly disoriented, I opened an eye as I tried to wiggle away from the thing holding me still but stopped as soon as my eyes finally adjusted to the environment around me and landed on sparkling blue eyes staring back at me.

"You should really stop doing that," Bryce mumbled, groaning as he hid his face into the crook of my neck and pressed a chaste kiss there. I ran my fingers through his hair lovingly as we lay there in each other's arms.

Last night had been wonderful, in a sense. Bryce opened up to me slightly and actually stayed after we both had a shower. We had spent the rest of the night talking, and I ended up telling him about how Angelo transitioned and about my life back in California. I had been more than a little surprised when Bryce had, in turn, told me about his life back in Britain although he did tactically manage to keep any mention of his mother away from the discussion. I didn't push him, though. I supposed all would come to be known in good time. After all, we had that. We had enough time.

"I love when you do that," Bryce mumbled softly as he pulled me closer against him, tightening his arm over my stomach possessively.

"Do what?" I asked, smiling at how relaxed we were right now. There was no tension, no running away.

He moved his hand towards mine as I continued to play with his hair, softly running my fingers through the thickness of his brown waves. He slowly grasped onto it. "This."

I tilted my head so that I could kiss his hair and place a loving kiss there. "I love us not standing on thin ice."

Both Bryce and I continued to lay there, just fiddling with each other's hair and clothes when suddenly, the double doors of Bryce's room shot open and slammed against the strong walls with a loud bang.

"Alex, I'm B—Who the hell is that?"

I immediately shot up from Bryce's grip and turned towards the screaming woman only to stop dead in my track. There in front of me stood a 5'9" blonde bombshell. Her shocked, glaring green eyes were quite apparent even from a distance. My first thoughts were awful, something I immediately cringed thinking about. I supposed Bryce sensed where my thoughts were trailing, and he quickly pulled the covers over us, and when I tried to move away, pulled me back against him almost lazily.

"Theia, meet Amber. We went to primary school and college together. Amber, meet my mate, my girlfriend, and eventually my soon to be fiancé and wife, Theia. Now, that the introduction is done. Amber, could you get your ass out of my room with the knowledge to never make an entry into my room in such a manner ever, if not at all."

I knew I was blushing beet red by then. The embarrassment and raw anger etched on the girl's face quite apparent as she stood in her position, staring at us.

"B-But Alex! I thought you didn't—I mean—you didn't want a mate!"

He didn't want a mate?

"I was scared that I would never find one, Amber. You know how rare it is for the men in my family to find their mates. It was a defense mechanism I had. I just didn't want to feel disappointed if I didn't find mine."

The girl still stood there, an ugly expression quickly taking over her face. "B-but I thought you didn't—I thought you wanted me…to marry me—"

"We were eleven for God's sakes, Amber! We were kids, barely even wolves! I don't see you as anything but my friend!"

"I-I left him for you! I th-thought we would eventually end up getting married! I left him for you!"

Bryce moved to sit in bed now. Apparently, lying down was not worthy of having a serious conversation. He pulled me up with him and pulled me closer. Halfway up his lap when we leaned against the headboard, I turned to look at him when my eyes widened. His golden eyes were furiously glaring at Amber. Knowing the only thing that could calm him down, I looked down at his lap before quietly climbing on it, grasping on the bedcovers as I did so that we both would stay covered. I didn't appreciate her ogling. Bryce was mine to ogle.

Immediately, his eyes were on me as he relaxed. He wrapped his arms around my waist, pressing me harder against him and breathing out a shaky breath before he looked at Amber again. "We both know that was only out of your own selfish reasons. I never have and will never entertain the idea of being with you. He loved you, and you just left him for me! We all three were best friends, Amber. You just don't do that. I tried to make you go back to him, but you wouldn't budge. If you remember correctly, that is the reason why I told you to stay the fuck out of my life. Please remove yourself out of our room."

"She's a little girl for fuck's sake, Alex! She is not woman enough for you! She's human!"

Bryce chuckled while I gaped at the woman. "Well, she's my human and the queen, so show some respect!"

"Also, I'm eighteen, and mind you, that does not classify me anywhere near being a 'little kid.' And well, you being 'woman enough' clearly didn't teach you not to throw yourself at someone who doesn't want you." I blurted out almost after Bryce finished.

Amber jerked forward almost as if to attack me but froze when a deadly growl sounded from behind me.

"Take one more step, and I will finish you, Amber," Bryce growled viciously, and even though the anger he was suddenly feeling wasn't directed towards me, I could feel it vibrating off him.

Amber stood staring at Bryce for a split second before turning around and rushing out of the room. I sat, muted, on an angry heaving Bryce's lap. The morning had been ruined.

"Say something." Bryce snapped as his hold tightened on me. I sighed before tilting my head towards him.

"Who is her mate?"

"That is not my story to tell."

"Then whose is it?" I retorted back almost immediately.

"D—" Bryce stopped and turned towards me. His frown was now gone and replaced with a grin. "Ah! You caught me there for a second! Must admit, that was pretty smart of you."

"That was not fair, but hey, at least I made you smile." I smiled at him softly and snuggled back into his chest.

Just then, the door shot open once more. Both Bryce and I snapped our attention towards it. This time, a very worried Meryl marched in.

"Get ou—Oh!" She blushed once her eyes landed on us. "Sorry, I thought that stupid girl, Amber, was back to sink her paws into my little Alex. I'm glad I found you here, instead. That must have gotten rid of her! Good riddance, I say!"

Meryl smiled brightly she spoke. She sent a secret wink my way and a look of motherly love towards Bryce before she turned around and made her way out, only stopping once she was at the door. "You two better come downstairs you know. It's almost noon."

Noon? I totally forgot about Cas and Angelo.

"I have to go home! What the hell would they think when they wake up to find me missing? Oh, God, what a disas—Bryce, let go!" I pleaded desperately as I tried to get out of bed.

Bryce, on the other hand, had other plans. Pulling me back against him, his free hand tucked underneath my shorts and then hooked his fingers around the lacy panties I had worn after bathing last night. Bryce had been quick to get me one from my room "across the castle." My breath hitched as he tugged on it, his breathing becoming heavy as he leaned in closer to press a kiss on the base of my neck.

"Is it a sin? I just can't get enough of you," Bryce groaned against my neck, his bold fingers moving further down towards my throbbing nub, his other hand sliding slowly against my stomach and quickly cupping my breast.

"You're so wet," Bryce growled, stroking me almost in a torturous pattern. His other fingers were pretty occupied with teasing my tight nipples.

A soft scream left my lips almost suddenly as Bryce plunged a finger into me. My hips began moving in rhythm with his fingers all the while pushing against his hard length from my back. I leaned into Bryce's shoulders as I arched my back to get some release when his lips touched mine.

"Master A—oh, Jesus!"

Both Bryce and I froze, his lips still on mine. However, he was quicker to collect himself as he removed his lips from mine and looked towards the outburst. I, on the other hand, only did so much as to hide my heated face against his chest.

"Yes, Mrs. Dracous?"

"M-m-master Mya apologizes for b-bursting in! B-but Madam M-Meryl s-said to just enter, and P-Prince Romanov brought the visitors! I-I'm sorry, Luna!"

"It's alright, Mrs. Dracous. No harm was done. We will be down in a few. Thank you," I silently smiled at how soft and comforting Bryce's voice sounded while he talked to Mrs. Dracous. The sounds of the doors closing softly helped me relax a bit against Bryce's finger as he plopped it out and quickly plopped it into his mouth, humming as he cleaned off all the juices. I couldn't help but blush more.

"I suppose we should go down," Bryce said chuckling, pressing a kiss on my temple.

I sighed as I stayed against him.

"Yes, I suppose we should."

CHAPTER TWENTY-SEVEN

As it turned out, the guests that Bryce had Roman pick up on that very amusingly chaotic Sunday morning almost a week ago were, in fact, Casey and Angelo. What made him decide, I still don't know, and probably, I would never know.

Bryce and I had made an entry, and perhaps, it was blatantly obvious what had transpired between us the night before because Angelo had immediately retreated into his brooding self while Cass and the rest of the boys gave me eyebrow wiggles.

As it turns out, though, by the end of the week Cass had made up with a very sorry Leo, and Angelo had been all too happy to leave, his former self now withdrawn and on the edge all the time.

I felt horrible about his darkening mood. He was, first and foremost, my friend and even though I could not give him my heart, I did still love him as a friend. He protected me, and he cared. And in the lowest of times, I felt guilty that I could never be able to like him back just to make him happy… even for a while? With me feeling so soft towards Angelo, it had taken a lot from Bryce not to hand him a knuckle or two on the face during one of our too many occasions.

And, well, things between Bryce and I? Yes, we had never been stronger. I supposed it was because of the patience from my part and strong will from his.

The full moon had come and gone. And Bryce really had chained himself with wolfsbane and silver shackles. It had been a horrible experience, not being able to sleep all night, hearing his yelling and growling.

The next day, he was exhausted, and so I had to stay in bed with him while he slept the whole day. It was necessary since his beast was on edge. But then the incredible task of actually removing his large, strong arms from my waist seemed impossible. He would even snarl at me in warning.

And so, like that, almost a week had passed. The holiday break had been partially shortened by Principal Williams with a promise of giving us a month break later in the schooling season. I was a little disheartened at that. With how things were going with Bryce and me, a little more time with him in the castle was always welcomed.

"You're quite deep in thought today," an amused voice spoke up from behind me. I smiled as I turned in my chair just in time to let Bryce lean in and place a kiss on my lips.

He made a move to break the kiss, but I pulled him back, not ready to let the warm feel of his lips go yet. A soft moan left my lips when Bryce groaned and pulled on my hand and off the chair before taking a seat and pulling me on his lap instead. Putting his arms around me, Bryce deepened our kiss. I smiled at the soft sigh that left his lips into the kiss.

"And there you go, lady and gentleman. They seem to be at it, again!"

Oh, God, not again!

The sound of quiet chuckles and happy coos reached my senses, and I tried to break the kiss. Bryce, on the other hand, snapped out of the kiss, pushed my face against his chest and turned towards our audience.

"Get out all of you! Aunt Meryl, you too!"

"Killjoy!"

"Fine, fine!"

"It is our right as citizens of this—."

"Roman, dear."

"Oh, alright!"

The sound of the door shutting close sounded through the now silent room. I couldn't help but smile against Bryce's chest, his spicy cologne blending like a blessing with his natural muskyscent as the smell of rain in a luscious green woods.

"They just don't know when to give up!" Bryce growled against me as the footfalls faded into distant taps. I couldn't help but chuckle and shift in his lap for a more comfortable spot.

"Well, maybe we should cut down—." My smile widened as Bryce nuzzled his nose against my neck, I leaned away. "— on this."

The room took a whole turn of mood when he snarled at me and grasped onto my shoulder before pulling me flush against him. "No one has the right to keep you away from me, not even you, Theia. You can forget everything but always remember that!"

My insides warmed at a strange type of feeling. I tilted my head to place a kiss on Bryce's chin before snuggling into him. "We've changed."

"Yes. I can't keep my hands off of you," Bryce stated with a serious tone.

I smiled as his fingers drew loose curls on my arms, his warm breathing heating my neck as he placed tiny occasional kisses here and there.

"That's pretty obvious."

Bryce chuckled as he wrapped his arms around me tighter. "Uh-huh."

I giggled. "Uh-huh."

Just then, there was a knock, and our eyes turned towards the tall, proud metal-crested Mahogany double doors.

"What is it?" Bryce yelled at the top of his voice, my eyes widened at how strong and deadly his voice could sound like.

"Your majesty, your aunt requires your audience in the main parlor; you and our Luna," A strong yet slightly shrill voice said from the other side of the door. Oddly so, the voice sounded confident and not in the least, bit scared.

Bryce turned towards me with a small smile and when I replied, got off the seat with me still in his arms. He placed a sweet kiss on my forehead before letting me slip to the ground as he began leading the way to the doors. Pulling on the doors tightly, we stepped outside, meeting Mr. Buckwood, the same man who had given us a tour around the castle during our schools visit trip. I smiled as the recollection of what had occurred that day floated into my mind.

"Thank you, Earl. We shall go now."

"Very well, Your Highness."

Descending the stairs into the regally beautiful parlor, I couldn't help but notice Meryl seated on an exceptionally fitting sofa. Its olive undertone and copper fringes blending perfectly with the shade and tone of the room. My eyes connected with her and instantly the decor was set aside, her foreboding expression now holding my utmost attention.

"Is everything okay?" Bryce asked me. I noticed that his voice almost carried a certain bit of anger. Apparently, he didn't appreciate being disturbed from whatever we were doing in the room a couple of minutes ago.

"Sit down, dear." Meryl's clipped tone instantly had me worrying a block more.

With an eyebrow raised up, Bryce complied, pulling me into his lap just as soon as he seated himself.

"This is so strange," I muttered under my breath, but Bryce obviously caught that, and his fingers pushed against my sides slowly in response.

"Speak."

"Son."

This seemed like a new voice. The strong manly baritone promising the sordid fact that once you heard this voice, you were probably never going to be able to forget it. I tried to turn in the direction of this voice's source but quickly huffed when my efforts proved futile. Now, I knew why Bryce had tucked my head under his chin.

"It's Your Highness to you, Prince Gerrath."

"Surely, you wouldn't alienate your uncle so much because of a foolish decision I made. I have apologized, haven't I?" The voice kept moving, and somehow, by the end of his sentence, I knew the man was standing before us. He talked about past apologies and mistakes. It was, however, clear that he meant none. He didn't seem very sorry to me. My dislike for this man grew a meter.

"Ah! I see you've finally met your mate, Your Highness. But I should add that by the way she's tucked into your arm, I am to assume that she is either an enthralling beauty or an ugly example of beauty and the beast; you being the beauty in this case. If you could please not find this offending and answer me, Your Highness, tell me which of the two is she?"

Bryce's sudden growl and a jerk forward caught me off guard, but I somehow managed to grasp onto his shirt in reflex, which helped me not embarrass myself by falling flat on my butt. I grimaced as his arms slid around me once again and a small chuckle bubbled out of the unknown man's throat.

At that moment, I couldn't help it. Not finding my head tucked underneath his chin, I quickly swept my face towards the source of the voice and glared at the man with the more ferocious hardness I could muster. He, on the other hand, stood still, his mouth slightly agape as his widened eyes took my form in.

Oldie really thought I was "an ugly example," but for his information, the beast was beautiful! And my beast is beautiful, stupid old pervert!

Behind me, Bryce took another growl before he pulled me closer and wrapped me against him again.

"Stop it," he snapped at the man, and I shuddered against him.

"Apologies. It seems that you have found a well-fitting mate, Your Highness. She is so unlike your usual contemporary beauties, blonde and model structured. You did well. And with the way you hold her, in a painfully controlled manner, I am assuming she is unmarked and unmated. You do remember that Royals can mark any unmarked royal mate they prefer, do you not? I suppose this is an open invitation to Alpha King Derrek. I have heard from the Lords that he is absolutely obsessed with another King'sm—."

"ENOUGH!" The ferocious growl that had erupted from behind me seemingly shut down the entire room.

There was a pin drop silence, and if I could help it, I would definitely try looking at the man just to see the expression of fear he probably had on his face. I could feel Bryce shaking now, deep dark growls rumbling from the depths of his chest. I could feel his fingers that were pressed against my sides beginning to grow and sharpen. A shudder passed me as I tried to gulp down some fear. Meryl, however, quickly acted on the unsteady situation and moved around the room to Bryce's side. Her face was now clearly visible to me.

"Calm him down, please." She mouthed desperately, flinging her arms in the air slightly.

I nodded, my mind still blank with whatever was happening. It was true. I had realized the increase in Bryce's hostility and possessiveness when it came to me. But it's turning out of control, and this was still a new thing to me.

"Hurry!" Meryl mouthed from where she now stood. Her stand almost desperate as if she were about to cry. *Why is Meryl so worried?*

"Bryce," I whispered against his collar.

I felt as he stiffened and let out a slow sigh. It was working, and with a smile, I continued.

"I love you, just you. You know that, don't you? I'm not leaving, not for Derek, not for anyone. Please calm down."

Prince Gerrath let out a thrilled laughter. "Looks like the little girl is not going anywhere anytime soon! Although I feel bad for King Derrek really, losing what he wants to you all the time. The man has the luck of a toad caught under a speeding car's tire!"

"You really should shut up, Prince Gerrath! If you value your life, that is, or I will forget that you were once married to Aunt Meryl."

Married to Aunt Meryl? My wide, shocked eyes had met Meryl's watery ones before she made a move to flee the room.

"Don't," Bryce growled, stopping her mid-run. I could only gulp as his hold on me tightened. "Now, Prince Gerrath, nonsensical things aside, what business brings you here?"

I tugged on Bryce's shirt to indicate that I wanted to move, but Bryce's arms only tightened on me. That is, until after a minute, his actions shocked me. His grip on me loosened, and I shifted on his lap to turn towards the prince. His eyes once again widened as they took me in before zeroing on a spot. It took only a minute to realize what he was now fixed upon. My hair had moved slightly, and my dark love bites were now exposed for the world to see. Behind me Bryce chuckled, helping Prince Gerrath's concentration move towards his right direction.

"Your grandfather's demise has left you with a sum of property, all of which I know you do not want. All of which you will have to leave for London to sort out. I want it. And so, I have come here to hand you a proposition. If you give me the property, I will take your Aunt back."

I heard Meryl's breath catch in her throat, and a small sob left her lips as soon as the old idiot uttered out that garbage from his lips.

Bryce however, chuckled. "Yes. I will be going to London tomorrow. But I'm afraid I have great pleasure in telling you this, but I have already decided to will properties to Aunt Meryl. That is on the condition that she and you have no contact, and if that happens, all that property will automatically belong to charity. I didn't regard grandfather's riches with any greatness, anyway. So you see, uncle, your service are not needed. You may leave."

The man stood frozen for a while. His expression altering from shocked to lividness. He turned to throw a distasteful glare at

Meryl before glancing at me before he proceeded to storm out of the large parlor.

"Every time I have the unfortunate luck of meeting him, he reminds me of how it was good that I had left him and that I had found him in that library with that fucking stupid blonde girl who couldn't keep it in her eighteen-year-old pants!"

My world stopped. My heart bled for Meryl as I watched her simper towards the couch and fall limp on it.

"But Meryl, how—? Isn't he your—?"

"Mate?" Meryl asked as she laughed bitterly. "I never found my mate. I was giving up. That's when I met Gerrath. Lord knows I rue that day."

As if sensing my awkwardness and regret at asking that question, Meryl quickly put her hands in front of her and shook her head as she said, "It's okay, dear. It's not your fault. I needed that. I thought he finally realized his mistake." She shook her head again and turned towards a silent Bryce and me. "I think it's time I retire into the kitchen, kids. The apple crumble won't make itself now, will it?"

Gone was the sorrow-filled expression. Her once lost bubbly self was back. But I could see through the facade. Seeing her douche of an ex-husband again had taken a rough edge on her.

"Do you think she'll be alright?" I asked Bryce as we both watched Meryl make her way out the parlor. Her strides showed a hint of slight unhidden anger.

"I don't doubt she will. She's a fighter," Bryce muttered back as he seemed to lean against the seat a little more, pulling me backward with him as he did so.

My mind reeled back to the one fact dear Mr. Douchery had let slip before he had fled, and I straightened in Bryce's lap. "When were you going to tell me about your grandpa?" I asked out loud, looking straight ahead.

"Back there in my office, But—."

"— Then this happened." I completed, sighing back against him as I raise my arms a bit to let him slip his around my waist.

"I'll be back in a week, you know," Bryce muttered, the feel of his lips moving against my hair as he spoke, making my arms tingle.

"I'll miss you. I'll probably spam your inbox. Heck, by the end of the week, you will be all done and ready to reject me!" I joked, a ripple of giggle leaving lips.

It was only seconds later when I realized that I was the only one laughing did I tilt my head back to glance at Bryce, only to stop and gulp. Fiery golden eyes glared back at me as I gulped down another burst of fear, a slight shudder running down my arms. This was not a good idea, being this close with an unstable Bryce, who had turned a little too territorial after our little make-out fest almost a week ago.

Bryce chuckled. My posture straightened almost immediately. Bryce's beast had finally made its rare but occasional visit. I knew because it held a deeper tone although how was not clear to me. Bryce always did have such a deep baritone himself. "You look scared, Theia?" Bryce said, leaning in as his intense golden eyes shone a little brighter, a strange twinkle present there.

Somehow, I knew his beast liked games. He liked to rile me up. Bryce had some reasonable explanations as to why, but my own theory was that he thought I was punishing him by not letting us mate; thus, the sudden sessions of intimidation seduction after last Sunday.

Everything would be great and jolly, and his wolf would suddenly make an entry out of nowhere, teasing and seducing like a pro I'm sure it was. The funniest thing here, though, was that I knew that Bryce secretly didn't even try to hold his beast back. Bryce wanted exactly what his beast wanted and somehow, as twisted as it was, his beast wanted what I wanted. But they didn't need to know that yet. Patience always made everything sweeter in the end. My eyes widened on its own accord as I realized what I was thinking about, and I blushed slightly, fidgeting in Bryce's lap.

"Should I take that as a yes?"

Trying my damn hardest to conceal my thoughts, I immediately pulled up my recently well-mastered smirk and turned to face Bryce. Now facing him fully, I straddled him. "Scared? Me? You don't scare me anymore, Bryce." My smirk widened as Bryce's surprised eyes moved towards the finger I was now jabbing into his hard chest playfully.

His lips quirked up on the sides as he quickly snatched my finger from his chest and brought it up to his lips. His eyes held mine as he lightly bit onto the tip of my index finger before slowly pulling it into his mouth and sucking on it.

"Bryce, stop," I whispered, afraid that if I spoke any louder, my voice would give away the tingles that were now terrorizing me.

"Make me." Bryce's eyes twinkled with mischievousness as he winked at me. I blinked, and the spell broke. My smirk returned, and before he knew it, I pulled my finger to safety.

"You're good, Anderson," Bryce grinned as he tucked a strand of hair behind my ear. His grin widened. "But I'm better."

It was all but in a startled gasps time span that I found myself pressed between a sofa and a smirking Bryce. I watched wide-eyed as Bryce leaned in closer until his warm breath touched my lightly parted lips.

"So tell me, beauty, are you scared of this beast yet?"

* * *

"I fucking hate it when you look at that thing."

Still smiling lightly, I gave my newly gifted ring a soft touch before turning towards a frowning Bryce.

"You have no need to be jealous, babe. He just wanted to give me something to remember him by."

"Yeah, something you apparently never take off anymore!"

I glanced again at the sharp-edged ring that only just a week ago belonged to Angelo's pinky finger, resting halfway up my right ring finger. It was something I had seen him wear ever since he was fourteen. He had given me a part of him and just as I had cherished the others that were handed my way by my loved ones, I cherished this jagged silver part of him too.

"Your jealousy is clearly messing with your memory, babe. I take it off before I sleep and while I take showers and cook."

Bryce slumped into the bed, his tan, strong bare chest illuminated perfectly in the glowing dim lights of the room. He looked at me blanked-face, clearly indicating that he was waiting for me to get in too. I rolled my eyes as I slipped off Angelo's ring before replacing grandma's ring. Braiding my hair into a loose simple braid, I quickly secured it with a band before turning towards the bed. A mischievous smile graced my lips as I looked at Bryce's quickly widening eyes.

"Theia, don't do it!" Bryce warned quickly, putting his arms out in front of him. I crouched slightly, preparing myself. "You'll hurt yourself!"

Still smirking, I let go into a speedy run before jumping straight into bed. My breath knocking off my chest as I landed on Bryce's strong chest. My lips smacking against the hollow part where both his shoulder blades meet in the middle.

"Goal!" I breathed, giggling as I quickly placed a quick kiss on the tough yet smooth skin.

My smile widened when I heard Bryce chuckle as he ran his fingers through my hair, loosening my braids even more in the process. "Sometimes, you're so impulsive and crazy. You remind me of something."

I tilted my head slightly to look at Bryce, and my eyebrows scrunched up in confusion. "Remind you of what?"

His arms tightened under my breast as he continued to let me smash him with the full force of my weight. A low chuckle left his lips when he replied, "Why you're designed perfectly for me."

"I love you,Alex."

"Alex?"

I nodded. "Alexander; I don't say it too often."

He hummed again, pulling me closer as he tucked his chin over my head. "My flight leaves before you wake up love, tomorrow."

"Can't you—? I have school tomorrow. I hate this sometimes," I grumbled against his chest, my sight turning blurry. I knew it wasn't goodbye, that he would be coming back home… to me. But something had me feel like this was my last moment with Bryce. I felt scared. I realized I was scared to lose him. Living without Bryce would be damn well hard. I would live. I would, maybe. But loving without Bryce was, well, impossible. I wouldn't love. I wouldn't… ever

Not being able to hold on much, I let a sniffle slip and quickly rubbed away my tears as discretely as I could. "You'll come back to me, won't you?" I mumbled lowly, trying not to show the strange desperation in my voice; desperation I didn't know why I possessed.

"Always, princess. I love you too, Theia. I don't say it enough, but I do. I love you."

I nodded against his chest before tilting my head and meeting his worried eyes. His eyes softened when they noted the moisture in mine, and he quickly leaned in to place his lips on mine. I couldn't help but let the strange tears flow as I kissed him back with everything I had. I kissed him like it was my last day, like it was his last day.

I love you too Bryce. I love you too.

CHAPTER TWENTY-EIGHT

If there was ever a chance of me learning even one magic trick, anyone could bet their wooly sweaters I would probably learn how to make people disappear. Sitting there in the cafeteria, my face resting on my hands, I continued to move my gaze from Marley to Jeff to Connor.

Apparently, Diandra had left and moved over to her aunt who lived somewhere in Seattle. Apparently, Diandra had never been a werewolf. It was as if her leaving had opened up this large canal of information about her that had been else wise buried behind her home walls.

I, for one, was still feeling incredibly guilty about how things had turned out for her despite the fact that her dad had regained his senses and made a point to apologize for blaming me for his daughter's faults. Maybe that was why I refused to be a part of the conversation the group was currently having.

A sigh left my lips as my eyes drifted towards a laughing Alex. It seemed like he barely cared how much of a downfall he had caused in Diandra's life. Although, he looked healthier and happier than he had since I could even remember. I suppose Diandra had been just as toxic as he had been to her that day throughout their relationship.

As if sensing my eyes on him, his gaze moved on mine, and he stilled. His grin now turning into a smirk. He wiggled his eyebrows in a mischievous manner only he could pull off, and I almost let out a giggle at the sight. That was until an arm slipped around my shoulder and a stiff growl sounded from beside me. I turned, surprised, towards the source of the sound and rolled my eyes when they found Roman's hardened features.

"That pup needs to know you're spoken for." Rome growled lowly as he continued to glare at an indifferent Alex.

Probably hearing Roman, Alex rolled his eyes and turned back to the girl in his arms as he continued to whisper into her ears to which she let out a loud, obnoxious giggle. It was my turn to roll eyes.

"I think Bryce made a mistake leaving Roman in charge of your safety, Thi. He has turned into an even more of an uptight moron," Marley chided suddenly, giggling as she leaned into Keith's embrace.

"Control your woman." Rome spat at Keith gruffly before he continued to glare at Alex.

I rolled my eyes again, ignoring Roman's protective hold on my shoulder. "Does anyone know why Matthew is not in school today?"

"Oh, he's supposed to pat—."

"His mom got a new pet puppy, and he's in charge today!" Roman cut Jeff off in the middle of his sentence. Getting up, he pulled me with him. "Let's go. We're getting late for art class."

I barely had time to think things through as I caught hold of my backpack before tumbling behind Rome as he made his way out of the cafeteria. I could hear Marley grumbling behind us, rushing just as we were to get out of the cafeteria. We had only just crossed the cafeteria door when the bell rang, alerting us that we were, in fact,and going to be very late for the following art class if we didn't put a step on it.

"Mr. Naight, I see you've finally given us the honor of having yourself in our presence since you informed me earlier today that you were finished. Would you mind showing us your assignment? I see Miss Anderson is well secured in your arms."

Roman smirked as he continued to maneuver me towards the center of the class, the wrapped up canvas resting on his arm. The class watched us with slightly wide amused eyes as Roman and I rounded around Ms. Sveen's table and stood in front of them. It would be a lie if I said that having Roman stand beside me acting, well, like he usually does was not awkward at all because it was. It always was. I almost laughed at the picture we were probably portraying, him being the big bad wolf, and I, innocent little Red Riding Hood. Little. Literally, Roman stood an almost good foot taller than I, my head barely reaching his neck.

"The class is waiting, Mr. Naight. Miss. Anderson?"

My head shot upwards, tilting just right to look at Roman. Our eyes met, and his smirk widened.

"Thank you, Ms. Sveen, our project is already done and ready. If you could only give me a second or two to unwrap it?" I mumbled, fidgeting a little under a couple of Diandra's well-wishers' scrutinizing gazes.

It just so happened that the school had suddenly found itself dividing between people who blamed Alex and me for Diandra's misery and people who blamed her. Well, then there were also people who just did not give a rodent's butt hole about Diandra, and those who played Switzerland. Personally, being under all those watchful eyes, all I wanted to do was fly off to Switzerland and get lost somewhere in the streets.

Ms. Sveen nodded softly, and I quickly got to the task at gently but quickly unwrapping the covers off of the canvas. The brown paper tore off, and my breath hitched in my throat. The collective number of gasps around the room seemed silent to me as I continued to watch dumbfounded at myself in the plain brown T-shirt I had worn on a very boring Thursday afternoon, the first week of our bonding week.

Now, looking at myself etched on the beautiful canvas with a softness only Roman's paintings seemed to possess shocked me even more than the rest of the people in attendance because he had picked this painting out of all the other ones, ones I had actually posed for, or I was actually aware of.

"Wonderful job, Rome! You have captured Theia beautifully!" Ms. Sveen praised excitedly as she shifted on the borrowed chair at the back of the class.

"I suppose I have," Rome agreed, a tone of indifferent arrogance. I rolled my eyes at him as I moved towards my seat, pulling on his shirt a little as I began.

If I didn't know Rome any better, I would have called him a jerk. But knowing him allowed me to see through things. I saw through Rome. He didn't like people. They were an acquired taste. It had taken me some time, but I had accepted this, and I suppose now I was fine with it.

"So I've got bills."

I turned towards a blank-faced Rome. My attention was broken from staring at the wonderful masterpiece Lionel had also managed to complete.

"I gotta pay. So I'm gone work, work, work *e'reday*."

Roman turned to look at me expectantly, a sudden smirk playing on his lips. I rolled my eyes letting a grin of my own form on the corners of my lip.

"I got mouth. I gotta feed. So I'm gonna make sure everybody eats!" I belted out as lowly as I could. Instantly, an even bigger grin lit up on his face, and he leaned in closer.

"Very good little, Theia. Looks like I have taught you well!"

I let out a very un-lady like scoff as I grasped my pencil and raised my gaze to the rest of the class. Immediately, a curious gaze or two caught my eye, and I stiffened. The girls were staring again. Upon the time of our friendship, I had found various students almost staring blatantly. A lot has even been so curious enough to approach me and ask me how if they had been right… if they had actually seen Rome smile. As if sensing my sudden knowledge of them staring, the girls quickly averted their gazes and turned to face the front.

"Hey, listen, I have to be at the council meeting this afternoon, okay? So I'll come by to play guard by six," Roman murmured, pulling my sketchpad towards him. I frowned as he flipped the pages until it landed on the drawing of Adam and Belle. He traced this finger along the edge of the page as he seemed to hesitate for a second before he finally spoke. "Maybe we could watch whatever it is that you drew here. The— The Beauty and the Beast?"

I was about to reply when the bell for next period sounded around the classroom. Immediately, everyone around us began to place their supplies into their backpack and move out.

"Sure, Rome. We can watch the cartoon," I giggled as I turned to pick my bag before beginning to shove everything into it.

"What?" Rome suddenly exclaimed loudly, "Cartoon?"

"Oh, yes! Disney's Classic too!" I smirked, getting up and already moving towards the door. "Don't worry, Rome! We will have lots of fun watching it!"

"We're not watching it, Thi!" Rome huffed behind me as I walked out of the classroom. The halls were less crowded than the usual normal days.

I couldn't help but turn to give Rome a mischievous smile, "Oh yes, we are."

* * *

It turned out that out last two classes were free since surprisingly both our Math and Gym teachers seemed to be caught up with some personal commitments, and well, that was how I currently found myself sitting under a large tree with the group. I watched warmly as Marley leaned into Keith's embrace. Internally, I couldn't help but desperately shove down an aching longing for Bryce.

"Anyone up for 'Insidious: Chapter 3'?" Jeff suddenly spoke up, pushing his nerd glasses snuggly into position as he continued to scroll through his phone.

A shudder ran down my spine as I recalled the horrifying trailer, and I immediately prepared to shake my head. There was no way in Neptune's throne that was I going to go watch that disaster.

"A disaster to your sleep you mean?" Connor chuckled as he lowered himself down beside me.

I face-palmed myself. "Said that out loud, didn't I?"

Connor chuckled. "Always do."

"Just so you know, we're taking you. I already booked us the tickets… non-refundable," Jeff grinned, making a final tap on his iPhone screen before slipping his cellphone into his front pocket.

"Oh, this is going to be fun!" Marley giggled as Keith landed another one of his kisses on her forehead.

I scowled at each and every one of them as I slipped out my phone from my pocket and quickly tapped on "Create New Messages."

Just then a ping sounded, and I smiled as I read the sender's name.

Guess what?Dad's taking us on a family vacation to Hawaii! Isn't that amazing? Angelo doesn't want to go, though. He has been sour ever since his return. Can you do me a favor, Thi? Message him, please. Maybe he might listen to you. Anyways, how are you? How are things with your Alpha male going? All good, I hope!

-YourBabyMommaCasey.

I couldn't help but smile as I typed back a quick reply and pressed on send just as my ringtone began blaring around the slightly moderately populated school grounds.

"Hello."

I stilled, my vision already becoming blurry.

"I love you." I breathed into my phone. I clutched my iPhone harder against my ear as I heard Bryce let out a shaky breath from the other side of the line. I knew the distance was affecting him too. "I miss you," I mumbled into the line again, letting his deep breaths as an answer be enough. "I hope you're okay."

"I love you, Theia" Bryce's deep voice sounded solemn, and for a second, I nodded, completely forgetting that he could not see me.

"I miss you," I repeated. Leaning to place my head on my knees, it was hard enough to control not crying in front of my friends. It was horrible crying because you couldn't stay away from your boyfriend for a few hours. How pathetic was I?

"I'll be there by Friday, love," Bryce mumbled back.

I sighed. Was it pathetic that a week seemed too long? *Damn it, I was becoming clingy!* I shook my head to rid some of the emotions before finally replying, "Take care of yourself, will you?"

"I will…" Bryce stopped for a second before he continued, "I don't want even a hair out of place on you when I get back Theia."

A soft giggle left my lips, and I rolled my eyes, a quick glance towards the group had me blushing bright red. Each and every one of them was making smooching faces, well, everyone except Marley. She, for the first time, was actually blushing her face off. It was then that I notice the darkened mark on the crook of her neck. I made a mental note of asking her about that later, as I quickly turned to my phone again.

"Yes, sir," I muttered back, a large smile etching my lips as I managed to get enough sarcasm in that reply.

"I'm serious, Theia. I don't want even a single hair on your head out of place!" I smirked at the low warning in his tone.

"Or what?" I grinned as I leaned into the phone more, the teasing remarks from behind me getting louder by the passing minute.

A shiver ran down my arms as I heard Bryce chuckle on the other side of the line. "I don't think your friends would like to know, Thi."

"Right on, mate!" Jeff mumbled out as he leaned back into the tree and closed his eyes.

The rest of the guys' and my eyes held wide as we waited for Bryce's reply. Lord knows Jeff knew nothing about whom I was talking to and what his position was both in my life and in everyone else' present.

"Tell your friends I said hey." Bryce chuckled, and I let out a breath I was holding. Lately, he had been getting a little too territorial and violent with people. I felt a little weight shift that he was not quick to temper at Jeff's little mumble.

"Bryce said Hi," I grinned at everyone. I was sure everyone saw the blush that was now on my cheeks. Thankfully, they seemed to avoid that as they all yelled out a "Hey" of some sorts. Bryce chuckled again from his side of the line.

"I love you," I mumbled slowly, turning away to face the vast expanse of a green. Rosenberg high school really did have a great amount of land to name its own.

"You know I love you too, don't you?"

I sighed. "I know."

"Is Rome taking enough care of you?"

A giggle left my lips, and I snuggled closer to my cashmere sweater. "Oh yes. He is great! In fact, we're going to watch Beauty and the Beast tonight!"

My smile widened as a deep laughter seemed to rumble from the phone. "I'm sure he will have fun."

"I'm sure he will!"

"I love you. You know that, right?"

I smiled. "You've told me that three times in this phone call. And you say it all the time, well… Most of the time. So yes, I know. I love you too."

"Will you two just keep repeating that? You love each other! We all know that! Now, move on, little kiddies!" Roman's sounded to me, and I quickly looked up to stare at him with wide eyes. My blush now burned my face.

"Shut up, cousin," Bryce growled playfully. "I have to go now, love, but I'm going to call you tonight, okay? Be safe, be good and I'll see you in three days."

The heaviness in my chest was back. I was acting like a little kid again, craving Bryce here with me. This needed to stop before I embarrassed myself.

"Okay. I miss you lots," I whispered back, trying to sound as broken as I suddenly felt. Why did it feel like I was about to lose Bryce?

As if he had caught the slight croak in my voice, Bryce growled. However, this time, it was not playfully. This time, he was serious. "Don't make me pack everything up and show up there by midnight."

My breath caught in my throat, and I almost choked on what my saliva. "N-no. You have work there. Sort that out, okay? I'm fine. Promise."

I could hear as Bryce sighed and moved about where ever he was. "Okay. I'll call you tonight, all right?"

"Uh-huh." I sighed as I closed my eyes, trying to let go of the panic that was fighting me within my chest.

"I love you."

My lips quirked up. "I love you."

The phone stayed still against my ear even when Bryce had disconnected the call. I couldn't help but keep it near and be still in my position. It felt like time wasn't moving. And somehow, suddenly, I didn't really want it to. Or if it did, I wanted Bryce here with me.

* * *

"You sure? I could always skip the council meeting." Rome asked me for the fifth time as we sat in his car in my driveway.

I shook my head as I leaned in to give him a hug before moving out of the car. Turning back, I leaned against the car window. "It's fine, Rome. I'll see you later tonight, okay?"

"Okay." Rome sent me one of his rare smiles. His rare smiles always made me feel better. They were beautiful. I supposed it was always a wonder to see the "always angry" ones blow into full smiles.

My smile still on I walked towards the door and upon reaching it slipped the key into the lock and pushed it open. The smell of freshly baked cookies scented the entire house, and I could almost hear my stomach beginning to grumble.

"I'll bring your cookies and warm chocolate up in a few, dear!" I heard Agnus call out just as I began to drag myself upstairs and towards my room.

"Thank you, Agy!" I yelled back, my mouth already salivating for the moment when I could simply devour my cookies.

I smiled as the familiar scent of my room hit my nostrils in full force as I opened the door and walked in— Gardenia and Rain. "I need to bathe," I mumbled to myself in an almost tired voice before flinging my bag on the study table's seat and marching towards my bathroom.

* * *

Freshly showered and sweat free, I moved into my bedroom with full-blown smiles. I had given myself a good amount of a lecture speech in the bathroom, and now, accepting that Bryce would be back in three days seemed easier. I noticed that there were some changes in my room as I walked in. One, a tray lay on a vacant spot on my study table, a still warm cup of chocolate and freshly baked cookies beautifully on full display. The other, however, was the wide-open windows. The rapidly cooling air almost breezily making their way into the room.

Almost immediately spotting the castle, I moved towards the window and leaned against it. I looked at the mist as it surrounded the neighboring mountains and trees, almost enveloping the castle as if it were its cashmere jacket. My gaze moved towards the floor I was once supposed to be in. I almost immediately caught it. It was slightly in the older part of the castle, and even though my wing and I had a lot of distance between us, I knew there was no claiming otherwise. That part of the castle really was magnificent even from a distance. Then in the next minute, my whole world came crumbling down.

A gasp ripped out of my lips as my hands moved to clutch my head. Bits of the object that had just a second ago slammed and broken against it still sunken into my skin. I could feel a wet warmth dripping onto my forehead and down my cheeks. The pungent smell of iron and blood now holding my full attention. My axis turned as I continued watching my white tank top soaking slowly in red. "I'm bleeding," I thought numbly as I tried to clutch harder to my head. "Bryce will save me."

Taking a short breath in, I tried to turn to face my assaulter. Maybe if I could turn around… Maybe if I could just see who would do such a thing… Between all the pain and periodic blankness, I gasped as I saw my assaulter. Everything stood stagnant, every feature. But what I knew I would never forget those sharp green eyes.

"Now, you'll know never to shatter someone's love. Goodbye, Theia"

My assaulter smirked and leaned into me. I glanced down as my assaulter's hand spread flat on my chest before with a quick ease, I felt myself tipping back out of the window. I was falling. My eyes were closed as the darkness overtook me. My eyes opened again numbly... *Mom… Dad…* Darkness evaded my senses again. *"I love you. You know that, right?"*

Bryce… I smiled as I opened my eyes. Bryce's face flashed across my eyes again. The first time I saw him in his room, his beast.

Roman… Matt… Marley… My eyes closed again, and I sighed. I was getting tired now. Was it okay to be too numb to worry about death? Bryce would save me. Casey's platinum blonde hair swam across my eyes, and I looked as Angelo's piercing gray eyes looked back into mine. My eyes opened again, I was still falling. The air rushed against me as gravity did its work.

"You belong to me, huh?" I felt a tear slip down my temple as I remembered that night. *"What do you think?"*

Realizing for the first time how this was going to end, Bryce could not save me. He was in London. I was falling. I was dying. I was never to see my family again, my friends, Bryce. Everything I had dreamt of was all a could have been.

"I love you Theia… I'll be there in three days."

"I love you too Bryce." It was barely a whisper, but it sounded like a yell to me. I was about to die. I didn't want to, but no one could save me. My vision began to blur, but this time, I couldn't bring myself to mind.

I knew I was closer to the ground now… Any minute now…

Darkness enveloped me again, and I fell into it. I was only just wrapping my arms around the darkness when I fell against something hard. That something began to speak, but I could barely hear it beyond the dark haziness. As if for the final time, the dark haze clears, and I manage to open my eyes, my withering gaze links on panicked brown ones. I let out a whimpering labored breath; the darkness was finally coming to embrace me forever. This was it…

"Matthew…"

My eyes traced the brown orbs above me. I could only whisper his name before the last bits of life was sucked out of me.

And it was at that moment that I knew… Death felt like a fall.

TWENTY TWENTY-NINE

BRYCE

"The southern borders have been secured, Your Highness. Also, Mr. Knockwood has called in, Sir. A complete analysis of the property has finally been made."

My mind swayed to the matter at hand as I nodded in acknowledgment. The property and title were irreversible. There was no chance I would be able to relinquish my hold on the title, and to manage that, I needed the properties.

Arriving here only minutes ago had only one fact standing strong and proud; I would have to capture throne to the U.K. *Well, inherit it.*

I huffed out a puff of air in frustration as I pressed the bridge of my nose. I did not want to expand my holds. I was perfectly fine with North America. And now grandfather had apparently written everything to me— power and position without my knowledge.

The grand meticulously carved doorway came into view as I rounded off into the corner of the hallway. Heaving in a deep breath, I prepared myself for what lay ahead. Hopefully, the no good of a lawyer found a way I could transfer everything to our closest cousin Benjamin. My life was in America. Theia was in America.

"Am I to assume you have found a way, Mr. Knockwood?"

The fidgeting man instantly began shaking like a leaf. My frown deepened. This man had better have found a substantial method.

"Y-your Highness! It's a p-pleasure!" The slightly balding man instantly rose from his seat and extended his hand in respectful greeting.

I stood looking down at him as I altered my gaze between his face and his extended arm for a second before grasping onto it and giving it a firm handshake.

"What have you found for me Mr. Knockwood? I prefer it if we cut to the chase. I do not want this," I spoke in a mildly business-like tone as I motioned around the room.

"B-but, sir, you will gain more power! You will be the most powerful Alpha King!"

"Do you have a method or do you not, Mr. Knockwood? You are wasting my precious time."

Instantly, the man stiffened in his seat and moved an inch back into his seat. I almost growled in agitation.

"Again, you're wasting m—."

It then hit me, an Earth shattering pain. It felt like my entire life was being torn away from me like my lungs had been hammered, and I could not breathe. I clutched my chest as I slipped from my chair and bent over on the floor. Something had happened to Theia.

"ROME!"

"Yes, Alpha!" Roman's voice came through our mind-link sounding very submissive. He understood that I was currently his King and not cousin. Good, I needed submission.

"Where is Theia? Theia is hurt. You were supposed to be her shadow. Get yourself to her!"

"Theia is fine, Alpha! I just dropped her home half an hour ago!"

My anger flared as I clutched harder to my chest. My life was being cut into half. I knew she was hurt badly.

"I said get yourself to her!"

"Okay, I—."

"Theia!" Matthew's intrusion into the mind-link left me with only one feeling: dread.

"Matthew!"

"Theia, Theia, Theia! No, no, don't die on me! Don't die on me! Theia, please! Please, Thi! Gotta go to a hospital! Oh, my God, Theia!"

My eyes widened as I realized Matthew wasn't talking to us but to his own self. His emotions seemed all over the place, and he didn't even know whom he was contacting. I could feel the bile pooling in my mouth as I now sat on the floor frozen.

"Matthew, mate, I'm coming!"

Then Matthew let it slip, and the thin thread snapped.

I let a tear fall as my heart cracked and crashed. I let another fall, then another, and as each tear fell my anger increased, I let it. I let my beast approach. My restraints were weakening, and my beast needed my mate. I needed my Theia.

Matthew unintentionally flashed another image of Theia looking just as lifeless as she had a few seconds ago, and that was when I lost it.

I let myself go to my beast. I could feel as my bones cracked, demanding a transformation, but I didn't allow it. I would endure the pain. My vision, hearing and smell heightened even more so. The feel of my veins bulging out of my skin left me feeling my position. I was the bloody Alpha King and whoever had dared hurt my mate would know just how much power that position gave me. I was going to rip the person's fucking life out with my bare hands. I shot up to my feet, and for a second, my vision blurred and just for that split second my beast took over completely.

Letting out a livid growl, I grasped hold of Mr. Knockwood's collar and moved him in front of me, lifting him up to my eye length.

"I accept everything. Prepare the damn papers and fly over to my castle. Get your damn self there in a day."

An already sweating Mr. Kockwood nodded vigorously, and I dropped him back on the floor as I speeded my way out of the room. Everything was a blur around me as I slammed through the closed doors, not even fidgeting when it flew backward, ripping off of its hinges.

"Alexander! Alpha, r-respond, please!"

I snarled at the sound of Roman's voice when he began linking me. It was all his fault.

"When I get back, I'm going to rip your arm off so you can feel a fraction of what I felt when my mate was fucking dying because you couldn't guard her!"

I could hear Rome's wolf whimper and break down, but I didn't care. I knew Roman never cried, and his wolf wouldn't be found in a weak state even if it killed him. But I didn't care! My Theia was dying. What if I never got her back? I needed to get there!

I knew I was probably still crying, but I kept speeding past hallways and doors, slamming and smashing everything I went through. Suddenly, I stilled when I heard Aunt Meryl's voice break through the pack link in a sob. Her hurt and desperation reached out to me as she unknowingly linked with me, sending me an image of my Theia on the verge of death lying on a stretcher.

I let out a strangled growl as I began running towards an open window, this time, taking the easiest way down. I leaped out of it. My feet touched the ground, and I speeded towards the man I needed.

"Get a jet ready. I need to fly back to Peidmond right now!" I growled as I reached UK's Royal Beta, Hugh.

"No offense but I—."

I had my hand around his throat before he could even finish his response. I grinned as I felt my claws sink into his neck, and his eyes began to bulge out with the pressure.

"I am King now! This is my kingdom! And I fucking want you to ready my fucking jet! My mate is dying! Fucking get to it now!"

* * *

The closer we had gotten to Peidmond, the more I lost myself to my beast.

By the time we were minutes into the landing, I was seeing red. I knew I was probably going to kill everyone within a meter radius to Theia, and so much as I felt like ripping a few throats, I let Matthew know I was coming.

I glanced up to see the stars shimmering silver against a moonless night as I speeded past trees, knocking over a few trees, trying to state the anger in me before I reached civilization again.

My feet froze when I ran out of the woods and onto the road. The hospital stood on the other side. Glancing at my hands, I felt my eyes heat up again. My Theia lay somewhere in there, fighting for life and death. *All this was my fault. I should have never left her alone. I traveled a lot, and now, it had given my enemies enough time to hurt her. It was all my fault.* I held back a strangled growl as I speeded across the street and into the hospital.

Theia's scent hit me like a ton of bricks, and I choked down a sob. *Fucking pussy!* I growled at myself as I entered the empty elevator and immediately pressed the button to close the lift doors.

"Intensive Care Unit, son. Fourth floor." I grimaced as Aunt Meryl's shaky voice cut through the link. Curling my hands in a fist, I swore at the speed of the elevator. When it finally did stop with a *ding*, I couldn't find myself to give a fuck's ass about the humans around me as I speeded past them. Their slow movements suddenly a blur around me.

I slammed against a door. The scents of everyone assaulted my nostrils, making me barely hold off a livid growl as they all mixed with my Theia's. I grasped onto the door handle and pulled the door open.

"Fuck!" I watched the fucking door handle in my hand as I held the now broken piece.

The door pushed open from the inside, and I looked up to see a disapproving doctor glancing at the broken door handle.

"I'll buy you a new door," I snapped at him as I looked past him into the room. "Get out."

"Alexander!"

"I said everybody get out!"

One after the other people piled out of the room: crying Marley, sobbing Mr. and Mrs. Anderson, Aunt Meryl, a shamelessly crying Matthew… My anger returned as Roman made a move to get past me. I grasped his shoulder as he did. My claws retracting to inflict all the damage I had planned on doing while on my way here.

Turning him with a rough swing, I stopped. Roman's bloodshot eyes and dead expression had caught my eye before his head lowered towards the ground. His shoulders slumped as if in defeat. I frowned.

How was I going to kill someone who already looked good as dead? How could I inflict pain when he looked like he was feeling hell? Fuck it! A growl bubbled from my chest as I pushed him out of the room and closed the door.

I knew everyone was looking in through the glass, but I didn't give a fuck. I kept standing frozen, looking at my feet, and too afraid to see what my absence had caused my Theia.

I slowly padded my way towards her, afraid to look at the frail face I knew was on the bed. My mind ran back to the first time I had caught her scent, the first time I had heard her voice and touched her hand. My mind ran back to the time when she had accepted me so easily, accepted my beast and loved my beast.

I glanced up and looked at her. I couldn't help it. I fell to the floor. Demented sobs ripped out of me. *It's all my fault. It's all my fault.*

"No, it's not. It's the culprit's fault, the person who pushed her, the person who tried to kill her. It's not your fault, son. Theia needs you right now. Be strong, for your people, for your Theia!"

Anger bubbled me as Aunt Meryl spoke. She was right. It was the culprit's fault. And I was going to hunt down whoever it was.

"You're right. You're right."

I swiped the back of my palms across my face as I got up and moved towards the bed, now looking at Theia and nothing else. I was going to make sure her pale cheeks found their warmth again if that were the last thing I would do. I would turn her if that could make it any better.

So mind made and will concrete, I walked around and sat on the chair beside her bed. Reaching out, I grasped onto her hand. My lips thinned as I felt the cold instead of her usual comforting warmth. But her heartbeats were still there, and I knew that as long as I could hear her heart beat. I would fight. And God forbid, if it stopped, then I would kill. I glanced at her comatose, bandaged self again, my grip on her hand tightened.

"I love you, Theia."

* * *

MATTHEW

Patrolling sucked like skunk and rotten eggs sucked.

My ears perked up at the sound of birds chirping in the far east direction. When Rome had informed me that I would have to patrol outside Theia's home, I had not given it a second thought. Theia was important.

A sigh left my lips as I whipped my tail a little. My light brown coat wavered slightly in the wind as I lifted my muzzle up and took a sniff. Something felt wrong. My instincts going on hyper drive I ran towards Theia's bedroom. My large paws thumped heavily against the ground.

"Fuck!" I swore as I looked up and saw a hand tipping Theia over the window. A golden jewelry of sorts caught my attention but only for a second.

The heavy scent of Theia's blood had me cringing with panic.

She fell with a great speed, and I didn't have enough time, so I took a shot and transformed just in time to have her land in my arms. I watched my Theia with wide blurry eyes as a content little smile eased on her bloodied, tear-stained face. Her eyes opened an inch as she took a shaky breath in. Our gazes met, and I couldn't help but let a tear slip down my face.

"Matthew" she breathed before the last remnants of her consciousness left, and she passed out.

"Theia!" I growled loudly. I was mad at her for being hurt, mad at her for being alone in her room. Fuck, I was mad at everything!

Her heartbeat weakened, and my breath hitched in my throat.

"No, she couldn't die!Theia, Theia, Theia! No, no, don't die on me! Don't die on me! Theia, please! Please, Thi! Gotta go to a hospital! Oh, my God, Theia!"

Not giving my state of undress a second thought, I ran. The fucker in her room would pay! I didn't get a scent, but I would get the person! That fucker would beg for death after I would be over with him! Hell, Al— my eyes widened, and I let out a scared scream.

Fuck, Alpha Alexander will go crazy!

Suddenly, an arm wrapped around my bicep and pulled hard. A growl left my lips as I felt myself lose control but only a second. There was no way in hell that I was going to let Theia fall! Digging my heels into the ground, I made a swift turn and crouched low, Theia still in my hands.

I will die protecting you if I have to, Thi. The fucker will not get you so easily again!

"Matthew, relax man! Give me Theia! I'll take her to the hospital, and you go change!"

I broke out of the red haziness for a while when I saw a red-eyed Roman standing in front of me, extending his arms out as if to hold Theia. I snarled at him threateningly.

"You've got to be shitting me if you think I will believe you so easily! For all, I know you could have done this!"

Rome's eyes hardened as he began walking towards me.

"Don't you fucking dare accuse me of that again! Just give me, Theia! We need to get her to the hospital before she bleeds to death, dammit! This is not the time for your suspicions!"

Glaring at him, I passed sweet Theia into his hands. Instantly, he took off.

"You better take her to the hospital, Roman! Beta or not, I will fucking hunt you down and watch as Alpha will rip into your chest!" I growled at him as I moved to put on my pants.

Even though I knew he was already half way to the hospital by now, I knew he could hear me, the perks of being a Royal. I growled as I hurriedly put on my T-shirt and shot after him, hoping Theia would be okay was the only thing on my mind.

CHAPTER THIRTY

BRYCE

The afternoon sun sunk lower behind the vast expanse of the concrete jungle that lay out in front of me. A sigh left my lips as I brought up the steaming cup of tea to my lips before leaning against the moderate sized window. The smell of bleach and soap hung around the hospital room, probably because it had just been cleaned and I had only just bathed minutes ago.

Lowering the cup from my lips, I broke my gaze from the view of the city and slowly turned towards the comatose girl lying on the bed only a few steps away.

I flinched. There it was. The familiar burning in my chest, the burning that reminded me that the love of my life was hanging by a thread, the burning that reminded me that every second I lost and wasted if I was not any closer to who had done this to Theia.

I didn't even know when it was that I reached her, but I found myself caressing her cheeks softly, just like I found myself doing so, often lately.

It had been a week since I had come to a brink of losing her, a week since she fell, and I broke. The warmth in her cheeks was returning and the blues in her lip slightly fading. My eyes touched the bandage covering her head, and I stifled in a growl. It had been a week, and I wasn't any closer to catching the scum who had done this to her than I was on the day she had been pushed.

But that had not stopped me from doing everything in my power to hunting the scum out.

I took another sip of my hot tea before turning and placing the cup back on its saucer.

"It's Tuesday today, Thi. Aunt Meryl and the lads will be here in the afternoon after class. Your mom and dad will be too. I'll have to leave for a while, okay? Going to the castle to have a meeting, love. I-I'm doing everything I can to catch the person who did this to you. You'll be fine, love. I won't lose you. I won't let you go. I love you, Theia," I whispered as I leaned in and placed a soft kiss on her petal like lips.

I smiled as I felt my Theia's heartbeat increase for a minute, already used to the reaction every time I touched her or kissed her. She was in a coma, I knew that, but I knew she was there. She could hear me and feel me. I knew it.

"Mr. Whilhem…"

Damn it!

A frown already forming on my face, I turned thin-lipped towards the unnecessarily inquisitive doctor who had the misfortune of being assigned Theia's case. He was the brightest and most talent specialist in the whole state, yes. But he was just too inquisitive and curious for his own good.

A grimace made its way to my face as I watched him ready himself mentally for the new question he was about to pop up on me. It really was his misfortune. Misfortune because I was very well on the verge of ripping his vocal chords out any day now. If only he weren't the best in his job…

"Yes, Doctor Lucian, how may I assist you today? Should I assume you are progressing with my ma-hmm-girlfriend? Are there any new reports?"

Doctor Lucian's eyebrows quirked with intense curiosity at my near slip-up, and I almost began readying myself for his death. My claws already retracted from my fingers.

The fool of a doctor should have put his curiosity for a good cause, really and found out how quick I was to losing myself lately. My beast was lost without Theia. And every day that passed, it moved closer to self-destruction or complete annihilation of everything around it. The thread was slipping. I was losing myself to my beast.

I glanced at my anchor lying on the bed. Her soft brown curls tucked in a bandage that hid multiple sutures needed for her wounds.

Whoever had hit her with the vase had a great amount of strength. The impact of her wounds was too much to be a job of a human. It was clear that the scum who tried to kill her was not human. That left only one thing… a werewolf.

But who?

"Mr. Whilhem, is it true that you are a titled Duke?"

My back straightened automatically as I tensed up. Reaching down to grasp onto Theia's hand, I shot the specialist a chilly stare before answering, "Yes."

The doctor reeled backward as if stuck. In what sense, I didn't know because, damn everything, if I didn't smash him myself if he didn't stop with his interrogations.

"Do you have any more questions, doctor?"

I couldn't help but smirk when a struck Mr. Lucian shook his head abruptly before he did a bow of sorts and nearly ran out the door.

"UK's Royal Beta and the Delta just arrived Alpha."

My senses peaked as I felt Roman's voice through the link. The boy was a wreck. And somehow, during this past week, I had come to pity him more than hate him for what happened. Roman hated pity. I supposed that was why our relationship had strained to such formalities. The worst part was. I didn't see it fixing anytime soon.

"When are you, Matthew and Aunt Meryl reaching here?"

"Matthew and Aunty Meryl are just about to get there, probably, in five."

That was another thing. Roman refused to visit Theia. He refused to see her. But I knew. I knew he visited her when he thought no one was here. His scent lingered around her bedside way too many times a night. At first, I was livid. The mere presence of him around my mate, sometimes lingering on her cheeks and her hands made me see red. But then one night… it stopped.

It had been one of the rough nights. My beast was seemed caught in the tangle of fury, demanding Theia, so much so that I had found myself standing outside of her hospital room's door only fifteen minutes after I had initially left for the castle.

I had been well on my way into opening the door and marching in, but Roman's silhouette bent over Theia's bed froze me on my knees. My initial reaction almost forced me to rip him away from my mate, to rip his hands off of my mate. But then his shaking form seemed to clear out to me. Roman had been holding Theia… and crying.

"Alpha?"

My eyes shot into focus, and I shook my head in agitation.

"Okay, I will be there as soon as they get here. Until then, let the Beta know who's in charge. I dislike his attitude extremely."

"Okay, on it."

A sigh left my lips as I felt the mind-link fading away. The image of a crying Roman flashed before my eyes every time I wanted to be mad at him for letting this happen to my Theia.

I turned to face Theia again and slowly leaned in to place my warm lips on her slightly cold forehead. Her heart beat increased again, and I almost smiled at that.

"I love you, Theia. You're my everything," I mumbled, pressing another soft kiss on her lips.

"Alexander dear…"

I shot up immediately and turned around. My eyes anywhere but at my aunt's and Matthews. I avoided their gazes because I knew what it would hold. They were waiting for me to break down, to have this room under lock to stick beside Theia and to not let anyone near her. They were waiting for me to break down and refuse to eat, bathe, sleep, and dammit, there were times when I was on the brink of it all, but I wouldn't.

I refused to make myself weak when I could be searching for the scum who did this to her. I couldn't lose myself and expect her to find herself. How could I break down in hopes of her fixing herself?

I had to be strong. And I was. There was no way in fucking hell that I was going to let that scum go or let my mate wither away. She was mine. And as long as my heart continued to beat, everyone could be damn sure hers would too!

"I will be back as soon as the meeting is over." I turned towards Matthew. "Have you figured out whom the human scent in her room belonged to? It's clear that the actual criminal masked their scent, but the human scent was left unmasked. We must find the human, Delta!"

"The scent matches no one in our territory, Alpha. That means…"

"It's someone else— an outsider." I finished his sentence, moving to glance at my unconscious, beautiful mate.

"Yes," Matthew muttered. His stance now alert and businesslike.

"Contact all the Kings. We need to find that scent. Each of the best Tracker Were's in our territory will travel around different territories looking for the scent. Hand them the pieces of bed sheet and sweater the scent is most prominent in. We must find him."

"Yes, Alpha."

Aunt Meryl walked past Mathew cautiously. She gave me fleeting glances as she neared Theia and settled herself on the chair beside her bed. I watched as she wiped away a stray tear and began softly humming slow tune to her.

"I must get going," I murmured before turning and making a swift exit. The earlier I left, the faster I would be done with the meeting and return.

Just as I made it out the door, I collided head on with Mr. Anderson. I stilled. Mr. Anderson looked away awkwardly as he tried to hide the misery on his face.

"H-how are you, son?"

"Not an inch better than I was yesterday."

My head turned towards my shoes. I, too, avoided his gaze.

I was a coward. I could not bring myself to look into my mate's dad's eyes to see the disappointment there, the soul ripping hurt. I couldn't bring myself to look at him after I failed to protect his daughter, after his daughter got injured, possibly, because of me. I had let him down. I let myself down.

My head lifted, eyes slightly wide when a hand reached out and thumped me on my shoulder.

"I don't blame you, son. Just… don't let this go unavenged."

I nodded, lowering my head again when I noticed the slight crack in his voice. What was worse than watching a mother and father cry for their child— their daughter?

"I won't, Sir."

Mr. Anderson gave me another shoulder pat before he silently walked past me and into the room.

I stood still in my place. Turning towards then closed door slowly, I shook my head off the pain and disappointment I was feeling before walking towards the elevator.

* * *

"The best of our trackers will start on the job as soon as tomorrow, Your Majesty."

I nodded briskly at the Royal Beta of UK. The good thing about the man was that he was talented and honest in what he did. The bad thing: for a beta, he was not truly royal.

I supposed that was what made the man want to prove himself so much, want to prove his worth between us Royals. Maybe Matthew did too.

"Very well, Beta. I suppose this conclud—."

"ALEXANDER!"

Ever had the feeling where everything around you seemed to spin in slow motion. While you, you stand still and unable to move? I felt it.

When Aunt Meryl's panicked voice spilled loud and clear through the mind link, I felt everything around me slowing down, and the thumps of my heart deafening. I knew in an instant. Something was wrong with Theia.

I ran. That was how that current moment found me, blurring through the forest. My tie and jacket discarded already miles ago. As seconds passed by and trees stretched out past me, I let myself go to my beast more and more. It was hopeless. There was no stopping it. A growl ripped from my throat as I sighted the Peidmond Hospital and speeded in towards the door, accidentally bumping into someone.

"Sor—."

Fuck. I turned, searching for the person I bumped into. *The scent… is so familiar.*

I couldn't help but cuss out loud when the only thing I found behind me was a dozen heads amongst the many people in the crowd. The person was gone.

"Mr. Wilhem, this way please!"

Looking the young male nurse with narrowed eyes, I took my time before nodding and then proceeded to follow him.

My wolf was not keen on anyone at that moment.

Maybe it was a mistake. I thought about this scent as I followed the slow man.

The feeling of my claws growing out of their bedding made my need to just get into the damn even more.

Fucking hell… This will take a year! I need my mate.

"It's safe to speed, Alpha." My eyes narrowed a notch further.

Is this man saying what I think he is saying?

"I'm in your pack. Well, I was. I mean, I'm hoping to j-join in again."

"We will discuss it later pup! Just take me to my mate without being detected now!" I hissed back. My eyes bolted shut, fighting off the beast that was overpowering me by the second.

The seconds that passed between the man and me reaching Theia's room undetected was a blur. The slight smell of burning rubber assaulted my nostrils as I stood in front of the closed door for a hesitant second. My Theia was inside… fighting to breathe.

I threw the nurse's white shoes a final glare before I stormed through the door, unable to hold my beast in anymore.

Everyone instantly moved against the wall as I entered. Their heads were slightly bent down. My beast snarled at their submission, pleased that they understood the delicacy of my state. My eyes zeroed in on my mate. The heart monitors told a very dangerous tale— dangerous for everyone present and responsible. The fool of a doctor, though, still stood, hustling over my mate, pressing the defibrillator on her chest and yelling orders to the scared nurses.

An aged nurse turned towards the heart monitor and shuddered.

"We're losing her."

Those three words, as soft-spoken as they were, managed to elicit an equal amount of reaction from everyone present in the room.

I heard when Aunt Meryl and Mrs. Anderson began to sob. And the men in the room tried to be as strong as they could for the women.

I… I saw red.

The last remnants of control left my body, and I let my senses go to my beast. A growl rumbled out from the depths of my chest as I began to stalk over to her side. My eyes did not once leave her now beautiful but pale skin. How had it come to this?

From the periphery of my gaze, I noticed the female nurses had retracted towards the wall while the specialist still stood beside my mate, frozen on his feet, shaking like a leaf and staring at me with wide, terrified eyes.

Foolish human! I snarled at the fool of a doctor before gripping him by the collar and pulling him away. *Fucking mortal!* I knew what I had to do.

I watched as the heart rate slowed in the monitor, even more. I leaned over her, my nose grazing her cool neck.

"I'm so sorry, baby," I whispered and a slow, broken smile wiped itself across my face.

I knew my hands were shaking as I brought my fingers and slowly peeled the hospital gown off of her left shoulder. I pressed a single fleeting kiss on her soft, cool skin as if for an apology for all the additional hurt she would have to go through because of this. But I had to do it… I had to save her.

And so with a final whispered declaration of how much I loved her and that she was going to be fine now, I bit into her skin.

* * *

ROMANOV

There comes a time in your life when you realize that death will always be a constant. That no matter how much you try to avoid it or how much you try to prepare yourself, death will always surprise you.

First, my mom… *as if that wasn't hell enough*, and now… Theia.

Theia— my best friend; the one single person who took her time out to figure me out, to know me.

I don't think I could ever forget the first time I laid eyes on her— warm porcelain skin, wavy long brown hair, and those big brown doe eyes… beautiful. Beautiful enough to be crushed.

I had hated her… the innocence and the bravery. Then it all changed.

No matter how hard I tried to be mean to her and to be brisk and nasty even if it had been in her own house, she always walked through it all.

And now, there she lay, slipping away. And it was my fault.

They say that one day, you'll be that loved one snatched away and taken. I had always thought about dying. I had always imagined dying at the brick of old age, finally living through it all. *If I had only just guarded her… If only I had just stayed…*

A long huff of breath left my lips as I moved out the hospital room and sunk lower in the seat provided just outside. It had only been a minute since Alexander had stormed into the room. I rushed out. I was not a coward. I was just ashamed. He was losing the only thing that came first and the only one that anchored his soul. And it was all my fault. Closing my eyes, I hoped everyone in the room would sit still. One wrong move and it would be a blood bath.

"Dammit," I muttered out loud tiredly as I pinched the bridge of my nose.

"He's marked her." Mathews shocked whisper echoed around my minds walls.

He had marked her. He had marked her before the mating process. Before… *Fuck*. Nonetheless, I understood why Alexander did it.

"I thought that isn't the way—."

"It's going to hurt her tenfold more."

"So why?"

"It'll link his soul with hers."

There was a minute of complete silence before Matthew finally understood.

"It will heal her."

CHAPTER THIRTY-ONE

MATTHEW

It seemed like a normal occasion to me these days, finding myself wondering if it's normal to constantly think of how much of a shitty pile life can be. One minute, everything seemed like peaches and kisses in the rain, and the next, you just found yourself falling off a cliff, head down towards your doom.

It didn't get better at home. In fact, it got worse. I constantly found myself thinking of how fucked life could be with my perfectly faked happy family. When in reality, my parents could never see eye to eye. And then here, I'd always find myself thinking how much of a letdown life is every time I saw Theia still unconscious, lying on the hospital bed.

I supposed it seemed stupid of me, running from one mess to the other, running from my parent's potential divorce to Theia's comatose self. Perhaps, I shouldn't even be shocked about this. This was something that should have been expected from two human parents—*adopted*— two human adopted parents.

Sometimes, I could even find myself wondering how hard it must be being a human, never being able to know your true soul mate out of the billion all over the world, and instead, just taking a wild jump in the dark… hoping every time that the one you are with now is actually the one. But then it doesn't turn out to be the one, swearing off love until you're ready to take a blind jump again.

I supposed that was why growing up love scared me.

At first, it was with finding people who could actually appreciate and love me for the abomination I had already known myself to be at the age of eight. Then when I did find that sort of love, it was with becoming attached to any new toy or thing. It was the fear of being disappointed, of being rejected.

Since the last few days, that fear has evolved, and now, I am just scared of love, *period.*

Alexander looked like he was dying each day. Roman stalked around, looking like a soldier on autopilot. I watched as Roman flinched beside Alexander while Alexander continued to caress Theia's hair. I looked down in understanding as I stood outside the hospital door.

Alpha Alexander's mind block seemed to be slipping again. It always did nowadays.

Whatever seeped through seemed to shake everyone around him to the core. I didn't know what it felt like to die, but I'm sure if I could feel death without dying, Alpha's thoughts would be it.

It had been two weeks since the incident and a week since Alexander took a risk and marked his mate— our Luna, our Queen.

Exhaling a huff of shaky breath, I looked up just in time to see Roman flinch for the second time. At this point, he stood with closed eyes and a tight jaw. Thankfully for the poor guy, only just a minute later, Alpha placed a final kiss on Theia's forehead turned and stormed straight towards the door. I moved back instantly, taking my position away from the door. I was to stay with Theia now.

"His thoughts feel like a sky liner crashing down on me. I don't think I can control this anymore, Matt. I'm staying back."

A sigh left my lips as I moved into the room and locked eyes with Romans red tortured ones.

"I'm just afraid Alpha might do something rash. We have not made any progress with neither Theia nor the culprit. Alpha seems to... to be on his last nerves."

"Tell me about it," Roman muttered loudly shaking his head as he slumped down on a sofa in the corner of the room. His fingers firmly pinched the bridge of his nose.

Another sigh left my lips as I turned towards the beauty lying on the hospital bed. Her warm pink cheeks looked better than it had a week ago. In fact, she looked better than she ever had, but the fact still stood, Theia was still in a coma. Our Theia was still comatose.

I slumped down on the chair beside her bed with heavy breath and looked down at her hand as I did. Mustering up enough courage, I grasped onto her palm and rubbed her soft skin in slow circular motions.

"I wonder if Mrs. Anderson is holding off better than she has been doing past the two weeks. You know ever since that doctor finally decided to keep his mouth shut and genuinely help Theia recover rather than expose us."

A loud snort escaped from Rome's lips as he leaned further into his seat. "Bet he loved Mayor Johnson's reaction."

"Bet he'll love the Alpha's reaction more if he ever has the misfortune of stumbling in front of him again."

Roman let out a bitter laugh. "That doctor should have known the Mayor would know. Hell, everyone important knows. That's how they know not to cross us." His expression softened as his gaze switched from the window to her. "Do you think she'll be okay?" he mumbled a bit shakily, twiddling his fingers together— a sign of nervousness.

I turned towards Theia. It hurt every time I did so, but I couldn't help it. Somehow, I always wished I'd see her awake, smiling at me. A soft sigh left my lips as I turned towards Rome and got off the chair, reaching him I laid a palm on his shoulder and pressed it comfortingly. "She'll be fine bro. She'll be fine."

Roman nodded as he switched positions and settled down further into the sofa. He closed his eyes as he let out a tired yawn. He had not been able to have a proper night's sleep. I turned towards the window and my gaze on the dark gray clouds, a telltale of how it would soon be raining.

I didn't know when I began walking, but soon I found myself at the open window, looking out at the dimly day.

A chilly gust of wind swept into the room, and I shuddered in reaction. "I should close the window. It's getting a little chilly," I thought as grasped onto the window and began pulling it to a shut.

"Matthew."

Then I stopped. Everything stopped. It had seemed like a weak whisper, merely brought by the breeze. But I knew.

My whole body did a "one-eighty" as I turned towards the bed. My heart seemed like it could beat right out of my chest.

Fuck…

"Theia!"

* * *

THEIA

Dark— everything was dark. But I could hear these silent hums. Sometimes, it felt like someone was talking to me. Sometimes, I could understand them. I could understand him, this one hum... This one deep hum that always sent tiny tingles in me. Sometimes, it felt like I even knew this hum. It felt like I couldn't live without this hum.

Still, everything was dark, and I couldn't move. I tried to respond to the hums, maybe move a finger when I felt as if they had touched my hand. I tried to hum back, but I could never.

It was as if everything seemed hazy. I couldn't even conjure up an explanation to where I was. Often times, only one thought stood stagnant in the darkness— death. Death felt like a fall. So, was I still falling?

"Bet he… The Alpha's reaction … misfortune… him again."

There it was again— the hums. This time, however, it seemed like I could understand it. I concentrated a bit harder. I needed to listen. I needed to get out of this dark. I tried and tried, but nothing came, just the silent blurry hums again. I waited and waited... And then, it came.

"Do you think she'll be okay?"

The soft, almost whispered voice, seemed almost alien but stronger than the normal hums. I tried concentrating on who it could be but nothing. What was happening around me? Where was I? The darkness seemed to be overtaking my senses again, but I fought through it. I wasn't going to let it win. I needed to hear that familiar voice again, the one that sent tingles in my mind.

"She'll be fine bro. She'll be fine."

Wait. I knew that voice. I knew. Who was this voice, this hum? I really, really needed to talk to these hums. I really needed to ask them about the one that sent tingles through me. I really needed to get out. It was at that moment that I felt myself land in strong, able hands. Familiar bright blue eyes shined down at me. Slowly, the bright blues dulled down to warm browns. The strong features turned almost soft, and the slightly wavy hair molded into straight strands. And then I knew… I knew whose voice it was.

The darkness in my head began fading into me as I ripped my eyes open. The blinding light in the room almost had me gluing my eyes back together. But I found myself blinking frantically instead. The dulling pain at the back of my head came rushing back, and I almost groaned out in pain.

That, however, was not the first thing I wanted to utter, so instead, with all the strength I could muster, I managed to utter the only thing I knew right now.

"Matthew."

It came out weaker than I had hoped it would, but somehow, he heard and almost lost his balance as he shot towards me. The warm browns I would know anywhere swirled with everything from disbelief to relief. And when he rushed towards me I gladly managed to put up a shaky smile.

"Theia."

That was when I noticed the other guy in the room— tall, shoulder length dark wavy hair with dark eyes that seemed to sear into my soul. He, too, rushed towards me. But I frowned. Glancing at Matthew for a second, I looked back at the muscular boy.

"W-who are you?"

* * *

ROMANOV

Fuck everything. She doesn't remember anything—nothing past her first day in school and nothing beyond Matthew and that preppy friend of hers. She probably doesn't even remember Alexander. Hell... She doesn't even remember me.

I swept my hand across the coffee table and glanced blankly at the whole glass table toppled over and crashed into the floor. The telltale sound of loud growls and havoc occurring in the room across the castle alerted almost every one of the current condition of our king.

The man had lost the final thread. Heck, even I could understand how devastated and angry he felt! Theia had clutched onto Matthews shirt almost all throughout the time until her parents, Alex, Marley and everyone came over.

Somehow, I found it strange that the Doctor Lucian allowed Mr. And Mrs. Anderson to tell Theia about everything: how many weeks had passed and how things had changed—everything but the truth about us werewolves, everything but the truth about Bryce. When Theia had managed to convince her parents to go back home, she had resorted to clutching Matthew's shirt again. I still felt like ripping Matthew and his shirt away.

It had been fifteen minutes into being alone when Theia noticed that I had not moved from my spot at the corner of the room. What she had done next almost shocked the pants off of me. She had called me by my name— *Rome.* Somehow, she had thought I looked like Rome. I was glad when Matthew told her of how we were good friends. It was only then when Theia allowed me to move closer to her. The hug that came next seemed automatic. Almost strangely, she didn't pull away. Her right hand, though, still clutch to Matthew's shirt. I suppose she felt safe with him. He had, after all, been the last person he had seen before going blank. He had, after all, saved her life.

Another loud crash echoed through the castle and followed by a tortured cry. I could understand Alexander's pain. Mr. And Mrs. Anderson had not allowed Alexander to visit Theia, laying out some crap about not stressing her too much on such a delicate day. I thought it was all bull. It was a practically a crime. No one could keep a mate away from the other. That was not acceptable. How Alexander had controlled himself, I would never know. But I knew that Theia, even though unknowingly, was looking for Alexander.

I had seen her looking into everyone's eyes before talking to them. Each time a slow disappointment flashed in her eyes, only for a second, before she put the mask back on again.

Letting out a growl of my own, I looked up into the mirror. The gashes on my fist were already healing. I rolled my eyes as the distant tinge of blood wafted through the air and touched my nostrils. Across the castle, Alexander also seemed to be having a blood bath. His blood always did have a tough iron pungent smell. Letting out a loud scowl, I marched towards my bathroom and shut the door behind me as I entered it.

* * *

THEIA

I never found him— the familiar hum I heard when I was in a coma.

Somehow, I felt like he had the bright blue eyes that I had seen just before they dulled into browns. I supposed that was how I found myself looking for those blues. The blues showed me a slice of the sky. However, that was only partial of what I was looking for. The slight tinge of brown on the upper edge of his blues matched mine. I couldn't even find those.

It was how I lay here now, thinking about the voice I could have very well imagined. The eyes I could have very well made up.

Had he just showed up today? Did he even exist? Was he just an angel that had sheltered me in the darkness of my coma? I didn't know. For now, though, I knew that the memory his familiar hums telling me that everything will be okay would help me through the night. I sighed as I closed my eyes and leaned into the soapy-smelling pillows. I could feel as the painkillers worked their way through my headache and into my system. Everything felt hazy as I pulled the bed covers over my chest. The knowledge of my dad sleeping on the sofa in the far corner of the room made it seem safer.

As the final waves of light faltered from my eyes, I let myself fall into the arms of Morpheus. Somehow, in my mind, though, he had those familiar blue eyes with the tinge of brown that reflected mine. It's was in no time when darkness took over. This time, however, it felt almost soothing.

CHAPTER THIRTY-TWO

I suppose it was only when I had stepped into my home after being released from the hospital that the realization of how much had gone past and how much I could not remember actually settled in.

It had looked like my bedroom was untouched in a sense that there seemed to be a layer of dust covering my study table. My study table was adorned with ornaments I could not remember buying. My bed was there, looking as homey as it had since its very first day under my ownership two years ago. Although, the bedspread that covered it was unknown to me.

My gaze had moved towards the one thing that I knew I had looked forward to— the window and the castle's view. I could still feel the feeling of excitement that I felt in the pits of my stomach as I had made my way towards the large window and opened it.

The very window I had fallen from according to Matthew, or I had been pushed down from according to Roman.

Now, I could understand why anyone would want to throw me out a window, figuratively that is. I admit I could be annoying and irrational as hell. But on literal terms, whose heart had I broken again?

Still feeling a bit annoyed to have been thrown out of my own window, I glanced up only to come to a halt. The man in white was standing on the balcony of the castle again, the very man who has stood there on my first day, probably the only day I can remember with great detail. The man and I stood staring at each other for a minute. Let it be known that all I could make out from his distance was his broad form and white shirt, probably even his wavy brown hair. Maybe he was the man with blue eyes and that tinge of brown that reflected mine.

Looking around I found the one thing I needed the most—my binoculars. As if hesitantly, the man had brought up his palm very clearly and moved it into a small wave. I had almost reeled back at his actions but found myself soon following his path and waving back. I remember wondering as I had closed the window if he really was the man with the blue and brown eyes and then thinking if I would ever find out.

* * *

"Are you sure you can go home on your own?" Marley asked me for the third time, her tone slightly nervous.

I raised my eyebrow as I stopped in front of her and held her in place. She had been going on and on about having one of the boys dropping me home since the morning. But I didn't see the point anymore.

"Ley, you know it's no use making one of the guys drop me when my folks got me a car. I'll be fine. I promise."

Marley rolled her eyes as she continued to drag me along with her towards my newly gifted car "That's not a car, Thi. That's a Land Rover, a Land Rover LRX Concept. That isn't any car! It's a god damn vehicle!"

"You really should stop saying God damn." I chuckled at her before getting in. Turning the key in the, I lowered the passenger's side of the window and bent to look at Marley. "You really sure you don't want me to drive you home?"

Marley stopped dead in tracks before she contained herself and shook her head quickly. I frowned at that. "No, no, it's alright. Keith wants to drop me home."

"Oh, well, have fun!" I wiggled my eyebrows at Marley while she scowled at me. Still giggling, I shot her a wave before driving past her and out of the school's driveway.

Looking at the passing trees as I drove on, I sighed, and I shook my head. There was no one in Rosenberg High with the voice that I seemed to crave and with the eyes that seemed to haunt my every waking and sleeping hour. A week had almost passed since I got home from the hospital and three days since I got back into school but nothing. Not even the man in the castle seemed to have any time to visit me now. In fact, the castle almost seemed barren.

I even noticed how strange most of the people were acting around me as if something seemed to be ripping at them; like how they knew something they pitied me for. I hated that. I didn't need anyone's pity. In fact, I was taking my amnesia quite well. The doctor had told me that it was temporary. I suppose that added to the relief of things. Not that anyone knew, of course, I had asked him to keep that bit confidential. I guessed a part of me hoped to surprise everyone when I eventually did get my memory back. Maybe the hope of getting my memory back allowed and encouraged me to make new ones while having a chance. Of rewriting things again while having a chance.

Rome and Matthew seemed to be the worst out of everyone around me. But Rome was the worst. Often times, he came to school looking demented and highly worn out. He told me only just three days ago that it was because his cousin's brother had flown off to London to take care of some things and instead, left Rome in charge of the large pack they had. Rome had slipped. He had said pack instead of family. I guess his tiredness allowed him to say things he normally wouldn't. It was then when I initially got the feeling of something very big being hidden from me.

I mean, who said pack instead of family? Everyone was acting weird. Matthew and the boys trailed behind me wherever I went. Roman nearly ripped throats at any glances I received from anyone. The boys nearly helped. Mom and dad couldn't look at me in the eyes for more than a second. Angus couldn't help but fret over me for the tiniest things, pulling Lilly to do the same. And Marley? Marley couldn't stop giving me retail therapy, always slipping bits and pieces here and there like watching Beauty and the Beast and possessive males and soul mates.

"Who says amnesia is a bad thing? See it my way; it gives them a chance to fall in love again." My mind hovered around what I had heard Roman's Aunt Meryl whisper to Matthew and him. Whom had she been talking about? Obviously, I was the only one here with amnesia, but who was the guy she was talking about? Meryl seemed like she knew so much. She was the only one who managed to tell me everything clearly when I asked her for it. Sometimes I wondered if I should ask her about the hum I was still searching for. The blues and browns that had seemed to have etched itself in my mind.

Often times, I felt like I was trying to find something that always stayed in the shadows— always close, but never visible.

I tapped my thumb against the steering wheel as I waited for the gates to open. My home looked as red bricked as ever against the nearing autumn golden hues. The gates moved open, and I quickly drove in through driveway and into the garage. Parking my Rover, I grasped onto my backpack and slipped out of the vehicle. Locking it as I walked towards the garage door.

"Agnus, are you home?"

Hmm… Maybe they aren't home.

Letting out a casual shrug, I began making my up the stairs and into my bedroom. I smelt like a dozen sweaty male colognes and Marley's expensive turd of perfume. Clearly, I needed to get out of this mess of a dress.

* * *

"So hungry," I couldn't help groaning as I rushed down the stairs, hoping I'd get something in me before my tummy decided to sing another one of its native's song.

Slipping into the kitchen, I stopped when my gaze met the refrigerator's silver door. I slipped the note from under the magnet and quickly read through.

Gone downtown to buy some groceries, miss. Might be back by six thirty. Kept your favorite roasted chicken and mashed potatoes in the fridge. Heat it up if you're hungry. Don't forget to lock the doors and windows.
-Agnus

P.S: Mr. And Mrs. Anderson will be out till late tonight so do not wait for them. They called around noon. Be safe, miss.

"Okay!" I spoke up against the silence of the house as I placed the note on the kitchen counter and moved towards the fridge again.

Waiting on the roast gave me time to think, and somehow, I found out I felt slightly awkward being alone in my home as if I couldn't fully trust what lay in the darkness of the shadows and something would grab for me if I didn't pay much attention.

The ping from the microwave sounded, and I easily made up my plate of delicious looking meal before quickly moving towards the living room.

A soft noise of something swinging aired through the current silence, and I quickly put the plate and glass on the coffee table before moving towards the source of the noise— the back door. I froze. I had never been to this part of the house, the backyard. I supposed, in this past week, I had been constricted to everything on the inside due to rain. Nothing on the outside could be explored. But now I could see…

The grass seemed slightly overgrown. The large tree branched out wonderfully, as it grew tall and proud. But what held my eyes captive and what seemed welcoming, almost alluring was the simple plank swing that hung from one of the stronger branches of the tree, swinging back and forth slowly in the soft breeze as if inviting me for a swing. I didn't know if it was some sort of magic, some sort of invisible string that pulled me towards it but before I could realize what I was doing, I found myself out in the backyard, running my fingers slowly against the coarse ropes.

This urge in me wanted to take a swing, to wait for something and to wait for someone because… because somehow, maybe I had before.

The food forgotten, I slid onto the swing and slowly grasped onto the rope. Almost immediately, I jolted forward when the warmth of another, a larger familiar hand, engulfed mine.

What the fuck? Frantically, I looked back, but nothing. A soft wind caressed my skin as if in a sorry, and I sighed. Somehow, the touch seemed so real. Somehow, the touch seemed so familiar. Somehow, I knew it belonged to the hum I was searching for. The tingles were proof enough.

It was hours later when I found myself back inside the house. I had fallen asleep on the swing. The light drizzles of the afternoon rain against my shivering skin and calls from Lilly had woken me up. When Lilly pulled me into the house with her, Agnus had given me a scolding of my life. I had a feeling Agnus knew exactly what I was doing on the swing, the knowing look in her satisfied, aged eyes told me enough, but somehow while she knew, I was clueless.

Who was I waiting for?

I supposed that was how I found myself here in bed. Glancing to my side a smile shimmered through, and I reached to bring the large mug of hot chocolate to my lips. I looked down at my lap again and grimaced. My draft for the history essay seemed only halfway through, and it was due tomorrow. So placing the mug back on the side stand, I grasped onto my pencil and began scribbling through the page once again. Aiming not to stop until the essays draft was finally complete.

* * *

There it was again— the strange clatter.

Stifling in a groan, I snapped my eyes open and instantly moved my palms to rub the sleep away. All my books seemed piled up on the edge of the bed. I supposed I had been too tired to place them over at my study table before giving sleep a go. Then it sounded again.

My eyes shot towards the direction from where the sound was coming from, and I instantly shot to my feet. The sound was always muffled as if it was intentionally being kept to the minimum of sounds. My hand grasped tighter to the empty mug as I edged closer to the window. The faint light from my bed stand's lamp illuminated the room only partially, and I gulped in fright of what lay ahead.

Just pull the damn curtain and smack whatever is there with your mug, Thi; then, call dad and 911, Do it!

Breathing in a final breath of the brave air, I quickly pulled the curtains open just as the clatter sounded again and immediately dropped the mug.

There hanging by my window… was a man.

I stood frozen.

Looking at the man's shadowed face as he stared back, it felt normal… Why?

The man looked down then back up at me as if thinking whether to make a run for it or stay. I felt my heart began to beat faster when the man slid the window completely open and jumped right into the bedroom. He straightened up in the shadows and stood extremely still. Somehow I knew, his gaze was never faltering. I felt confused. I felt as if this had happened a million times before. I felt safe. This was where I was supposed to be. My breath hitched in my throat. I glanced at man's arm, his fists stiff and clenched beside him.

Gulping down slightly terrified of what was to happen next, I slowly reached out for his hand and sighed when my palm wrapped partially around his wrist. *The tingles…* My gaze found his hidden ones as I hesitantly but surely began taking steps back into the light. He started to clear out— black shoes, dark blue jeans, black t-shirt, his neck…

My steps grew braver as I lead him slowly away from the shadows. He dipped his head low as we completely moved into the light as if he were ashamed. I frowned at his actions; then, I frowned at mine. This was hardly something ordinary. I ignored my crazily beating heart as I spoke the next words, "L-Look at me," I stopped. P-please… I need to know."

The man stiffened further, but thankfully, I managed to stand there in front of him, my grip on his wrist forgotten. Slowly, he lifted his gaze to meet mine, and the whole world froze.

His bright blue eyes shined through with unshed tears, but my gaze stood stagnant on the tinge of brown. I looked at the man standing in front of me while the rest of the world shifted off its axis.

I had found him— the hum. Glancing up at him, I closed my eyes as the tears I never knew where there slipped out. *Why was I crying? Why did I feel like my world was safe again? Why did I feel like holding him as he stood there in front of me looking as vulnerable as a man could ever come to look?*

I don't know what prompted me to say what I said next, but I did. I looked him in the eyes, a small smile on my lips, and my grip on his wrist tightened as I stood in front of him.

"Bryce."

CHAPTER THIRTY-THREE

My eyes swept along the trees as they continued to tremble in the drizzling rain. The scent of wet soil smacked against me in an onslaught as another strong gust of wind passed against me, almost rattling me from my bones. I felt a shudder run down my spine as I watched myself rush out from the back of my house and into the rain. A black umbrella shielding me from the harsh fall of the rain. I felt like screaming, like fainting because clearly, I could not be here and feet away at the same time. But I was.

I was standing here in broad daylight, watching myself run out the back door of my house as if I was watching a movie about me. But instead of the screen being just at one place, it was all around me. The other me, however, didn't take any notice of the actual me standing here in plain sight. That got me thinking… Was I dreaming right now?

A movement in the corner of my eye broke me out of my revere, and I quickly refocused my concentration to the other me as she quickly walked towards a man sitting on the exact swing in my backyard. How had I not noticed him earlier?

She stopped in front of him. I watched stunned as he looked up, and the tension in his bright blue eyes faded immediately into a smile.

"Hi." The hum…

I felt my breath hitch as darkness began spreading around the scene in front of my eyes. I found myself standing still as I watched the other me and the man melted into darkness before a whole new scene began painting itself out.

"Let's go."

My eyes shot towards the large door that stood on my left. A second later the strong, elegant-looking door shot open, and the same man with the bright blues stormed out of the room. I stilled. He was pulling me out of the room!

"Leave me!" The other me hissed at him as she tried to pull herself away. The man, on the other hand, only turned towards the other me at a speed I could never fathom possible and slowly brushed his nose against hers— my— her— mine… Oh, never mind!

I felt slightly less sad when the darkness began spreading on this scene. Somehow, it felt like we were seriously up for some face fisting and such. And honestly, I did not want to witness that.

It wasn't even surprising when another scene began molding its way around me. This time, I knew my surroundings. I was back in my bedroom. From the beads of light shining through the large open slightly open window, it was obvious that it was early in the morning.

"What the fuck!" I almost screamed when a slow moan sounded from behind me. Instantly, I jumped to face the sound and immediately froze.

The man lay on my bed, quite obviously shirtless, but what shocked me wasn't the man with the hum. Instead, it was the girl who was cuddled against him— the other me.

I watched myself as the other me slowly reached out, put her fingers on the corners of the man's mouth, and he pulled his lips up into a smile.

The scene began to fade again. My mind reeled, but I stood still, thinking, digesting and evaluating. So what? Were we dating? This really isn't a dream. Does that mean…? My thought broke as I turned my head to look around at the darkness that was greedily surrounding me. I was now standing all alone in a black room. *What now?*

Suddenly, the scene around me changed, and I almost fell on my face as the beast with yellow eyes pulled me over its shoulder. It pulled me and touched me this time, not the other me. This time, I was her.

Everything went black again. There appeared to be an intense silence.

"Let me go." I turned in my position with a gasp, almost cringing when I realized that the venomous words had come from my lips. The scenery had melted into place all around me, and now, I seemed to be in someone's bedroom. My breath hitched as my eyes found what I was looking for. The beast was still here. In fact, he was directly in front of me. His golden eyes stared straight into mine. I could actually feel his claws stabbing at my arm as I stood in front of him. Somehow, though, I didn't feel afraid. Instead,he felt like home.

"And what if I say no?" The wolf-man muttered back. As he said that, the jet black fur all over his body pulled back into his skin, and his claws retracted into his nail beds. It seemed only a minute, but as fast as he turned into a beast, he turned into a full grown man in front of my very own eyes— the man with the hum.

Darkness swept into space once more. I felt myself turn around, trying to distinguish my surroundings in the dark. Where was my beast? Where was… *Bryce?* His name came in like a loud wave, crashing in all over me and pulling me in with it into the depths of blue. And I floated in the dreamily stormy blues unable to do anything… to move.

The recollection of already knowing this feeling began easing in when I finally determined that I couldn't see anything and couldn't make out anything. It felt like I was in a coma again. It felt like I was stuck in my head again. I was stuck. The silence seemed eerie, but I held on, trying to channel the calmness I always had when I was in a coma.

"No one has the right to keep you from me, not even you, Theia. You can forget everything. But always remember that."

I kept floating. Those serious words floated into my mind like a promise. One I knew would never go away.

"I love you, Bryce."

I so desperately wanted to bring my hands to my lips. My lips had moved. I felt them. But how was I not in control of things? The soft-spoken statement resonated around the dark room, but I kept floating. It felt like a while when I finally felt the tingles settling into my skin. I had reached shore. A low groan ripped from my throat as the darkness slowly began parting, and the blurry lights began to shine in from the door that stood partially ajar. I turned into something soft and then turned again.

I felt my hand brush against someone else's and immediately shuddered at the feel of a thousand jolts of electricity coursing through my skin. It felt like each and every nerve in my body had suddenly come alive. Another groan left my lips when I twisted and turned but couldn't find the touch again. I needed that touch. I almost craved that touch. If it was possible to fall so quickly into addiction, then heck, I was addicted. *Fuck!* It only took me a minute to grow agitated. I needed that… I needed it, damn it! What's wrong with me? Fed up, my eyes ripped open on their own accord and as if on instinct I turned my head towards the man kneeled on the floor, beside my bed. His bright blue drops of Caelum met my brown pools, and I froze.

"Bryce!"

The swings, the fights, the portrait, the castle, the room, the kisses, the pain, the smiles, every phone calls, every conversation, those golden eyes… they all came rushing back.

* * *

My eyes refocused on Bryce's, and only in that moment did I notice how completely broken he looked.

His hair seemed like it hadn't seen a comb for weeks. His beard reaching a week or twos neglect. The shades of dark under his eyes spoke lengths about just how much sleep he had been able to give himself. But what stood most saddening, what broke my heart was his guarded eyes. Since when did he begin guarding himself against me?

I edged closer to him but stopped when he stiffened. His unreadable expression only made my heart drop further into the pits of my rib cage. Releasing a soft sigh, I reached over to him. Soon enough, my fingers touched the corners of his lips and slowly but surely pulled his lip up into a smile.

"Guess what?"

A confused frown marred Bryce's face. He glanced towards the window for a second before he looked back at me. "What?"

I ignored the slight break in his voice as I pulled a small smile.

"I love you," I said, not caring for the tears as I reached over grasped a handful of his shirt before pulling him over me. "I love you. I love you so, so much. I love you."

"Th-Theia?" Bryce looked down at me with wide, glazed eyes as I lay underneath him. A wet drop fell on my cheeks, and I nodded back, giggling despite my own tears.

"I remember! I remember, Bryce! Why didn't… why didn't you come? It's been days."

My curiosity grew when Bryce looked away. The sudden drumming's of heavy rain swept into the room with a cool breeze. I ignored the goosebumps as they rose on my skin and I held his chin with my thumb and finger before gently turning him towards me again. Bryce visibly shivered against my touch.

"Y-your condition was fragile. So Mr. and Mrs. Anderson decided that you needed some alone time for recovery."

"So, actually, Mom and Dad told you to stay away from me?" Bryce's chin tightened as I watched him direct his gaze to mine.

He dipped lower, and not before long, his nose gazed soothingly against my neck. I almost jolted forward when it touched a particular spot and my whole body set on fire.

What the hell was that?

Immediately, Bryce's arms wrapped around me and pressed me back into the bed. A slow smile began to carve on his face.

"Well, I'm here now, aren't I?" Bryce murmured softly as he dipped his face into the crook of my neck again.

My mind, however, was still reeling over what had just happened to my whole freaking body only just a minute ago!

"Wh-what the hell just happened to me when you touched my neck?"

Bryce's smile suddenly turned into a nervous grin as he shifted off of me and took a seat beside me.

"I marked you."

What the fuck did he just say?

* * *

"I still can't believe marking is possible without mating!"

Bryce's grip around my back tightened as he smuggled into the bed more.

An owl hooted somewhere in the near distant. A good few hours had passed since Bryce had jumped through the window. Glancing towards the digital clock that nestled beside my bed alerted me that it was nearly two in the morning. Somehow, we had ended up spending a good three hours just talking and cuddling.

"It is possible but just not appreciated amongst the royals because it's excruciatingly painful when done without… mating."

I sighed as I leaned into him, my face snuggling in closer to his chest. Lying here with Bryce and straddling him felt like the most calming thing ever. It made me wonder of all the other changes that would now occur since Bryce and I were intimately connected now.

"I was wondering, love."

Lifting my head up I looked at Bryce. "Hmm?"

"Do you remember who— who pushed you?"

I felt my feelings dampen. Somehow, I had hoped he wouldn't ask me that. I had hoped he wouldn't because I couldn't remember a single thing about that afternoon, still. The only thing that shined through the hazy memories of that afternoon was the bright green eyes.

"N-no, all I remember is green eyes."

Bryce's slightly nervous demeanor changed completely into that of a man completely alert. I could practically hear the keys in his brain whirring. As if sensing my eyes on him, he quickly got up and walked towards the window, pulling it completely open. I frowned.

Did he need air?

"What's happening? Are you okay?"

It was only after a minute of looking out the window when he turned towards the room, walked in and got into bed again.

"Everything is fine. Let's wait for the boys to get here, okay? Then I'll tell you everything."

What's happening? I was still confused. The serious expression on Bryce's face was enough to know that whatever he was thinking about was extremely important. The question here was, "What was cooking in that mind of his?" My head shot towards the window when a soft thud alerted me to someone's arrival.

Matthew smiled at me proudly as he walked further into the room. Then his gaze found Bryce's and immediately hardened. He grabbed a chair and placing it in front of Bryce, dropped down on it.

"I suggest we keep it a secret, Alpha, for now."

A secret? What secret? Keep what a secret? Bryce glanced towards me before nodding. Just then, another, a lighter thud sounded around the room, and I smiled slowly, knowing who it was already. Then I stilled.

Now that I remembered much of what had happened since I arrived in Peidmond, I finally understood why Roman refused to talk as much to me after I woke up from a coma. And if he did speak, it would be deeper than usual.

My mind settled to when I had visits from him in the hospital, especially… to the night he had cried. My heart broke a little. Mustering up a little more courage in that situation, I finally turned to look at Roman. He however still stood by the window, looking guarded. Our gazes met, and I launched out of bed. Instantly his arm wrapped around me, and I began shaking in guilt. How had I not remembered him?

"It's good to have you back, Thi," Roman mumbled as he patted my back as warmly as he could.

A warning growl erupted from behind us, and I instantly let go. Pulling Roman with me, I walked back up to the bed and got in, immediately being pulled and engulfed by Bryce. I was sure he was glaring holes into the wall right now.

"You might not want to do that right now. My wolf is still unstable," Bryce whispered into my neck, and I nodded slowly, looking over to Roman in an apology.

I always seemed to put him under the hot light.

"Considering Theia has her memories back..." Matthew looked at Bryce. "... Well, most of them. I'm suggesting we keep this down for a while."

Roman nodded in agreement. "I think so too, Alpha." I supposed he knew better than to test Bryce's wolf right now. "The attackers might feel threatened if they thought she had regained her memories back or was to regain it back soon. They might try to complete the unfinished business."

"And we can't let that happen. Theia doesn't even know who to identify at the moment," Bryce muttered stiffly, nodding, as he seemed to be thinking a theory up in his own head.

I turned towards Bryce, twisting slightly in his lap to get a good look, "So you're all telling me to hide my improvement from my parents and everyone else. Can I at least tell Marley?"

"No." I almost moved back to Bryce's chest when three distinct "Nos" shot out of each of the man's mouths.

I frowned, clearly as confused as ever. "And why?"

"Just no, okay?" Matthew muttered between gritted teeth.

My eyebrows automatically lifted in question. "What's gotten your panties in a twist?"

Matthew heaved out a frustrated breath and leaned into his chair further.

"She won't be able to hide it from Keith. And Keith can't help himself to keep his mouth shut," Roman murmured tiredly, leaning further into the bed. *Any more leaning and he will be asleep on this thing.*

Still not content with their reasoning, I turned towards Bryce again. The feel of his thumb rubbing circles on my hips was incredibly distracting, and as if to top everything off, my nerves seemed to be on fire. As if sensing my trepidation, his lips smirked a little, and he leaned in to press a slow kiss on my temple and then one on the sides of my cheekbone and another on my jawline.

As quickly as I could, I moved away slightly and turned towards a now slightly red Roman and Matthew. I felt myself redden as well. Quickly thinking of a way to save this situation, I cleared my throat and ignoring Bryce, who was now slipping his palm under my T-shirt to lay it against my bare abdomen.

"So, what's the plan now?"

"You go to school and come home with Matthew either in the same vehicle or trailing in front of him. Try to act like you don't know much and try to be normal with everyone although don't be too trusting. One of the boys will always be with you in case you might need them."

Hesitantly, I nodded and then frowned.

"And how will I meet you?" The two boys almost scoffed out loud as soon they heard the question.

Bryce, however, pressed a kiss on cheeks as he began caressing my abdomen again. I twitched in his arms. "I'll always be here, love."

Roman cleared his throat loudly before he suddenly stood up and glanced towards Bryce as if in a silent request to leave. Matthew followed the lead. I felt Bryce nod to both boys, and they both glanced at me.

"Good night, Thi!"

"See you tomorrow, Theia."

I giggled at the contrast in their goodbyes. "Night, guys. See you soon."

I watched with immense interest as both boys leaped out of the window gracefully, but not as gracefully as Bryce did. I then noticed Bryce's warm breath on the back of my neck, his fingers lazily grazing my bare hips as I now nestled between his legs.

"I'm a beast starved, Theia. You can't condemn me for not being able to keep my hands off of you. Not—." He stopped; then, took in a shaky breath. "—Not after being away from you for so long."

There was a small minute of silence around the room, and I thought about the week after I had woken up from a coma… the searching, the unexplainable need and the guttering feeling of not being complete.

"Do you know what death feels like Bryce?"

Bryce stiffened. "No."

"It feels like not having you in my life."

* * *

"Theia, dear, breakfast is ready!" Agnus's sweet voice called loudly from the hallway.

"Coming, Agy!"

I sighed as I picked my books up and shoved them into my backpack. Glancing back to my bed, I smiled as I saw Bryce still asleep soundly. Bryce groaned in his sleep, and I turned just in time to see him move his arms about as if trying to search something. Rushing in, I moved closer to him, and instantly, he settled. I frowned.

Was he looking for me?

He groaned again and leaned forward, hugging him as I sat on the bed, and immediately his arms wrapped around me and let out a content sigh. I felt my sight turn blurry. He really did seem starved.

After the boys had left last night, Bryce and I just went back to talking about anything and everything until Bryce fell asleep. It took me some time, but his warmth and the comfort of just having him close had me welcoming my share of sleep too.

Waking up in the morning, getting out of bed and into the bathroom seemed like a very difficult task. Our limbs were tangled beyond what I could imagine complicated. But I managed, and gracefully at that too because, by the time I was out of bed and in the bathroom, Bryce was still asleep. My eyes wandered towards Bryce's lips, and I smiled to see it slightly pouted. No matter how strong a king and how dangerous a man, asleep, he was the same outside as he was in, Bryce— my soul mate.

Touching a finger to his temple, I slowly brought it down in a gentle caress as I leaned down and planted a kiss on his chin. Immediately, his eyes opened, and the pout was gone. His features settled into that of what he was outside— regal.

His eyes met mine, and his gaze softened. "I thought it was all a dream. For a second, I was so fucking pissed."

I smiled. "Well, it's not. I'm here, aren't I?"

He pulled me closer against him. "You're turning me into a softy."

A laugh escaped my lips, and I placed a kiss on Bryce's lips.

"Oh, don't you worry. You're still my Big Bad Beast."

CHAPTER THIRTY-FOUR

Lies hurt people. Lies destroyed relationships and destroyed a person's life. But what if you were lying to protect yourself from having a good outcome, was that lie… still wrong?

It seems understandable that everyone lies to protect themselves in a sense. A cheating husband lies to protect himself from his infidelity, a divorce and losing his image in the society. A killer lies to save his horrid ass. A mother lies to protect her daughter from everything she once did wrong when she was young like dating the wrong guy or smoking and falling for her English teacher. A girl lies to herself every night when she looks in the mirror and tells herself that she isn't good enough. A guy lies when he thinks acting manly will make people respect him more.

Lies hurt. Lies destroyed lives.

So why couldn't I feel guilty about lying to everyone around me, about not telling them that I could remember? Was it because, at the end of the day, it would do a lot of people good? Was it because I didn't even know who it could be anymore? Was it because I was scared?

A sigh left my lips.

The afternoon air cut crisp and cold against me as I made my way out of the Rover and pushed the door close. My grasp on my books tightened as I immediately began walking towards the school. There was no time to feel guilty. I had nearly died. This had to stop.

"You forgot to lock it."

I stilled. Then glanced sheepishly at a grinning Marley before looking locking it.

"Good Morning," I smiled brightly at her as I hooked my arms into hers and then proceeded towards the door.

My smile faltered a bit when I sensed someone's eyes on me. I quickly whipped my head towards where I sensed it came from. I felt my feelings dampen as I tried to search the stare out of the many people that were currently crowding around me, walking towards their own destinations. I sighed as I agreed to myself that I was doing exactly what Bryce had warned me not to do. It was true. I was on edge. And by the concerned look on Marley's face was making, it was very obvious.

Yes. I needed to lie.

My mind faltered back this morning. I realized, waking up in Bryce's arms was the best feeling in the world, from what I had experienced so far, anyway. Well, it was the best except for when he tried to transform himself into a tightly wrapped cocoon, and I, the caterpillar.

"You okay, Thi?" Marley asked, concerned as she turned to look at me. Her hand rested comfortingly on my shoulder.

My eyes widened for a second when I realized I wanted to tell her. Then, I remembered. So instead, I calmed myself down and smiled. *Be calm Anderson. Be calm.*

"What? Yeah, everything's fine! Why wouldn't everything be fine?" *Lie harder, Anderson! She still looks unconvinced!* "I just... feel like I'm missing something. Marley, was there something in my past that I don't have now?" I mumbled, looking down at my sandals. Would she tell?

Marley paled. She looked around and then at me, her eyes still a bit glazed. I watched curiously as she opened her mouth and then, shut it close before shaking her head. "N-no! Everything is the same. Maybe you're feeling tired... Do you want to go home and rest?"

I shook my head. Feeling slightly disappointed that she of all people denied me the truth.

Lies. Lies hurt.

"I'm fine, Ley. Let's just get to class," I mumbled back as I managed a smile to occupy its abandoned spot.

Reaching the math class seemed to take a lot more time today than it usually did, but once entered, both Marley and I took no time in settling in our usual spots on the further right corner of the class.

"You look gloomy." My head shot up, and I instantly felt myself relax.

Matthew. Quickly grasping his jacket, I pulled him down and towards me.

"I feel like it's eating me up, not telling Marley," I whispered as low as I possibly could. Keith was sitting right behind me.

Matthew had stilled for a second before he leaned in closer. "We need to careful, Thi. The fewer people who know about it, the better."

I nodded. How it was possible for him to speak so low was beyond me, but after straining my ears to hear every word he said, I was just glad I at least understood him. I guess I wouldn't tell Marley, at least, for now.

"Good morning, guys! I'm sorry for not being able to make it yesterday although I'm sure you all spent the class productively completing the problems on page 487 like I had asked you all to?"

Oh, crap. My eyes widened in alarm when I couldn't find my math book. Had I left it at home?

"Miss Anderson?"

Dead as a duck in a restaurant! My alarmed eyes met Mr. Phelps quizzical ones and I immediately sunk lower into my seat.

"I suppose you had other more important situations to handle too, Miss Anderson."

I looked around to see almost all of the class having the same alarmed expression I wore. *Saved by the majority! Let us fall to our dooms together, brothers!*

Looking back at Mr. Phelps I tried not to flinch at his serious expression. "Sorry, sir. Yes, sir."

Mr. Phelps nodded. "Very well. Will you all please spend today's class completing your important but quite obviously neglected assignments? Yes? Thank you!"

I could swear I heard everyone let out a sigh of relief. Mr. Phelps was an amazing teacher and all but honestly, his temper skyrocketed quite quickly. And it was very explosive. Reaching for the ruler, I stopped as my fingers collided with Matthew's. Looking at him, I grinned. He was reaching for the ruler too. That only meant one thing— a stare off.

"Miss Anderson, can I have a word?"

I immediately let go of the ruler. I narrowed my eyes at the ruler now grasped by only Matthew.

"Miss Anderson?"

Glancing up at a slightly amused Mr. Phelps, I nodded when he motioned towards the door. Then I proceeded to follow him out. He turned towards me as he closed the door behind him. The hallways looked very calming and clean without the crowds of the students.

"You are aware I'm sure that due to your… accident, you have missed quite a lot," Mr. Phelps mumbled, coughing to clear his throat when he reached "accident."

I nodded. "Yes, sir."

"Yes, well, Principal Williams has been suggesting putting you up with a study mate. But since you're one of the two brightest students in class, Emogen being the other, I have offered to help you catch up since this is your final year… Grades definitely matter, Theia."

"Mr. Phelps, I assure you—."

"I'm afraid before you try to refuse, I should let you know this is not an offer. It's a requirement. Here is the letter from Principal Williams explaining so."

I stared at the letter for a second or two before taking it. I looked up at Mr. Phelps. "Where are we required to study sir?"

A smile made its way on Mr. Phelps' face, and he leaned against the door. "Wherever you are most comfortable, Miss Anderson."

"May I let you know tomorrow?"

Mr. Phelps nodded, stopped and thinking quickly, grasped my hand before writing down his digits. "This is purely for educational contact only, Miss Anderson. Please do refrain from sending me a drunk text or something."

I almost laughed to that. "Sure, sir. I don't drink, anyways," I replied as we made our way back into the classroom.

Everyone stilled as we entered the class, frowning in confusion. I made my way back to my seat.

I leaned towards Matt. "Why is nearly everyone here acting weird?"

"Alpha Alexander nearly lost his socks when he found out you were outside the class without any one of the pack there with you."

"What! Who told him?"

Matthew shook his head in regret. "Sorry, Theia. I did. I'm sworn into telling him everything about you."

"Possessive Alpha Mate Mode" activated.

"I feel like the president."

Matthew let out a low laugh as he picked up the ruler again.

"You're our queen, Theia. You're kind of more important here."

* * *

"And the presidential award for killjoy goes to—" Beside me, Connor made his best drums impression. "— Roman Naight!"

Rome gave me a thankful smile for a second before he growled again. I knew better than to call him Romanov in public. He despised that name.

"Mr. Phelps tutoring you seems pointless, to be honest. That's all I'm saying. And nothing is wrong with thinking Prom is pointless!"

"Prom is the only time I get to wear fancy dresses and get to see the idiots here in a tux, so just stop, okay?" Marley jumped into the conversation as she put another French fry into her mouth. She let out a happy moan. "This is some good French fry."

Keith immediately growled from beside her. My eyes widened.

"That's it," Keith muttered as he quickly grasped Marley by the hand and pulled her out of the cafeteria.

"What's wrong with him?" I spoke up, all the boys at our table turned to look at me with alarm.

"Frisky love," Connor sang out loud after a minute of silence and that too, quite off beat. *I wish I hadn't asked…*

Shaking my head, my cheeks burning from the embarrassment, I quickly looked down at my tray in time to catch Matthew stealing my burger.

"Hey!" I swatted him on the hand, halting both him and my precious burger. Immediately, he left the burger and turned towards the fries, popping four into his mouth.

"What am I going to do with you?" I muttered tiredly as I shook my head before taking a bite of heaven, well, as much of a heaven the cafeteria could provide that is.

* * *

"Alexander might not be over tonight, okay? But our defenders will be."

I turned towards Roman and nodded slowly.

"He's changed, hasn't he?"

Rome's gaze met mine.

"What do you mean?"

I shook my head as I looked back down at my lunch tray.

"More aggressive, more possessive and more emotional towards me."

Roman smiled as he took a sip from his juice box.

"He was a complete wreck when you were in a coma, Thi. He destroyed his complete wing at the castle. Everyone was very scared of him and still are. But sometimes he would let his walls slip, and the whole pack would feel his pain. I think the whole kingdom did, the United Kingdom included. I found myself withering on the floor in the intensity of it all a lot too many times, Thi. It felt like hell." Roman shuddered as he leaned forward.

The table stood empty except Rome and me at the moment. The rest of the boys had left early because they had to meet up for a football meeting. Roman and I opted to finish our lunch in peace.

"I never want to feel that way again. So I understand why he has changed and why he is as he is. I don't blame him, Theia. That feeling… it's not something someone can just walk through unaffected."

"I understand," I mumbled slowly. Imagining Bryce feeling that way made my heart constrict in the violent of ways.

Roman looked up and met my eyes. His eyes never faltering from mine.

"I'm not scared of many things, Thi. But I'm scared of that feeling, that pain. It scares me."

I felt my eyes water.

Oh, Roman…

* * *

It would storm today. I watched as the thick, saturated dark clouds hung above us all, slowly swaying towards a direction as if too heavy to move. For three o'clock, it seemed like it was already twilight. And on normal occasions, that wasn't meant to happen till hours later.

Another loud boom of thunder. I shook my head when I heard a dozen girls screamed in fear and in shock around boys and me. Yes. It would storm today.

"Hey, do you… do you suppose you could drop me home today?" Marley mumbled from beside me as we made our way towards my Rover.

Smiling at her, I nodded, "Sure! Let's go."

As we settled into the Rover, a loud *ping* resonated around the car, and I immediately reached towards my bag for my cellphone.

Missed me? I didn't mean to hurt you. I promise. I just wanted you all for myself. I'm going to call you. But let's get home like a good girl first, all right?

Hurry! Hurry!

-S

Till that very instant, I had only just heard and read about "blood running cold." Reading that message, I got the first hand of experiencing that as well.

I felt a chill ran down my spine. I felt my blood freeze in my veins. Everything stopped. Beside me, Marley seemed to be talking the phone with Keith, obliviously telling him that I was going to drop her home in a few. I, on the other hand, could hear nothing.

Another *ping.*

Drive, Theia.

Fuck!

I found myself turning in my seat like a maniac, trying to spot at least one person who seemed suspicious, at least one person who was looking at me, or at least one person who I could picture doing me harm.

My eyes moved and settled on a smiling Lionel. His gaze met mine and stayed. Pulling up his hand, I watched frozen as I saw him wave at me while Mr. Phelps hurriedly made his way towards the teacher's lot behind him. I pulled a hand up of my own and began waving at Lionel for a second before turning towards my ignition. I turned on the car and drove out of the parking lot, passing a slightly fidgeting Jeff with his phone in his hand. A dark hoodie hid almost all of his face.

Why is this happening to me?

"Thi, I need to tell you something," Marley murmured as I drove into her driveway and stopped. She turned to face me in her seat. My mind was still on the text messages I had received. It was obvious that person went to Rosenberg High, but who was it? And why was he terrorizing me?

I shook my head to clear myself of the thoughts before turning towards a nervous Marley. "Has something happened, Ley?"

She shook her head before reaching out and grasping my hand between hers.

"Remember in the morning you told me that you felt like you were missing something?"

I nodded. My heart now raced for a whole different reason.

"Alexander Bryce Wilhem is your… soulmate."

I smiled slightly and reached for my blazer's collar before tugging it down and showing her the mark. She nodded solemnly.

"We didn't tell you because the doctor said that it—."

"I know."

Marley froze. Her expression hardened and then softened immediately. "You know?"

I nodded. "Everything."

Her mouth fell ajar. "But— how?"

"Bryce finally paid me a visit," I replied, my fingers softly caressing my neck in a loving manner.

"So… can you… remember… everything?"

"Not exactly. I don't remember that day. You can't tell this to Keith. He can't exactly…"

"Keep his mouth shut? Trust me. I won't."

A giggle left my lips as I pulled Marley in for a hug. "I can't believe how happy I am now that I have him, Ley. The past week felt like… death. I don't want to experience it again… ever."

Marley patted my back as she hugged me. "I'm glad you're back, Thi. We can do lots of fun now! Did you tell Mr. And Mrs. A?"

A sigh left my lips as I shook my head. "No, I'd rather not tell them right now, though. I don't know how to handle them not allowing Bryce to see me. He could have just been a friend or something. But they didn't even allow him near our home."

Marley smiled at me sadly as she patted me on my shoulder. "It's all better now. Don't worry. Hey, I should go. Do you wanna come? We can have a charmed marathon."

"I'm sorry, Ley; but how about this weekend? I have to get home today and discuss this Mr. Phelps thing with my folks."

"Sure, sure, tell your parents our hot Mr. Andrew is tutoring you. See how they react" Marley giggled as she got out of the car and leaned into the window.

I rolled my eyes at her before sending her a wave and driving out of her driveway. The ride to mine seemed longer than it usually did. By now, the storm winds had begun to dance their waltz, occasionally making wailing sounds of the thunder and lightning.

I walked up the stairs and into my room with slow steps. Clearly, as much as I wanted to yell at the stalker to leave me alone, I was afraid his voice would meet someone else's, and everything I have known so far would shatter.

I sighed as I closed the door behind me and turned to face my room. The flimsy white curtains danced in the air as the chilly breeze twirled it around in its arms. Their union hitting me flushed against my cheeks as a thousand goosebumps made their way up, all over me. The loud sound of my iPhone ringing jolted me from my "momentary loss," and I quickly plunged my hand into my front pocket and dug it out, accepting the call from an unknown number without much thought.

"Hello!"

Silence. What the hell?

"Hello! You call me and not even speak to me? What do you even want?"

Nothing.

"Speak dammit! What do you want from me?"

"I thought that was very clear by now, Theia. I want you."

I shifted on my bed as if getting away from something invisible. His deep baritone sounded like the epitome of evil, even inhuman and almost like Bryce sounded when his Lycan took over but evil. *So… I was dealing with a werewolf, a beast?*

"Well, I don't want you! Please, just… leave me alone."

The person on the other side of the line let out a laugh as if he had heard the funniest joke on the planet. His laughter stopped suddenly.

"No."

I felt myself tremble, my vision already getting blurry by the mere frustration of not being able to do anything about this situation.

"Why?"

My voice came out in a whisper, cracking with the helplessness of the situation. There was a period of silence before the man finally broke it.

"You're my mate."

***

"You're my mate."

You know that moment when you're quite an oblivious child. You watched Conjuring, and you find out it is based on a real story? Everything in your whole plane of axis shifts. You start to wonder. Is this real? Do they exist? No. How can they? But do they? Everything you know comes to a stop and then scrambles up like an egg. You view things differently. You wonder if the wildly deranged house next door has skeletons of their own. You try to tell yourself that it possibly couldn't exist because, heck, you had never experienced it. But this lingering voice in the back of your mind keeps whispering, "What If?"

That one sentence had turned my world from a zero to a hundred eighty. Had left me at a loss for words. How the hell was this possible? No, this was a lie. I was Bryce's mate. There could be no one else. Another chuckle rang through the phone just as the window in front of me slid open, and Bryce slipped through. I froze.

"Funny. I would have thought you would have more to comment on this revelation. Have I rendered you speechless, love?"

Bryce's eyes, currently on mine, hardened as he quite obviously heard every word the man said very humorously.

I watched, still in shock of things as Bryce quickly but quietly made his way to my bed and leaned on it. His glare now very bluntly directing itself from my phone's screen to me.

"Is someone there, Theia?"

Fuck.

"Say, no," Bryce mouthed as he neared the bed.

"No. I'm just shocked. You are obviously mistaken. I'm not your mate!"

I couldn't move an inch because I didn't know what to expect if I did. Everything was happening so fast. What was I supposed to think? Bryce, however, continued to move on the bed, ignoring completely the very conversation that was occurring right now. Sliding his arms under my leg and back, he quietly picked me up and perched me on his lap, his nose immediately finding solace in the crooks of my neck. I sighed in his warm embrace. At least, he didn't seem mad at me.

"If one thing stands solid in this world, Theia, it is that you're my mate. I have known since you were ten. This, love, years of manifestation, isn't that proof enough?"

Bryce's hold on me had tightened for a minute before he placed his own iPhone before my eyes.

Talk to him. Mates just don't throw each other out of a window.

My eyes widened as I read the message, and I turned a little to look at Bryce. His hard eyes met mine and softened. "I love you," he mouthed assuring before he leaning in and placed a small kiss on my forehead.

"Mates don't just throw their mates out of a bloody window," I muttered into the phone. My grasp on the device so tight, it was beginning to hurt. The man growled.

"I didn't do it. I tried to save you, but that fucking Matthew took you before I could. I took care of it, though. Yes. Yes, I did." He let out a chuckle and then went silent. I pressed my ears closer into the iPhone and frowned when I heard the all too normal sound of the city traffic. *He was in the city.*

"I may call you later, Theia. As you can hear, traffic is very… aggravating. "

The sinking of my chest must have been obvious because Bryce pulled me back into his arms and quickly wrapped his arms around me.

"Won't you say goodbye?" The man mumbled sadly from the other side of the line.

"Forever," I spat back. Everything was getting so suffocating. I just wanted to break away. He let out a bark of laughter, almost sounding on the verge of hilarity.

"Oh and, Theia?"

"What?" I snapped, trying to let him know my anger and ignoring the soothing circles Bryce was now making on my sides.

"Say goodbye to Alexander for me will you?"

The man chuckled, sounding very amused, and before I could even reply, he disconnected the phone call. I let the phone drop to the bed before, without even thinking, turning into Bryce's lap and crushing myself against him.

"He knew. That you were here, Bryce. I'm so scared," I whispered, the burns of the trailing tears already making themselves known. *When had I started crying?*

Bryce moved me back a little and stopped when I was at arm's length from him. "Look at me."

"No," I mumbled back, my voice cracking slightly.

"Theia." Slowly, I lifted my gaze and stopped when it met his sharp, bright blues. "You are my mate. You are mine. No one else's but mine. Do you understand me?"

Sobbing a little, I nodded and then looked back down at my hands.

Why was this happened to me? I didn't want anyone else. I wanted Bryce, just Bryce.

"Give me a kiss," I mumbled against Bryce's shirt as I tucked my head under his chin.

I heard Bryce sigh against me before he flipped us over. One second, I was straddling him. And the next, he was lingering over me. Bracing himself on one arm, he softly wiped at my tears. And then giving me a small, soft smile, he leaned down towards me and captured my lips with his. Breaking the kiss, he moved back and sighed, caressing my cheeks.

"You're mine, Thi. You're mine when you wake up in the morning. You're mine when you get out of the shower. You're mine when you're crying, puffy face and eyes. You're mine when you're smiling, the sun shining through your eyes. You're mine every second you're breathing. And hell, when we both get old and wrinkly, and we both take our last breaths together, you'll be mine then too. Don't you see, Theia? It's just us— you and me— no one in between."

I couldn't do anything but look up at a warm Bryce. He rubbed his thumb across my chin before leaving in and placing a kiss on my forehead.

"Okay?"

I nodded. Fresh tears slipping down my cheeks.

"Okay."

* * *

Everyone in my room seemed tense. I watched as the three tense males continued verbally battering back and forth with each other as they so diligently continued to wear down the wooden floors. If the situation didn't seem too fragile and deadly, I would have probably remarked at how they were showing such military mannerisms.

"Theia, darling, are you feeling okay? Dinner is up, sweetie, why don't you come down and help with the table?"

Mom's voice seemed like a surprise bomb attack because, in an instant, Matthew, Rome, and Bryce were frozen on their spots, fully prepared to bolt if mom so much as decided to enter my room. I met Bryce's eyes and nodded. I would have to go downstairs.

"Coming, mom," I called back, trying my best to sound as sick as I could. I wasn't taking chances in case I didn't feel like going to school tomorrow, faking sickness from the night before would help build my case for the next morning.

Yes, lies hurt. But how could keep my parents away from this whole affair, keeping them potentially safe, hurt?

"Okay, darling, be down soon," Mom replied instantly, the relief in her tone clear even through the thickness of the walls between us.

"Want me to get something for you and the guys?" I asked softly as I tried to settle out my hair. My cheeks seemed already flushed from today's occurrences, and all the crying that had followed along helped me pass the "ill" category. I hoped.

Bryce let out a sigh as he turned me around, held me on the shoulder and began pushing me back. The cold feel of my concrete wall touched me suddenly catching me by surprise. I moved forward waiting to smack nose first into Bryce's chest. That, however, didn't happen. Just when I expected collision, I felt myself being hoisted up and pushed against the wall again. On reflex, my legs immediately wrapped around Bryce.

"Would you mind if I kissed you, Theia?" Bryce whispered airily as he caressed my face with his nose, pressing tiny kisses on random spots along the way.

I shook my head. Bryce had chuckled before he nestled his nose on the base of my neck. His mark on my neck tingled only millimeters away from his lips. I almost felt like inching in and gracing my neck against his lips, but as if he knew what I craved, he leaned in and placed an open mouthed kiss right on his mark.

My whole world went white. A half cuss, half moan ripped out of my lips as I felt myself arch against him. My whole body felt as if it was on fire; every nerve, raw, incredibly sensitive. *Is this happening because of the mark? Is my body going to be an eternal goo of sensitivity for Bryce now?*

"The boys are still outside" Bryce whispered in my ear after he chuckled seductively.

I turned my heated face quickly away before holding him on his shoulders and trying to push away. If he wanted to play dirty, then so be it. He could. I, on the other hand, was escaping this! Bryce, however, seemed to have different ideas since instead of moving back, he pushed back against me, placing an open-mouthed kiss on his mark again as he rolled his hips deliciously into mine.

Another moan ripped out of me, but I quickly bit into Bryce's shoulder, muffling it half way. Bryce let out a loud groan of his own as my teeth bit into his shoulder.

"The boys are still outside," I breathed against his neck. It seemed like the only sentence I could formulate in my head at the moment as I hung there clutching on to him.

"Uh-huh… And you have to go downstairs," Bryce hummed against me as he slipped his palm underneath my sweatshirt. His deep baritone caused goosebumps to pop on the sides of my neck.

I quivered in his arms as his fingers caressed the lace of my bra strap, teasing me cheekily. "Will you stop that? I want to actually be able to walk downstairs, okay."

"Only if you give me a kiss."

I rolled my eyes as I giggled at his adorable expectant expression. "That's so cheesy, you know?"

Bryce narrowed his eyes and moved closer, his nose touching mine. "A kiss, Luna."

I felt my heart skip a beat. Seeing the corners of Bryce's lips tilt up, I knew he had probably noticed too. I bit back the blush stemming from my neck and thinking of the most effective thing I could do to wipe off the smug look on Bryce's face. I wrapped my arms around his neck and pulled him towards me, meeting him half way. Nibbling on his bottom lip, I smirked as I felt him beginning to respond, but before he could, I pulled away instantly and grinning at him, loosened my legs, letting them drop to the floor.

"Don't want me going downstairs looking freshly kissed when I'm supposed to be alone in my room, now, do we?"

A growl sounded from behind me as soon as I had managed to open the door and move out into the bedroom, but I only grinned as I continued towards the bedroom door and walked as calmly as I could downstairs.

* * *

"Um… Honey…"

I looked up from my table setting to catch my mom eyeing my neck with a weird expression on her face.

I shuffled on my feet awkwardly. "*Er…* Yes, mom?"

Mom's gaze faltered from my neck and met my eyes. She moved closer slightly, and my frown deepened. "Honey, what's that on your neck?"

What the hell? Where? My hand flew to my neck immediately, and I rushed towards a silver tablespoon, angling it just right so that the obvious reddening bruise that stood just near Bryce's mark shown proudly.

"Well, honey, are you…? is it a…? Do you have a… boyfriend?" Mom stuttered hesitantly, clearly sounding disapproving of the idea.

"Who has a boyfriend?"

Oh, great! He just had to come right now! I'll just go and bang my head on the wall now!

"No one, Dad! Apparently, mom is mistaking bug bite for a boyfriend," I mumbled hurriedly as I quickly brought my hair in front and hid the area.

I turned towards mom. "I fell asleep on the rocking chair by the window last night. The window was open."

"Now, Theia, darling, I thought we taught you to stay away from the window," Dad spoke up sternly. I sighed as we all settled into our seats.

"Dad, I'm eighteen. And I know it may not be twenty-three, or I may not be that old, but I'm old enough to have a little bit of common sense; hence, the rocking chair instead of the window bench."

My mom scoffed as she cut into her steak. "Still left the window open, dear. And now, look? The 'big bad bug' made a love bite on your neck."

My mother laughed as I gave her the stink eye, and Dad coughed awkwardly. The poor man didn't know how to participate in a conversation which involved key aspects such as daughter and love bites. I almost smiled at his obvious awkward state.

"Mom, I think you meant 'bug bite.' Please don't tell me you're reading 'those' books again."

This time, it was I who chuckled while mom gave me a stink eye.

"Theia, you're grounded for an hour. And you're doing the dishes."

I grinned at her cheekily before digging into my own steak as well.

* * *

"You sure you don't have a boyfriend?"

I looked up to see dad leaning against the counters awkwardly.

I shrugged. "Would it be really bad if I did?"

Dad mimicked my actions, shrugging casually as well. "Maybe, I mean, I think you should wait for the right guy, Thi. These boys in school…"

"Dad."

He looked at me with a concerned look.

"I'm not dating anyone in school, okay?"

I watched as dad's expression lightened, and he nodded happily. Clear relief flowed through his features. Nodding again, as if this time to himself, he gave me a soft pat on the back before turning around and walking out of the kitchen. I turned towards the sink again. Smiling slowly, I resumed to what I had been doing before dad's intrusion. I somewhat felt guilty in lying to my parents because lying always brought pain, but at least, I hadn't lied completely about not dating. I mean I really was not dating anyone in school. Bryce was not even in school.

That was clearly not a lie, right? Just a simple manipulation of the truth. Surely, not bad a deed?

I shook my head in agitation and began scrubbing the dishes faster.

The boys must still be waiting upstairs.

* * *

Walking up the stairs and then attempting to open the door with a large bottle of milk and two large packs of Oreos and Chip Ahoy was clearly not a great idea. It took me a minute or two of diligently trying to turn the door knob with my face before I gave up and just gave into banging my head against the door a few times instead. Apparently, the boys knew I needed help and opened the door just enough for me to move in and shut it close with my back.

I scowled at the smug grins on the Matthew and Roman's faces as they marched towards me and took hold of the goodies. Bryce, on the other hand, opted to remain being seated on the window bench, a half-smirk on his face.

"So we have a theory," Matthew blurted out as he munched on a piece of cookie.

"And what's that?" I asked. An eyebrow peaked in curiosity as I made my way to my bed and slumped down on it. Bryce followed a minute later.

"We think that the fu-stalker was throwing a hook in the dark when he mentioned Alexander before. He was just trying to determine whether you had your memories back or not, whether you remembered Alexander or not," Roman spoke seriously as he moved forward and took Bryce's seat on the window bench.

"Pretty smart, actually. We have to give him credibility for that!" Matthew nodded as he took another cookie and continued to rock back and forth in the rocking chair.

"Whoever he is, he knows you from your life back in California," Bryce muttered, moving to lean against the headboard before he grasped my arm and tugged on it, motioning me to join him.

"Do you think you remember someone from back there who could have had a serious obsession with you?" Bryce muttered again, seeming unfazed as he leaned forward and picking me up to rest beside him. I sighed in his arms.

I shook my head. "Not really. I mean I know Angelo, but he wouldn't just throw me out of the window. I-I don't really know who it could be."

"You trust that man a little too much," Roman muttered darkly before he reached out and grabbed a hand full of Oreos for himself.

I sighed as I slumped against Bryce. "I can't just say that it's Angelo. I mean the man is supposed to be here, at our school, he's… everywhere. Whereas, Angelo is stuck in a dorm in Romania!"

"Something you cannot be sure of Theia," Matthew butted in, wavering a cookie at me.

I shrugged. I noticed how Bryce didn't have any input in the conversation but didn't push it much. Somehow, I rather let the topic of Angelo being the potential stalker not continue. Childhood had been enough. We both had grown into being who we really are.

We both had grown to be more mature. The Angelo I knew now would never throw me out the window. I was sure. *I hoped.*

The room set in silence for a minute while Roman and Matthew continued to munch, occasionally passing some to Bryce. While I began skimming through my Math textbook, going over everything I would be tutored on, I felt my heart give a shaken jolt when I realized I hadn't told Bryce about the tutoring I had been involuntarily signed up for.

Damn, everything just seemed so messed up.

I shook my head but stopped. My heart sunk in my chest. I felt every male in the room straighten up in tension. Their whole attention was now solely directed towards the iPhone resting on the bedside table. I tried to calm down my erratically beating heart as I finally turned towards my phone.

My heart sunk further.

Private Number Calling…

CHAPTER THIRTY-FIVE

The room was at a standstill as the phone continued to ring. It was as if Chronos had decided to freeze time in layers of the iceberg, guarding it with the haunting silence that seemed to be resonating around the room in volumes. There was silence Except for the persistent tunes blaring from my iPhone.

My eyes met Romans for a second before he got up and with speed no normal human could possess, reached the iPhone.

"Stay the fuck away from, Theia!"

A chuckle cut through silence surrounding the rest of us in the room. Roman, however, turned to look at Bryce with a near incredulous yet murderous look.

"Ah! It's little *Prince-y* Romanov, daddy's little heir, always so lonely and afraid. Scared Theia will leave like mommy did, Romanov?"

I shriveled as three loud growls rung through the room roar. I felt like I was being watched; like I was about to lose everything I was holding dear. I felt helpless. I felt bad for Roman. He didn't need this! Bryce's arms tightened around me as he brought me closer into his embrace.

"Tsk, tsk, tsk, for a royal that growl came out like a joke! Have company, Romanov? Surely, not your cousin; my Theia seems to have forgotten all about his pathetic self. Ah! Where is my Theia by the way? Tell her to receive her phone calls in the future, will you?"

Roman's gaze shot towards me, but I shook my head aggressively, motioning Roman to just disconnect the call as if disconnecting the phone call would get rid of him.

There was another titter before the man spoke up again, "You're always so easy to rile up, boy. Tell me, will you run away this time too, Romanov, just like you ran away from home all because of that sweet gypsy's premonition?" The man chuckled from the other side of the line. His sarcastic titters sent shivers down my spine, and I shuddered at the sight of Rome's face. He had lost it. Now, glaring in his place stood a Roman I had never been exposed to yet.

"I will kill you." Roman spat darkly.

I shuddered at the promise in it.

Matthew, now alert and fully prepared for Roman's unsteady state, glanced at Bryce before he strode between Roman and me. Roman caught that and snarled at Matt. Matthew jerked back a little. Bryce pulled me deeper into his cocoon.

The threat seemed to amuse the man because he let out another bark of cold, shrill laughter.

"Fucking bitch," Bryce cussed under his breath against me.

"Speaking of kill…" The man chortled amusedly, "You might want to retrieve someone out of the old mill downtown. Poor thing must be smelling like the worst parts of purgatory. Clean your territory up a little will you, Romanov?"

"Fuck you," Roman retorted coldly before swinging the phone at the opposite wall. The man's shrill laughter came to a sudden death as the iPhone collided and crashed into the wall, falling to the floor in pieces.

Roman turned towards me with an unreadable expression. "I'll get you a new one."

"Her room isn't bugged." Bryce crisply broke the silence.

"So isn't her house. I checked personally, so this means there are no cameras anywhere." Matthew joined in, moving to sit on the edge of the bed.

Roman let out a huff of breath as he dropped to the floor, bringing his hands to his hair and clutching it in a death grip.

"How did he know… about everything… about me?" Rome looked up at Bryce wide-eyed, and I jerked back at the vulnerability in his face.

"The fuck is a psycho!" Matthew declared, hard-eyed and with an extremely serious expression.

"I agree with Matthew. It's obvious he knows what he is dealing with. Sources tell me that he isn't even from our territory. Logic tells me that he isn't just a common wolf."

Roman's eyes widen as he finally got up and moved to take a seat of his own on my large bed.

"He's Royal?"

"Without a wolf scent? We can't just rule out 'human,' guys," Matthew muttered thoughtfully.

Beside me, I felt Bryce nod against my temple. "I agree. He could be anything. We'll get him, though. Just one slip, one scent, and we will have him."

"You might want to retrieve someone out of the old mill downtown…"

I shot up in bed, catching all three guys in surprise.

"He has killed someone!"

Three voices hitched in their throats as the fact cut through the three guys.

"Fuck."

"Wait! Maybe it's a trap," Matthew spoke up quickly, just as Bryce picked me up and began walking towards the window.

"Well, he fucking better be ready to die either way," Bryce growled as he looked down at me and mumbled, "You'll stay in the car, okay?"

I nodded and clutching to him with my dear life, closed my eyes. Then, I felt him jump.

* * *

The soothing sound of a violin coming from somewhere down the lane seemed like the opposite portrayal of how I was feeling right now. The run to the castle had barely taken more than a minute or two. The drive downtown, however, was mind-wrecking. I felt sick in my stomach.

Matthew sat on the seat beside mine, and I could feel as he fiddled with his fingers, glancing at me from time intervals, always so alert. His brown eyes glowered light brown in the darkness, announcing how vastly equipped he was for this, for hunting like the actual wolves. They all seemed to be made for this.

"Fuck!" Matthew breathed out, sounding shocked.

Just then loud police sirens began sounding around the area, echoing back from all the surrounding concrete buildings. Matthew and I watched, tensed, as Bryce appeared out of the mill and began talking to the two officials who now stood outside their cars. The men nodded and bowed before one began punching in some numbers in his cellphone.

"He's calling the crime scene investigators. They found Amber's body."

I stared at Matthew, shocked and unable to formulate the chaos in my mind into words. *What the hell was happening here? What the hell did the man want?*

A blur later, both Rome and Bryce entered the car and slid into the front seat, their hands and chest bloody.

"What the hell happened?" I exclaimed, finally able to convey the loudest of my thoughts.

"She was suspended in mid-ai—." Bryce's explanation was cut short when suddenly Rome's cellphone went off; blaring out a tune I had never heard.

"Matthew, mate, can you get that? My hands are a mess," Rome muttered as Matthew leaned in and grasped his cellphone from his front pocket.

Bryce turned to give me a reassuring look. He motioned me to lean forward and when I did, placed a tiny kiss on my forehead.

"Everything is going to be okay. We'll get him, love."

"Fuck!" Matthew suddenly cursed loudly. His head shot towards Bryce then Rome.

```
Little Romanov,
Behold the dead body of Theia's culprit!
Apologies for the foul odor. The body is, after all, a few weeks old.
Hopeful you got the CD beside the body. Watch it. It holds the confession. I name the CD: The Last Few Minutes of Amber; The bitch who died.
Sweet dreams!
-S
```

I cringed in my seat as the other three men sat frozen.

"The scum will die next," Bryce promised to the silence before he turned the keys in the ignition and began driving away from the old mill.

We drove past as the Crime Scene Investigators rounded up around the corner. The driver gave Bryce a salute to which Bryce stiffly nodded before pressing on the speed.

"You sure you'll be fine?" Matthew mumbled as he got me up my window again.

I looked down, trying to make out Bryce and Rome in the darkness, and when I couldn't, I turned towards my bed and began walking towards it.

"Yeah, I guess," I mumbled back, pulling off my sneakers and disposing them beside my bed.

"Everything is clear," Matthew muttered out loud as he got out of the closet.

He turned towards me and smiled before moving towards the window. "Alpha will be here in a while. I'll be here at the window till he doesn't get back, okay?"

I nodded. "Okay."

"I'm going to take a shower," I spoke up just as I walked out of my closet with a hand full of clothes and supplies. Somehow, I felt dirty.

Matthew turned to me from the window before nodding and returning his gaze outside. A slow sigh left my lips as I began walking towards the bathroom. How had life come from peaches to pain?

* * *

Light. It always takes just a second to destroy it, just blow out the candles. The darkness, however, is always there even while the candles are lit. The darkness is always there in the shadows.

I supposed that's how life is. Every happiness can be so easily extinguished, and evils hide in shadows.

My sigh echoed back from the mirror as I watched the girl in it, wet, scrubbed until red, and raw. I wiped at the tear that slipped down her cheeks. The girl staring back at me looked like she was tired, on the edge of giving up, And so, so terrified.

I reached out and placed my hand on the mirror just as she mimicked my action. Our palms now touching with just the glass between us. I sighed again and turned away, quickly working on drying myself and fitting into my clothes. The room stood in darkness, and I almost reeled back into my bathroom at the fear of it.

"Theia?"

I watched frozen at the doorway as Bryce walked out of the darkness and into the bathroom's light. His hair freshly washed and combed backward, a stubborn strand somehow managing to fall on his forehead, caressing his right eyebrow. He walked up to me slowly as I stood rooted to the spot. A sigh left his lips as he slipped his hand around my waist and pulled me forward against him.

"You okay, love?"

I visibly relaxed in his arms. His voice melting into me, relaxing every tense nerve. "I am now."

"Let's get you in bed," Bryce mumbled as he bent low and swinging his arms under my thighs, picked me up bridal style. He began walking towards the bed.

A little giggle left my lips as my back collided with the bed. With a thud, Bryce slipped in beside me. The silence around us stretched forever, and all we did was lay tangled in each other's arms. Occasionally, Bryce would turn and twist me to fit him better or slip his hands under my tank top just to lay it against my bare skin. But the silence still stood.

"It was Amber. We saw the video."

I turned to face Bryce.

"I want to see it." Bryce fidgeted beside me, and I looked at him seriously. "I want to see it. Please!"

Bryce sighed as he stretched towards the bedside stand and grasped his cellphone. Fiddling with it, he handed me the phone before pulling me into his cocoon again.

"Isn't it clear by now why I did it? I did it because I love Alex! Alex belongs with me, and that bitch was just a hurdle in my path! And look… I know you wanted her but—" Amber turned in the video and looked straight into the camera. Her expression changed from smug to furious in a second. "YOU'RE RECORDING THIS? What the hell, Se—?" The camera suddenly turned out of focus before clearly falling to the ground. Blood splattered all across the screen. The scream that followed had me letting out a scream of my own.

Bryce quickly snatched at his iPhone before pulling me against him. "It's okay. It's okay! Calm down! Ca—."

"Theia, honey, are you okay?"

I whimpered as I heard dad's concerned voice as he knocked on my door.

"It's okay. It's okay," Bryce whispered in my ear, rubbing circles on my bare back.

"I-I'm fine, dad, just… a nightmare." I yelled shakily back, hoping he would go back to bed without worry.

"Are you sure, honey?"

I sighed and hid my face in Bryce's chest, clutching his shirt in my hands. "Yes, dad, promise."

"Okay, see you in the morning then."

"I love you, Dad," I called out, already hearing him take steps to turn away from my door.

His footsteps halted. "I love you too, fuzzybottom."

"Fuzzybottom." Bryce chuckled into my ear, and I felt my face heat with embarrassment.

I smacked a fist against Bryce's hard chest and almost cringed when raw pain shot through my hand. "Shut up."

"Okay, okay…"

I smiled and leaned into him.

"So… Fuzzybottom, huh?" Bryce chuckled huskily again. Only this time, moving back, he grasped at his shirt and tore it off of himself. I stilled as the first sight of hard chest came into view.

When had he gotten so... refined?

"I love it when you do that," Bryce said as he slipped back beside me, slid his arms around my waist, and nestled it just under my tank top, skin to skin.

I look up at Bryce curiously. "Do what?"

Bryce chuckled as he brought his pointer and poked me in my cheeks, softly. "Do that. I love it when you blush. You glow."

Feeling my blush deepen, I stretched up and pressed a kiss on Bryce's chin. "I love you."

Bryce's grin widened as he dipped in lower and caught my lips with his. Sighing happily, he pulled away.

"I love you too, fuzzybottom!"

* * *

"Honey, can you pass me the butter please?"

"Sure, mom," I smiled as I picked up the butter dish and passed it to a very curious-looking mom.

Waking up in the morning had been a task. Untangling myself from Bryce's strong limbs had been a task even more difficult. But I had managed, and as soon as I managed to get my feet firmly on the rugs, Bryce had been up and ready to murder. It was taking him a minute or two of glaring to realize nothing to be concerned about, and he was worrying for nothing. When all was settled, and he was calm, he gave me a little kiss on the forehead before jumping off the window like he always does.

"I can swear those bug bites are increasing by the night. Are you sure we don't have to call the bug exterminators in to clear all the… bugs, honey?" Mom gave me her more dad-like smirk before she proceeded to butter her toast.

I sighed as I tried to angle away from mom and discreetly tugged on my collar, trying to hide the love bites.

"No, I just have very sensitive skin. I'll close the windows from now."

Mom put her hand up in surrender, "Whatever you say, honey. I mean I'm just saying, if you really want to keep Alexander out, It's no problem at all."

I thanked Lord when I didn't get a whiplash from turning to face her so fast. My eyes were wide in alarm. I was literally freaking out.

"W-wha… *pssh*… Wh-who's Alexander, mom?" I frowned in an awkward angle, trying to look as serious as I could while wiping my sweaty left palm against my jeans under the table. My right, however, held onto the cup of tea it was holding.

Mom giggled as she waved her hand around as if it was no big deal. She leaned into the table, and automatically, I found myself leaning towards her too.

If dad walks in on us while we will look like we are conspiring for World War III, that would be a hard thing to get out of— a suspicious Dad. Damn, Theia! Couldn't one day be just… calm?

"Are you even listen to what I've just said?"

My eyes focused on mom again, and I frowned. "Hu— oh, no!"

Mom sighed as she brought the cup to her lips and took a long sip.

"Theia, Alexander was your… boyfriend before… you know? I don't know how you've come to accept him so quickly." My mom had eyed my neck before she looked back up at me again. I felt my face heat with embarrassment.

"But maybe I do know. Anyways, with your amnesia, I actually thought that having Alexander around would be a good thing. It might... you know... help you remember? But the doctor requested it was a bad idea and that it would do you more harm and well. Your dad didn't say anything about it, and we just wanted to protect you so much. We..." Mom shook her head as she wiped the tears now trailing down her cheeks.

I reached for her hand and squeezed it in comfort before getting up and walking around the table to her. Dipping low, I pulled her into a hug, burying my face into her hair like I always did when I was a kid— Lavender, the same scent like always. I smiled as she tightened her hold on me.

"I love you, sweetie, so, so much."

"I love you too, momma."

"What's going on here?"

Both mom and I stilled in each other's arms before I moved back and turned towards dad. Beside me, I saw mom pull on a soft smile.

"Just a little bit of mother and daughter talk. You hold no business here, husband!"

My dad grinned as he reached over and placed a kiss on my forehead before leaning down and kissing my mother on the lips. Her face was still wet and blotchy from the crying. I felt my heart swell looking at them.

He settled himself on his seat before replying, "Everything concerning you and my FuzzyB is my business, wife. Now, pass me the butter, please!"

My mom laughed as she shook her head before picking up the butter and extending it towards dad. She then quickly dabbed at her face with her handkerchief, grumbling about how it was great she hadn't done her makeup yet. I only grinned as I settled into my own seat, bringing another spoon full of frosted flakes into my mouth.

* * *

"Theia, seeing as you're 'not feeling well enough' for going to school today, can you clean the table up, Honey? I have to go get ready."

I put up a thumb up as I got out of my seat and began picking on the clean bowls and butter knives. "Sure, mom!"

"Thank you, darling!"

Humming to a tune I couldn't quite remember, I opened the cabinet doors before placing the clean bowls into their proper place when a throat cleared out beside me. I closed the cabinet and turned towards dad, hopeful that my now open hair would hide the love bites on my neck.

"So… *er*… the weather is great today, isn't it Honey? Kind of like how it used to be in Berkeley."

I nodded awkwardly. "Agreed…"

Dad looked around awkwardly as he shuffled on his feet.

I frowned. "Um, Dad, Are you okay?"

He shook his head as he reached for my hand and pulled me towards the high chairs, taking a seat on one himself. He pulled something out of his pocket and placing it on the island edged it towards me. My eyes widened when I realized it was a concealer. I looked up at dad with wide eyes.

"I heard you telling Marley how… yours finished last week. And well, with all the love bites and your mom not knowing, I thought… you know you might need it.I-I asked the sales representative. She said this is the best one that's out… out right now. And well, our complexion is the same and she—" Dad cleared his throat. "— may have tried it on me. I am not confirming anything! But yes, I also have another request to make." He looked up at, his eyes warm and serious.

I nodded numbly.

"Could you tell Alexander to stop it? It's frustrating knowing your daughter… knowing your daughter is all grown up, okay? Just… I don't need to see these too and your mother, definitely not."

What the f—? Oh, my lord…

I looked around the kitchen in alarm, trying to find any nook or cranny to escape from. Finding an open window, I sighed in dismay. It was too far away.

"I don't know what you're talking about."

Dad chuckled as he shook his head.

"You know… when you woke up from your coma, I thought about how easier it would be for Alexander to be with you. You might remember something, but then Dr. Lucian insisted it would put too much pressure on you, and you might collapse back into a coma, and well, your mom didn't say anything about it. We just… wanted to protect you, Thi. Although thinking of it, he can protect you the most. Your mother and I, we'd die for you, honey. You're our only child. Alexander…" Dad shook his head and pushed the concealer towards me, "… take it. I'm going to go get ready for a lecture I have in an hour." His mouth cracked into a smile, and I immediately got up and rushed towards him. Steps distance away, he pulled me into a hug.

"I love you, Fuzzy."

"I love you too, papa bear."

* * *

"Okay, Agnus please lock the doors and don't let anyone in and lock most of the windows on the ground floor, okay? Where is Lily by the way?"

Agnus nodded at mom kindly as she moved towards the front door. "She's out sick, poor girl, looks like she's been through a storm at sea! I told her to rest up and that I'd come and tell you."

Mom nodded in sympathy. "That's alright, as long as she has a good rest."

"Ready, darling?" Dad called as he came down the stairs, one hand handling his bag and the other his cufflinks and watch.

Mom laughed from the doorway as she waited for dad to join her. "The question here is, are you ready, Arthur?"

Dad frowned at mom as he reached me. "I am!" He grumbled as he leaned in and placed a kiss on my forehead. "We'll be home by eight, honey. Order in some Chinese for us?"

"Nonsense!" Agnus exclaimed from the sidelines. Everyone turned towards her. "I'll make you all my very own specialty, Shepherd's Pie!"

I grinned. "That sounds like an offer I can take!"

Both mom and dad nodded in agreement. "Alright, Mrs. Szhmit, that sounds great! Thank you."

"Bye, honey," mom and dad chorused as they closed the door behind them.

I laughed at their synchronization.

"Bye, guys!"

The sound of their Jeep drive off sounded into the house, and Agnus turned to me with a hard look on her face.

"Can you not cover that up, miss?"

I looked around in bewilderment.

"Cover up what?"

Angus walked towards me briskly before pulling my hair in front of my neck.

"The King's love marks! Surely, your parents do not know that you remember, and neither does anyone else. Let's keep it at that, shall we?" Agnus smiled warmly as she pushed my hanging jaw back up in place with her slightly soft, quivering fingers before patting me on my cheeks twice.

"Ag—"

"So much to do, so little time!" She cut me out smiling warmly as she rushed towards the kitchen in a blur.

I turned towards the staircase, shaking my head. *Today is such a peculiar day.* The sudden sound of the doorbell stopped me in my movement. I turned towards the door before walking towards it curiously. The doorbell went off again.

"I'm coming! I'm coming. Who is it?"

The person on the other side remained silent, and I stopped, my hand holding the knob. Quickly looking right to see if the chain was secure, I slowly turned the knob and pulled the door open. My eyes widened.

"What are you doing here?" I hissed, looking around to see if Agnus was listening.

"I use the front door, Theia. The window, that's Alexander's job."

I shook my head as I undid the chain and pulled the door open completely.

"No, I meant, why aren't you in school, Rome?"

Roman shrugged as he moved into the house, dusting his boots on the mat outside before he did.

"I had to buy you a new iPhone, didn't I?"

My face brightened, and I wiggled my eyebrows. "Oh, yes, come on come in!"

Roman immediately rolled his eyes and closed the door behind him. "You look like The Grudge when you smile that hard, stop it."

"Hey, that's mean!" I swung a punch at Roman's arm. "Your face looks The Grudge twenty-four seven!"

Roman scoffed as he followed me up the stairs. I turned to glare at him.

"I'm a sexy beast!"

I scoffed before giggling and quickening my pace. "No, you're just Beastly."

"Oh, no, you didn't!" Roman shouted after me as I made a run for it.

"Oh, yes, I did!" I giggled as I quickly reached my room and bolted inside, trying to close the door on his face.

Rome, however, was stronger and faster than that, stopping me in the process.

"Say that again!" Rome yelled as he ticked me on the sides. I wiggled against him, laughing before I couldn't take it anymore and slipped to the floor.

"S-stop! Stop! Okay, I'm sorry." I laughed hysterically as I tried to wiggle away from him on the floor, Roman kneeling beside me on the floor and laughing at my horribly loud and obnoxious laughter. He stopped as our eyes locked together and stilled.

"What if Matthew or I turn out to be the man Alexander is looking for?"

I froze. The feeling of his fingers tight against my sides.

"You're kidding me, right?"

"Answer the question."

I shook my head and made a move to shuffle to my feet. Rome let me. I quickly walked towards my bed and sat down, facing a now blank-faced Rome.

"You wouldn't do that to me. We're best friends. Besides, when you want something, you take it out in the open. You would rather fight Bryce than play mind games. And Matthew? Let's not even go there, okay? Can I just go and change now?"

Rome grinned as he nodded.

"Alexander so totally owes us money."

I turned around to a grinning Matthew. My hands now on my hips, I stormed towards him.

"Why aren't you in school, mister?"

He brought up his hands in surrender. "Hey, Hey, I'm just here to give you this, okay?"

He reached out and grasped my hand, turning it over so that my palm stayed outstretched before him. He brought up his other hand and quickly dropped the chain into my open palm.

"You broke it when you fell. Alexander thinks it's lost. I fixed it."

I watched Bryce's family heirloom glistening gold in my palm before quickly putting it on.

The same warm fuzziness spread itself in my chest just as it had the day Meryl first gave it to me, and I smiled at the comfort it brought me.

Matthew had grinned at my content smile before he turned towards Rome. "Alright, man, you take care of her. I'll be off to Mr. Bishop's boring History Class now!"

I watched smiling as Matthew quickly turned around and jumped out of the window. Quickly moving to the window, I peeked out just in time to see him land on the ground perfectly on his two feet. Although my home was barely three stories high, it stood on the edge of quite a decent cliff. The distance between my room and the ground was immense. My mind was boggled.

"Yes, that's how we do it. Now, March! You need to change!"

I rolled my eyes and began walking towards the closed closet door.

"Yes, sir."

* * *

"I like this color."

I turned to where Roman was standing, a golden iPhone 6 Plus in his hands. My face brightened, and I moved to stand beside him.

"Yes."

Rome looked at me and frowned.

"Yes?"

I nodded, grinning. "Yes. I will marry you—" I took hold of the iPhone from his hand and turned it over "—oh, wonderful iPhone 6."

Roman scoffed as he turned towards the sales representative. "iPhone 6 Plus, at least know the name of the phone you're married."

I stuck my tongue out to him, and the sales representative giggled.

"Girlfriend's birthday, Sir?"

Both Roman and I turned towards each other before breaking down in chuckles. Rome nodded. "Eighteen."

"Well, Happy Birthday, Madam!"

"Theia," I corrected her.

She stilled, and immediately, her eyes went to my neck. She froze even more.

"B— How can you—?" she looked at Roman before freezing even more.

"Y-your Highness, y-you're with our Luna? But K-king Alex, you're joking with me, aren't you?" She groaned she caught the grin on Roman's face.

"Yes, I am Margaret. Can we get Theia her phone now please?"

"Certainly, sir." Margret almost bowed in her seat when the person next to her turned, and she stopped.

Her gaze met mine, and I smiled comfortingly. The poor woman had looked like she was about to have a heart attack.

* * *

"You sure you'll be fine?" Rome asked as we sat in his Audi outside my house's garage.

"I'll be fine. Don't worry." I leaned in and gave him a hug. I moved his face to the side before placing a kiss on his cheek.

Rome groaned as he rubbed at his cheek, and I grinned and pat his shoulder. "Oh, my dear Romanov, I can't wait till you find your own mate."

Rome froze under my hand, and I looked at him curiously. "Not going to happen," he muttered bitterly as he looked away.

I frowned. "And why not?"

Rome turned to face me, and I almost reeled back at the intensity of his expression.

"Because I'm never going back there again."

What's he talking about?

"Wh—?"

"WHERE HAVE YOU BEEN?" Both Rome and I turned towards my open window. Marley's furious bewildered face looking in on us.

Rome rolled his eyes beside me, and I smacked him on the arm, frowning at his lack of it all.

"I wasn't really feeling well enough to come to school today. But since Rome accidentally broke my phone, he took me to get a new one."

"Oh," Marley continued to frown as she moved back, her arms still folded in front of her. She glared at Rome for a second to which he rolled his eyes again. "Well, I got your homework and stuff. Also, Mr. Phelps was asking about you. I didn't know what to tell him, so I just said you weren't feeling well."

I shrugged and closed the door behind me as I got out. The sound of the car rounding off out of the driveway had me whirling around in surprise.

Roman left quite suddenly. I wonder what it's about.

"It's funny how fast the weather changes in this city, isn't it?" Marley chuckled as she hung her coat on the coat stand beside the doorway.

I shrugged off mine and shut the door just as a strong gust of wind blew into the house. The day had gone from sunny to almost twilight dark in only a matter of hours, and somehow, unlike all the other times, this made me feel slightly uncomfortable.

"It is," I mumbled back as I hung my coat beside hers. "Do you want something to munch on? I'm actually really hungry."

Marley grinned as she nodded. "I'll be in your room then. Get me some cookies, yeah?"

I rolled my eyes as I blew a raspberry, the rebel strand flying high before falling back over my eyes.A grin brought itself to life on my lips as I saw the leftover pizza from the night before and quickly reached for it. Just then the all the lights shut down, and I stilled. The shrill scream of Marley echoing through the now silent house.

"Theia, I'm scared of the fucking dark! Get here now, please. Oh, my God, I need my Dad!"

Something told me to shut up. Something told me not to reply, not to make a single sound. But Marley seemed scared beyond her wits. I quickly yet carefully shut the refrigerator door before quietly edging closer to the kitchen island and placing the pizza there.

"Okay, okay, everything is fine. No one's here. Just… make a run for it. Make a run for it," I mumbled to myself under my breath as I turned towards the kitchen doorway.

Immediately, a large shadow pushed into me, pushing my back into the island. A whimper passed my lips as his arms slipped around my waist, and he pressed himself against me more.

"It's not really nice of you to just shut off your phone like that, Theia… really not nice to throw away your sim. How was I supposed to talk to you now?" He whispered into my ear, lingering his lips on the shell of my ear. I shuddered at this. Everything in me was telling me to run away from him, to run away and never look back because he felt wrong. He felt completely wrong. But then, there was something about this man… something that had me held.

"L-leave me alone, please. Please!" I whimpered as I felt his lips trail down my neck.

"You're my mate, Theia. It's not that easy, but I came here for something."

He breathed against me. "Ah! Here it is."

I felt his hand slip into my back pocket and pull out my iPhone. He hugged me closer.

"Passcode?"

I stiffened. "No."

The chilling chuckle sent shivers down my spine as I felt his arms tighten around me. "Theia, Theia, Theia… you underestimate me, darling." I tried to wince away when I felt him nibble on my neck. "I will do anything for you… anything. Give me the passcode."

"No," I snapped at him, moving my head as farther away as I could.

The man chuckled again as he pressed a strangely soft kiss on the edge of my lips and moved around, making me move within, slightly in a waltz. "Okay." He pressed another kiss to my forehead, and I broke down in tears.

Could he just stop touching me?

"Please don't. Please, don't touch me. I'm not you—."

The waltz stopped.

"You won't complete that if you're smart, darling."

I sobbed harder. The man pressed another kiss to my forehead, quite awkwardly before he moved away. I looked up at his dark figure. Somehow, I knew that even in this darkness, he was looking at me straight in the eye. I turned towards what I felt was the kitchen way and without thinking twice, made a run for it in the dark.

"Thank, God," I breathed under my breath as I got out of the kitchen and quickly rushed towards what I felt would be the hallway to the stairs.

"Ah!" A scream ripped from my throat when suddenly something pushed against me, knocking me down to the floor. Its heavy weight completely crushed me.

"Calm down! Calm down! Don't scream!"

I screamed harder. Suddenly the lights came back on, and I stopped. An alarmed, angry-looking Lionel's lay on top of me. His eyes were bright and alert.

"Thank, God! I was just starting my shift, guarding your home. Are you okay? Marley is fine by the way. Keith is here. Why were you so scared?" He asked as he quickly got to his feet and pulled me to mine.

Bryce… Bryce… Bryce…

"Theia?"

Lionel visible reeled back when I turned to him, my eyes wide and wet. I tried to bite down on my trembling lips as I looked at him, "Please. I want Bryce. I need… please"

His eyes hardened, and he nodded. Just then, the doorbell sounded through the house. My head had peeked towards the door before I turned towards Lionel again. He nodded as we both moved towards the door. His arms stretched in front of us as we reached the door.

"I'll open it, okay?"

I nodded shakily. My mind was still on Bryce. I wanted Bryce. It only took a second before the door was pulled open, revealing a suited Mr. Phelps with his briefcase in his hand. His eyes settled on Lionel for a second before he turned to me.

"I suppose this is a bad time?"

I couldn't move and couldn't speak. I watched dumbly as Mr. Phelps stood there. Thankfully, Lionel quickly spoke up instead.

"Yes, sir. Theia isn't feeling very well."

Mr. Phelps nodded in understanding.

"Take care, Miss Anderson." Mr. Phelps turned towards Lionel. "Lionel, I hope you'll be ready for all your assignment tomorrow."

"Don't worry, sir, it'll be done."

Mr. Phelps nodded and with a small nod in my direction turned around and began walking towards a navy blue car. Lionel moved further into the house as he closed the door. I stood rooted to the floor. As if he realized I wasn't walking with him, he turned towards me and sighed.

"His highness is on his way, Luna."

* * *

The sound of water rushing down the drain seemed soothing as I slipped under the strings of warm water. I felt dirty and disgusted with my own self. Everything just felt wrong.

"You're my mate, Theia. It's not that easy…"

A shudder ran down my spine the evenings scenes played in my mind. I couldn't help but let the tears flow as I felt them slipped down my cheeks. It seemed like forever when I felt like the shower was now suffocating me. I had scrubbed myself repeatedly until I felt slightly cleaner. But still, walking out of the shower seemed hard. The shower felt like a safe haven. The sound of the door bang open caught me off guard as I jumped off the shower. Fast footsteps sounded as they approached the shower.

"Theia!"

As quickly as I could, I wrapped the towel around me as I shot out of the shower and into Bryce's ready arms.

"You're safe, love. Nothing will happen to you. I won't let anything happen to you," Bryce mumbled as his arms slipped around the small of my back, and he hugged me to him.

I nodded into his chest as I clawed into his shirt like my life depended on it. I supposed at that moment. It did. Kneeling slightly, he picked me up in his arms and began making his way out of the bathroom.

"After we get you dressed, we're going to the castle, okay? You're not staying here anymore."

It was then that my eyes caught the red covering his hands.

I looked up at him in surprise. "What happened to your hands?"

A smile had cracked on Bryce's lips before he looked down at me, his blues and a tiny bit of brown meeting my complete browns.

"It's nothing. It's healing, isn't it?"

I frowned and turned away as he strode into the closet. "I'm mad at you right now."

"Why?"

I narrowed my eyes at his still bruised hand. "That's not healing."

Bryce sighed as he began walking towards me.

"You're such a handful," he grumbled as he picked me up and moved into the bedroom.

I got under the cover as soon as he placed me on the bed. "Can we stay here for a while?"

Bryce nodded as he got into the bed from the other side and immediately pulled me towards him. I felt myself melt into him like butter on toast.

"I see you have the pendant on. I thought it was lost," Bryce murmured undecided against me. I hummed in reply and then stopped before formulating my own set of words.

“It broke when I fell.” I stopped. I didn’t fall. I was pushed, “… when I was pushed. Matthew got it fixed, though.”

Bryce nodded as he randomly leaned in and placed a kiss on my lips, deepening the kiss as soon as I began responding. It was only when we both felt out of breath that he broke away and awkwardly rubbed the back of his neck, moved back to lie on his side instead of on top of me.

“Thi.”

I looked at him. “Hmm?”

Bryce turned to his side as his eyes met mine. It stayed.

“The full moon is this Sunday.”

CHAPTER THIRTY-SIX

The storm outside roared away as it continued to make its grand entrance. The impact from the worsening winds created a chaotic feel as it caused branches to hit the glass windows with a sharp, loud smack every few minutes.

I sighed in my bathtub as I sunk further into the deliriously warm water, pulling over all the bubbles towards my chest as I continued to scrub my skin raw. My thoughts trailed to the conversation Bryce and I had had a night before and then shook my head with a sad sigh.

"The full moon is this Sunday."

What had started with a soft reminder ended with a slight disaster. We had left for the castle just minutes later. UK's beta and trackers had arrived. They had brought news. Roman and Matthew, on the other, had seemed to have a nugget of suggestion that completely rattled everything we had based my stalkers identity on. The three likely suspects that had come out from the long berating conversation they had, but they would not tell me.

Slipping further into the tub, I shook my head and tried to rid the sour shades that were beginning to show itself in my memories.

It was made clear to me only as I had eavesdropped on the men that although we were in the same castle, I was back into the same bedroom Bryce had exiled me to when we were here before and when he had wanted to restrain himself from me. And somehow, although I knew that we were beyond such communication blockage, it still felt like we were falling back to square one. I was also beginning to have a serious issue with the full moon.

My initial thought when I had confronted them on including me in their discussions and Bryce bluntly refused was to wave a backhand at all the five men present there because I was that frustrated. How could I be denied being included in a conversation about a situation that clearly revolved around me?

But I took a second to think about it. And when I had thought about it, I had simply turned to the UK's Beta, looked at him straight in the eye and told him that this was my life they were discussing, my stalker, and my so-called "mate." Bryce growled at that, but I had ignored and continued. As long as anything was about me, it would do great to everyone if I actually knew about things too!

I had simply continued to hold the stare for another minute before the Beta had looked away, and victorious, I had walked back into "my bedroom" smiling because I knew I had made a point.

A bubble popped near my toes, and I wiggled them again, leaning further into the warm water as I took a final inhale and exhale before getting up. A sigh slipped from my lips just as the first beads of water began falling from the shower and down on me. My still aching muscles hummed in thank you, and I stood there, just basking in the contentment of things.

It had been a long day today. Who knew researching about the first settlement in Peidmond could be so extensive? Or maybe, it was the library in the castle that was actually extensive. I wasn't sure which, maybe both.

I leaned into the further right wall as I still stood under the warm running water. Again, my mind drifted towards Bryce, and I felt my shoulders slump.

Bryce had gone back to restraining himself again, ignoring me by being as cooped up as he could with the stalker case. That was his excuse. They had a lead; they had suspicions; they were on it. But I supposed deep down, we both knew that his excuses were complete shit. It wasn't hard to tell that it was. The agonizing growls I heard the night before was proof of how much he was lying. He was trying to stay away, and I slept alone.

My hands moved to rest on the glass wall, and I caught sight of my wrinkly fingers. Immediately, I reached for the shower knob and turned in close.

It could have been a massive issue, but thankfully, on the afternoon of my stay here, mom and dad had decided to take a trip back to California to check up on mom's businesses and grab hold of a few journals dad had forgotten back at his previous university. A huge coincidence that moved in just in the right time slot for me needing to stay at the castle for my safety. Apparently, it was. And silently, I was relieved they would stay out of all this. They planned to stay for a week. I hoped it would all end in a week.

Another gust of wind flew across the castle, and the balcony doors began to rattle at its impact. I watched mesmerized for a second as the raindrops smacked against the windows and doors and then slid down to its doom. The branches of trees lashed at the windows in the wind. In total, the wind seemed like the master.

I sighed as I turned towards the warm fluffy bed in front of me before looking down at my state of undress. A small smile slipping on my face, I shrugged as I let my towel uncoil from my hair and the other towel slip from down to pool on the floor. The night was a stormy one, and I was tired. And alone. *Who would possibly know?* I laughed bitterly at that, shook my head as I turned and walked towards the towel hanger, and hung the towels.

No one. No one would know. Bryce will definitely not know, even refusing to even dine with you tonight and all. I snapped at my subconscious as I slipped under the covers of the bed, already goosebumps making a presence on my body.

No, I love Bryce. My subconscious mind soothed in reply, and I sighed as I turned and smiled slowly, my head sinking into the cushiony pillow.

"Love Bryce."

It was only a whisper, but somehow it made me calm. It made my smile brighten. I nodded as if confirming that it was what I was going to do before letting my eyes shut for a minute. I was really tired from all the walking I had done around the library today after all. I had only just begun to surrender myself to Somnus when the loud sound of something crashing on the floor woke me up. I jolted up in bed immediately, clutching the bed covers to my chest as I turned towards the sound, my heart beating frighteningly.

The balcony doors swung close and open in the wind as the curtains danced crazily in the wind. The light from the tiny night lights around my room illuminated the broken pieces of the mud vase on the floor.

Just then, a loud boom sounded from the opposite side of the room just as the room's door flew open, and Bryce stormed in, the deadliest look I had even seen on his face. He had practically partially morphed into his beast.

Immediately his eyes sought me, and I pushed back into the headboard, pulling the covers even more up as my hold on them tightened. What had I been thinking? I was alone! Heck, no one was alone with an Alpha King. I groaned under my breath, squinting my eyes shut as I pressed my head deeper against the headboard if it was possible. Instantly, I felt movement and snapped my eyes open. Bryce stormed towards me, and I put a hand in front of me.

"Are you okay?" Bryce growled almost urgently as he stopped in his steps. His eyes snapped from my outstretched hand to me.

I gulped and brought the sheets further up. "J-Just stay r-right there. I'm fine!"

Bryce snarled at me as he took a step closer. He now stood at the foot of my bed. "Don't ever say that again, Theia."

I frowned. My wavering outstretched hand moved in motion again to stop him from getting to me. "I don't know what you're talking about. It was just the wind. Don't worry…" I looked towards the open bedroom door and the lit hallway beyond it "… Y-You can go back to bed n-now."

He growled. His golden eyes blazed in the dark. "Stop it!"

I stiffened.

"Please, Bry—."

"Stop… it." Bryce seethed; his nose was now buried in my wet hair.

Sometimes, I hated Lycan speed. Suddenly, Bryce moved back, and I shivered as I watched his eyes rake down from my face to the sheets before zeroing at the clutched sheets His now dark eyes found mine again, and I felt myself look away, my face hot with whatever was happening.

"You're… naked?"

I squinted my eyes shut. His warm breath hitting my neck did nothing but compliment the shudder that passed down my spine upon hearing his husky growl. It strangely excited me. It was official. I was a complete idiot. The hell of an awkward situation seemed more arousing than anything. *Was this the bloody moon's doing too?* I sighed as I tried to move underneath Bryce, a warning growl rumbling out of the core of his chest.

I sighed again. "Bryce, please, just don't make this harder on us, okay? Go."

Idiot! Just kiss him already and put both of yourselves out of your miseries for God's sake, Theia! I cringed at my subconscious mind's rant. I supposed it was right. But I couldn't. What if…? What if he pushed me away? What if he rejected me?

Bryce moved back for a minute, and I tried my best not to look at the solid naked torso that was illuminated beautifully in the night lights as it lingered above me. I internally sighed in relief when instead of leaving; Bryce leaned closer and buried his nose against my neck. My eyes widened, and I gasped when I felt Bryce press a very wet kiss right on his mark. I clenched my legs together.

The wetness pooling down there increased with each kiss on my neck.

Bryce stilled suddenly and pulled back again. I felt myself redden when Bryce's nose flared, and his gaze snapped to mine. A slow teasing smirk found its way to his lips; then, it died down.

"Are you sure you'll be okay?" Bryce mumbled as he suddenly got up and moved towards the balcony door, closing it as he reached it.

I felt myself deflate. *Say no!* I met Bryce's blank stare. My mind was made. I grasped the sheets around me as I got out of bed and took a step towards Bryce and then stopped. His gaze slipped down before he carefully dragged it up my form again. I stood patiently waiting for his now golden eyes to meet mine again.

"Come here," I mumbled softly when it did.

Bryce's golden eyes blazed, and he visibly stiffened. "You don't want to do this."

I frowned. "And who told you? I never said that. You're the one who runs away all the time. And I'm supposed to be the *virgin* here!"

Bryce's eyes burned golden again, and he took a threatening step towards me. His canines were now on full display. "Do you even have any idea how much it takes for me to stay away from you around the full moon?"

I brought my left hand up in exhaustion and immediately grasped at the slipping sheets with the other. Usually, the embarrassment of that would have deterred me, but not at that moment. I was on a roll.

"THEN DON'T!" Both Bryce and I froze. His eyes bore holes into my face, and I shyly grazed his neck. I lifted my gaze to his. "Then don't."

His eyes hardened, and he looked away. I let out a chuckle, losing hope as I rolled my eyes and turning around got into bed again.

Turning again towards him, I found his gaze on mine. I motioned towards the door, managing to crack a smile. "It's okay… It's okay. You can go back to bed. I'll be okay."

Bryce frowned as he watched me sink back into bed and turn away from him. I heard as he let out a frustrated growl, but I heard no footsteps walking away. The thick silence around the room was cut through when the sound of my cellphone began blaring quite loudly. I felt my face flame as I quickly leaned to grasp it.

Numbercalling...

I stared at the screen blankly for a while and after a minute with a carefree shrug, answered the call.

"Hello?"

"Called at a wrong time?"

A smile cracked on my lips, and I literally shook my head.

"It's fine. Don't worry about it. How's Romania?"

Angelo chuckled from the other side of the line and despite the awkward situation my smile widened. I was glad to know that my stalker wasn't Angelo. I was happy. Angelo deserved a normal life without any complications. If he were on an Alpha King's radar, his life wouldn't be anything but complicated.

"Romania's great. Thought I'd just call and ask you if you've left the billionaire yet."

I heard Bryce growl, and with a weary glance his way, I got back to the conversation.

"Very funny, Angelo." I chuckled as I shook my head.

Angelo let out a bark of laughter and then a sigh. "I miss you."

I smiled. "I miss you, guys, too. I called Cass yesterday. I'm glad you called."

"I'm glad too. But I called you to ask you an important question."

Bryce stiffen on his spot.

"Yeah?"

There was a small silence on the other side of the line. "Do we really not have a chance?"

I stilled and then gasped when the phone was ripped out from my hand and into Bryce's.

"BRYCE!"

"SHE'S MINE! GET YOUR OWN MATE, PUP!" Bryce had roared into the cellphone before he threw the phone. Thankfully, it bounced back on the bed.

I quickly grabbed it.

"Theia, I get that he's there. Call me later, okay?"

My eyes on Bryce, I gasped as he launched at me and pinned me on the bed.

"She'll never call you!" Bryce snarled into the cellphone as he snatched at it again and threw it away. I gaped. *What was it with these people and my phones?*

I glared at Bryce. "You're buying me a new one!"

Bryce glared back. "Fine! I don't even regret it. The rotter deserves it."

My glare hardened "Don't call him a ro—!"

Bryce groaned. "You talk too much!" I couldn't even finish my reply before Bryce's lips landed on mine.

I stilled beneath his lips for a second before I finally gave in and moaned into the kiss, kissing him back with everything I had. Bryce growled as he pulled the sheets, and I held on. His golden eyes met mine.

"I'm a very possessive beast, Theia, dangerous and deadly. I do not share. I keep thinking about not hurting you because I'm clearly not human. I am more. But you are mine like I am yours. I know that. You know that. But that's not enough. It's never enough. My beast, theother half of me, it's not enough. If you've changed your mind, tell me to go. Tell me to leave. Tell me right now. Right now, Theia! Because if you don't… I will not stop. I won't."

I held my breath as we stared at each other, his golds never leaving my light browns. *Foolish girl, do it!* I broke the contact and directed my gaze to his broad chest. Closing my eyes, I let out a shallow wavering breath as I opened them back and let my grip on the sheets go. I heard as Bryce's breath caught in his throat, and he immediately caught my chin between his fingers before tilting my head up. A growl left Bryce's before leaning in and pulled my lower lip between his lips.

"You feel so good." Bryce sighed as he slipped his palm down my naked chest. Moving his palm to cup my breast, he gave it a soft squeeze.

A loud moan slipped from my lips as he trailed a path of kisses down my neck and captured my nipple between his lips. The jolts of electricity did nothing but increase the all too familiar tingles everywhere.

"Bryce." I breathed, moaning right into his chest as I felt his fingers caress my thigh. I rocked my hips against his hand, allowing the tiniest bits of friction.

Bryce groaned as he rolled his back against mine, his hands now gripping my hips.

"Look…" Bryce groaned again into a roll, "… at me."

I could feel my hands visibly shake as I lifted my gaze and met Bryce's golden ones.

Bryce lowered himself down, and I met him halfway, capturing his lips in mine. His lips strayed downwards, and I tossed my head back into my pillow. Arching my neck, a string of electrical pops burst around everywhere in me. I felt like my whole body was on fire.

My mind was hazy, so much so that I didn't even know when I had my hand tugging on his sweat pants, pushing it down with shaking impatient hands. I felt my fingers slide into Bryce's sweatpants and boxers, and Bryce stilled, above me, his ragged edge breath increasing a notch. I tugged on the pants again, and as if Bryce couldn't contain it anymore, he blurred out of bed before being back in bed within a second, only now, naked. A shiver ran down me as Bryce climbed over me and took a nipple into his mouth again, pulling it slightly as he teased it.

I couldn't believe he was my soulmate. Everything about him displayed power. His body was definitely the definition of primitive masculinity. Everything from the hard planes of his chest to the large thick hardness he had resting on my abdomen at that moment showed how powerful a man he was.

I could feel as it throbbed against my skin. A moan slipped from my lips when it throbbed again, and I felt a pool of wetness gush out from my core. Almost immediately, Bryce stilled into the kiss and leaned back, his eyes on me.

"I want you so bad." I found myself moaning out loud as Bryce rolled his hips into me again. His balls hit my clit with a surprise impact, causing a jolt of pleasure to course through me. The tip of his length rested just above my belly button, and I hummed in pleasure as he rocked against me again and again, one of his fingers slipping into my tight wet passage.

My eyes widened, and I found my hands immediately grasping the white silks of my bed sheets as my back arched into the movement.

"Want what, love?" Bryce growled into my ear as he nipped at my earlobe before pulling it between his lips, slowly nibbling and sucking on it.

A gasp left my lips as he added another finger into my core, pumping it in and out at a lazy pace while rubbing my clit with his thumb, quickly as if sensing my orgasm, Bryce leaned in and captured my lips with his. My scream muffled in his mouth. I came undone.

"Want…" I panted against him, my hand reaching and grasping at his hard length as the high from my orgasm depleted slightly. "… You."

A flash of bright gold had glazed over Bryce's eyes before his eyes turned darker, he had seemed to still in my arms, and a shudder ran down my back when I saw his Adam's apple bob up and down lazily as he gulped even that seemed masculine.

"Theia," Bryce growled in a warning as I rubbed my thumb against the head of his dick, spreading the wetness all over its head.

"Please," I mumbled softly as I ran my fingers along his long thick length before grasping it and giving it a long stroke. Bryce's head fell down into the crook of my neck as his body quivered above me, he hissed out, and I felt him licking his lip against my neck, a shaky breath leaving his lips.

"Theia," Bryce growled again against my neck, his warm breath hitting my skin. I bit back a moan as I felt another jolt of electricity hitting me where only he could get a reaction.

It felt strange, but I felt powerful. His reaction and his slight vulnerability towards me shocked me as much as it turned me on. I knew he wanted this as much as I did. All the "staying away" hurt him just as much as it hurt me; maybe, even more.

I grinned. By the end of tonight, we would be mated.

"Hmm," I hummed as I pumped the length of his thickness again, feeling a spark shoot in me everywhere when Bryce groaned against my neck, rocking his hips against me, trying to get more.

My grin turning into a smirk. Instead, I removed my hand. A low growl rumbled from his throat at the loss.

"That's it," Bryce growled as he moved back. A gasp left my lips as my head pushed back into a pillow when a blur later, Bryce loomed over me, covering my body with his.

A gasp left my lips as he rolled his hips into mine, and I felt the tip of his length pushing at my core. My breath hitched in my throat.

I watched spellbound as Bryce entwined both his hands with mine and brought them above my head. When he lowered his lips to mine, I moaned into the kiss and kissed him back, nibbling on his lower lip.

I shivered as I felt him nudge my thighs open with his hips, and he settled against me again. I felt him inhale a sharp, ready breath and opened my eyes just in time to see his dark golden eyes staring back at me as he moved his hips back and then thrust forward.

A loud scream ripped out of my lips as Bryce stopped and stilled in me. His gaze moved, and he brought his finger to my cheeks before he brushed away the tears I didn't even know I was shedding.

His face dipped low again, and he brought his lips to his mark again. Just as he pulled back, almost immediately, he thrust back into me in one long thrust, breaking through the barrier, completely. Another hoarse scream left my lips as the pain began passing and the tightening of my coil in my belly began making all sorts of pleasure burst in me. I felt hips bucked into his.

"You're… so… beautiful!"

I moaned and tightened my grip on Bryce's hand, turning my head to lightly kissing his arm.

"I… uh… I—" I panted as I felt his tongue lick at his mark, "— so full."

A growl ripped from Bryce's throat, and he immediately thrust in harder, increasing his pace and tightening the coil in my belly faster. I moaned as his lips met mine again, and I moved my legs and hooked them around his hips. A hot groan emitting from his throat let me know how much he liked the new angle. He rocked in faster and moving down, brought my left nipple into his mouth and tugged on it in the motion of his thrusts.

"So close," Bryce growled into my breast, his thrusts increasing to almost a crazed pace. My own coil began to tighten as I matched his movements, moaning and groaning out his name in pure pleasure as I did.

The coil tightened to its last extent before it finally exploded. My release caught me off guard as it slammed into me, spreading throughout my body as I felt everything go limp, bursting with shots of electrical sparks everywhere, leaving me yelling out his name as my body convulsed under him.

Bryce kept on plunging as he dropped tiny kisses everywhere, before reaching down and as if on impulse sinking his teeth into my neck, just where his mark was supposed to be.

A couple of thrusts later, I felt Bryce's release, a quite loud groan ripping out of his throat before he finally dropped on me. The full impact of his weight only made me feel warmer instead of uncomfortable. The feel of his canines retracting from my now highly sensitive skin only had me shivering underneath him as I tried to bite down a tiny moan.

"I love you," Bryce groaned against me softly as he lifted his head to look at me.

My eyes swelled with tears, and though sore, I leaned forward to captured his lips with mine, breaking free I smiled.

"I love you too. I love you so much."

And that was how Somnus found us just minutes later, in the aftermaths of lovemaking, completely spent, and cuddled into each other's arms.

* * *

There it was again, the sudden knot of pleasure pulsing through my belly. I tried to move my limbs and turn away, but again as I seemed to make progress, I was pushed back, and the knot pulsed again. A soft moan stifled through my lips, and I ripped my eyes open, groggily blinking away the black haziness as I tried to adjust to the light. My hand reached down as if looking for something and stopped as it found itself grazing through a short soft hair. A muffled groan reached my ear, and I nearly moaned at the jolt of pleasure it sent coursing through my belly. I looked down and gasped.

Looking back at me was Bryce, wide awake and smirking at me as he lowered his face between my thighs again and pulled my nub into his mouth, making the similar knot of pleasure run through me.

"Babe." I moaned out loud as he ran his tongue along my soaking wet slit.

Smirking wider, Bryce removed his tongue from my pussy and moved up, spreading both my thighs as far as it could go with his hand. He positioned himself against me, and I already knew I was wet and ready for him. I watched as his dark eyes met mine, and looking me straight in the eye, he plunged in hard and deep.

"Oh, God, Bryce!" A loud moan ripped out of my lips while I arched into him, wrapping my legs around his hips as I sunk my nails into his back, dragging it down as the pace increased.

Bryce looked at me and smirked. Leaning in, he thrust from a different angle, and for a moment, I saw the stars. My vision cleared, and our eyes met again. He was still smirking.

"Good morning, babe."

The next time I broke free from sleep, it seemed like it was already noon. This time, however, Bryce was comfortably sound asleep beside me as he held me with a loose arm around my waist.

A muffled groan left my lips as I tried to move my sore muscles and a sharp discomfort shot from my center. I grimaced and tried to move again. The need to freshen up and clean myself really seemed important enough to act on, immediately.

A deep blush bubbled up as I let my thoughts wander back to last night and then earlier that morning. The man seemed insatiable. A slight grin reaching my lips, I leaned in to kiss Bryce's forehead as I wiggled my way out of bed. Thankfully, Bryce took my pillow as a temporary substitute, and as quickly as I could with every muscle in me sore, I rushed towards the bathroom.

* * *

The taste of the peppermint toothpaste instantly freshened my senses as I shoved my toothbrush into my mouth, brushing the bristles on my teeth. I looked up into the mirror and smiled at the reflection. My cheeks seemed to be glowing and my lips fuller, an eternal pink tinge gracing it. I looked completely sated. As I cleaned my tongue and spit the gunk into the basin, I concluded that I liked this look on me. I looked happy.

"Theia!"

I froze and then turned towards the bathroom door just as it flew open, breaking free from one of its bolted hinges. I stared wide-eyed at a seething Bryce. His eyes blazed at me as he stormed towards where I was standing, instantly wrapping his arms around me when he reached me. I rested my face against his chest, holding him back as I patiently waited for him to let go.

"So why the sudden rampage?" I mumbled into his nude chest. Seeing a thin silver scar running down from the center of his chest up to his first abs, I pressed a chaste kiss there before snuggling in closer.

"Thought…" Bryce stopped, his voice a husky gruff and his arms tightened around my waist, "… thought someone stole you."

I smiled, amused. "Well, I'm here, aren't I?"

Bryce moved back, and I frowned when his narrowed eyes met mine. He quickly closed the gap between us before hurling me over his shoulder and began walking out of the bathroom.

He stopped suddenly just in front of our bed. His eyes were locked on the floor.

I, however, looked at our bed or more specifically, at the red taints on the white silk sheet. Bryce kissed my cheeks in loving comfort, and I smiled.

"I love you."

I hummed happily into Bryce's chest, basking in the warmth of his endearments. His arms slipped tighter around my towel. Rubbing tiny circles on my abdomen, he moved his palm towards my pelvis in a soft caress.

"Does it hurt?" He murmured into my ear as he leaned in forward. I shivered at the impact of his warm breath hitting my neck and face.

"It's sore," I mumbled back, and he immediately rubbed a circle or two before moving his hands up lazily, his caress a soft whisper.

"I'm going to go clean up now, okay?" Bryce spoke as he pressed a parting kiss on my temple and moved towards the bed, pulling the sheets out of bed and towards the bathroom.

"Okay," I smiled back before I slowly dragged myself into the closet. Now, that Bryce was not holding me in his unnaturally warm arms, the chilly morning air did nothing but send unwanted chills down me, truly discomforting.

A groan left my lips as I slightly dragged myself out of the closet. Another soft groan left my lips as I dropped down on the coverless bed. Moving was achy. The door to my bedroom shot open, and still sprawled on my bed, I turned my head towards the open door and the freshly showered Bryce. Sometimes, lycanthrope speed was a stunner.

My bright yet tired eyes met Bryce's bright ones as he chuckled and strode his way towards me. Leaning in, he slipped his arm under my butt and back and in a quick whoosh scooped me up in his arms.

A grin placed on his lips, his eyes finally met mine. I closed my eyes as if on impulse, and he kissed my nose. "Should have warned you about not being able to walk properly for a few days."

My eyes widened in fright, and Bryce chuckled, "Don't worry, I'll carry you everywhere."

I rolled my eyes but have a startled yelp as soon as Bryce began striding towards the door and out into the hallways. I knew where we were going. That seemed like one of the paths I knew properly. We rounded the corner, and Bryce's grip on me tightened, but he continued to stride casually forward. A soft smile played on my lips as we reached the kitchen doors and I pushed it open. Everybody in the room stilled.

Aunt Meryl simply sparkled with happiness as Matthew and Roman became red with the strangely shy looks on their faces. I groaned as I felt my face heat into a blush, and I hid my face into Bryce's neck. Bryce, I was sure, was grinning with pride.

"Oh, good Lord, finally, it has happened! She smells like him. Theia, sweetie, I am so proud! Very proud! I quite understand your limb dilemma at the moment, so I promise none of the boys will tease you about it," Aunt Meryl cooed brightly as she moved towards us and placed a comforting hand on my legs. What caught me by surprise was that Bryce snarled at the contact, and immediately, Aunt Meryl removed her hand from my leg with a knowing smile.

"I need to get used to this," Roman muttered as he scrunched his face up, his face getting redder.

"Yeah, man! Never thought— damn, I don't even want to think about it!" Matthew mumbled with wide eyes and a constipated look on his face.

I frowned at them and waved a hand in front of me widely. "Shut it! I'll see what you have to say when you find your mates."

My frown turned into a smirk as Roman shook his head turning more wide-eyed. Matthew, on the other hand, blushed beet red.

"Alright, you two—," Bryce suddenly spoke up from behind me as his thumb rubbed tiny circles on my skin. I nearly moaned when I realized what he was doing. He continued, "— get out of the kitchen so that my mate can eat without you two blushing like nuns in front of her, and my beast can still control himself and not actually kill you whenever you glance at her."

I blushed as I watched both boys fumbled out of the kitchen in quick blurs but only after grasping hold of a few muffins each. The sound of the door close shut sounded back to us, and Bryce immediately leaned into my neck as he placed a slightly open-mouthed kiss there.

"You have no idea how much I want to take you right now on the kitchen counter."

I moaned as he whispered into my ear in a deep husky tone. Turning my head, I found his lips and collided them with mine.

"Please, children, not on my kitchen counter and definitely not when there are muffins on it."

Bryce and I stilled; then, turned to face the woman we had forgotten still occupied the room. Aunt Meryl grinned at us knowingly before she sent a wink our way and walked out of the kitchen effectively. We both stared as she walked out of the kitchen and closed the door behind her.

I felt Bryce turn towards me, and I looked at him. Immediately, he leaned in and pressed his lips to mine. A soft growl ripped out of his throat before turning around, Bryce speeded us out of the kitchen and into his bedroom. He dropped me on his bed with a thump and only seconds later, joined me himself, his lips meeting mine.

CHAPTER THIRTY-SEVEN

The fall always seemed like a pleasant time for me. It seemed like I could just… breathe whenever the autumn rain decided to hit the city. It was peaceful, and it was calming; plus, as it neared, so did the start of a new school year. It was late spring now… And after summer, fall was coming. With it was prom.

That was how Tuesday evening found me, smiling as I inhaled the lighter gust of winds and gazed at the already weakening leaves. I glanced down at the packaged ball gown before heading at a quickened pace towards my SUV.

June was ending, and so was my last year in high school. The smile on my face flattered as the knowledge of all the five college applications that lay tucked under my pillow settled in my mind together with the scholarship responses. I was currently screwed. I knew that I'd have to open them. I was just scared of the response. Moving up my gaze met the view, and I slowed my footsteps in relief. My SUV was parked in the same spot I had left it, in the same condition.

I shook my head as I disregarded the awful worries I had only just had a couple of minutes earlier. Somehow, being on the same sofa as Matthew and Roman while they played Grand Theft Auto last night had taken its toll on me.

A loud gasp ripped itself out of my lips as I moved back. I could hear my heart thumping in my chest as I stared wide-eyed at the smirking man already occupying the seat.

"I see you're already mated to Alpha Alexander. Knowing him must have taken a lot on his part not to hurt you. Pity. How are you, Theia?"

I frowned.

"Alpha Derek, don't you think this is a very inappropriate place to visit someone?"

Derek chuckled as he reached out and quickly ripped out my things from my hand before turning around and placing them on the back seat. Waves of panic crashed in my stomach as I looked at him, wildly thinking of what he might be up to and how I could escape.

"There is no escape."

My eyes snapped to Derek's. He smiled. On normal occasions, I would have found that smile normal, just like any other friendly non-verbal gesture, but today, I found it weirdly frightening.

"I suppose that's what you were thinking of, am I right? Don't worry, Theia… I'm not here to cause you any harm." Derek had stopped for a second before he continued, his eyes now gazing at the other parked cars in the lot. "Tell me, what was the date of your official commencement of being the Luna?"

I scoffed at him as I pushed down the bile of disgust and the familiar burn on my cheeks. I moved away.

"You must be crazy to think I'm going to tell you!" I snapped back at him and continued to control the shaking in my hands.

I had thought that threat would hurl my way after that reply, but Derek surprised me when he chuckled humorously. He shook his head. "Well, then, let me have another go at the guessing game, aye?" He paused for a second or two and pretended to tap his temple. I watched shocked as he did a poor enacting of "pretending to think" before clicking his fingers and turning towards me like he actually had my answer. "Three days."

I couldn't speak. And before I could hide the shock on my face, his smirk widened as he took the shock on my face as a confirmation.

"Correct then?" He grinned.

I felt like breaking out of the car like rushing out and breaking the door if it meant my freedom. I felt like punching Derek's face and knowing it would hurt him or maybe just calling Bryce… Oh, God, Bryce.

"I'm telling you nothing!" I snapped back as I turned away.

Then it hit me. *What if… Derek was my stalker?* I froze. I screamed!

A pair of livid golden eyes stared right at me as it ripped open the car's door and threw it against a wall. The collision hit with a bang, and immediately, the large black beast pulled me against it, shielding me from the impact of the collision. A gasp left my lips as it let out a deadly snarl, and I looked up at its face. My brown eyes met his strong jaw, and I smiled softly. Bryce, on the other hand, kept his eyes on his threat as if evaluating a prey, challenging the other to make a move first.

"I feel wounded, Alex. Is that how you treat an old friend, mate?"

Bryce growled louder and crouched forward, encasing me against him. His claws erupted further, and I stared in wonderment at their deadliness.

Turning my head, I caught just as Derek brought his hand up on defense and took a step forward, his eyes bright golden eyes and glowing back at Bryce. "I'm not here to rouse a fight. I'm just here to help… to avenge Amber."

I frowned. Why would he avenge a mate who left him for his best friend? Was the mate bond *this* strong? Bryce, however, seemed to act on plans of his own as he leaped from behind me and pinned Derek on his back.

"You're really pushing it, mate." Derek gritted out as he bared his teeth at Bryce. Bryce bared his back.

I didn't know what happened next, but suddenly, both kings stilled and looked at each other. I could only conclude that they were communicating. I watched as they seemed to have a long conversation, occasionally growling and snarling before Bryce suddenly got off of Derek and extended a hand towards him. Derek took it.

"You better go change before some human sees you, Alex. Driving a car is certainly not a good thing in the book of Beastly Indulgences."

Bryce grunted beside Derek as he suddenly dragged himself towards me, grabbed my arm, and pulled me towards a dark corner. I sighed as Bryce's body transformed from his Beast to his human form right in front of me. The thick black coat of fur covering his body instantaneously receded back into his skin, leaving it to his original self instead.

"You're hurt," Bryce muttered quickly as he almost speeded his way to me and immediately pressed his fingers on my forehead. I placed my hand over his and smiled at the warmth it always seemed to bring.

"You should probably wear that before someone catches you standing here nude, you know?" I mused, pointing to the trousers tied to his thigh.

* * *

"So… what did you deduce?"

All four heads except mine turned to face a calm Derek.

All three men made moves to speak first, but Aunt Meryl spoke before they could even begin. She glared at Derek. "Well, my dear, I deduce I'd smack your head with a frying pan for scaring the poor girl to death! Theia could have been really injured!"

Bryce shot up as he snarled at everyone in the room before ripping me from my seat, between Roman and Aunt Meryl, and placing me on his lap.

Derek chuckled awkwardly. "Now, now, Meryl, don't be so crass! I was only having a laugh!" He turned to face me before looking at Bryce. I found myself moving back into Bryce's chest. Derek, however, did not notice. "Does he do that a lot?"

Bryce snarled at Derek in a warning, and Derek immediately brought his hand up like a white flag.

I rolled my eyes. *Oh, you have no idea, Derek, no idea at all!*

"If I may speak, Alpha?" Matthew spoke out loud, breaking the glaring spell between Bryce and Derek.

"Yes, go on, Matt."

Matthew nodded before beginning to speak. "If what Derek has said is true, as it seems to be with the text messages to prove it, then, I believe Amber had revealed her accomplice's identity before she died, which suits our suspicions, Alpha Alex. We have our man."

"What text messages?" I muttered out, looking at everyone in the face. They were still not telling me even if it concerned my wellbeing My eyes stopped at Derek. He looked amused. I wanted to punch him to Argentina and back. "May I see the text messages?"

"No!"

I stiffened. "I didn't ask you, Bryce." My gaze turned back to Derek. "May I?"

I ignored Bryce's low growl as I reached out and took the iPhone from Derek's hand. Looking down, I found what I was asking for.

I fear time is less, but I must tell you before I leave… I have made a big mistake, Derek. I was wrong to choose Alex over you. He has found his mate! And I am alone. I'm scared of telling you this, but I just have to tell someone… I did something terrible… I pushed the girl out of her window… She's… Dying.

Derek, I know you hate me. But please don't. I just wanted Alexander… And you know me, I didn't like to lose. I had someone helping me. He wanted Theia. And now that Theia's hurt, he's going to kill me.

I'm texting you instead of calling you because I'm a coward, Derek. I can't face you after all I did. I don't want us back... But I just want forgiveness. Please.

It will probably be the last thing you'll ever give me. The last thing anyone will ever give me.

I forgive you, Am. But who is the accomplice, Amber? We can't hurt Alex. He is our best mate! Please, at least, pick up the call!

I can't, Der. I'm in hiding! But I'll give you the name... This just might be the only good thing that I could do before dying...

Andrew Sevrik Phelps.

Please, tell Alex I'm sorry! Thank you, Der. Thank you.

The whole world around me crashed down. *Mr. Phelps* — the man who I had been around for so many hours per day? The man who had been to my home to tutor me for my Math finals only just a day ago? I didn't feel as the phone slipped from my fingers and landed on the rugged floor with a soft thud. I was too shocked to think of anything but what I had just found out.

Suddenly, it made sense… He takes a personal interest in tutoring me, the leeway in class and appearing out of nowhere when I had that encounter with the stalker in my house. I groaned out loud as I brought my fingers and grasped at my hair, closing my eyes at the whole impact of the revelation. My math teacher was a psychotic maniac. And I still had school for another two weeks.

"That's it. I'm calling the cops," I exclaimed as I made a move to get up. Immediately, Bryce's arm around me tightened and pulled me back against him.

Aunt Meryl jerked up in her seat, her warm, concerned eyes on me.

"It's not that easy, Theia. He is human for all we know. We have not found any traces of Beast on him. He will directly link to the human authorities and the media. I admit although all the powerful people know of our existence, it would not be wise to mingle with the whole human population," Roman murmured from his side of the sofa as he turned towards me with a look that spelled pissed off.

"Yeah, especially those crazy scientists!" Matthew butted in before he leaned forward, a disgusted look on his face.

"Also, love, we have no proof. We need to catch him red-handed. Brutal confrontation, however, as much as I want to break every bone in his body one by one, is not a wise choice."

I heaved out a frustrated huff of breath before ripping myself out of Bryce's embrace and walking to Aunt Meryl. I kept eye contact as I neared her. "What would you do?"

Aunt Meryl smiled. "I'd plan, dear, I'd plan."

A sigh left my lips as I nodded before walking out of the room. Before closing the door, I put my hands up and gave the audience in the room a wave though I didn't turn around. "Good to see you, Derek. Thanks for helping!"

* * *

The view from the castle windows was marvelous. Dots of sparkling gold down below and silver stars high above, it was enchanting gazing at the night lights of the city and the neighboring villages from this height. I smiled as I watched a golden sparkle make its way slowly around what I thought would be the highway. My toes curled into the black sheets of Bryce's bed covers. My smile faltered as I looked back down at my toes curling into the black silk.

Why can't things just be simple for once?

A short scream escaped me when suddenly I was pushed back against the covers and a pair of lips landed on mine. A soft moan escaped my throat, and I could feel as Bryce smiled into the kiss, pushing himself closer to me.

It felt like awhile before nibbling on my lower lip softly. Bryce broke the kiss and leaned back a little, a small soft smile on his face. "Okay now?"

Despite the blush that was blooming on my cheeks, I scoffed. "Your kisses don't hold that much power, Wilhem."

Bryce grinned as he leaned in closer, his blues piercing humorously into my browns. "Want to try again?"

I couldn't help but let out an amused laugh at that. "You're insatiable!"

My blush deepened when Bryce groaned theatrically and hid his face against my neck, pressing a soft kiss on my shoulder as he did. I could feel the amusement dripping out of his lips as he spoke the next words. "Well, it's good then because you love it."

We lay in bed dimly for what seemed like an eternity, undisturbed— *Yes, people had finally learned to knock or not disturb at all while Bryce and I were in the room*— completely calm until Bryce broke the peaceful yet worrying silence.

"It's okay to feel afraid, you know?"

I sighed, as I looked away, the sparkling white diamonds in the sky seemingly more interesting now. "I don't want to talk about it, you know?"

My lips pursed when I heard Bryce slip out a determined breath beside me before turning on his sides to face me. "Well, we have to, love. It's okay to feel scared, but you should always know that you don't *have* to. You're not getting hurt again. We've got it all planned, really. It's all in the matter of sitting back and waiting for Phelps to strike. We'll be waiting."

Planned?

All the endless wheels in my mind turned as shifted to look at Bryce, a soft, confident smile appearing on his face. I couldn't help but smile back. "Well? What's the plan?"

* * *

"You ready, love?"

I watched as the students around us walked towards the school looking as oblivious as I wished I could feel today. Turning around, I smiled at Bryce before turning to face the two boys at the back.

"I'm ready. You guys ready?"

Roman grinned as he leaned forward, bringing a confident looking Matthew forward with him. "Always. Let's get this plan started!"

CHAPTER THIRTY-EIGHT

Normally walking into school always seemed so bland and dull, but today, every fiber of my body was vibrating with a newer sense of a feeling. Maybe it was fear. Maybe it was the whole anxiousness of just getting this over with. Then again, maybe it was fear. I nodded my head discreetly as I walked between the two tall forms of Matthew and Roman. Yes, it was definitely fear.

A sigh left my lips as I darted my eyes up towards Matthew and locked gazes with him. Instantly, a teasing smile lit on his lips, and he wiggled his eyebrows at me; clearly indicating towards the incident that had just happened in the car only minutes ago when Bryce had lost his rationality for a minute or two and had suddenly decided against letting me come to school today.

Naturally, it was perfectly normal to say that fitting myself between the steering wheel and Bryce's chest while managing to keep my back away from blaring out the car's horn in that period was an accomplishment, and I needed a well-deserved award for it too.

"Shut up," I grumbled out when I realized Matthew's grin had widened while I had drifted off to thinking about the incident again.

"Hey, it isn't my fault it was so funny. I mean really! One minute you're getting out and the next you're on Alexander, and he's crushing you into his chest, muttering, 'No, no, bad idea. I'll just kill him. Yes, yes.' Whipped, that's what we get when we find mates."

"Well, it won't be long till you find your mate." I winked at Matthew cheekily. My hand, however, reached out and gripped the edge of one of Rome's long sleeves.

Immediately, I felt him move closer.

"You're a little quiet."

Matthew and I frowned at each other when Rome heaved out a sigh.

"I've been trying to calm my nerves, Theia. I have to, or Mr. Phelps won't survive through the day."

A dark chuckle ripped out of Matthew's lips just as we rounded towards homeroom, and I turned towards him with wide eyes. I'd never heard him use that tone before.

"Well, then, we'll just have to kill him now, won't we?"

I shook my head and took an extra leap before them. Turning towards them, I stopped on the track.

"We need to catch him, red-handed, guys. You know that. Everything that has been found out about him suggests that he is human, and we can't say that he isn't because it was Amber who smashed my head and pushed me, so you can't be impulsive…" I stopped for a second, waiting for my rapidly beating heart to slow down. "… I know, I'm scared, but I know you're here. He won't hurt me. Heck, he wants me. So let's just be as calm as we can about this, okay."

"Wow."

I blinked. Roman and Matthew blinked with me.

"Did you just hypnotize them?"

Gasping, I turned immediately and hit flush against Jeff's chest.

"No," I mumbled, frowning to myself. Behind me, I felt Roman and Matthew scoot closer.

"Yo, Jeff, mate! How's it going?" Matthew butted in, saving me from verbally falling into a jumbled, confused mess. He, however, didn't wait for a reply. Grasping my elbow, he continued to steer me towards homeroom. "Oh, hell, mate, we're late! I'll see you in math, all right? Mr. Phelps keeps hinting at a quiz!"

"Yeah! Sucks, man. See you on the field!"

"Thank, God!" I breathed as soon as we were in walking distance.

"You used the Luna command," Rome muttered darkly from beside me.

I stiffened but kept moving. Matthew dragging us closer to the room. We reached the door and pulling it open, slipped in as quietly as we could.

"You used the Luna command," Rome muttered again as we slipped into our seat. I turned to him with a frown.

"I'm sorry. I didn't mean to… order you, guys. I was just trying to make you both understand."

"It's not that. We're just disgusted because that reminds us that you're finally mated to the Alpha King and all."

I flinched in my seat.

"Okay, awkward! Stop being weird around me. Can we jus—?"

"Ah! Miss Anderson, Mr. Jefferson, Mr. Naight, good to see that you've finally arrived."

Mr. Bishop spoke up sarcastically. I closed my eyes tightly, waiting for the berating that was about to come next. It didn't.

Slowly, I opened my eyes and felt myself flush red when I noticed Mr. Bishop was looking right at me. As if having my attention back to him, he heaved out a sigh and began speaking again,

"Alright, everyone, so today's revision periods have been switched up a little bit. Math will be happening in this classroom, right after homeroom period." Mr. Bishop paused and did a sweep around the room as if making note that he had our unconditional attention. Nodding to himself, he continued, "Alright then, go back to your gossiping and all the other nonsense you, kids, do."

As if his last sentence were a blessing, everyone around the room began talking again, well, everyone except Matt, Rome and me. We three sat as if we were waiting for war. *And heck we're going to win! I hope.*

* * *

The class sat in a stand still. Not even one of us was speaking. Hell, not a single one of us were breathing.

"Damn, I mean, I knew Mr. Phelps was decent looking, but… Damn." A whisper drifted to my ears from somewhere around me, and I fidgeted in my seat.

"I know, Tess. Mr. Phelps is hot!"

And a crazy lunatic! I yelled at them in my head, scoffing at the girls who were busy staring at a roughly tumbled looking Mr. Phelps sorting through his papers. The whole class seemed to be in awe, well, the whole class except Matt, Rome and me. I was suddenly scared. Matthew and Rome, on the other hand, had transformed into their Beta and Delta selves.

As if finally sorted the papers, Mr. Phelps looked up and grinned. I swear I heard a few of the girls around me sigh dreamily while I suddenly found my book and yellow pencil quite interesting.

"Morning, everyone! I'm just going to distribute revision guides that will help you for the finals. You may spend the rest of the class working on it. I'll be right over there if you need me for any clarification."

I didn't care to look up at him while he talked. I could barely sit in this room anymore. It felt like the majority of me wanted to run away, scream "Teacher Danger!" or just confront him. The overwhelming feeling was making everything harder on me. Every desk he went to, I was aware of. His every movement sent my nerves spindling in alarm waiting for the moment he would reach mine. I hoped he wouldn't reach mine.

"Ah, Roman, how's prep going for the finals?"

I thought I heard Rome growl.

"Never better, sir." Rome grounded out, his palms fisting against his dark washed jeans as he said, "sir."

If Mr. Phelps noticed the bite in Rome's remark, he didn't show it because he darted to his next student quite happily. "Great then! Theia, how are you doing today? Here's your revision slip."

I looked down as he slid the paper towards me on the desk. My voice refused to make itself known. *You have two options, Theia: you fight or you flee.* I sighed. *Or shut up.*

I finally coughed and spoke, "Well, t-thank you, sir."

Mr. Phelps leaned in and gripped the edge of my desk. "Theia, are you okay?"

"Why, the fucker?" I heard Rome ground out under his breath beside me. Matthew leaned in closer on instinct.

I sighed before finally looking up at Mr. Phelps. I put on a small smile. "I'm fine, sir. T-thank you for asking."

"Good, good. Enjoy the revision guide!" Mr. Phelps eyes flashed as he smiled down at me and nodded approvingly. He then moved on to the next student.

"Fucker!" Rome gritted out angrily, and I almost nodded in agreement.

Rome turned towards Matthew, and I looked up at him and then to Matthew As if answering to a silent question, Matthew nodded. I frowned.

"What's up?"

"Just gave the King a report."

I shot Matthew a knowing small smile to which he smiled back reassuringly. He had used King. That meant Bryce was really mad, and that meant Matthew had had to hear a good load before he had withdrawn from the conversation. Beasts really were feral and wild tempered. And after the "pushed from the window" incident, Bryce had become a little too touchy about my well-being even in the smallest of things.

"He's really pissed," Matthew mumbled as if trying to frighten me. I felt the tips of my lips quirk up. It wasn't going to work.

Beside me, Roman scoffed. "Nothing Theia can't fix after school."

Immediately, he stilled. Matthew and I already stiff beside him. We all turned towards each other.

"Holy fuck, I can't believe I just said that!" Roman blurted out quite loud. The whole room quietened down.

Wide-eyed, my gaze immediately darted to Mr. Phelps and then back to Rome. A sudden burst of loud laughter suddenly boomed out around the room, and everyone's head shot towards a hysterical Matthew, laughing his brains off. I frowned, confused. *What's he up to?*

"C-crap, man, that was… that was awesome!"

When Mr. Phelps arrived before us, I didn't even notice, but before we all knew it, he was in front of us, looking extremely curious,

"And what's happening here?"

Matthew settled down a little and chuckled as if Mr. Phelps were one of his friends.

"Oh, nothing, sir. Rome was just sharing the worst pickup line he has heard to date. It's really funny."

"Really?" Mr. Phelps drawled in as he leaned against a vacant seat in front of Matthew and folding his arms in front of his chest as he did. "What was it?"

"Something I'm sure is very much improper to use on your grown male math teacher, sir, especially when you're straight."

Everything was silent. The whole class sat back and watched in awe as Matthew performed the "Act 1, Scene" 1 of Genius Matthew. Only, they didn't know that Matthew had in fact just saved Roman's ass. Matthew and Mr. Phelps stared each other silently; waiting for the other to crack before Mr. Phelps finally gave in and looked away.

"Alright, then." he sighed as he shrugged and moved back to his seat.

Triumph and gloriously basking in it, Matthew leaned back into his seat and turned to us with a smug grin, "And that, little children, is how it's done."

"Smug basket," Roman grumbled from behind me, and I turned towards him with a stern look.

He sighed. "Thank you… basket."

"Roman!" I sighed as I threw my hands up in exasperation. Funny really, there wasn't much Math going on in Math class.

"What?" Rome rolled his eyes; then, looked at Matthew and grinned.

"That's the best you will get out of me."

* * *

"I asked her! I finally asked her, so no more teasing."

I grinned at Matthew as we watched Connor slump down on the seat beside me with an accomplished look.

"Finally asked Hannah out for prom?"

"And she said yes, I suppose?"

My grins widened when Connor nodded.

Hannah really was a beautiful girl, the perfect protagonist for most teen fictions. And the fact that bad boy extraordinaire, Mr. Connor, had a massive crush on her (and that she was his mate) was like a romance novel out of my library.

"We are so proud of you, little Padawan." Matthew chuckled as he patted Connor on the back.

Connor crinkled his nose and made a mock annoyed face. "I'm a friggin Jedi!"

I couldn't help but chuckle with Matthew. "Not when it comes to Hannah, you're not."

Matthew burst out in hysterics when Connor turned pink. I couldn't help but feel bad for the poor guy. Maybe we had been a little too tough on him.

"Anyway, why are you still here, though? Waiting for someone?"

Connor's blush deepened. "*Er*… yeah… Hannah. I, well, I said I'd drop her home."

A warm smile lit up on my face. "Oh, that's great!"

"What about you two, though? And where's Rome?"

I turned as Matthew began to answer but a loud screeching sound of a fast rounding car pierced through the afternoon air cutting him off his reply. All present heads turned towards the Lexus that stood, glaring in the middle of the parking lot. I didn't need to see the driver to know who he was. It felt like the whole energy has shifted around me. I could feel it. Bryce really was mad.

It didn't take long before the door swung open, and Bryce burst out of the vehicle.

Ignoring all the gaping mouths and all the wide eyes around him, he quickly stormed towards me, and as soon as he reached me, he tossed the keys to Matthew and hauled me over his shoulder, blindly running out of the car park and into the woods with the extreme speed only werewolves possessed.

"My beast needs to spend some time with you. It's anxious, and I need to calm it down a little. Theia—" He darted his eyes to mine, an unsure look on his face. "— do you think… you can handle that?"

I, on the other hand, was trying my best not to let my swirling mind win from the great speed he was actually walking. This should not be humanly possible!

"Yeah, don't… ah!"

Bryce suddenly stopped, and I jerked forward on his shoulder, preparing to be thrown over from the sudden stop. Just in time, his hands darted forward and grabbing me, pulled my back flush against his chest. Then, he began to transform.

I could feel it in the way his muscles spasmed and twisted against my back; how the feel of his smooth skin suddenly turned into thick, soft fur against my hands that held his against my waist. My voice hitched in my throat when I felt his sharp claws slip out in the place of his nails. He instantly moved his fingers so that he held me with the pads of his fingers against my tummy instead of his claws. He jerked forward for a second, and I moved with him, knowing that was his spine remodeling itself.

I felt his beast. I felt him in the way he felt taller. I felt him in the way he growled softly behind me and the way he hid his face against my neck, his soft muzzle contrary to the hardness I had always unconsciously linked it to. I felt him… his beast… my beast. I smiled… my Bryce.

"Hey." The deep rumble of his voice instantly sent shivers down my spine, and I leaned into his chest.

"Hey."

"I missed you."

A laugh left my lips, and on impulse, I twisted in his arms to turn around. With a little hesitance, he let me. I slowly looked up at him. My breath hitched in my throat. Bryce looked regal. Everything a King would look like. He looked dangerous and deadly. He looked… furious.

I frowned. "What's wrong?"

He looked back at me blankly. "I'm ugly."

My frown hardened. "Oh, shut up. You're beautiful in what you are. There is no definition of beauty if it's personified, Bryce. You are beautiful. And I love you when you're human or when you're a beast… all of you."

Bryce's blank stare stayed, and we both stared at each other before his face crumbled, and he pulled me against him again.

"I can't lose you. You know that, right?"

A smile lit up on my face, and I buried my face deeper into his furry chest. "I know you won't. You're stuck with me forever, Mr. Wilhem. I'm afraid to say it, but you're mine."

Bryce's beast chuckled, and I felt him place a kiss on my hair.

"I love you, mate."

A sudden question popped up in my head, and I pondered on it for a second before blurting it out.

"Say, how often do you all take baths in this form?"

The laughter that rumbled afterward echoing around the two of us in the quiet forest had me humphing and moving closer into a hysterically laughing Bryce's chest.

* * *

"Stand still!" I scolded Bryce as I folded my arms in front of me determinedly.

The soaking wet beast before me growled before it straightened up and stood in a manner which perfectly articulated that of statues. Rubbing my shampoo on his silky black fur, I scrubbed and shampooed him before turning up to his head and doing the same with that. My beast was getting a bath.

"I'm going to freaking smell like passion fruit!"

I laughed and scrubbed him harder, moving to his hands.

"You already are a big lump of passion fruit."

Bryce stiffened and turned to me, his golden eyes flashing at me with something more primal.

"You don't want to go there right now, love."

I felt my face heat, and I nodded, wide-eyed to realize how bold I had been a minute ago.

"Forget I said that!" I breathed out quickly, moving to his back.

"I don't reckon I can *ever* forget that. I don't reckon I *want* to."

I groaned when I detected the amusement in his tone.

"Shut up!" I mumbled as I quickly but thoroughly finished with his back. I handed him the bottle of shampoo and moved back, letting the water from the running shower wash down the foam from my already wet self.

Bryce's beast was apparently too big to fit into the bathtub.

* * *

"Theia?"

"Yeah!?" I yelled as I moved towards the bathroom door, towel in hand and still completely wet from bathing Bryce.

"I'm done!" Bryce called out loudly just as I opened the door and moved into the bathroom.

Two steps in and my feet hit something slippery. The last thing I remember before the blackout was the sharp throbbing pain in the back of my head. Then… nothing.

CHAPTER THIRTY-NINE

A groan slipped out of my lips as I tried to make a grab for my head. *Damn, it felt like a loaded bookshelf had fallen on it.* After what felt like a long time, I gave up and decided to just get up and out of bed. Twisting against the softness I knew could only come from our bed, I slowly opened my eyes and waited for the darkness to disappear.

"Oh, thank, God!"

"Why does this always happen to me?" I whimpered, shoveling my head into the pillow.

Where's Bryce?

"Bryce?"

I quickly turned and shot up in bed, looking around at the people in the room. I couldn't see Bryce.

"Well, get to her then, you big oaf!" Aunt Meryl suddenly scolded from my left.

He is in the room! Relieved, I burst into a smile and Then turned towards Aunt Meryl who smiled back me warmly. My smile brightened when Bryce appeared from behind her, his golden eyes wide and a little panicked. I frowned. He was in his beast form.

Confused, I looked towards Aunt Meryl who rolled her eyes and waved her hand up in the air. "The boy panicked, dear, when you slipped on the soap that he threw because his beast form hates the smell of strawberries." My eyes widened as Aunt Meryl explained with a bit of a tired tone, rolling her eyes quite a lot. "He blamed himself, and well, rage plus panic equals hello beasty. So here he is, being a complete nutter, and so irritably childish, not able to turn back."

I turned toward Bryce who gave me the "don't judge me look." Instantly, I put both my palms in front of me and shrugged. I wasn't judging. Aunt Meryl smiled warmly as she watched us; then, narrowed her eyes at her nephew.

"Now, Theia, will you please control your Alpha King while I go and check if that good for nothing lousy doctor has arrived yet, darling? Yes? Thank you!"

Sending a warm smile my way, she turned towards Rome and the rest of the unfamiliar guys, who I suppose were here as Bryce's guards. "Come along, dears." I noticed as all of the men in the room quickly filtered out of the room one by one, looking really relieved.

I turned to Bryce.

"What happened?"

"I hurt you."

I sighed. "Come here."

Immediately, the large furry beast that I had come to know and love began walking towards me, the shiny dark fur receding back into his skin. His head changing right before my eyes into my familiar Bryce.

By the time he reached my bed, Bryce was back to being his human self. Reaching for his maroon sweater, he shrugged it on. I kept my eyes firmly pressed on his chest. Even though we had had sex, I still could not come to terms with just eyeing him as I pleased. I suppose the shyness would stay for a while longer.

"I'm sorry."

"No biggie," I sighed happily against Bryce's chest as soon as he slipped under the sheets and snaked his arm around my waist.

Fifteen minutes later, I was just as comfortable and tingly as I had been when Bryce had slipped into bed. I let out a happy sigh as I felt Bryce edge closer and tighten his heavy hold around my waist. I wiggled into a more comfortable position but suddenly stilled when Bryce let out a loud groan, and his grip on me tightened.

"You might want to stop that, love." My face now alight with embarrassment, I stayed as still as I could while I felt a large bump beginning to poke me on my thigh.

Despite myself, a knowing grin had found its way on my lips, and I grinned cheekily. Trying my best not to hurt my still slightly sore head, I wiggled my back against his front again. Another loud groan tumbled out of Bryce's throat, strangely mixed with a husky growl. I nearly moaned hearing that.

"Naughty, naughty, little mate. You need to be punished," Bryce growled huskily into my ear. I whimpered as I felt him brace his hand behind me, now clearly towering me in bed.

A loud gasp ripped out of my lips, my eyes wide and my mouth open in an O. My hand darted towards Bryce's and gripped onto his. He, however, continued to slip his hand under my panty, finding the already wet spot he was clearly looking for.

"So wet, love, just perfect for my di—."

I smacked my palm against his lips. He pulled the skin of my palm between his teeth and then flicked his tongue against it. I shivered in his arms. *Change the topic! Change the topic!*

"S-so you changed m-me out of my wet c-clothes?" I stuttered as he caressed my nether lips.

Bryce chuckled, and I gasped as his fingers found me.

"Correct for two—." He plunged a finger in, and I moaned out loud. He chuckled. "—points."

Another finger joined the first.

"Mmm," Bryce echoed as another moan slipped my lips. My hips moving in rhythm to his, I jerked forward when he hit a sensitive spot.

"Your moans—"I moaned loudly. "— are the sexiest thing in the world, baby."

"Don't—" I whimpered as his movements increased speed. "—Stop."

Bryce chuckled and then stilled. I whimpered, annoyed.

"Thinking about it, I reckon I just might. Stop, that is," he whispered into my ear, pulling my earlobe between his lips he nibbled. "Never tease the Alpha King, love. Big mistake."

I couldn't help but growl. Everything was aching. I needed something, and Bryce had just let me undone as if suddenly a lightbulb lit and exploded on my head. I knew what I wanted. I'd take it. Bryce chuckled as he made a move of getting away.

"You're such a tease." I breathed just as a loud groan left Bryce's lips.

My hand moved back from cupping his bulge and neatly slipping under his pants and boxers, found his hardness. A smirk pulled up on my lips as I circled my thumb against the large tip and then… pumped. He bucked forward. Quickly, I removed myself before Bryce could pull me back and straddled him.

"What are you, doing?" Bryce cocked an eyebrow up as he asked, honestly curious.

The veins on his neck were thick and ready to burst out because of all the teasing. We both needed this. Or maybe, falling earlier had me wired completely wrong, but damn it. I was going to do it!

I smiled at Bryce cheekily as I leaned forward and placed my lips on his. Nibbling on his lower lip, I quickly moved back and as I did, grabbed the waistbands of his pants and boxer and pulled them down. Instantly his length sprung up— tall, thick, proud and angry. Bryce's eyes darkened, and he growled, now knowing exactly what I was doing. Launching forward, he made a move to grab me. I moved away before he could, a triumph teasing smile firmly placed on my lips.

He wasn't going to dominate this… well, yet.

I slipped out of my tank top and panty quicker than I could say, "one potato, two potato" and moved back to straddling him. Bryce made a move of grabbing me again, and this time, I simply leaned back against him.

Bryce smirked. "Minx."

"Uh-huh," I smirked back, my hand already holding his length against my core.

Holding in a breath, I moved up and then in one swift slightly painful go slid down on him.

* * *

"Looks like the Dr. Lucian's here."

I grinned as Bryce slipped my sweater on for me. Quickly leaning down, he slipped his hand under me and scooped me up into his arms.

"We don't really need him, you know?" I mumbled as I snuggled closer to his chest.

Bryce growled as he continued walking towards our bed. "We do. I don't want you hurt. Your head might still be sore."

Rolling my eyes, I hid my face against his shoulder. "The only place I'm sore right now is…"

"Okay, and they are just here!" Bryce cut me off tactfully, albeit loudly.
I looked at him a grin loud and clear on my face. Bryce, on the other hand, looked away, the sure but rare sign of him actually blushing.

"You're so cute," I cooed, knowing how much that would irritate him.

"No, I'm not!" He immediately burst out, looking at me with an intense frown and his cheeks and neck still red.

"You are," I cooed again, ignoring his pissed off self.

He dropped me on the bed. I giggled as I bounced on the bed before settling back into place.

"Think I'm cute, huh?" My breath hitched as soon as Bryce climbed over me. His lips found my neck, and I nearly jumped out of bed when his fingers found my sides.

"Bryce! Oh, my God, stop!" I twisted under him, hysterical bursts of laughter poured out into the room.

"B-BRYCE!"

Warm tears slipped down my cheeks as I continued to laugh, twisting and turning trying to get away from Bryce's tormenting hands.

"Say Bryce is the hottest man alive." It was only then I noticed Bryce's loud laughter was actually rivaling mine.

"No."

"No?" He tickled me harder.

"Never." I gasped, screaming in between loud laughter.

"Say it, Theia! Say it. Come on."

I gasped for my breath as I clawed at his arms. Out of breath because of the laughing, I gave in.

"Okay, okay!" I heaved in a large gulp of breath. "Alexander—," Bryce growled at my usage of his first name. His eyes getting darker, I gulped and continued.

"Yeah? Come on."

"— Bryce Wilhem is the h-hottest man alive."

"There! That wasn't too bad, was it?" Bryce instantly stopped. Grinning, he leaned down and took my lips into his.

"Holy Lord, doctor, please turn around!"

Bryce groaned against my lips but continued to nibble my bottom lip for a second or two before he firmly pressed a soft peck on my lip and moved to his side. Looking towards the door expectedly, my eyes widened when I saw a scared Aunt Meryl and a blank-faced Dr. Lucian.

Aunt Meryl spoke firs, "Well, you did say come in, and well, I thought— and this room is sound proof— I… Oh, God… I apologize."

"I said, 'Come on, Aunt Meryl,' that too, to —."

"I think they get it," I whispered urgently from beside him.

Immediately, the doctor made a move towards me, and Bryce growled.

"Touch only where you have to Dr. Lucian. Thank you for visiting us on such short notice by the way."

Dr. Lucian looked at me for a second before he turned towards Bryce and slowly smiled. "Of course, Mr. Wilhem, I completely understand. As Miss Anderson is my patient, it's important to check up on her."

Bryce nodded.

Dr. Lucian took another step towards me and then stopped. He looked at Bryce. "May I?"

I cocked an eyebrow up when I noticed the underlying bite in his tone. Apparently, Bryce noticed this too.

He handled it better than I did. Nodding curtly, he motioned towards me, "Sure."

I, on the other hand, continued to stare at Dr. Lucian with an eyebrow tipped up.

His gaze met mine and warmed. Instantly, he smiled. "Hello, Theia, got a bit of bump I heard. Do you mind scooting forward a bit, please?"

I blinked. "No, no."

Blinking again, I scooted forward. A minute or two's probing and examination later Dr. Lucian turned towards Aunt Meryl. Again, my eyebrows tipped up. Why was he so stiff with Bryce?

"If you and Mr. Wilhem won't mind, could I please have a minute alone with Miss Anderson?"

Naturally, Bryce growled. I almost rolled my eyes at that. *That was so expected.*

"No."

Dr. Lucian continued to look at a blank Aunt Meryl when he replied, "Miss Anderson is still her parent's responsibility, Mr. Wilhem. I suggest you let me and yourself respect patient-doctor confidentiality and have a little chat with my patient alone."

Bryce turned towards me as if asking me whether to destroy Dr. Lucian or not. I reached over and placed my hand on his, then pulled him closer.

"You can barge into the room as soon as the one minute is over," I whispered discretely. I could feel as Bryce let out a chuckle.

The light mood, however, was only there for a second before getting out of the bed. Bryce turned towards the doctor.

"One minute. A second longer and you can kiss your license and your life goodbye."

Dr. Lucian stared at Bryce for a second before he nodded briskly and looked away. I waited till an unwilling Bryce and a curious Aunt Meryl walked out of the room before turning towards the doctor.

He motioned towards the bed. "May I?"

Looking dumbly at the spot where his hands were pointing, I quietly nodded.

"Thank you," Dr. Lucian replied nicely as he sat on the edge of the bed. He turned towards me, and our eyes met.

"I know this might be very weird for you, and you might be worried why I asked to talk to you in private."

I nodded. "Yes, actually, that's what I'm thinking about right now."

Dr. Lucian smiled warmly. "Now, I want you to know that you can trust me, and please do not take offense if the matter is not as I am perceiving. But—" he paused and looked at me straight in the eye, his gaze serious. "— does Mr. Wilhem, your… boyfriend, physically abuse you, Miss Anderson?"

I blinked.

Then, I burst into a bubble of laughter. "I-I'm sorry, what?"

Dr. Lucian, however, didn't look amused. I calmed down. "Does your boyfriend hit you, Miss Anderson? You're getting quite a lot of hits on your head, and you cringe when you move. I want you to know that I will help you if you need me to. Is there something that's troubling you?"

I couldn't help but chuckle. Shaking my head, I looked up at the concerned doctor. "I want you to trust me when I say, Dr. Lucian, that my boyfriend does *not* hit me or abuse me in any form. It was just an accident, and I cringe because… well, just because."

Dr. Lucian stiffened. Then nodded. "So you cringe because of other reasons?"

"Dr. Lucian, seriously, I suggest you—."

"One minute is up!" Bryce growled out as he burst through the door and moved towards me. "The door is right over there, Dr. Lucian. Thank you for stopping by," Bryce muttered, not even sparing the doctor a glance as he sat down on the bed beside me.

Dr. Lucian turned towards me before smiling politely. "I'll see you around, Mr. Wilhem. It appears Miss Anderson is fine, no concussion. The shock made her black out for a bit. If pain persists then, please give her pain reliever. Goodbye, Theia, I'll see you soon!"

Biting on my tongue, I nodded. "Thank you for coming, Doc."

Dr. Lucian left the door open as he walked out of the room.

"What did he want?"

Tell him the whole truth and watch him bash a doctor or just not tell him everything.

I groaned. "He wanted to know if I was under some sort of stress."

Bryce narrowed his eyes at me.

On second thought… tell him everything

"And if you were physically abusing me…"

The chaos that ensued afterward was seriously something I would not want to relive again. Thankfully, though, Dr. Lucian had managed to get himself out of the castle and the castle gates well before Bryce had run down with a speed that could almost surpass Flash.

I, however, wasn't that lucky. Let's just say that Dr. Lucian was definitely never going to see me again. Or Bryce hoped.

* * *

Two Days Later

All course finals were done. We were free, and prom was tonight. Naturally, I was pretty nervous. Somehow, I felt like something big was about to happen. But then, the stalker hadn't messaged me in days, and well, maybe it was *just* prom nerves. I sighed.

Apparently, Bryce couldn't come to the prom with me. Therefore, Roman, Matthew and I had planned school domination instead. Marley seemed over the moon when I had asked her if we could dress up together. And well, here we were. An hour before prom, our hair being worked on, courtesy of Marley's over excitement. I smoothened the fabric of my light blue dress for the millionth time as I watched the lady working on my hair carefully twirl a loose piece of my hair back and secure it.

"You look amazing, Thi," Marley said from behind me, and I smiled at her. Eyeing her dress, I grinned.

"Ah, you look incredibly sexy. What's for dinner Marlene?" I winked, Marley clearly getting my implication blushed beet red.

"I stand guilty," she grumbled as I got up, and she took my place on the seat. The lady, amused, began working on her hair next.

"I think Alpha Alex will explode when he sees you," the lady cooed, and I smiled at her, blushing.

"I hope not. I need him alive."

Marley giggled and winked. "Oh, why?"

I grinned at her cheeky sarcasm and then smiled, thinking of Bryce.

"Because I love him."

The sun seemed to be fading earlier than usual today. I watched as the oranges swirled with the blues, creating an image worth stealing on a canvas. A warm smile rose on my face as I thought about the room Bryce had set up with each and every portrait I had made of him hanging on the walls. We had come so far.

"You ready?"

Turning around, I grinned at a near to "vibrating with excitement" Marley.

"Let's do this," I declared as I met her halfway, positioning my arm in a gentlemen's manner. I waited for her to hook her arm into mine before we both walked out of the room and began descending the stairs.

Walking down the stairs, holding our dresses just right, praying that I wouldn't catch my feet in my dress and fall on my ass, I breathed a sigh of relief when we finally stepped on the lower floor. Everyone else stood watching quietly.

My eyes immediately sought Bryce's. Looking at him with a grin, I wiggled my eyebrows and in the whim of things, bowed down in a curtsy.

"How do you do, sirs?" Marley giggled as she followed the lead and bobbed a curtsy.

The spell broke, and the boys blinked. Marley and I let out discrete sighs of relief. I could only twirl around before Bryce's arms finally found my waist. He held me close.

"It's only because today is your prom that I'm letting you go. I feel like hiding you in our room and never letting you out, love. You look breathtaking."

I giggled. "How very cave man of you, babe. Thank you by the way. Maggie, the hairdresser, helped a lot."

Bryce growled as he hid his nose against my neck. I held onto his biceps.

"The lads and I have everything set up if something happens. So you don't have to worry, okay?"

I stilled. "You-you think something will happen tonight?"

Bryce stiffened and then moving back, looked me in the eye. He gripped me by my shoulders. "We can never be too cautious, love."

"So you'll be around, right… if something goes wrong?"

Bryce had smiled before he nodded. An identical smile lit up on my face, and I mirrored his nod. Immediately, he burst into a laugh.

"Oh, Theia, what am I going to do with you?"

I grinned as I cuddled back into his chest.

"Love me, *Alexander*, love me."

* * *

"Dance with me, woman!" Matthew laughed loudly as he pulled me over for a spin, I gripped onto Roman's suit just in time to twirl him around with me.

After a minute of glaring at Roman, all three of us burst into laughing. The DJ was playing some EDM track which I had no idea of, personally, but it sounded too fun to sit around during. We were almost an hour into Prom. After photo booths, avoiding the clearly spiked fruit punch and munching on delicious muffins, we were finally taking the Winter Wonderland-themed prom dance floor by storm.

Even though I didn't have my boyfriend here, I considered myself extremely lucky to have had *two* prom dates.

A smile popped on my face when I remembered the fear I had while moving over to Peidmond, spending prom alone at home. And here I was with not one but two best friend dates in tow; an amazingly great boyfriend, a blessed family, great friends both here and back in California if only this stalker disappeared into thin air.

"I think he has."

Startled, I looked up to find Rome looking at me calmly.

"What do you mean?" I shouted into the music. I knew I didn't need to shout because he would hear me all the same, but I still did out of habit. A few steps away, Matthew was pulling up a storm dancing to the song that was playing now.

"Well, maybe you're okay. Maybe the stalker is gone. He hadn't bugged you in days."

I frowned. "Maybe… Maybe you're right!"

"Of course, I am! Now, let's get back to enjoying prom, okay?"

Chuckling, I nodded but then stopped and smiling sheepishly, put up my pinky finger. Roman chuckled, understanding my unspoken information.

"Be back in a jiffy!" I giggled as I turned around and quickly made my way out of the gym and into the bathroom.

I hurriedly made a beeline for an empty cubicle. It had seemed like a minute before I walked back out, happy and light in the bladder. Walking towards the bathroom mirror, I chuckled as Matthew's weird dance moves flashed in my mind.

"Guess who?"

I froze. My ear buzzed with the cold echoes of the whisper.

"Running is futile."

My breath hitched in my throat as my heart pounded up a storm in my chest.

"It's time to say good night."

Immediately my eyes darted up and widened when they met bright green eyes.

Bright green eyes…

And then, my whole world came crashing down.

CHAPTER FORTY

Earlier That Day

"Oh, Theia, what am I going to do with you?"

I grinned as I cuddled back into his chest.

"Love me, *Alexander*, love me."

Bryce's chuckle hung loud and clear around the slightly occupied room.

"I love when you call me Alexander."

I smiled into our embrace.

"Do you want me—?"

"No."

I tilted my head up to look at him, a surprised expression on my face at being stopped by him before I could even complete my sentence.

Our eyes met, and he smiled, bringing up his hand and lovingly caressing my cheek with his thumb. "I love it more when you call me Bryce. No one else does. No one else can, just you. It's… It's a way of showing what you are to me in my life. No one can take your place. You will always come first, Theia. I love you, you know."

I blinked rapidly, trying to get rid of the tears. Bryce chuckled again and pulled me against him.

"I know. I know. I'm the most romantic man alive." Bryce chuckled as he held me. I couldn't help but break out into a giggle at that, my voice still cracking and trying not to cry.

"You're delusional," I mumbled, still chuckling at Bryce's proud stance. "Henry Cavill is."

Bryce stiffened at that and turned to look at an amused Rome. I frowned. "Find this Henry Cavill and make him *disappear*."

I gasped. "You wouldn't!"

Bryce turned to me with a wicked grin. "Oh, I would."

I watched, shocked, as his smile softened, and he turned to a more serious expression, "But I won't. We have more important issues to take care of. I won't be there at the prom with you, visibly, but I will be there."

I frowned. "Why hide?"

Then my eyes widened, and I asked him the same question for the second time that night, "You-you think something will happen tonight?"

This time, however, Bryce gave me a different reply. "It's the perfect timing. He will be there, and you will be there. Chances are he will do something. But Theia, if he does, I want you to know that I am here. Just be calm and have faith in the boys… in me. I will not let any speck of harm come to you. I will not let him steal you."

I nodded, believing every single word Bryce said, but I couldn't help asking, "What if he takes me away?"

"I'll be there in the shadows."

* * *

BRYCE

Growing up, I had been an only child. My father and mother had been the epitome of a happy couple, and each night before going to bed, I had prayed that nothing would ever change.

Life had been splendid. And *that* was where I got it wrong. Life was an equilibrium— the good and the bad. When I reached the age of fifteen, the bad caught up with my family.

My parents died.

A bloody drunk driver was all it took to take down one of the most powerful Lycanthrope king in the world and his wife.

My mother lost a lot of blood; so much blood that even our advanced regeneration abilities couldn't help. There was no hope. And my father knew. He stopped fighting. They both went together in each other's arms. Everything changed after that. Overnight, I changed from a boy to a man, a king. But hope remained.

Years passed, and I healed. I hoped and waited for my very own mate.

Then, Theia came— tiny, beautiful, innocent Theia. I saw her from the window, and she was perfect. But life is an equilibrium. And after all the weeks of good, the bad was here to make its due.

I sat in the large chair, watching the dozens of camera monitors on the wall before me with a steely gaze. I watched as a hooded figure slipped out of the bathroom with my Theia in his arms. A heavy breath left my nostrils, and I stood up from the seat. Andrew Phelps was going to die tonight. Just then the monitor room's doors burst open, and Matthew, Roman, and Alex rushed in, looking just as deadly and ready for battle as I felt. I watched as all three men bowed even Rome. My beast growled in approval. I stepped forward.

"He took her."

I nodded. "The Warriors?"

"Right behind him."

I nodded again. Turning around, I grabbed my black jacket and turned towards the boys. Looking each one in the eye, I spoke, "Anyone of you has doubts?"

Alex stepped forward, and I stiffened.

"Your majesty, Agnus, Theia's housekeeper stopped me on my way here today. She had a confession to make."

Agnus? No…

"Go on," I growled, impatient.

"She believes the younger maid, Lilly, has something to with this as well. She found Lilly fiddling in Theia's room earlier in their employment, right about the time your number got blocked."

My eyes flared, and I made a move towards the door, my gaze seeing red.

"Lilly has been missing for a few weeks now, your majesty! Agnus kept that a secret because she didn't want the young girl to lose her job when she came back," Alex called out from behind me, the desperate need of putting out information evident in his tone.

I stopped in my tracks, my hand on the doorknob, and turned to look at the three men behind me.

Roman's eyes met mine, and he nodded, stepping forward. "Let's kill the bastard, cousin"

"Let's go."

The halls swept passed us as we walked in Lycanthrope speed. What seemed during the day as the safest, brightest of places now held their own secrets in the shadows. We passed the open doors of the gym area when I suddenly stopped in my stance.

"How the fuck is he here?" Matthew growled from behind me, and I agreed.

Within another second, Matthew had speeded into the brightly lit gym, grabbed the man by his collar and was in front us in the dark hallway.

Andrew Sevrik Phelps trembled under my blazing eyes.

"Okay, okay, I give up! I'm a rogue!" He cried out, his hands up defensively.

I had my hand around his throat in a manner of seconds. His eyes bulged out of his sockets as he fought for air.

"Why Theia? Where are you taking her?" I spat in his face. His fingers clawed at my hand around his throat.

I let go of his throat, and immediately, he fell to the floor with a slump.

"I don't know what you're talking about. I'm a rogue. I had been hiding my scent with wolfsbane lacing because I wouldn't get a job, otherwise. I came here with my friend, Finn. He's a nurse. You've met him… Your Majesty!"

"YOU'RE LYING!"

Andrew Phelps stood his ground. "Am I?"

"I see Theia as a student. I wanted to get on your good side so that you would let me join this pack. That's why I was taking so much care of her education. I swear! I don't know what you are talking about."

I waited for the telltale increasing in his heartbeat, the perspiration, fidgeting eyes— anything that would give away his lie to my beast. Instead, my beast smelled the truth coming off of him. I turned towards the rest of the men. All of whom looked shocked.

"It's someone else." My hand fisted on my sides, and I fought myself the need of throwing my fist against the wall. The rest of the students didn't need this. Instead, I turned around and stormed towards the exit.

Andrew Phelps ran with us. My beast growled with approval.

If Andrew Phelps were right that he was not involved in this, my entire kingdom would gain two wolves by the end of tonight.

My heart sparked, and my thoughts turned to the one person who sat on the pedestal in my heart— *Theia.*

* * *

THEIA

I felt nothing, not even the tightly wrapped ropes around my hands and feet or the deadly promises the darkness around me brought. I sat in the awkward office chair quietly as I waited for my impending doom to make an entrance.

It was funny, though; I couldn't remember how I got here at all as if the past hour of my mind had completely been erased. Only what had happened while I had decided to go to the loo. But I knew Bryce would get here sooner than later. He was always around *in the shadows.*

"He's not coming, you know."

I felt myself freeze all over. The chill paralyzed me from the tips of my hair to my toes.

The man walked out from the darkness and under the single light bulb that swung flickering weakly in the dark room. His slightly disheveled blonde hair swept back. The man could very well be ten years older than I am. I blinked.

"Dr. Lucian?" I mumbled almost to myself, trying to think over what had happened in the moments I couldn't seem to remember.

Dr. Lucian chuckled as he moved in closer. "Don't trouble your pretty little head, Theia, you won't remember. I gave you *Flunitrazepam.*"

I cringed as he leaned down to me and grasping the handle of the office chair, swung it around.

"S-stop!" I shouted out as I tried to push away the hot bile beginning to fill my mouth, telltales of vomiting.

Dr. Lucian broke out in a hysterical laughter and with a sudden hand, jolted me to a stop; his nose barely an inch away.

"A thousand nights I've moaned, it was your name that leaves my lips each night. A strange face graced my dreams. A stranger I knew before I met."

I gasped. *The text messages…* Dr. Lucian grinned and rubbed the tip of his nose against mine. I closed my eyes shut tightly, moving back into the seat.

"Hello, mate," he murmured softly, and I almost puked.

"You've ha-have me mistaken, Dr. Lucian. I… I already have a—!"

"D-don't!"

I stopped. Dr. Lucian's eyes glared red and puffy as tears trailed down his cheeks.

"Y-you're mine, please."

I couldn't help but sob in helplessness as Dr. Lucian fell on my feet, putting his head on my lap. A few breaths later, I stiffened. A new sense of courage was encroaching my insides.

"No," I spoke out boldly, pushing the fact that I was still crying aside.

Dr. Lucian's head snapped up, and he snarled, more tears slipping down his cheeks. "No? No? Yes, you are!"

"No, I am not!" I screamed into his face. *I am not his mate! Where is my mate!*

"Oh, poor Lucian, she's quite a heartbreaker, isn't she?"

My eyes widened as I watched the next figure move out of the dark and into the light of the bulb. Her green eyes met mine, and I felt everything around me fall down to its death. *She* was supposed to be dead.

"A-Amber?"

Amber grinned at me maliciously as she moved closer. Her black heels clicked against the stone pavements of the floor.

Reaching us, she leaned a hand down and placed it on Dr. Lucian's head, ruffling his hair softly. Dr. Lucian closed his eyes and sunk his head further into my lap, humming soothingly.

"You're a strong one, Theia. When I pushed you over the window, I expected you to be dead. Poor Lucian didn't talk to me for a whole hour, thinking I had pushed you, his mate." She sneered the word *his mate,* and I almost spit on her face.

I cringed as I felt Dr. Lucian's arms moving around my waist and his nose nuzzling my lap even more. Then I looked at a triumphant Amber, and she grinned at me happily.

"You were supposed to be dead!" I spat at her, wanting her to hurt, to let her feel a fraction of what I had the past few months. Instead, Amber bubbled out in a fit of loud laughter.

"I was in London when Derek messaged me telling me to come back to him because Bryce had found his mate. Fool thought I would go back to him! Instead, I began planning. A plan to get rid of you. My maid, Lilly, agreed on working for you to be closer to you, and per my commands, she blocked Bryce's number from your cellphone. I had hoped that would help, but *alas*, you worked your dark magic through that too. You two got closer, and I couldn't stand the thought of Bryce touching someone else, and that day, I made my presence felt… I thought he would see how hot I have become and take me instead of a fresh virgin like you, but he didn't… All he fucking saw was *you*!"

Amber's eyes blazed, and she reached forward, grabbed my hair and yanked at it. I shrieked in pain, and immediately, Dr. Lucian growled and smacked her hand. Amber reeled back before she threw a punch at Dr. Lucian. I watched wide-eyed as he scampered down on the floor, blood pouring out of his lips.

"Ungrateful bastard!" Amber shrieked as she kicked at a whimpering Dr. Lucian. "I gave your delusional ass everything—sanity, sex, hope, and this is how you repay me? I fixed your depressed ass. I gave you your mate!"

Amber suddenly turned to me and smiled. Moving over, she lazily undid the ropes and moved back to look at her work.

"Don't move a muscle or I will mutilate you. Thank heavens that I can kill you without killing my Bryce. If someone killed my Bryce, you would die too. That wouldn't be so nice, would it?"

I watched as Amber turned to look into the dark. On the floor, Dr. Lucian extended a bloody hand towards me as if wanting to just come closer. Looking at the poor madman, I felt my heart bleed and reached over to grasp his hand. Immediately, he whimpered and moved closer, fresh tears leaking down his face as he leaned against my lap again and broke down into a sob. I felt myself cry with him. *What had Amber molded this man into?*

Amber turned to face me, and her grin brightened. "See? You're warming up to the *man-boy* already! Always so compassionate, Theia, always so understanding and compassionate. Ready to *help* the helpless." She reached over and gripped my jaw. She leaned in, her bright green eyes glaring into my browns. "Who will help you now?"

"You always were so messy, Amby."

Both Amber and I stilled in our places. Dr. Lucian, however, continued to cry into my lap, as if completely unaware of his surroundings.

"Hello, Derek, welcome!" Amber giggled as she did a swooping curtsy. She suddenly stopped and turned towards Dr. Lucian and me.

"Shut up, Sebastian!"

Dr. Lucian immediately whimpered and dug himself into my lap, quieting down immediately. Despite my disgust and fear, I pat his head soothingly before moving my hand away.

"Another toy, Amby, Really?" Derek chuckled as he moved further into the room and grinned. His eyes moved around the room and then finally to me.

Amber stiffened and took a slight defense position. "How did you find us?"

"Oh, I didn't find you *AmbyBamby*," Derek cooed as he moved his weight from one foot to the other, his hand coming up and folding in front of his chest.

"I did."

My heart did a happy swoop hearing Bryce's voice.

A strangled gasp left Amber's lips as she moved forward and then stopped. The woman actually thought Bryce would hug her for a second.

I wanted to run to him and wanted to jump on him, but I was held down… Dr. Lucian was still whimpering.

A tiny *click* sounded around the room and suddenly the whole room…*no*… Factory came into clear view. My eyes trailed over Matthew, Roman, Alex, Lionel, Mr. Phelps and a dozen more warriors, all standing behind Bryce, ready for an attack. My gaze moved to Bryce's, and I flinched at the glare he was sending to my lap. I put my arm around the poor mad doctor, and immediately, his glared moved to me. I shook my head. Dr. Lucian continued to sob although it seemed to be almost gone now.

As if understanding, Bryce composed himself and quickly turned towards a stiff Amber. "Funny really, I had expected to find the maid Lilly here, not the *dead* Amber."

At this, Amber giggled as if Bryce had actually said something flatteringly funny. "Oh, no, silly. That's what you were all supposed to think. Poor Lilly laid herself out for slaughter when she agreed to get plastic surgery done. All I had to do afterward was kill her, mutilate her, bleed her out, clean her and lend her a couple bags of my blood. Anything for you, though, Alex."

I watched as the other Alex cringed and mouthed *psycho* to himself.

Amber, however, wasn't done. Motioning towards the now quiet, almost sleeping doctor on my lap, she giggled. "Poor Sebastian here was suffering from an alcohol problem and was almost suicidal when I met him. His wolf wouldn't come out because of all the depression. His human mate was married to someone else. Well, I found him and fixed him; just a few of those pills that cause delusions, lots of sex, a little redirecting and *bam*— a crazy stalker!"

She turned to Bryce and giggled again, motioning towards all the warriors behind him.

"Don't you think you're a little overboard here, though, Alex, a whole army going to war with a single royal for a pathetic human? I don't know if I should be insulted or flattered!"

Bryce moved forward, and Amber breathed when he was almost chest to chest with her. I cringed, not liking the closeness. He narrowed his eyes and snarled at her.

"All is fair,*and* love *is* war, Amber."

Immediately, as if Bryce's reply was the key, all havoc broke loose. A dozen more wolves moved into the clearing from behind us and growled at Bryce's warriors, who now were also in their beast forms. Dr. Lucian whimpered against my lap and made a grab for my hand just as Bryce snarled at me warningly. I watched silently as a dozen warriors circled around me, protecting me from all the other wolves which I supposed were on Amber's side.

"You're right, Alex, love is war. And look, I have an army too!" Amber giggled as she moved towards her large wolves.

"You're such a delusional, bitch" Derek growled as he shook his head, watching as Amber made a futile effort of attacking me.

Immediately, Rome reached over and flung her away, running after her as he leaped and pinned her down. I cringed as I heard her shriek. Derek cringed too.

He looked towards Bryce and Bryce nodded. Derek turned towards me gave me a soft broken smile and ran away in a blur. My heart pained for the man who knew that his soulmate was going to die today, the one who was made for him and rejected him was going to die today. I knew he couldn't stay. Despite all the hurt she gave him, he couldn't stay and participate in her destruction. I guess in some corner of his heart Derek still loved Amber.

I sighed as I shook my head and looked down at Dr. Lucian. Amongst the chaos in this abandoned factory, the blood being shed, bones being broken, rogues being left disabled, Sebastian Lucian was asleep on my lap like a one-year-old baby.

"We could have had it all!" Amber shrieked at Bryce as she tried to block his attack.

Bryce's beast leaped forward, and instantly, Amber transformed into her beast as well. Her light brown coat glistening under the light. They both took a blow at each other, moving further towards the open window.

"You're Derek's mate, Amber! You still have time! Stop this madness!"

Suddenly, as if that was the wrong thing to say Amber ran towards Bryce with a loud shriek.

"If I can't have you, she can't either!"

Bryce's black beast crouched and flung his hand at the brown beast out of defense. I watched with an open mouth as the brown beast flew backward and with a loud grunt pierced through a sticking metal rod on the unfinished wall— straight through the heart.

With her dying breath, she lifted her head and turned to me. Her knowing eyes were dying and haunting. I whimpered as the last breath of her life left her lungs, and her head dropped. Her whole body transformed back to her human self. Derek's mate was dead.

The whole room fell silent except for Roman, who had not even transformed. His head moved towards me instantly. I sat still and blank. As if finally in his senses, he quickly leaped and threw a large dirty cloth over the dead woman.

"Take all the wolves to the retention center," Bryce's beast ordered a dark gray wolf who immediately transformed into a naked Alex. I looked away.

"Matthew, Rome, please remove the… body."

Bryce's beast stalked over to me, and I whimpered when his eyes turned to the bloodied sleeping man on the floor, head on my lap. His eyes glazed with red, and I quickly put my hand over the sleeping deranged man. His glare moved to me.

"Phelps, remove him and take him to the hospital. Take two of my guards."

Mr. Phelps immediately transformed and scooped the sleeping man in his arms. Mr. Lucian instantly woke up.

"N-no!" His eyes found mine. "T-theia!"

I shook my head, feeling suffocated and incredibly sad.

"One day you will thank me, Mr. Lucian."

Mr. Phelps led the crying doctor away, and I looked down at my feet. I knew Bryce was standing a step away. I knew the rest of the warriors had arrived and were spilling kerosene everywhere. But I stood frozen.

"Come here," Bryce muttered gruffly, and almost at once, I ran forward into his arms, my feet taking blind flight.

I let out a loud sob as my face collided with his chest and picking me up into an embrace. He buried his nose in the crook of my neck, and he sobbed with me.

"I didn't mean to kill her… I was just…"

"I know," I whispered. I kissed the side of his face and held him closer to me as he continued to sob. For losing his best friend's soulmate, for losing his childhood memories. His best friend.

We held each other for what seemed like ages before Bryce finally calmed down and moved his head back to look at me.

"Let's go home," he mumbled, his voice gruff and gravely.

Leaning forward, I placed a kiss on his forehead.

"Let's go home."

* * *

Two Days Later

Memories never left, deranged memories, most definitely not. They attached themselves to your mind and sucked at your soul day by day. And one day when your poor withering soul cannot take it anymore, it claimed your life instead. Deranged memories killed you. And added with guilt, I was on the verge of withering away.

The purples and oranges of the evening sky swirled above the vast amount of green land, and I sat on the window bench in my room, gazing at the castle that sat on the mountains.

I was back home, sitting in my room and gazing at my other home. A sigh left my lips, and I looked down at my lap. I tried to be happy and not feel guilty for being the reason someone's mate died, but the guilt was getting to me. The lights in my room suddenly lit on, cutting out the darkness in the room. Looking up, my gaze met my smiling mother.

"Come down for dinner, honey."

Seeing mom smile, I smiled slowly and nodded, getting up and moving out the room after her. Rounding towards the kitchen, I came to a sudden stop. Derek grinned at me as he reached over and took my hand in his.

"Great, you're finally here! We were starving!" He chuckled as he led me into the heavily populated kitchen.

Aunt Meryl beamed as I sunk in beside her. Her palm instantly covered mine. "I've missed you, dearie. Don't you ever stay away for more than a couple of hours."

I couldn't help but chuckle at that. "I was there yesterday."

"Exactly! That feels like ages ago!" Roman chuckled as he neared me and pressed a kiss on my head before sitting down beside a still grinning Derek.

I watched Derek, and his grin fell a little, leaning forward his hand found mine.

"I'm over it, Theia. It was not your fault. If it weren't her, it would be you. You would be dead. Alexander would be dead."

It felt like I had a cold bucket of water. The actual sense of his words crashed on me. I smiled, moving my fingers to grasp his hand tightly. King Derek Mcgall was a fighter.

"Yes! I am going to steal half of your dinner," Matthew exclaimed excitedly as he plopped down on the seat beside me, and I grinned at him immediately.

"You wish!"

"Steal her food, and I will cut you, Matthew!" Marley scolded Matthew from beside him and sent a wink my way. I grinned at her appreciatively.

My smile suddenly faltered. The whole kitchen was filled with people: Derek, Aunt Meryl, Matt, his parents, Alex, his parents, Roman, Marley, her folks, Agnus and even Keith! Everyone was here, trying to cheer my mood as well as theirs and giving in to a fresh new start. But the one person I was actually looking forward to seeing was not here.

I felt my spirits fall. Bryce had been trying lately between getting me out of depression, fixing Dr. Lucian into a rehab center and sentencing the convicted Weres. I understood, kind of. Derek seemed to have caught my expression because he reached for my hand again.

"I'm sorry, Thi. We couldn't find him."

I nodded, managing a small smile.

"It's okay. I understand."

* * *

"Oh, no, sweetie, it's fine! You, kids, go up, and we'll take care of the dishes and table. Go on." Mrs. Jefferson ushered us out of the kitchen.

All the ladies already at work with clearing things away while the men took to the lounge.

"Just come back when we call for dessert." Aunt Meryl winked at us, and Marley moved forward.

She grabbed the older woman's hand. "You know, I think I might just be in love with you."

Aunt Meryl giggled as she shooed us all away. We made our way upstairs. Marley and I giggled at the boys as they talked about which football team they liked best. I sighed as we rounded towards my room. The whole dinner had ended, and Bryce had not shown up.

"Why was Alpha Alexander not here?" Marley whispered in my ear. I shrugged.

"He left before I woke up yesterday. I haven't seen him since," I muttered. Marley heard embraced into one big hug.

"It's going to be fine. Maybe, he was busy."

"Maybe." I shrugged as I cut through the crowd in front of my room's door and twisted it open.

I stopped in my track, everyone behind me echoing my move.

Bryce stood near the open window. His light blue shirt rolled up at the sleeves with two packages in his hand.

"Okay, then! We'll talk to you later, Theia! Good night!" Alex blurted out quite loudly as he and the rest of the gang quickly removed themselves from the scene.

Bryce's eyes stayed on mine, and after a minute of staring at each other silently, I sighed, walked into the room and closed the door behind me.

"I brought Chinese," Bryce mumbled, still standing by the window.

"Uh-huh," I mumbled back, already halfway across the room. It felt like home when I finally slipped my arms around his waist and melted against his chest. Instantly, his arms came around me, holding me back in our hug.

"I love you," I breathed into his chest, inhaling the expensive musky cologne that I could only recognize as Bryce's.

"I love you too, love," Bryce murmured before I felt him press a kiss on my forehead.

"So, dinner?"

My already full stomach turned in protest, but I moved back and smiled, anyway. "Sure."

Bryce chuckled as he shook his head and made his way to the bed. I grabbed my TV's remote and jumped in behind him.

"Here." he handed me a Snickers bar. "Dessert after dinner."

I sent him my brightest grin before reaching over and giving him a very sloppy kiss on his cheek. Bryce burst out laughing as I wiped at his cheeks afterward.

"This is why I love you. You bring me Snickers!" I said as he opened his Chinese takeaway packs and tucked in.

I switched on the TV and changed the channel until it stopped on The Flash.

"So… I found these." Bryce pulled a bunch of envelopes, and I immediately tensed in my spot— University application replies.

"Why aren't these open, yet?" He spoke softly, and I shrugged.

They weren't open because I would have to leave and move away from him.

"You're going. You do know that, don't you?"

I sighed and nodded. I knew I wouldn't give up college.

"Thought I saw Cambridge somewhere over there. You up for studying in the UK?"

My head darted towards Bryce's, and he looked at me expectedly. "Well, open it?"

I shook my head, "We'll be so far away."

Bryce chuckled as he brought in another one of those delicious smelling chicken up to his lips.

"Nonsense. Open it, we'll find a way."

"Ugh," I groaned, giving in as my fingers already began nimbly moving along the envelope and opening it neatly.

Dear, Miss Anderson…

I stared at the letter for a whole minute or two, reading and re-reading it over just to make sure that what I was reading was correct. I couldn't believe it…

"Well?"

I looked up, and my wide eyes met Bryce's. A grin formed on his lips, and he leaned in to press a kiss on my nose.

"Accepted." I breathed the word as if it was something so alien.

"Accepted," Bryce echoed. His tone was proud and strong compared to my disbelieving whisper.

"Just wait here, I'll be right back," Bryce whispered as he packed the empty takeaway packs into the bag and sped out of the room.

"Oh, hello, Alexander dear, you really should start using the front door, you know." I heard mom loudly but timidly scold Bryce and chuckled at the thought of how his expression might be.

His response was covered by the massive distance, and I slouched further in bed, taking a careful bite of the chocolate bar. It was a tradition. My first bite was always a decent one. The rest that followed was savage mutilation. I wasn't proud. But, hey, it made me feel good.

I was just taking another bite when the lights around the night dimmed, and the various decorative night lights around my room came to glow like fireflies. I smiled knowing Bryce had returned. Looking up, my gaze met Bryce's as he got into bed from the other side and sat down facing me.

"It's been a long two days," he finally mumbled, and I quietly nodded in response.

"You shouldn't feel guilty, you know?"

I sighed as I looked away at the sparkling yellow lights. "I know." Hesitating, I looked back at him. "But it still feels wrong."

Bryce looked at me for a minute before he replied, "She would have killed you if she hadn't died. I admit she could have gone to jail, but what happened was not intentional. It was an accident. Now, all are lighter. Derek is too, trust me."

Our gazes never faltered as he spoke, and finally, I nodded for the first time in two days. He was right. I had to move past it. Everyone else had.

"I trust you."

Smiling, Bryce leaned forward and placed a kiss on my forehead, his palm holding my cheeks soothingly. He moved back, and I smiled.

"I had something made… for us."

Instantly, I narrowed my eye at my large Adonis of a boyfriend. "What did you have made?"

I watched curiously as reaching for his back pocket, Bryce pulled out a small black box. I instantly held my breath.

Opening it, he looked back up at me. I, on the other hand, looked down.

"Promise rings because your father would hunt me down if I proposed to his eighteen-year-old daughter."

Looking back up at him, I couldn't help but let the laughter flow. I leaped on him.

"You're amazing! I love you so much."

Laughter bubbled around my dimly lit room as we both fell backward in bed.

"So will you wear it?" He asked as we lay on out back and looked at each other, smiling.

"Yes. If you make me wear it, that is."

Bryce grinned as I felt him reach for my left hand and finding my ring finger, slid the crown-inspired ring on it. I knew there was another ring there, but Bryce made no move towards that. My heart warmed when I realized he wanted his ring to be *my* decision. I couldn't help but smile, plucking the thick platinum band from its cushion and fishing out his hand, I slid it on.

The night stayed beautiful as the open windows slipped light cool breezes into the room, twirling and turning under my room's nightlight before it touched me. I scooted closer to Bryce.

"You know I think I loved you from the moment that I saw you from the castle."

I turned towards him, bracing myself in my sides. He turned his head towards me. His eyes met mine, and I sighed.

"Alexander Bryce Wilhem, you have no idea how much I love you." I chuckled as I pecked a kiss on his nose. "There's no escaping me now, you know? Theia Wilhem sounds great by the way! For future ref—."

I could only complete half way before Bryce's lips touched mine. A hot growl emitting from his lips, I smiled into the kiss as I pulled him closer, deepening the kiss.

At that moment I couldn't think of a single thing I would change— from the beginning to our rocky but exciting journey to our intense climax, not one single thing.

I realized I wouldn't even change the bad. It made us who we are.

Sure, our story was far from over. We still had such a long way to go, a long journey to live. But I knew. No matter what the ride, our ending would always be the same.

Happy and together.

Forever.

EPILOGUE

It's not about the journey but the ending. They said that.

What did I think?

It was all about the journey because without the journey, I wouldn't have this ending— Through the change, through the love, through the hate, through the highs and the lows, through each and every tiny aspect of my journey, of our journey.

Looking back, sometimes, it had felt like he was the wave, and I, the shore. We craved each other. We needed each other. But every time we got close, the wave broke, and the shores were left abandoned.

Looking back, seeing the beginning and everything that happened afterward, I was sure that was not the end. Sure, the villain had been vanquished, and my King in Armani had saved me, but that was hardly the ending.

"Do you think that woman knows her butt-crack is showing?"

Beside me, Roman choked on his orange juice, and I groaned, shaking my head.

"Well?" Charlotte urged as she leaned in closer.

I fidgeted in my business class seat as I turned to look at her. I groaned again, and she narrowed her eyes at me.

It was three years ago when I had found myself settling into an apartment with Roman as my neighbor— a new country, a very different environment, without Bryce. Well, for the first initial weeks, that is. He couldn't resist for more than two weeks, not that I minded. I didn't mind at all.

Charlotte and I had become friends quickly when we had found each other seated in the same row, in the same class. It was safe to say, then, that Charlotte, Casey, Marley, and I had spent most of our free nights playing cyber sleepover during these three years. I supposed it's great in a sense that despite different colleges and countries we had all managed to maintain such good friendship.

Glancing at Rome and Charlotte, I sighed if only I could say the same about them… Charlotte lived on campus and Rome and me in apartments just a bend away. It had still been a miracle Rome had refrained from killing her yet. Naturally, if that wasn't indication enough Charlotte was the Neville Longbottom to Rome's Severus Snape. Roman detested Charlotte.

"I think you should stop talking, Char," Rome hissed at her while dabbing a tissue paper on his jeans.

"Well, aren't you a jolly jellybean? As expected really, three years and you're still as dry and horrifying as the Sahara!" Charlotte snapped back while grasping at my hand she tugged lightly.

"Hey, how long before we land?" I quickly butted in, knowing exactly well how easy it was to distract Charlotte.

After subtly putting out the fact that she would come over for the break, Charlotte had finally voiced out her interest last week. Bryce invited her. With the trip being official and Charlotte's very amazing father informed, we were all packed, washed and ready. Secretly, however, I supposed it was the princess in Charlotte that made her want to visit Bryce's castle more than to actually visit Peidmond, but I couldn't blame the girl. After seeing pictures for the past three years, I would be super interested too.

"We're supposed to land in a couple of minutes. I'm sure the announcements coming along any second." Roman leaned further into his seat just as a deep voice began speaking to all of us passengers.

Grabbing at my iPod and iPhone, I was just packing them in my bag when I noticed Charlotte leaned in closer. Curious, I moved towards her too.

"I bet Alexander is already at the airport just waiting to get you in those huge arms of his," Charlotte whispered in a sing-a-song tone. Instantly, I blushed a deep red.

I admit even though three years had passed, it still felt new like we were only just in our initial months of dating. I felt my blush deepen as I smacked Charlotte on her arm and looked away. The scenes from that day she once walked on us played in my head. It wasn't a day to easily forget. After all, it was the day Charlotte found out about werewolves.

Shooing the mental images away, I groaned as I slumped further into my seat and bent over so that my hair covered my face and hid my blush. I groaned when I heard Roman and Charlotte's chuckles.

"It was a good sight to see, to be honest. You on his lap while he was full werewolf mode and just hugging him. Too cute!" Charlotte whispered teasingly.

I groaned again. It was true. Bryce and I liked to do that a lot, just talk and spend some time with him in his beast state. I had noticed earlier on that he was a little sensitive about his beast. A little digging and one night, he finally admitted that it made him insecure.

It had taken me a while to register that he was actually scared I would be disgusted by the large black beast. Yes, he was scary and looked deadly, but in the end, he was Bryce. And he was mine.

After that confession, I'd found myself coaxing him to change and just spend time with him like that. Over time, I realized him in his beast form had a personality of his own. Aside from his own deeper gravelly voice, he was easier to anger, deadly possessive but very eager to play games and just... cuddle. Bryce in his beast form was more a cuddler than in his human form.

It had just been one of those days when Char had decided to just crash in, or maybe, I shouldn't have given her a pair of keys the day before. I supposed it was my fault.

But hey, at least, she took the fact quite nicely! The tiny voice in my head scoffed, and I almost snickered out loud.

"It's Lycanthrope for your kind information. Know your beasts right!" Roman hissed at Charlotte before straightening in his seat. He tapped his hand on mine. Surprised, I turned towards him.

He cocked an eyebrow up. "We're here."

* * *

"Reckon Matt missed you?" I snickered as we walked towards the arrivals lounge.

Roman looked at me as if I was even crazy to ask the question and scoffed. "Of course, he did. He hates being Beta, for the time being. He'd be glad I'll be taking that up again once I'm done with University."

This time, however, Charlotte was the one who scoffed. "Oh, please, you won't be done for another four years!"

"Who thought you'd pick Law, Rome?" I added, nudging him as we continued to move towards arrivals lounge.

"Oh, God, please! You both have four more years to go too!"

Both Char and I snickered at that. "At least, psychology is fun!"

I was still grinning at Roman when I felt strong arms wrap around my waist. I smiled into the all too familiar embrace as I hooked my arms around Bryce's neck and pulled his face down, smiling at him as I placed a soft kiss on his chin.

"I missed you," he grumbled into the embrace, and I grinned.

He'll never change…

"I missed you too, babe."

* * *

Driving though the city seemed like a dream, it had been ages, months, since I had last come back home. My nerves buzzed with excitement and anticipation of seeing everyone.

The permanent smile that I had for a while, now, widened when my thoughts wandered towards mom and dad, and then there were Aunt Meryl, Mrs. Smith, and Agnus as well. Even though I was finally twenty-one, my treatment still stood. I was still an eighteen-year-old to them. I supposed I was even younger to my parents!

The welcoming warmth radiated through me when I felt Bryce's hand find mine. I squeezed our entwined hand lightly. I smiled harder when Bryce squeezed back.

"Peidmond seems so English! And it also rains here a lot! Reckon it's meant to be, really! After university, I'm bloody moving in!" Charlotte exclaimed excitedly from the back seat, and Bryce and I grinned at each other, waiting for Roman to respond. We both knew he would.

"Delusional, this one!" Roman muttered out loud, and we broke into a round of chuckles. Charlotte, however, only grumbled even more.

"Oh, and since Roman is never going to find his soul mate because he's so heartless, I guess I'll just move in with him!" She snapped. Everybody in the vehicle except for her stilled.

Looking up in the review mirror, Roman's stormy eyes found mine, and I shook my head, squeezing Bryce's hand harder at the same time. Bryce got my message. Immediately, Roman's eyes glazed over, and I watched as slowly but surely he calmed down, relaxing again. Charlotte, on the other hand, still sat clueless as she watched the houses on the last street before my home with great interest. I couldn't blame her. I found myself doing that a lot too. Both Charlotte and I blamed it on the psychology.

"We're here," Bryce announced as he rounded into our driveway and cut off the engine.

Instantly, my doors were flying open, and an ecstatic Marley rushed forward and pulled me in for a hug.

"Oh, my God, I'm so glad you're back for the holidays!" She squealed, and I giggled along with her.

"I know! I'm so glad. I've missed you," I exclaimed, hugging her back.

It was only minutes later when we realized no one around us was talking did we turn around. We both froze. A wide-eyed Charlotte stood just a step or two away, eyeing the now very tensed Matthew in front of her with an extremely alarmed expression. She looked scared, and if I didn't know Matthew, trust him, or what was happening, I would have jumped right in. But I did know him, and Matthew would never hurt his mate.

Charlotte's scared eyes on me widened, and I shook my head comfortingly, bringing my hand up and down in a comforting way. Telling her, it was okay. I mouthed an apparent soul mate just as Matthew finally decided to touch her, and thankfully, Charlotte got the memo. She let out a relieved sigh.

Bryce's arms slipped around my waist before automatically, he began rubbing my belly soothingly. I couldn't help but smile at that. Both Bryce and his beast wanted kids or pups as his beast called them. But we weren't planning. We both knew there would be a time for that. I was only twenty-one. There was no rush. Bryce, however, still loved to caress and rub my belly. Somehow, it always put a smile on his face. And his smile put a smile on mine.

Still, pushing the slow tingles around in the back of my spine away, I quickly refocused my attention on the two mates that were now glued together.

Charlotte hugged Matthew back, rubbing his back like a child soothingly, while Matthew buried his whole soul into the crook of her neck.

"Oh, can we please just get in already? It's almost fourteen degrees, very chilly by my standards!" Marley suddenly groaned, and immediately, Matthew jerked around to snarl at her.

Keith was in front of her instantly.

"Mine," Matthew growled coldly, one arm at his back around Charlotte while the other in front of him positioned to block any attack. His glare was solely stuck on Keith.

"And the stamp has been placed, ladies and gentlemen. I am officially a mate!"

Everyone blinked. Then, I groaned while trying to pin down my laughter. Charlotte winked at me. Oh, Char, what am I going to do with you?

Beside me, Marley stood behind Keith not at all ashamed as she laughed her sanity off.

* * *

"Guess who's here?" mom spoke after all the hugs and kisses.

I leaned into my dad's embrace as I answered, "What?"

"Someone's here to meet you, Fuzzy." Dad chuckled. I moved back and turned just in time to spot a sprinting Casey just seconds before she collided with me, and I fell back to the sofa.

Bryce let out a loud warning growl as he now stood beside me, and Casey quickly quipped up a sorry before turning to me.

"Surprise!" She grinned, and I pulled her in for a hug again.

"I'm so, so glad that you're here," I mumbled back softly, knowing too well not to ask about Angelo. It was expected. Angelo hadn't shown. And sadly, I didn't mind.

"My turn," A deep voice mumbled from behind us, and Casey stilled. Her cheeks turning red.

Turning around, my eyes nearly fell out of my body—Lionel, taller, muscular Lionel.

Lord, save Casey.

And by the way, Lionel was looking at Casey, Lord, save Lionel.

What was today? National Find your Mate day.

"Good to see you, Luna" Lionel nodded solemnly, and I laughed out loud before pulling him in for a sibling hug.

I strangely felt so proud of him. From being the pack's late bloomer to being the acting Delta and best warrior, he had achieved a lot.

"You've come a long way, Lionel. Don't let the fear of rejection stop you from telling her. I'm so proud of you," I whispered into his ear as I hugged him tightly. My smile widened when I felt him hug me back.

"Thank you, Thi," he whispered before we broke away.

My eyes met Bryce's proud ones, and he smiled, nodding approvingly. I knew he had heard.

"Okay, she's my best friend, guys. I think I deserve a hug!" Matthew declared as he marched into the house. Just as I noticed, Lionel led Casey out. Charlotte smiled at me brightly. I winked at her knowing that secretly, she had wanted this, this fairy tale love story.

Although, I wasn't sure that if this story were in a fairytale if she would be the mated to a werewolf. Still, maybe it could be one— a 21st-centuryfairytale.

Strangely, Matthew reached over and pulled me towards the back patio. I walked behind him patiently. My eyes lingered on a now laughing Bryce who stood talking to my dad, my dad's arm on his shoulder. His eyes met mine just as Matthew and I slipped out.

The door shut close as we stepped out, and Matthew immediately pulled me in for a hug. I sighed happily against his chest as I hugged him back. I actually missed my boys a lot, together like in Senior Year.

"Scared?" I whispered against his chest, knowing exactly what was troubling him.

I felt Matthew sigh.

"Yes," he mumbled into my hair. I tightened my arms around him.

"There's no need to be. I'll always be here for you. Bryce and Rome will always be here for you."

Just then, another pair of arms wrapped around us, and I felt Matthew pulled his arm from around me. I looked up to see a softly smiling Rome. I couldn't help it. I let the tears flow as I wrapped an arm around Rome too. All three of us had been through a lot together. It felt great knowing everything was falling back together now. And everyone was finding their mates.

Now, if only Rome finds a girl that can stand him! That would be great!

The sound of the patio door open and close was more apparent now, and soon after, I felt another person bring his arms around the group, hugging everyone.

"Is everything okay here?" Bryce asked curiously, his hand finding my waist while the other found Matthew's shoulder.

Despite my tears, I laughed.

"Yes, yes, everything is fine. Everything is great, actually. I'm here with all three of my boys. What could be better?"

"Ugh, stop, you sound like my mother!" Matthew groaned as I continued to laugh.

* * *

"What are you doing?" I smiled as I swung forward.

"Remembering."

Bryce chuckled before moving behind me and pushing on the swing, a loud giggle left my lips as the swing swung higher, taking me with it. I soared. I let my eyes close as I felt the wind sweep past my cheeks. Everything felt lighter this way. Suddenly, Bryce's hands clamped over mine as he grabbed the swing to a stop. A loud gasp ripped out of my throat as my body nearly jolted forward.

"Bryce!" I gasped, turning to look back at the grinning man.

Grip still in place, Bryce moved to stand in front of me. Slowly, he kneeled in front of me.

"You know what's coming, don't you?"

My eyes widened when he grasped my left hand gently with his right and then brought his left hand to hold that hand too. Both our promise rings shone under the afternoon lighting. My eyes began to tear up. Bryce's smile widened before caressing my palm. He slowly slipped out the promise ring from my finger and slipped it on my right hand. I held my breath as I watched. Bryce reached for his back pocket and quickly retrieved a tiny dark velvet box. Looking back at me, one hand still holding mine he flipped it open.

A ring.

"We have come such a long way from where we began. I came from my edge of my world, and you came from yours. But we both met here in the middle, and I'm so glad we did." Bryce stopped, looking overwhelmed, and I nodded, smiling brightly and already crying because of the intensity of that moment.

Completely red in the face, he continued, "During these four years, we've had tears, we've had anger, and we've had smiles. But what I'm grateful for more than anything is that, during these four years, we've had love… each and every day. And I want that for the rest of my life, not just the love but-but everything! I want us for the rest of my life."

His grip on my hand tightened soothingly, and we both smiled at each other.

"Theia Anderson, will you marry me?"

I knew it was coming, but still, my breath hitched in my throat.

Bryce suddenly looked panicked. "I mean we don't need to get married right now. We can wait until university is over if that's what you want. I'll wait until next year. We'll even get married tomorrow if you want to! But please will you marry—?"

"YES!"

I couldn't help it. I jumped on Bryce, crying, laughing and kissing him all over his face. Bryce laughed with me as he held me by the waist. We were both on the ground now.

"YES! YES! YES!" I exclaimed happily, still kissing him everywhere!

"I love you, Theia!"

My blurry, happy eyes met his sparkling one, and despite me crying, I smiled brightly.

"I love you too. Oh, my God, won't you make me wear it?"

"Of course, but first, a kiss, Luna?"

Everything felt perfect as I leaned forward and captured his lips with mine. The kiss was slow, possessive and passionate with an underlying promise in it. I felt Bryce smile into the kiss before I felt him slip the ring on my finger. My fingers untangled from his hair and immediately wrapped around his neck, hugging him closer. We were officially engaged.

My heart fluttered with the newness of it.

"I love you," Bryce grinned as he broke the kiss, placing a small peck on my lips and then my nose, still grinning.

He wiped the tear that slid down my cheeks as I smiled back at him.

"I love you too. I love you so much!"

"Theia, Bryce, the dinner will be re— oh, dear!"

Both our eyes darted towards my mom standing at the open patio door, her expression stunned. Her eyes had raked over Bryce's position and my face before she let out a very loud squeal! Still squealing, she rushed back inside. We were sure to spreading the news. I was sure my dad wouldn't be that happy.

I turned to Bryce, and he winked at me before hurling me to my feet and then bending down scooped me up in his arms. Meanwhile, I basked in the feel of being in my soon-to-be husband's arms. Husband— I shivered when I felt the whole zoo in my stomach.

* * *

Walking back into the house had been a task. By the amount of cheering we had received, I was slightly surprised that the roof was still intact by the end of it.

By the time we had gotten back inside Blond's parents, Mr. And Mrs. Pheper had arrived. Sadly, Blond wasn't able to make it. He's flight had been canceled. I was glad, though, that Alex, or as I liked to call him Blond, had made it into Princeton. He had gotten the scholarship, so that had sorted out everything wonderfully. He was now doing double major in literature and creative writing.

It was a shame I had never gotten to know that Alex was interested in being an author which I supposed he already was— a best-selling author of "Luna."

I read it. It was after all based on me. Bryce was happy about that, though.

A smirk made its way to my lips when I felt Bryce move towards me nervously again.

"You best keep my daughter happy, Alexander, or else… it won't be good!" My dad warned Bryce for the fifth time. I squeezed Bryce's hand comfortingly.

Just then, there was a tap on my shoulder. I turned around, and immediately, my smile brightened.

"I suppose I owe you, 'Congratulations'?"

I welcomed the hug that came my way. "Thank you, Derek. It feels like a dream." I stopped and moving my head back to look at him, mumbled, "Soon when you find your love, I'll be congratulating you. You'll see."

Derek only smiled as he pushed a loose strand of my hair behind my ear with great concentration.

"Everyone gets their happy ending, Theia. But it's not always that they get their happy ending with someone else. Sometimes, their happy ending is just… them." He looked back up at me, and he smiled. "Trust me, I am happy."

Mom then made her entrance, her eyes sparkling and her face set into a beautiful ecstatic expression only she could pull off, a beauty they could only possess especially when they smiled for their children.

"The dinner's ready, guys. Please make your way to the dining area."

"Shall we?" Derek smiled as he extended an arm towards me.

Smiling, I took it. Looking up, Bryce's warm gaze was on mine. I moved closer to him. He smiled.

"We shall."

* * *

"How is Dr. Lucian doing?" I whispered to Matthew as we settled into our seats.

"He's great, to be honest! Everything seems to be normal. He does, however,still have a strong bond with you. He's able to call on his wolf now. That has helped his recovery immensely."

I nodded. I knew Sebastian had bonded with me in some twisted way Amber had managed to do to a very weak man. The bond was now clearer, though. Sebastian now had a life debt to me. As strange as it sounded, he was now my protector, and I was his. I nodded again smiling, my concentration back on Matt.

"That's good. Hopefully, he'll be fine before we know it."

Bryce leaned in and placed a kiss on my forehead when just then a loud shrill ringtone began blaring out at the dinner table.

Roman immediately stood up, his hand clutching his iPhone.

He looked up at everyone, "I've got to receive this; please, excuse me."

I watched smiling as everyone at the table chattered and ate dinner. The happiness radiating from everyone seemed contagious. Roman reentered the dining room, and everyone at the table fell silent. He looked up, and I felt my blood run cold. Roman looked straight at Bryce as he spoke the next words.

"Father's… dead"

Bryce stiffened beside me. Everyone at the table sat froze, watching the two men. "When's the next flight?"

"In three hours."

Mr. Smith moved forward into his seat, recovering from the shock, first.

"My family and my sincere condolences Prince Roman," he spoke out, his voice strong and genuine.

My head turned from Marley's dad to Roman's. His gaze met mine. His jaw hardened, but he didn't blink.

"It's King Romanov now."

Dear Readers,

And so this part of the ride has come to an end. My love has been found. My story has been told.

But how can we completely say goodbye when there is so much more to live for? How can we completely let go when there is so much more to hold on for?

So I suppose this isn't the end. This is only yet another beginning. This part of my story isn't over yet. And I suppose it just won't be told.

It's a secret, and you may wonder, as you wish, how things really will end, how we raise our kids, our lives. It's all part of the story I still have yet to live.

But I promise you this, whatever that part may hold, it will have a happy ending.

Thank you for joining me on this ride.

Yours faithfully,
Theia Wilhem.

THE END

BOOK YOU MIGHT ENJOY

BEASTY
Jennise K

They say we all have our own soulmates—the ones we're destined to spend our whole lives with. But orphan Olivia Fredson has no time for that. She has an infant niece, a family business, and her college education to take care of—all on her own.

Even multibillionaire Romanov Naight is too busy to even think of one. When he's not managing his law firm and the university in which he's one of its governors, he prowls the night together with his pack to keep their kind safe from meddling humans.

But it takes only one night, a car crash, and a school project to change their minds.

Suddenly, Olivia finds herself in the complex world of werewolves and in a complicated relationship with Berlin's Alpha King himself. No matter what she does, she always gravitates back to Romanov—his castle, his presence, his arms.

Little does she know that behind all the sweet caresses and hot kisses is a thousand-year old curse not even the strong Romanov can protect her from.

For how can you protect your soulmate if you yourself are the danger?

BOOK YOU MIGHT ENJOY

HIS TO CLAIM
Ashley Michelle

Shortly after reaching maturity, Scarlett finds her mate… only to face a painful rejection that threatened to cut her life short. No one told Scarlett reaching maturity would hurt this much, but she came out the other end stronger, braver, smarter, and a little less naïve.

Seeking to pick up the torn pieces, she leaves her pack for a town well away from her home, far away from her ex-mate who just can't let her go even after claiming someone else.

All seems well until she wanders into Alpha Noah's territory and she finds an unfortunate blessing. The Goddess has given her another chance at a mate—only it has to be with Noah, a demon wolf plagued by his own dark past. With tainted hands and a shattered heart that almost drove him to madness once more, he has turned ice-cold.

Their wounded souls push and pull, but some things just won't heal. Rogues have been ravaging their world, and in a war where hundreds of lives have been lost, revenge is all that's left.

Is the Goddess playing a cruel game this time? When utter carnage surrounds her, will Scarlett's inner luna rise to the challenge? Will Noah ever get to claim her as her mate?

In a world where families are pitted against families and bonds are severed as soon as they are formed, there are no guarantees.

ACKNOWLEDGEMENT

Thank you, first and foremost, Google, for never letting me down. You really do know everything.

I'd like to thank Wattpad, for providing me with a platform that has allowed me to grow so much, and connect with so many incredibly nice, dorky and sassy human beings. I'm so happy to be a part of this community.

Thank you MUM, for never asking me to leave writing and always supporting me. You make my roti go round.

My heartfelt thanks to Le-An and AJ. Guys, thank you so much for always being so patient with me while I took my precious time getting back with the manuscript and bonus materials. You've truly helped me achieve something I'd never dreamed of achieving while writing MTTAK.

Saara, thank you for the late nights we spent discussing details about MTTAK when I was stuck. Thank you.

My warmest of thanks and hugs to Victoria, Fatima, Anagha, and Tanya. For all the times, each one of you have encouraged me, advised me, complained about certain aspects in the book or just made me smile, thank you.

Most of all, I want to thank my readers—each and every one of you who've been with MTTAK since the get go. Thank you. Thank you so much. For every comment, vote and message. For every fangirl moment, every tears you've spilt over this book, and even every rant—thankyou. I'm so happy I've got to meet every one of you. I love you guys.

AUTHOR'S NOTE

Thank you so much for reading *Mated to the Alpha King*! I can't express how grateful I am for reading something that was once just a thought inside my head.

Please feel free to send me an email. Just know that my publisher filters these emails. Good news is always welcome.
jennise_k@awesomeauthors.org

Sign up for my blog for updates and freebies!
jennisek.awesomeauthors.org

One last thing: I'd love to hear your thoughts on the book. Please leave a review on Amazon or Goodreads because I just love reading your comments and getting to know you!

Can't wait to hear from you!

Jennise K

ABOUT THE AUTHOR

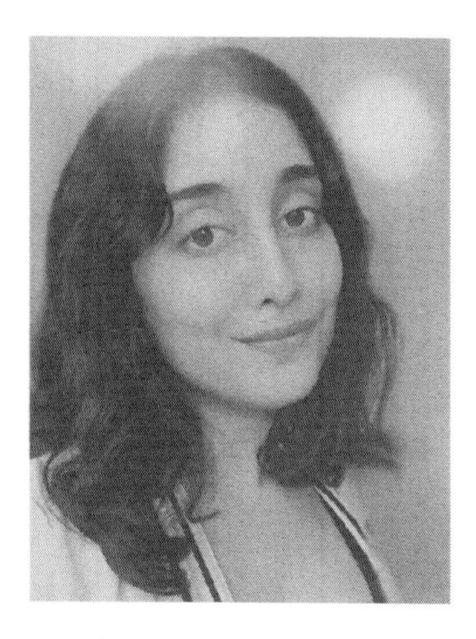

Jennise comes from the beautiful country of Fiji, holds a Bachelors degree in Biology and Psychology, and is currently progressing towards eventually becoming a Dentist.

When she is not writing, she spends time with her family at home, either watching an Asian drama or up-taking one quiet hobby or another like the introvert she is.

In the future Jennise aims to work full time, write part time, and travel to other countries in order to taste their cuisine in her spare time… or well, whenever she can get some free time.

Printed in Great Britain
by Amazon